Under

the

Same Sun

Books by Mariam Kobras

The Stone Trilogy:
The Distant Shore
Under the Same Sun
Song of the Storm, coming in 2013

Under
the
Same Sun

by

Mariam Kobras

Book II: The Stone Trilogy

Buddhapuss Ink   Edison NJ

Cover Art *Sunday Morning* @ 2011 Eric G. Thompson

Author Photo by Sarah Fulford

Cover and Book Layout/Design by The Book Team

Library of Congress Control Number: 2012943431

ISBN 978-0-9842035-5-0 (Paperback Original)

First Printing October 2012

PUBLISHER'S NOTE

To contact the artist, Eric G. Thompson, or learn more about his works, go to:

www.ericgthompson.com

Buddhapuss Ink LLC and our logos are trademarks of Buddhapuss Ink LLC.

www.buddhapussink.com

This book is dedicated to
SHILOH JOSEPHINE THOMPSON

PROLOGUE

NAOMI SIGHED IN relief when she realized her flight wasn't full. She would have some privacy.

The first-class passengers were called just as she began to wonder if there was time for another cup of coffee. In the tunnel, she waited for a woman in a wheelchair to board and unfolded the magazine to have another look at Jon. Her husband—there he was on a glossy front cover.

She hadn't flown first-class on a commercial flight for quite a while. Before Jon, she'd not allowed herself the luxury; and with him it was always a private plane, one of those small, well-appointed jets that whisked them across the continents to wherever he wanted to go.

Settling down in the wide, comfortable seat she watched the other passengers board before she turned to look out the window. It had begun to rain, the sky hung low and dark over the tarmac. From afar she could see the blinking lights of runways, of planes slowly sinking and landing in a spray of water as their wheels touched the ground.

A man sat down across the aisle, nodding a greeting toward her.

Naomi remembered seeing him in the lounge, by the bar, and she nodded back before she closed her seat belt and opened the magazine to read the article about Jon.

"I saw you earlier," he said. Surprised, she looked up.

The plane was moving, its big body shuddering with the power of the engines. Raindrops pelted against the window.

"I saw you in the lounge. You caught my attention right away. Name's Parker. Pleased to meet you."

She didn't reply. He wasn't her type, with his blond hair and fair complexion, but he looked pleasant enough, his blue eyes smiling at her.

"It's a pleasure to have such lovely company on a long flight like this."

The flight attendant began the safety instructions while they taxied toward the runway.

Once they were in the air and the announcement that it was now safe to use "approved electronic devices" was made, Naomi pulled her headphones from her bag and clamped them over her ears shutting him out. It took her a moment to fish her MP3 player out of her purse, but soon Jon's voice flooded her mind.

chapter 1

HE HAD BEEN holding the apple in his hand the entire time it took the bus to cross London.

Beside them, the river was a golden band shimmering in the late afternoon sun, the few ships on it collecting ripples in their trail like lace on a satin gown.

Quite successfully, he'd ignored the chatter of the others as they commented on the sights and on how excited they were to be back in England, back on the road.

His fingers had gripped the apple. It was like a good-luck charm, the promise that all would be well, something to dispel the loneliness.

Jon had felt that loneliness like a terrible ache on the bus ride to the venue, like a deep silence settling in his heart. He had woken up alone in his hotel room and stared at the curtains blowing in the morning breeze, the other side of the bed empty and cold, untouched. He'd listened to the sound of the birds in the park across the street, remembering when they had been in London together for the first time. It had been a day much like this one, perhaps a little cooler, and it had been the day he had decided. He could remember opening his eyes and seeing her black locks on the pillow, a pale shoulder partially covered by the sheet, and he had known it was the day he would propose. How nervous he had been, afraid she would refuse. But she had said yes, and after breakfast he had taken her out and bought her a ring. The elation of that moment, of the moment when he had put it on her finger had come back to him when he had retraced that walk only this morning. He had stood outside Tiffany's and had felt the crazy urge to bend down and run his hand over the pavement, trying to find a memory of her footsteps there. Furtively he had looked around, but no one had noticed him. The stream of early pedestrians had parted around him, ignoring him as if he was nothing more than a garbage can that had been put out in the wrong place.

IT HAD BEEN three weeks. Three weeks since he had let her go, watching with a heavy heart how she had left, fleeing their life, and the aftermath of the shooting. He had tried to talk her out of it, had made her breakfast and hoped with every fiber of his heart that she would change her mind; but seeing her sitting at the kitchen table, her head lowered in defeat, her hands folded in her lap, the omelette untouched, he had told her to go. Very softly, softly enough that his voice wouldn't crack on the words, he had offered to let her leave and find her peace. Naomi had looked at him, a small spark of hope in her eyes, and he knew it was the only thing he could do.

She hadn't said where she was headed, and he had been too afraid to ask, afraid to hear her say it was none of his business or that she would not be returning. He stood in the doorway as the car pulled out of the driveway and vanished into the morning traffic, then returned inside, alone, desolate.

The house had seemed dead without her, an empty shell left behind, and he had wandered through the rooms, listening to the echo of emptiness. At last he had found enough energy to make coffee; and while he was standing in the kitchen, dolefully watching it drip through the machine, the phone had rung, and it had been her.

"I'm at the airport," Naomi had said, her voice as normal as if she was calling from a shopping trip, asking what to buy for dinner. "I'm going to New York first, to see Joshua, and then I'll go to one of my family's hotels on the Eastern Shore to rest a bit."

Jon had offered to join her, first in visiting their son and then in her exile, but she had declined. But, she had promised, she would be there when he started the tour; she would be in London.

So now, as the bus took drew close to the venue, he closed his hand around the smooth surface of the apple.

"Your fans," Sal said from behind him, "faithful as ever. Do you feel like giving some autographs today?"

The bus had to wait a moment before the gate swung open.

"Sure." Jon didn't care one way or the other. He didn't even care about the concert. It had been meant for her, and she wasn't here. He had dreamed of going on the stage again. Never mind the thousands of people in the audience; he wanted to sing only for her.

Once off the bus, he took the pen Sal held out to him and began walking toward the group of fans, Sal, Russ and Art by his side, security surrounding them. He was so used to this, his smile fell into place before they had walked halfway across the parking lot. In the back of his mind he realized he was still wearing the same shirt he had put on that morning. It was a bit rumpled, not exactly suited for public appearances, but Jon didn't care.

They were wearing T-shirts with his picture on them. Jon hated his own face on shirts, and he hated it on blue shirts even more. It had never been among his favorite colors, and even less on middle-aged women.

There was a speck of red hidden behind the two matrons holding out CDs for him to sign, and his heart skipped a beat. He tried to see around them, get a closer look, and just then she stepped forward.

He had not expected to see her again, ever. And yet here she stood, in a dress much like the one she had worn the day he had asked her to marry him, her braid falling over her shoulder, unchanged. Her lips curling into a small smile when she saw his stunned expression. She moved forward to take his hand when he held it out.

"Forgive me," Naomi whispered, so low only he could hear it. "Forgive me, and please take me back."

"Forgive you." There was nothing to forgive. He wanted his arms around her. Wanted to take her to a quiet place where they could be alone, if only for a moment; and he wanted the fans gone so he could kiss her right there and then.

She pressed his fingers slightly, the corners of her mouth twitching. "Don't stare, Jon. Let's go."

He heard the murmur of discontent from the waiting group, but he couldn't be bothered. There would be no autographs today.

Russ led them inside, where they were greeted by representatives of the venue, of the British tour management and the press, but Jon waved them away and asked for his dressing room.

"Later," he said, "I promise. I'll take the time to talk to you, but not now."

Sal stayed behind to answer some questions, and Jon closed the door behind them, even locked it, relieved that they had at least a few minutes of solitude before he had to go and join the sound check.

"You're here."

Again she smiled. "Of course, I promised. Have you forgotten?"

It was so hard to believe that she had really come. "And you stood out there, with the fans. Just like you said you did last time, only then I walked by and didn't see you."

"Yes." She sat on the corner of the dressing table and picked up the

eyeliner. Carefully she pulled off the cap and drew a thin line on the tip
of her finger.

"I could hardly wait for you to find me. I was so scared you'd decide
not to give autographs at all and I would have to call Sal to come let me
in. Then my surprise would have been wasted."

Jon could hardly speak. Her composure was too much to bear, her
cool, sensible words as close to a taunt as she had ever attempted.

"I'm rested," Naomi went on, a little gentler; "I needed a break."

The morning she had left came to his mind again, and how she had
sat at that table, miserably staring at the steaming eggs, like a prisoner, a
captured animal, so defeated and hopeless that he had let her go, had in
fact sent her away even though it broke his heart.

"I never wanted to put pressure on you, never. I only wanted to see
you healed and well. I just wanted our life back." He balled his fists, the
fury at what had happened to her boiling up again. "I wanted you to
forget and be your real self again, not that broken husk on the verge
of death."

"I am myself," Naomi said softy. "I'm okay now."

It was a lie. Jon could see it. She looked tired, and she was still too
thin.

"Perhaps you should have stayed where you were. It was too early for
you to come back." He could hardly believe what he was saying. "You
need more rest."

Instantly he could see he had hurt her.

Naomi lowered her head. Very slowly she laid the eyeliner back on the
table and stood up. With a shaking hand she smoothed her dress and
tugged her jacket into place.

"Jon, I've come all this way. I flew overnight to get here, and you want
to send me back?.I thought you had forgiven me, but it seems you are
still angry." She looked up at him, her eyes swimming with tears. "I
could not wait to be back with you again."

"But, baby…" Jon wanted to kiss her. He wanted it so badly he could
feel his lips tingling, and he reached out to her. "Baby, I'm so happy you
are here! I can't begin to tell you how much I missed you, how desolate
I was without you and how scared that you'd never come back. Don't
you know how much I need you? Only, Naomi…"

"No buts, Jon. No more buts."

He wanted to drown in that kiss, wanted her body close to his so he could feel the soft warmth of her skin under his hands. Three long weeks she had been away, and to him it felt like an eternity.

"Missed you so much," Jon breathed into her mouth. "You have no idea. I wanted to go after you, find you and stay with you, give up the tour, everything. Nothing makes any sense if you're not there."

From outside he could hear Sal's voice, not yet impatient but loud enough to remind him of where he was supposed to be.

"They are waiting." But he didn't let her go. It felt too good to have her in his arms again.

Naomi pushed against his chest. "In a minute Sal is going to bang on the door, and that will be so awkward. I'll be right here, darling. Give me a chance to get some coffee and then I'll join you, I promise. But I just got off the plane, and I need to freshen up a bit before I see the rest of the group."

"But how will I be sure?" It sounded a little plaintive, and it made her smile.

"You'll just have to trust me, I'm afraid. I'll make Sal take me to hospitality and get me a backstage pass so I can move around without being a nuisance." She rose on her toes. "But first, one more kiss."

Jon didn't want to let her go, so afraid she would be gone when he returned from the sound check. He had done it once before, taken her with him onto the stage and sat her down next to Sean on the piano bench, just to make sure she would not vanish, and he was very tempted to do it again now so that he could keep her in sight the whole time, only he was sure he would meet with resistance.

There was a knock, diffident and not too loud, and he sighed.

"Go," Naomi urged. "Don't make them wait. I promise not to go anywhere."

"I can't." His hands dug into her hair, loosening the braid, freeing the locks. "How can I, with you here, after not having you in my arms for a month."

"Three weeks, Jon. Don't exaggerate so. And we talked on the phone all the time." But she didn't try to get away again.

"The phone," he mumbled against her temple. "Can't make love on the phone. Can't feel your breath on my skin, can't touch you, can't see you when I wake up."

Her body softened against his, but only for a moment. "Jon."

"Ah, Naomi, you're breaking my heart. All I get is a moment's solace, and then you send me off again. I've hardly had time to say hello to you."

"And little wonder." She undid her braid to put it in order. "You were too busy kissing me to speak in proper sentences."

He had been on his way to the door, but turned and shot her a dangerous glance. "I haven't even begun kissing you, my dear. Just wait until we're back at the hotel. And then."

FOR THE FIRST time in his life Jon didn't want to go onstage. He made his way slowly, carefully; and when he was at the bottom of the narrow stairway that would take him up at the back so he could make a decent entrance, he stopped. One hand on the handrail, he looked back, dithering.

Sean had started the band. They were rehearsing the orchestral intro, a short piece out of the movie soundtrack that had won the Oscar just a few months ago. Jon could hear Sean giving directions to their sound engineer and Russ talking to Sal, could see them still fiddling with the recording computers at the side of the scaffolding and the lighting people climbing along the crossbeams like monkeys. Their rope ladder dangled down onto the stage, almost exactly on the spot where he was supposed to be, right by his microphone stand.

Someone had set up his guitars for him, but not in the right order, and he cursed silently. His attention wavered. Part of him wanted to go back to where Naomi was so he could look at her and have her in his arms, but this bothered him.

Over the years they had all developed a routine full of small rituals; and now someone had broken them, had changed the setting, and the obsessive part of him was upset. Calling for Sal, Jon jumped up the few steps. He pushed at the ladder hanging in his way and pointed at the guitars, a harangue on his lips, but Sal was already there, putting the instruments in their place.

"Goodness," he grumbled, "you are insufferable. If you can't stand being here, then go and smooch some more with the wife. Don't dump your sour mood on us."

Jon didn't reply.

"You've already wasted fifteen minutes. You have another forty-five for the rehearsal, and then the press and the fan clubs will be here, Jon.

You know we promised them a press conference."

As if he didn't know, after a quarter century in the business. The first show of the tour, and they needed a good write-up. Everyone in the music world would be looking at the London concert, and everyone who was still thinking about buying a ticket for the later performances too.

"Yeah." He still didn't feel like playing, let alone singing. She had said she wanted coffee and that she would join him shortly, but she wasn't here yet. It made him restless. "Let me just go and make sure she's all right."

Sal sighed. "For heaven's sake, Jon, she doesn't need a babysitter. Let me go and see what Naomi's up to; but please, just do your job." Without waiting for a reply he left.

The guitars were well polished, not a single fingerprint from the tuning on their glossy surface, just the way he liked them. Lovingly Jon ran his hand over the koa twelve-string, its bold grain and coloring like the curly auburn hair of a lovely woman. It was an old friend, as old as his career. How well he remembered playing it in the sun-drenched open-air stadium in Geneva all those years ago when he had met Naomi, and the turmoil of his feelings when he realized she was the one and only, the one girl he wanted in his life.

Beside it was the ebony acoustic, his lover, the one that had been custom-made for him ten years ago. He had seen the black wood in the workshop—the fine, wavy red stripes like the highlights in Naomi's locks—and he had known he wanted it. The sound of the instrument, when it was delivered, had first surprised and then nearly hurt him. It was soft, melodious, with a sweet, mellow timbre; and it had an echoing, haunting quality that reminded him so much of her that he could only bear to play it when he was alone.

Now, of course, everything was different. She was back in his life; and he could easily pick up the guitar during a concert, could even play their most intimate song, *The Secret Garden*, on it and no longer cry.

Sean launched into the opening chords.

Jon raised his head to look up at the high ceiling, listened to the intro and let it inundate him. He wanted to stretch out his arms and float on the melody, feel it carry him like a wave. It was his music, the extension of his soul into the real world, a shining cloud that surrounded him, the fabric of his existence.

He picked up his twelve-string, swung it over his head, and settled it into place against his body. The guitar pick in his raised hand, he waited for his cue, then dove into the ocean of his creation.

chapter 2

SAL FOUND HER in the hospitality area, sitting quietly in a corner sipping coffee.

He stood in the doorway for a moment before going over to her. She had changed, but not as much as he had feared. It was true, she was still frail, and there was a residue of fatigue around her eyes and mouth; but Sal hoped it was more from the overnight flight than from her injuries.

"Hey," he greeted her softly, "it's good to see you back. He can be such an asshole when you're not around."

A small smile appeared on her lips. She tried to hide it behind the cup, but he saw and grinned in reply.

"So how was your flight?" Grabbing a cup for himself, he sat down beside her, his back to the wall.

"It was okay." Naomi shrugged. "I had this guy sitting across the aisle, and he kept pushing champagne at me, wanted to talk, talk, talk; and all I wanted was to really get some rest. That's the downside of traveling commercially. No private space, for hours."

With a little sigh, she gazed toward the hallway leading to the stage. "But I wanted to be here as soon as possible. I promised."

Sal didn't point out to her that with a private plane she could have traveled on her own itinerary, and without unpleasant company, so he only replied, "Someone wanted to impress you. I'm not suprised."

She pulled up her shoulders in that well-known gesture of denial. "It was more than that. He was just a bit too inquisitive. He insisted on telling me his name. Parker, he called himself. Just that." For a moment she seemed lost in contemplation. "He was really rather cute, now that I think of it. Very charming, in an English way. Very European. A bit like a puppy, eager to impress. I turned my back on him and went to sleep. Ah well." A wave of her hand, a cool dismissal. "It's over now, and we're all here."

Sal had the feeling there was a little more to it, as if a shadow of that flight was still lingering in her memory, and he was on the point of asking. But then, seeing her face soften as the music drifted toward them, he said, "Come on, you know where you're supposed to be. He's on the stage and being petulant because you're not around, and

I promised to take you there, drag you by your braid if I have to. You have such a way of unsettling the routine."

Naomi rose. "But I promised to come to London. Would you rather I leave again?"

"No!" The thought alone was enough to make him break out in a sweat. "Don't even think that! If you left now I know there'd be no concert tonight. He'd go after you like a mad dog and to hell with a sold-out house!"

The red dress looked good on her. In fact, Sal thought, trailing after her toward the hall, she had regained some weight and was well on the way to being her old self, to being the beautiful, healthy woman she had been before the attack at the Oscars.

"You look great." He held the door for her. Naomi gazed at him over her shoulder.

"I mean, you look well. Rested," he added hastily. "The break did you good. You even have a tan. Good!"

Without replying she walked to the stage and put down her cup on the edge, right at Jon's feet, and propped her elbows on the wood. It was a little too high for her, but she managed. Jon, in the middle of a verse, gave her a smile without missing a beat. He stepped forward and leaned down to her, still singing, to kiss her, and when it did not work went down on his knees, his guitar slung on his back.

Sean, picking up the mood, changed to a gentler measure, changing the character of the song; and the lighting engineers, at their tables at the back of the house, pointed a mellow, pinkish beam at them. The image was so perfect, so made for a romantic moment somewhere in the show that Sal wondered if they should repeat it with a female fan, but he dismissed it right away, knowing full well Jon would never agree. He would never sell himself like that, not for anything. Sal sighed. It would have been a nice snapshot for a front page.

A COUPLE OF pieces later Jon called an end to the sound check. They had, he announced, rehearsed more than they needed to already, and he was ready for some food and a rest before he had to face the press. Before Sal could get in a word, he had vanished, Naomi in tow.

In the dressing room, quiet welcomed them. Naomi's ears were still ringing from the volume of the music, her heart beating fast, bones throbbing with the rhythm. She sat on the corner of the table again to watch as Jon was transformed into the icon, the star who would make thousands of women swoon only a little while later.

"This one?" Jon took a shirt from the rack, one among many. It was cream silk with colorful embroidery on the shoulders and down the sleeves. He held it up for her to see, a grin on his face. "I'm going to wear this one. What do you think?"

Her breath caught. "Really, Jon?"

"Yeah, I think. Does it remind you of something?" The supple material seemed to flow through his hands like a small waterfall.

Of course it did.

The concert had been only a couple of years ago, and she remembered all too well how she had stood outside with the fans back then, hiding from him, wanting to see him but not wanting him to see her after their long years apart. Cold rain had dripped down her neck and soaked her coat, and Jon had walked by, eating an apple, unconcerned. She had told him, of course, once they had found each other again, how she had sat through the concert afterward, desperate and lonely, and how terrible his shirt had been.

The makeup artist came in, towels over his arm. Muttering at seeing John still in his jeans, he turned and left again.

"Well, yes or no? I have to change." He began to strip, right there in the center of the room, tossing his clothes on the couch. "And don't look at me like that. There's no time for that now. Don't make me regret that I have to go onstage in a little while."

Deep inside her heart she heard him sing as he had that night—sad, lonely, his voice breaking on the songs they had written together—and she recalled so well sitting in the third row, crying, mourning their past.

"Not that one, Jon." She couldn't bear to see him in it again. "Please, pick something else." And, with a wave at the rack, "Pick a new one. There are plenty. Give me that one. It's my memory, and it still hurts, and I want it all for myself."

He laid it in her outstretched hand, bemused. "Okay, so which one do you want me to wear? You tell me."

Naomi slid from the table and went over to the collection of stage outfits, all still covered in protective plastic covers, pristine, waiting for their turn in the spotlight. For a moment she hesitated, then she took a dark red linen shirt down, and black trousers.

"Here," she said, "dress like a gentleman. Dress the way you should.

You don't need those crazy American outfits to stand out on the stage. Your music and your voice alone are good enough for that."

"I am American." Jon's eyebrows came up in amusement. "And you are married to me, so that makes you one too, more or less."

"Never!"

The vehemence of her reply made him chuckle. "So tell me. What was that place where you were these past weeks? Your family's?"

She returned to her perch, the discarded shirt crumpled in her lap, and told him about the hotel where she had gone to rest, one of the many that belonged to her family, this one in Maryland, on the Eastern Shore, in a small town with the name of an archangel.

"It's right on the water," her legs dangling, her fingers once again playing with the eyeliner. "With its own dock and a small swimming pool on the deck. It's been ours for ages. Well, for twenty years." She shrugged. "I don't like the weather there. It's okay now, but in a couple of weeks it will be as hot as hell, too hot to be outside." There was a bowl of lemon candy on the table behind her and she picked one out. "I got up every morning at dawn to watch this couple go out to catch crabs. They would take a boat and row across the bay, their dog with them, and he would stand in the prow, all excited and yapping. I think it was a very young dog. He could hardly wait to get to the beach, and sometimes he jumped into the water just before they got there. It was fun to watch him shake himself and spray the water all over his people. They didn't seem to mind though." She smiled in reminiscence. "Then a little later the fishing boats would come in and I'd be there to watch the cooks buy what they wanted for the day, and then I'd go to the kitchen with them and have some coffee. And then…" She gazed into the distance, right past him. "And then there would be nothing for me to do. Mostly I sat on the deck and tried to write. They wouldn't let me work the desk. And I hated it. I wanted to do something."

Jon, on the point of pulling on the shirt, let his hands sink to look at her and listen.

"It felt a bit like being back in Halmar, for a while. But then I realized it wasn't, and that was when I knew I was ready to come back to you." A smile brightened her face. "And about time too, it seems." Her attention returned to him. "Look at you, daydreaming when you should be getting ready. Here, let me help you."

Patiently he stood still as she buttoned the shirt for him and straightened the shoulders, the urge to draw her into his arms strong. He even held out his hands so she could fasten the cuffs.

"You look good, Jon Stone. You look good enough to make the ladies wilt. I'm jealous." Naomi stepped back to look at him critically. "How I hate sharing you with all those others. You know you're mine alone, don't you?"

"Yeah. Three weeks, and you have no idea how I missed you. You can't begin to imagine how lonely I was and how grueling the nights were—me, alone in that bed, your scent still on the pillow." He tried to embrace her, but she stepped back, shaking her head. "And now you won't even let me kiss you. What's the use in being married?"

"You will get rumpled. No hugging and fondling before the show."

Before he could react, there was another knock on the door, and he sighed. It was time.

She was there. That was all that mattered. Naomi once more sat on the corner of the dressing table, in the way of the makeup artist, forcing him to work around her, creeping ever closer as the eyeliner was applied, fascinated by the procedure; and Jon, a deep burning in his heart, recalled how she had done the same thing right before that interview, after they had won the Oscar. Moments, it had been only moments later that she had been shot. He felt the urge to jump out of the chair and be done with it; take her hand and walk out of his old life; forget the stage, the concerts, the publicity and hide somewhere, in a quiet corner of the world where no harm would come to her and he could be himself.

"Just a minute more," Ralph murmured, feeling his impatience.

"So you miss Halmar?" Jon asked around the puffs of powder Ralph was producing around his face.

There was no answer for a while, and he closed his eyes. The smell of the makeup was irritating.

"No." Her voice was steady, calm. "No I don't. I want to be here, with you."

When he dared to look she was smiling directly at him, her eyes bright.

THERE WAS A way of dealing with the press that they had developed over the years; and now, walking into the room reserved for them, Jon said, "Stay with Sean and Art. You don't need to be out there with me. Not this time," and quickly pressed her hand. There would be no more kisses before the show; he was ready for the limelight now.

"HELLO, DARLING." SEAN touched her shoulder lightly. "It's good to see you. Are you well?"

She had missed him, and everyone in the group. As much as she had needed the silence, she needed this more.

Standing between Art and Sean she felt safe, at home in a way she didn't feel anywhere else, and so she leaned into him briefly.

"I'm well, Sean, and so glad to be back with you all."

He left his fingers on her shoulder.

The last time she had been at a press conference with Jon it had been before the Grammys. Then she had gathered all her courage and joined him, faced the many questions, cameras, and curious eyes; but now, she knew, she would never be able to bring herself to do something like that again, ever. The lights scared her, the hum in the large room seemed deafening, the crowd—focused on Jon—as threatening as a clown with razor teeth.

"Steady," Art mumbled when he felt her draw back. "We're all here. Don't be spooked. No need to be afraid."

But she was. For the first time since the shooting, the well-hidden panic surfaced: black bile in her throat, a silver flitter behind her eyes, red knives in the veins of her arms.

Naomi gasped. She could feel Sean's steadying arm around her waist and Art moving to stand in front of her, shielding her.

"Do you want to go?" Sean asked softly. "If you want to go I'll take you back to the dressing room, or Art can take you to the hotel. What do you want, darling?"

She clasped the frame of the door. Sal was speaking, thanking the press for being there, giving some details of the tour program, praising the venue and the organizers, then he introduced Jon and invited questions.

"I'm okay," Naomi said. She didn't want to leave, didn't want to give in. There was the taste of metal on her tongue, and breathing seemed hard.

"What I would like to know," someone in the audience said, "is how you deal with what happened to your wife at the Academy Awards? You are launching a big concert tour today, and where is your wife?"

Abruptly, silence fell. Naomi felt Art and Sean shift, felt them move closer to her as if to close ranks, and saw the security men around them change their stance into one of alertness. The woman, LaGasse, hired by Jon to be her guard, moved in front of her with the easy elegance of a cat, her hand on her back, under her suit jacket.

"This is not a topic for tonight." It was Sal's voice, contained and cool.

She couldn't see Jon from where she was standing now, inside her tight ring of people, not even when she rose on her toes to peer around LaGasse.

"It's also none of your business. She is well, and that's all I'm going to say about it." Jon was furious; she could hear it in his tone.

"It was your former lover, was it not, who shot her? A young woman named Sophie? A movie director's daughter?" The interrogator was still the same. "It was she who shot your wife, is that not correct?"

No one spoke. Then Jon replied, very softly, "Yes. That is correct."

"Your wife was severely hurt, correct? She lost part of her lung? And her bodyguard was killed. The girl Sophie died too, if I remember correctly. So what about your wife? Where is she now? Here you are, starting a tour, and where is your wife?"

Naomi tugged LaGasse's sleeve, and she moved marginally, just enough to allow Naomi a view without being seen.

The man who was putting these questions to Jon, who was verbally pushing him into a corner, was the same one who had bought the champagne on the plane, the one who had introduced himself as Parker.

"My wife." Jon rose. He was formidable in his stage outfit, and now, staring down at his opponent, he looked intimidating. "My wife and her well-being are my concern. Neither her health, nor anything else about her, are open to discussion."

"Oh." Parker stepped forward. "So you are keeping her hidden?"

A murmur went through the group of journalists, some of them stared at him quizzically.

"I'm not keeping her hidden, what utter nonsense." Jon threw a quick glance in her direction. "It is her decision alone how much she wants to reveal about what happened, and to whom. If you are that interested in this, I suggest you ask her for an interview and not disrupt my press conference." He grinned wryly. "I wish you the best of luck. You'll have to deal with her managers first, and they are as tough as nails. I'm glad I get to see her sometimes, they protect her that well."

Most of the reporters chuckled, breaking the tension.

"Stupid," Naomi heard Art whisper. "How stupid of him. Why did he react like that? I'm not getting it; he could have told them you were here and fine and looking forward to the tour. What made him take the bait like that?"

Strangely, her fear seemed to dissolve. For the first time in months she felt the urge to talk about the incident in Hollywood, to tell someone and lay the burden aside. Only once, way back when she had still been in LA, had she tentatively spoken to Art; but she had been shy, scared, worried, not wanting to bother any of them.

"So you don't mind if I ask your wife for an interview?" Parker was asking, "because I will. I'd kill for an exclusive interview."

Jon, on the point of leaving his spot by the microphone, turned around to stare at him. "We do not," he said slowly, "we do not use that word. We do not talk about killing. We are musicians, artists, writers. We do not enjoy death, or pain, the way you reporters do. Something terrible happened at the Oscars, and we still bear the scars of that day. My wife nearly died. The trauma we all suffered is awful, but it's nothing compared to what she had and still has to endure." He leaned forward, his palms on the table before him, and the glamour of the rock icon was broken when he added, "I beg you, leave her alone. She is only now reclaiming her life. Don't hurt her."

"Come." Sean gripped her arm and led Naomi away.

SHE DIDN'T SEE Jon again until it was nearly time for him to go onstage. Naomi knew the entire band and the technicians were together for a last pep talk and a few jokes, and no one else was allowed inside, not even Sal. The door to the room they were in was tightly closed. Together with Art and Sal she stood outside, leaning against the wall, tired, feeling the jet lag at last despite sleeping on the plane.

She felt displaced, as if she was walking in cotton, almost as if she had just woken from anesthesia, with the same taste of electricity on her tongue and dullness behind her eyes. It wasn't tiredness but something else, as if her body was off-kilter, and her mind too.

From inside they could hear snatches of laughter, a voice raised in singing for a brief moment, not Jon's though, and then, at last, they piled out, exhilarated, hyped, ready for the stage and the thousands of waiting fans.

Jon came out last. He gave her a smile, standing still as one of the techs attached the in-ear monitors and clipped the little transmitter box to the back of his trousers.

"Baby," he said, his arms outstretched so the cables could be hidden under his shirt, "you look tired. Are you sure you want to stay and listen to this nonsense? It's only me up there. And you know very well how I look."

"What you said," Naomi replied, "the things you said in there, Jon."

His look grew pensive. "You shouldn't have witnessed that. I'm sorry, my love. I should have made Sal interrupt the conference right away. They had no right to ask those questions."

"But maybe they do."

"What?" He had been busy tucking the shirt into his trousers, but now his head came up. "What are you saying, Naomi? This is private."

"Yes…and no. They won't stop asking." His collar was lopsided, and with a deft twist she put it in order, letting her hand rest on his shoulder. "Someday I'll have to face it. It might as well be now.."

Someone handed Jon the microphone. Without thinking, born of the many years onstage, he softly spoke into it and adjusted his monitors. For a moment he was far away, their discussion forgotten, as he said, "A little more bass, Russ."

Naomi took a step back from him. Every second that passed now, every breath he took, moved him farther from her; she could see it in the absent gaze, in the set of the mouth and the way his posture changed. He was Jon, and yet he wasn't; he was more, as if—with the eyeliner, the face powder, and the sleek shirt—he had turned into a new being, a vessel for the music, the core of his band.

His body was moving with the rhythm he was hearing through the monitors, his lips whispering the lyrics, his fingers twitching as he imagined the chords he would be playing in a moment.

"I love you," she said softly, "I love you, Jon Stone. No matter what, remember that."

And Jon, his attention drawn back to the real world, gripped her tightly around the waist and kissed her fiercely, mindless of the cables and the fact that everyone onstage had heard her words through the microphone in his hand.

chapter 3

THERE WAS A seat for her in the first row, right in the center, but Naomi refused, saying she didn't want to be among the steaming crowd when Jon started to flirt with them.

"We have," Sal offered carefully, "A VIP lounge reserved. I think he meant it for you, just in case you showed up. I don't think there's anyone else there. You would have it all to yourself."

It wasn't exactly what she wanted either, sitting so far up and away from it all, alone, but she was too tired to stand upright anymore.

"Here." Carefully, he took her arm. "I'll take you there."

They could see Jon from where they were standing, his back turned to them, at the bottom of the stairs that would take him up on the stage, hidden in dimness. He looked unreal, bathed as he was in the mist of the fog machines, colorful beams flitting across his hair, a still, tall figure, all his attention focused on the music.

"Okay."

There was an elevator, for which she was more than grateful. Stairs would have been too much, she knew, and she was sure Sal did too. She also knew that he had made sure she would be comfortable.

They could hear the opening bars of the intro even inside the elevator, and she wished it would move faster so she could see Jon when he entered the stage, when the beams caught him and the applause surged through the air like a huge wave. She fidgeted, impatient, and Sal grinned, but he didn't say a word.

The lounge was the best in the building, as close to the stage as possible, and there was no one in it. A guard was standing just outside the door, a stern, hefty man with cropped hair, his suit smooth over well-developed muscles and the dreaded bulge of the gun. The sight was enough to make her feel exhausted, scared, and in a way despondent. He gave her an attentive but humorless nod, no trace of a smile, not a hint of personality; and Naomi wondered if this was something they learned during their training, to distance themselves from their charges, not to be attached in any way. Stewart had died for her during the shooting. He had been her bodyguard and she had liked him, had even enjoyed his company when she went out for a stroll on the beach at dawn. Jon hadn't allowed her to see his family when she had been well enough to mourn him, so instead she had made a pilgrimage to the cedar groove on the grounds of their estate where Stewart had lugged a large piece of driftwood one morning at her request. There, she had at last cried for Sophie, for herself, and also for Stewart, so senselessly dead.

"Your name?" she asked the strange man, and he looked at her in surprise.

"Alan," he replied after a second, "madam."

"Well, you don't need to stand out here like a statue, Alan. Come inside and watch the show, if you want to." It was pathetic and unprofessional, and she knew it.

He did not even move. "Ma'am, my place is right here."

Sal listened to the brief exchange without interrupting, patiently holding the door for her.

Someone had taken care to place a chair on the balcony so she could watch without being locked in the secluded room. On the table, on spotless white linen, was a large bouquet of roses, and a cooler with champagne and a single flute.

"Try to get some rest," she heard Sal say. "I'll be back shortly and keep you company, okay? But right now I have to get back down there and see that everything is going the way it should. I'll make sure the waiters look in on you and get you anything you want." He hesitated. "Are you all right? Are you sure you want to do this, Naomi? You don't have to. I hate to leave you here like this, but…"

"It's fine, Sal, don't worry." She rather liked the privacy and seclusion, at least for the moment. It would give her a chance to rest and get her flight-muddled mind sorted.

"It's good to see you." He was still standing in the doorway. "I'm glad to see you." He left before she could answer.

The music soared. It filled the hall and made its way right to her heart, made her sway a bit with the impact, sorry for the decision to be up here and not down there with the others, perched on a stool beside Russ at his computers, right next to the stage. From there she could have heard Jon's breath when he came over for a drink of water between songs, could hear him crack a joke with the band and catch a glance from him, a smile.

A young woman entered, a tray in her hands, to offer her coffee or wine, food and cake; but she declined. With a glass of champagne,

Naomi sat down in the chair on the balcony where she could see across the audience and right at Jon.

"Here you are." The voice was quite close, and by now, well known. Parker was stepping out of the lounge right next to hers. He had taken off his jacket and rolled up his shirtsleeves, showing off well-toned underarms. His hands were strong, square, his fingers sturdy. "I have the feeling we are meant to meet again and again."

She turned her head away.

"And I'm very happy about it, I have to say. What great good fortune—the press lounge is right next to yours!" He leaned over to her. "So, you're having champagne again? Mind if I join you?"

"Yes."

There was a brief pause. "I'm thinking it's not right that they leave you up here all by yourself. You should not be all alone. Someone should look after you, pour your wine. Will you let me do that for you?"

"No."

"I never thought you'd be this monosyllabic. Really." The music was loud enough to nearly drown out his words, the beat throbbing, demanding.

Naomi loved how it sounded, almost like a big band was playing: full, harmonic, balanced. Jon had taken up the koa and stood nearly at the edge of the stage, close enough for the fans in the first row to touch. He picked up his cue from Sean and began to sing, his voice well modulated, carrying, seducing the crowd. She could see them standing up clapping, waving, singing along, diving into the song with him; and she leaned forward, her hands on the railing, wishing she was down there too.

Without her noticing, Parker had gone back inside and now returned with a bottle of wine that he offered to her. "If your husband prefers the adoration of the multitude to adoring you, let me keep you company for a while."

Without looking his way, Naomi placed her glass on the far side, well away from him.

"Come on," Parker said, "I can see your glass is empty. Are you angry because of the press conference? I assure you, I was really concerned about you. What happened at the Oscars, it was nearly too much to take."

The song had finished, the cheering ebbed, and Jon took the microphone in his hand. "Two years ago we were here," he addressed the audience. "I remember it was cold, and it rained that evening. I wasn't in a very good mood, I have to admit. The coffee was lousy, and I hadn't slept too well the night before. I guess I needed a miracle to happen to make me happy."

Laughter rippled through the rows, which made him hold up his hand.

"Yes, and some god must have smiled on me, because that miracle happened. And that's why we are here again tonight. Welcome, all!"

His hand came up well above his head, guitar pick between his outstretched fingers. "Let's rock the house, guys!"

And they did, launching into the fast, hard *River Song*, one of her favorites, and the reason for being where she was now.

Excitement welled up in her, and a sudden joy, a kind of happiness she hadn't felt in many months. Not since she had woke from her coma and found herself in a hospital bed, in a sea of injury and pain. Her heart beating fast, Naomi jumped up. They were playing the old version of the song, the one she had first heard on the radio nearly twenty years ago, the same one that had made her send a sheaf of lyrics to Jon.

"Take it, Sean!" Jon called, and Sean, smiling softly, hit the piano keys. It was their most famous song, the steamy rock rhythm like the beating heart of a huge beast, and Jon moving with it, giving himself up to it.

She was ready to cry. They had never again performed this solo, not after she had left Jon all those years ago, not in a single concert, Sean had told her. It had always been her favorite piece, and Jon knew.

He stood below, on the stage, legs apart, shoulders straight, chin raised, steadying the guitar with one hand and with the other pointing straight at her, looking up and nodding slowly, triumphantly.

Naomi's fingers gripped the cold metal of the rail tightly, and she didn't care at all that many faces turned her way, that some flashlights went off, this time not directed at Jon but at her; and she even leaned forward a little in her desire to be closer to him.

The song ended. Jon handed his instrument to a waiting tech and took up the microphone to start on the quiet, soft *Secret Garden*, the first song she had written for him. The lights turned mellow, the audience quieted down.

It was time to go. The lounge, Naomi realized, was not the right place for her at all. She needed to be at the heart of the music, in the place where she could smell the dust of the stage and the sweat of the performers, where she could feel the beat in the soles of her feet and maybe, in a passing instant of glory, touch Jon's hand when he came close.

PARKER SAW HER leave and hurried to the hallway to follow her, only to stop in his tracks after catching sight of the the massive security guard who accompanied her.

"Thank you, Alan. I'll find my way, no worries. I don't need an escort."

"Ma'am" was the reply, "those are not my orders. It would cost me my job if I let you go all the way to the backstage area on your own. Mr. Stone told me not to let you go anywhere alone. He was very adamant about that."

Defeated, she folded her hands and lowered her head.

"If I may," Parker interrupted, "I'd be more than happy to take you wherever you want to go."

"Ma'am?" Alan moved to block his way.

"Please take me backstage." She shot one last, blistering look at Parker and walked away, followed by the guard.

"Naomi," Parker called, just before she entered the elevator.

The way she stopped, the way she held her head while she waited for what he was about to say, seared his heart. She was still in the same red dress she had worn leaving the plane; her braid hung over her shoulder just like before. "I'll ask you for an interview. I'll call your manager and ask for an interview. Will you agree?"

Slowly, she came back into the hallway, the lift doors closing with a discreet hiss.

"Why," Naomi asked. "Why do you keep pestering me? Why were you at the press conference? Are you stalking me?"

He had to think, and quickly. "No. No, please don't think that." He moved toward her but stopped when Alan raised his hand in warning. With a shrug, Parker explained, "I'm a journalist. And you…" A softening of her mouth, just barely noticeable, but good enough for him, for the moment. "I would like to give you the opportunity to tell the world what happened, give your view of the affair; no scandals, nothing you don't want written." Once more he fumbled for his business card, just like on the plane, and held it out. "Give me a call? Think about it, at least?" He drew a deep breath. "And if I annoyed you or overstepped, please put it down to bedazzlement."

She did not take the card. But, very gently, said, "Call Sal Rosenberg. Tell him I told you to. Then we'll see."

This time the doors closed behind her, and he was left alone, his hand still outstretched, with the memory of rose perfume and the swirl of a red skirt around slim legs.

One step. He was one step closer to her.

ALL SHE HAD to do was follow his voice. Like a lighthouse beacon, it reeled her in, the safe harbor waiting. Doors opened for her swift and smooth, security personnel eased her through and let her pass.

The huge hall was like an aquarium turned upside down, a bowl filled with music instead of water, the beams of light skipping over its surface, like sunlight breaking on a river, the standing, dancing people in it algae and ferns rooted to its bottom yet swaying in a rhythmic current. Jon was speaking to the audience while he played the intro bars to his next song. Naomi went to stand next to Art and Russ at the computers right at the side of the stage, and Jon saw her then. His face lit up, and with a movement of his hand the next song took off, his voice carrying it away across the thousands of listeners. He had turned slightly toward her, as if he was singing to her alone, flirting with her until she smiled back at him.

It ended too soon. A last encore, a last bow, and he left without turning back once. It took a while for the audience to accept it, even after the band had taken their leave.

"Let's go," Art said. He rubbed his hands in satisfaction. "Brilliant, they were really brilliant tonight. Wow, Jon had some steam in him for a first show! What a grand opening to a tour; he really rocked them. I think, boys and girls, we will have to discuss a new live album, and don't you just love the idea!"

Sal, a very wide smirk on his face, nodded. "Hell, yeah. Feels like the old days, doesn't it? And I had thought he was too old for it."

"He's not old." Naomi slapped his shoulder. "Don't say that. We are not old."

"Of course not, baby girl." The smirk turned into a friendly grin.

"Well, you aren't. But forty-six in this business can be difficult. Not for your man though."

A tech came by carrying Jon's guitars. "Here, I'll take those myself." Fondly he stroked the wood, now smudged from Jon's touch, the ebony one rattling when he shook it. "The stupid bastard. He dropped one of the picks inside again. We should really tape the damn things to his fingers."

They met Jon in the hallway. The assistants were around him, draping a large towel over his shoulders and handing him a bottle of water, relieving him of the cables and monitors while Ralph was carefully wiping makeup and sweat from his face to give him some comfort.

"Naomi." His voice was raspy, rough from the singing, his features under the grime tired, ashen, the glamour gone. Yet seeing her, he smiled. "Babe, just let me take a shower and change, then I'm all yours. Can't wait to get you alone now." Impatiently he waved the others away.

"Will you wait here for me? It'll only take me a minute, I promise."

"I'll come." She blushed at the way he pursed his lips and drew up his eyebrows.

It had been so many years, Naomi had no idea if his routine after a concert had changed since she had last been with him, but she didn't care. She wanted to be there when he turned back into a normal man, into the husband she loved.

"I can't promise you I won't try to kiss you," Jon said once they were inside the dressing room. "I can't even promise we'll leave here anytime soon."

"Didn't you book a hotel room?"

His shirt was sodden when he peeled it off and dropped it on the floor. "Don't tease. It's bad enough being without you for so long."

"Hurry up, Jon."

Surprised, he looked up. "Hurry up? You want me to hurry? Nah, there won't be no hurrying, I can promise you that. It will be soft and slow, and you'll enjoy every second. Need to remind you why you're married to me. The sad days, and the lonely days, those are over now, my dear."

chapter 4

DAWN WAS STRETCHING its first cool wisps into the room when Naomi woke. Disoriented, she lay and watched the curtains dance lazily in the breeze and listened to the sounds of the traffic, trying to remember where she was, and why. Just yesterday she was greeted by the scent of a warm sea, the cry of gulls and the chugging of boats leaving for a day of fishing in Chesapeake Bay. Now, it was the lumbering rumble of buses passing on the street below that greeted her.

Breath touched her shoulder, arms held her enclosed, her body lay nestled into another, warm, safe, familiar.

"Can't wait," he had said, and whisked her away to the hotel despite Sal's shouts and the waiting throng of fans outside the venue. The drive had taken forever, but he had not touched her, had even sat in the other corner of the limo's large backseat, well away.

"If I kiss you now, mayhem will ensue." had been Jon's words. "I don't know that I'd keep it together." And he had pulled out another bottle of water from the small fridge, his eyes never leaving her.

Once in the privacy of their suite, though, it had gone differently. Jet lag had its claws hooked into her flesh and mind by then, and it had been like a wild dream. Jon, whispering to her in the darkness, coming for her, claiming her, a dark, sensual fantasy, right here in their bed. She had felt like the prey of a big, feral jungle beast, caressed into submission, gently mauled, loved to death. Her aching limbs told the story.

"Never again," he had said to her when she was sobbing in ecstasy. "Never leave me again. Every time you do, I break. Promise, I want to hear you say it."

And, clinging to him, his in every way, she did.

CAREFULLY SHE TRIED to slip out from under the sheets, but the arms around her tightened.

"Where do you want to run off to now?"

The touch of his lips on her ear made her shiver. "I thought I'd go for a walk and get some coffee. It's so nice outside, and the sun is just rising.

It's a lovely morning, Jon."

"Not yet. Please don't go yet. I'm sure I can make it worth your while."

Naomi turned on her back. "Oh, I know you can. But I'm really hungry. There was no proper dinner last night, and now I want pancakes, and bacon, and a very big mug of coffee. And butter and syrup."

"Hungry, dear heart? Really?"

She looked up at him, at his dark eyes and the beautiful shape of his mouth, at the face she loved so much. There was no way she could tell him how much she had missed him in her exile, how great the impulse had been to return, and how hard she had fought it. He would never understand. The scar down her side was healing well; it didn't pain her anymore, and she knew that it would, in good time, be little more than a thin white line, barely visible. The surgeons had done a very good job. But it was there; she saw it every time she looked in a mirror, and it reminded her of what had happened. She could feel it now when Jon ran his fingers down her body, and she flinched.

His lips tightened briefly, but he did not pull back and did not take his hand away either.

"Does it hurt?" Jon asked. "Did I hurt you? Last night, was it too much?"

That made her smile and stretch under his touch like a cat. "Oh no." Her arms came up around his neck. "Never too much."

"Ah, okay." His voice turned into the soft, deep drawl that made her melt. "If that's so, I have some more to give. Or do you want me to call room service for your breakfast now?"

"No." She moved against him. "I'd rather go hungry for a little while longer."

JON WAS STILL groggy from the concert, but when she said she wanted to go out for breakfast and not order room service, to spend some time strolling through London, he agreed.

There was a coffee shop just down the road, right across from Harrods, and he knew she always had gone there when she had been in town before, and then, after sitting and watching the passersby and the traffic, walk across the street and shop for tea at the notorious department store. He had seen the tin boxes in her kitchen back in Halmar, placed in a neat row on the top of the fridge, sorry, dusty things filled with stale, unused leaves. Perplexed, he had asked why she spent her money on them at all, and she had given him that impossible shrug of hers and replied that it was a ritual, nothing more, something she did to remind herself that she had actually been in London.

"But you can go every weekend if you want," he had argued. "Order a damn jet and just go! We can go right now!"

And, once again, she had given him that small, thoughtful smile and replied, "But where would the fun be in that."

The breakfast selection was not the best. Ruefully, over a sticky cinnamon roll, Jon pondered the fabulous buffet they would be serving back at the hotel. He could almost taste the fried eggs and bacon, the sausages he was rather fond of, and the creamy, fruity cereal they served there.

There weren't many people around at this time of the day. The baristas stood behind the counter, chatting, their aprons still fresh and clean, the display well filled with baked goods. At the other end of the café a lonely man sat, a newspaper on his knees and an espresso in his hand, doing the crossword puzzle. Beside him on the floor sat a battered briefcase, an umbrella balanced on top. Jon wondered how his day would look, where he was headed, what would wait for him when he got back home. Loneliness seemed to hover around him like a shadow, and for a moment the sight made him sad. It reminded him too much of his own long, empty years without Naomi.

"There are no pancakes and bacon here," he said in an attempt to dispel the feeling of melancholia that was rising in him like a fog. "We could have had all that back at the hotel."

Naomi, as always, had picked a seat at the high table just inside the window where she could look out and watch the world as it passed. Her elbows on the top, mug between her hands, she gave him a sidelong glance but did not answer.

"I'm sure there is syrup too."

Her hair was loose, the locks falling over her shoulders and back in that cascade of black he loved. Her features were sharper than they had been before, the sweetness had gone out of the shape of her cheeks and chin to be replaced by finely chiseled contours during her recovery, but her eyes had retained their clear, velvety expression.

"I love you." He was helpless against the storm of emotions.

Her lips curled. "I know."

"I thought I loved you even more when you were gone. I believed missing you would tear me apart." Jon took her hand in his to gaze down at her rings. "But it's not true. Seeing you here, now, this tears me apart. You are here, I can touch you, and I don't know where to go with my love for you. It's nearly more than I can take."

There was no reply right away, so he looked up.

"That's the weirdest declaration of love I've ever heard," she said thoughtfully. "I'm not sure I want to be compared to a headache, Jon. There is no pill for this."

"No, there isn't. I'll just have to bear it, live with the pain, endure it every day of my life. I embrace this ache. It's a part of me; without it, I'd be a hollow, silent shell." He wanted to kiss her again, just to make sure she was really back. "Without it, I'd be nothing."

Naomi sighed and slipped from the stool, brushed the crumbs of her muffin from her skirt, and pushed her hair out of her face. She picked up their empty mugs and carried them back to the counter, nodding to the young man who took them from her.

"Okay, then." With a small wave she indicated he should get up too. "You may stop whining. Let's go back to the hotel and see if we can find you some pancakes."

And that, Jon acknowledged as he followed her out into the crisp London morning, was what he loved about her. She always knew how to drown his more sentimental outbursts.

"I TOLD THAT journalist to call Sal for an interview with me."

The information was delivered so offhandedly that Jon hardly took any notice at first. One of those red double-decker buses was rumbling past them, close enough to almost touch, tourists staring at him and the view from behind the glass panes. For a morbid moment he wondered what would happen if one of them recognized him and called his name. Maybe everyone would cluster on this side of the vehicle and it would tip over, and he would be buried under his fans, literally. It was such an outrageously funny image that he grinned and even raised his hand in greeting, but he was ignored.

"What?"

"I said," Naomi repeated patiently, "I've thought about it and yes, I think I want to talk to the press, but only to that one reporter, the one from the press conference."

Jon stopped in his tracks, right there in the middle of the sidewalk, forcing a woman with a baby buggy to take a detour around him.

"Why do you want to do that, baby? You don't have to talk to any of those vultures. We pay Sal and Art a lot of money to take care of that."

She put her arm through his to pull him forward before someone noticed him and they got into trouble.

"I want to do this, Jon. There will be no rest until someone tells the story, and you know that very well. The sooner, the better too, or you will be asked the same questions at every stop."

"You talked to him? When?" He did not budge.

"Jon, please. I talked to him after Sal took me to the lounge you had reserved for me. The press lounge was next to mine, and when I went out onto the balcony to see you better, he approached me. It was okay. He is quite nice." She tugged his sleeve. "Come on, Jon. Breakfast."

They had slipped out on their own without guards, and he had not objected because it had been so early and so few people were around yet, but that was changing now, with the morning rush hour beginning. Traffic had picked up considerably. Shops were beginning to open; tourists strolled by on their way to Harrods. Often enough he had gotten away when he had left hotels early enough, and returned unmolested. The attention of the fans was focused on the elevators where he was expected to emerge, never on the entrances. In a way it was hilarious, and he had sometimes stood in the lobby for a while, even leaning on the counter, to watch their excitement.

"Sal left you up there alone? Alone, in a lounge? All by yourself?" He could hardly believe what he was hearing.

The way she was standing at the top of the steps, one hand raised to hold down her blowing hair, the valet in his red coat opening the heavy door for her, Jon thought she could well be on the cover of a hotel brochure.

"Of course he did, Jon. There was a concert about to start, remember? His place was not up there in that stupid lounge but with you, and beside your stage. He does not get paid to keep me company."

Slowly, thoughtfully, he followed her inside. The lobby was fairly empty; only a couple of clerks were working the reception desk. A man in a very dapper uniform was busy vacuuming the dark green carpet; someone else had just put down a big bowl with fresh apples on one of the tables. From the desk, a large bouquet of nodding roses spread their sweet aroma. Jon loved this large, old hotel. He loved the quiet elegance, the high ceilings, the tasteful rooms, and the total discretion. Here, he felt private.

"But alone, Naomi, anything could have happened to you. I hate the thought of you running around alone in that huge building. What if someone had seen; you might have been abducted, harmed."

"Yes." She inserted the keycard into the slot. "That's happened already, the being harmed. And in the best secured place on Earth. You can't impress me with that, Jon."

As always, an entire floor had been closed off for them. The moment the elevator door opened guards faced them, ready to block any stranger's access; but seeing Jon, they moved swiftly aside.

"I'm not trying to impress you." There were voices from down the hall, the sounds of cutlery clinking, plates being stacked. A whiff of coffee and toast drifted toward them. Jon pointed in that direction. "Breakfast."

Reluctantly, Naomi followed.

"Sal should not have left you there alone. He knows it wasn't safe, even with a guard outside the door. See?" He stopped. "See what happened? A bloody reporter got to you without any of us being there to take care of you. That's not supposed to happen. Ever."

Something in her face changed, a tiny little tightening of her mouth, but he knew he had offended her. It didn't matter.

"You can't do this on your own, Naomi. Please trust me. You are just too nice, too friendly; and someone like that—he would wheedle everything he wants to know out of you, and you wouldn't even notice until you read it in the tabloids the next day. You have to trust me. I've been there! Don't think I learned this overnight. It was a bitter lesson, and I want to spare you that. Baby, please?"

"Okay." Delivered in a soft monotone, it was quite clear that she wasn't really okay with it at all but was giving in for his sake.

"I promise, Naomi," Jon said. "I promise, I won't make this hard on you. I know you want to go out and enjoy the towns we go to, and I will take you out. We will have fun on this tour."

At last she smiled. It was a small and rather sad smile, but it was a start.

Jon held out his hand. "Eggs? Bacon? I'm sure there will be some mushrooms for you, and an omelette."

"How do you know?"

Her fingers were cool, and he closed his own around them firmly to warm them up. "Because, my love, I asked them to cook some every morning just in case you would be there for breakfast."

SHE COULD SEE, from where she was sitting with Art and Sean, how Jon had cornered Sal, a napkin and a spoon in his hand. His shoulders were tense as he stood in front of his manager, his back to her as he talked to him, not at all loud, but his voice carried well enough.

"...and not leave her there by herself," he was saying, "Those weren't my orders, you idiot. She is not to be left alone, ever."

Mortified, Naomi pushed the mushrooms around on her plate. Art, beside her, said nothing, and Sean listened with narrowed eyes.

"What were you thinking? Did you dump your brains in the gutter somewhere?" There was more venom in Jon's tone than she had heard in a long time.

They couldn't hear Sal's reply.

"Yeah, I don't care." Jon dropped the spoon back on the buffet table, where it landed on a pile of used cups with a ringing sound. Art raised his eyebrows. "I don't care what you thought. Don't think, Sal, it's useless anyway. Just do as you're told."

Without waiting for an answer, Jon came over to her table, fury painted on his face, and sat down beside her. He was still clutching the napkin, and he had not brought any food with him.

Sal, still standing where Jon had left him, gave her a resigned glance. One corner of his mouth tried to twitch into a smile, but instead it turned into a smirk of resignation. With a shrug he turned away and left the room, everyone in it staring after him, their expressions a mirror of Naomi's feelings.

Carefully she laid down her fork, appetite gone, the joy of being back with Jon lost.

"That was harsh." Art stole one of the cooling mushrooms from her plate. "Jon, that was really harsh. Did you have a bad night?" And then, realizing what he had said, grinned at Naomi. "Yeah, I guess not, but why attack Sal, and in public?"

"Don't talk to me, Art." Jon poured himself some coffee. "Just don't talk to me, okay? The stupid bastard..." He broke off and took a deep breath.

Art waited patiently.

"Okay, yeah, it was a bit harsh. Sorry you had to hear that, but I'm so angry with him. He left Naomi all by herself in the bloody VIP lounge when I told him to look after her. And promptly someone jumps on her and tries for an interview. We need to discuss security, Art. We need to tighten it considerably." His breathing calmed after a sip of coffee. Gradually his body relaxed; he leaned back in his chair, eyeing Naomi's discarded food with regret. "I'm sorry, babe. Didn't mean to yell at Sal right here, but when I saw him it just broke out of me. God, I'm so angry I could strangle him."

"He left you alone up there?" Art asked incredulously. "Was he out of his mind? With only one guard?"

Jon's fist hit the table, shaking the coffee pot dangerously. "Just my words! There you go, Art, I can't believe it."

"That is really hard to believe."

Naomi rose. "No, don't bother," she said when both of them began to jump up. "I'm only going back to our room." Her hand on Jon's shoulder, she added, "And I don't want to listen to you any longer. You should be ashamed of yourselves. Sal would lie down and die to protect me, and you know that. I'm done with you for now," and walked out without so much as a glance back.

THERE WAS NO luggage.

She hadn't brought anything but the change of clothes she was wearing now.

The door closed behind her, and it was only then that she realized she was still holding her napkin. It was a very nice one, damask linen, the hotel's logo elaborately embroidered in one corner, larger than a handkerchief, heavy. Sadly she gazed at it, rubbing the fine material between her fingers. Only a few weeks before Jon had appeared on her doorstep in Halmar she had ordered nearly the same design for the hotel there, only they had been pale green. They had used them at their wedding a few months later, and she had flushed with pride when her uncle commented on them, complimenting her good taste and how well they went with the interior of the dining room.

Longing for the Seaside spiked in her like a sharp, sudden pain.

It was June. In a few days they would be celebrating Midsummer Night there, and she would miss it.

She would miss putting on her white cotton dress, the one with the lace trim, and sitting in the meadow down by the sea with Solveigh and the other girls, watching the sun dip toward the water but never set. There would be no Norwegian folk songs for her this year, nor the spectacle of the bonfire or the taste of the fish grilled over it, no scent of dill from the vat with the crawfish and no tangy sip of aquavit, brewed by a local distillery and brought out only for special occasions.

Her hotel had always been fully booked for Midsummer, and most of the guests were the same ones, returning year after year like the geese traveling over the bay on their migrations. Often enough she had stood on the deck to watch their flight, wishing herself away with them, to warmer places, out of her loneliness and longing, dreaming of seeking out Jon and ending her exile. But the birds had vanished beyond the hills, and she had returned inside to her work, and everything had been as before.

chapter 5

THERE WAS A desk with a computer near the elevator. A security guard sat behind it to document who came and went.

He pointed, very courteously, toward Sal's room door.

For a few seconds Naomi stood before it, hand raised to knock, a little scared, uncertain what to say.

"Hey." Tired lines were etched around his mouth, but they melted into the dimples of a smile when he saw her. "I'm sorry, darling. Never meant to get you into trouble. He's really pissed, isn't he?"

"I don't know." She stepped past him into his room.

Sal raised his eyebrows.

"I didn't bring any luggage," Naomi said. "When I left DC I thought I'd go shopping here. I love to go shopping in London. But..." She hesitated and glanced at the open door. "I have the feeling Jon is not in the mood for Harrods. Would you like to go shopping with me?"

"Not really."

Surprised, she blinked at him. For some reason this dry, calm response shook her; it was so unusual coming from Sal, who normally always did her bidding, and gladly.

He pushed his fists into his jeans pockets and shrugged, still standing in the open doorway as if he was afraid to be alone with her, afraid of incurring more wrath from Jon. "I'm really sorry, Naomi, but I don't think I can go out with you. He's right. I shouldn't have left you alone; it was my fault you were bothered. I'm too upset to be good company now."

His room was neat, tidy, nothing lying around, not even a shirt on a chair somewhere. It was a very nice room too, large and sunny, but nowhere near as grand as the suite she and Jon were staying in. There was only muffled traffic noise from outside; birdsong and the tinkling of a fountain were louder. She remembered the hotel's yard from last year, and how much she had liked the white gravel of its winding paths.

"It wasn't your fault. You said you would come back right away and keep me company. Only I left before you could return. Sal."

He raised his head.

"Sal, I want you to do something for me. That reporter, the one who grilled Jon yesterday and who approached me in the lounge. You know who I mean?"

The corners of his mouth came down in disdain, but he nodded.

"I want to give him an interview, and I told him to call you about it. So when he does, make an appointment, okay? I'm ready for this. It's time to move on." Naomi could hardly believe these words had just left her lips. She could feel their residue on her tongue, the echo in her ears, and it seemed as if a distant door fell softly into its lock, leaving behind a kind of deafness, a muted, breathless silence.

"Time to move on." Repeating it didn't change anything; the phrase still fell dead.

Sal didn't notice her surprise. Relieved, he took a deep breath. "All right. If that's what you want, I'll do it. But, Naomi, we will have to be very circumspect. Let me handle it, okay? You know we have to watch what we want the press to know about the background of the whole thing; this could destroy Jon's career."

"Whatever." Somehow, right at this moment, she could not muster any enthusiasm for Jon's fame at all.

BACK IN THE hallway, she was alone. The guard was still sitting by the elevators, but otherwise there was no movement. Most of the band would still be at breakfast now; she could hear their voices. She still had her purse in her hand from their early-morning stroll; and now, on an impulse, knowing full well what the consequences would be, Naomi walked up to the elevator and, as casually as she could, pressed the button.

With a frown, the security man was about to speak, but she said quickly, "Spa appointment. Be right back," and he stopped.

It was that easy, and standing once again on the broad steps outside the entrance, she breathed in the warm, fume-scented London air.

She was free. For a fleeting moment Naomi wished Solveigh was with her to share the fun of a shopping trip, but Solveigh was back in Halmar, probably off work at the hotel by now, waiting for her baby's birth. She and Russ had yet to celebrate getting married. Everything had been overshadowed by the shooting, even her best friend's wedding to Jon's producer. There had been a very brief civil ceremony back in LA, she knew, before Russ had sent her off to be with her family for the baby's birth while he was touring with Jon.

Naomi recalled them sitting over lunch, right after the dull and unromantic procedure, and how she had suggested that Russ go to Halmar with her.

Russ had looked like an owl in his shock, his fine brown hair literally standing on ends.

"Are you out of your mind?" had been his words. "How could I ever do that? Thirty containers, Naomi, which means thirty trucks, and that's not even our personal stuff! If one of them goes missing there will be no show! We'd lose millions!"

And Solveigh, her fingers knit through his, her new ring shining in the California noon sunlight, had nodded, a wrinkle of exasperation between her eyes. A wedding feast, she had informed Naomi, could always happen later, when the tour was over, when she didn't look like a pig in a potato sack anymore, when there was time and she, Naomi, could hold the baby and be the godmother.

NAOMI WOULD HAVE preferred to be on Oxford Street. She liked the lively bustle there, the casual crowd, the tourists and the street vendors.

Before, when she had been just Naomi, an unimportant hotel manager from a small, Norwegian town, she had spent hours sitting on one of the benches there, a take-out container of Thai food in her lap, eating, watching, like a potted plant in the stream of life around her.

But for now, Brompton would have to do, and Harrods.

Tourist trap, she knew the Londoners called it, and sniffed in disdain when she professed her liking for it, overpriced, ostentatious.

She loved it. She loved the stupid splendor of the Egyptian floor and the marble restrooms; she even loved the silly souvenir department, and she could spend hours gawking at the artful displays in the food court.

"I'm a tourist," she had said to the lady who ran the B&B where she had liked to stay, "so it's okay for me to go there."

And every time she had brought back a tea tin, a useless but cherished memento of another trip to London, bought and then forgotten on the top of her fridge.

Now, shopping for clothes, she used her own credit card, the one for her own account, as if she felt she had to make a point, as if it was a short foray into freedom.

She needed a suitcase, or a bag, and another purse, shoes, and sandals. She took her time. A couple of times her cell phone rang, but she didn't take it out to look to see who was calling.

Dresses, she wanted dresses, underwear, a couple of pairs of jeans, shirts, a jacket or two. And she was in the mood for a good manicure, massage and all.

Out of sheer willfulness she picked a dark red nail polish and later, when it had been applied, looked at her hands in astonishment. They looked elegant in a new, strange way, not like hers at all, as if they belonged to a strange, strong, independent woman; and she liked it. It made her buy the matching lipstick, and when the salesgirl offered to freshen up her makeup she let her do it, amused by the fact that she had not been wearing any in the first place. She saw a different self in the mirror, an enhanced and altered self, with an arrogantly painted mouth and skin as glowing as pale satin.

In a new, dark blue skirt, its hem well above her knees, and a cream lace blouse, matching high heels on her feet that clicked with every step, she returned to the hotel.

JON WAS WAITING in the lobby.

All by himself, a cup of coffee on the table in front of him, he was watching the door.

"Does it give you that much satisfaction," he said when she walked up to him. "Is this something you need, to take off without telling anyone, leaving me in misery and fear?"

"Yes." She wondered how long it would take Harrods to deliver her purchases.

"Yes?" A short, bitter laugh, then, "So this is what I get, Naomi? I have to live with this, you doing as you please in the face of danger?"

The lush red varnish looked even better in the muted light of the lobby; it had the satisfying gleam of blood now.

"Danger. That is all you can think about, isn't it? Danger, Jon? I'm trying to get my life back, my life. Not yours, not Sal's. Mine."

Without waiting for a reply she left him there and returned to their rooms.

Jon followed, slamming the door behind him. "I'm so tired of your attitude. It's not as if I'm locking you in or anything. I just want you to let me know when and where you're going, and to take someone with you. Take LaGasse. Alan. For crying out loud, take Sal if it pleases you, but don't run off on your own!"

Naomi ignored him. She opened the balcony door and stepped outside. Just below, cabs and buses had come to a halt because a woman had dropped a bag of oranges while crossing the street. They were rolling everywhere, sunny little orbs fighting for their freedom.

"What am I supposed to tell you, huh? What is it you want to hear? I'll not apologize to Sal for shouting at him this morning. It was his job to look after your safety and he blew it. For that he deserves all the shouting I'm capable of." Fury and fear made his voice sound rough, nothing like the famous singer's at all.

One of the cab drivers had gotten out of his car and was helping the woman collect the oranges. She was awkwardly trying to hold them in the crook of her arm. The shopping bag was torn and useless, and when she bent down to pick up another one, they fell from her again. Intrigued, Naomi watched how the driver tossed the oranges into the taxi and waved to the woman, offering her a ride, and how she thanked him with a sweet smile. It was a meaningless little scene, but it lifted her spirits considerably.

With a sigh, she turned back inside and toward Jon. "I needed clothes. You were busy fuming and making dire plans with Art, Sal was too scared of you to go with me, and I didn't want a bodyguard trailing me while I shop for underwear. And you can stop ranting now."

"I'm not ranting! I'm…God, Naomi, why do you keep doing this? Why do I have to go through this again, and again: you gone, and I dumb-struck with panic because I don't know if and when I'll see you again?"

There was a knock on the door. Without looking Jon reached behind him and opened it, only to step aside in surprise. Two liveried men carried in her purchases, neatly bundled in the famous green sacks; and another one, right behind them, brought in the new suitcases, saying, "Madam, do you wish us to unpack for you?"

Distracted, Jon stood by as she directed them to the bedroom and gave her orders.

"You bought all this in the short time you were gone?" he asked when she returned. "And you got a manicure and a facial? How?"

Anger rose to pool between her temples. "Yes, Jon, I did. I was on a plane and at your concert during the last forty-eight hours, and then you go and have that fight with Sal about nothing and ruin the morning, and I felt like something nice, like some fresh clothes. You can go and fume somewhere else. I'm tired. I'm sad and upset, and I don't want to hear you carry your fury into the bedroom where I'm going now to have a look at my pretty new dresses."

"Is this what this is about? You wanted to go shopping, you wanted that more than anything else? Really? Well, baby, I would take you anywhere you want! You should have said something!" Helplessly, he spread his arms in a gesture of defeat. "I've never had a wife before; how am I supposed to know what you want if you don't say so?"

With a little gasp, her anger flew away, only to be replaced by a resigned fatigue, a tired indifference, and the wish to be somewhere else.

"I don't know, Jon. I don't know why it is so important that you have to be told about every little step I take, who I talk to, or what I want. I just don't know. All I do know is that I was able to take care of myself very well before we met again, and no one ever told me what to do. And I liked it that way."

He trailed after her into the other room, where the hotel personnel were busy with her things.

Naomi, her arms wrapped tightly around her body, did not move away when he stopped right behind her, and so he laid his hands on her shoulders, rubbing them gently. "You look beautiful. That lipstick makes me want to stare at your mouth all the time; you are outrageously glamorous." There was no response, so he plodded on, "I talked to Sal. I didn't apologize, it's true, but we talked. You will get your interview— he will see to it. But Naomi, why that reporter, I want to know? He isn't even a real one, did you know? He owns a newspaper. I have no idea why he wants an interview with you. Do you know him?"

Her heart jolted a bit. "I don't know anything about him, no." The lie stuck to her tongue like a piece of chewing gum licked off the pavement, gritty and vile.

"And another thing, my love. If you really want to, you can talk to him alone. But I'd be more comfortable if someone was there with you. If you don't want me or Sal, please take Art with you, or Sean, for all I care. It's a pity Solveigh isn't here." His fingers toyed with a stray curl just behind her ear. "I'll be right outside the door though, just to make sure he doesn't drag you away to his lair. I would, in his place."

For once his teasing did not have its usual effect on her; he could feel it in the stiffness of her stance.

Her hair smelled nice, like lavender and roses. It was in a pile at the back of her head. The mass of curls was right under his chin, tantalizing, inviting him to sink his hands into it, her body close enough for him to feel her warmth.

"That's a lovely dress. My favorite color on you, rose." He pointed at the one they were unpacking just then.

"I know." She shifted as if to shake him off.

"Did you think of me when you bought it? Did you buy it because you knew I'd love to see you in this?" He could feel the bones in her shoulders move under his hands, fine, fragile like a bird's.

"Yes. No." With a sigh she signaled the valets to leave, which they did, closing the doors softly behind them.

Naomi moved away from him to hang up the last two shirts herself.

"I'm sorry," Jon said, "I really am. Baby, look at me. I'm just so scared. After what happened I want to make sure you're really safe, and being on tour we're exposed all the time; there are so many possibilities for someone to hurt you."

"I'm sorry too." Said so softly that at first, he thought he hadn't heard right.

"I'm sorry I ran off again, Jon. I don't know what makes me do that; it's an impulse, a crazy urge to be free, and I don't even know of what. Everything I want is right here, right in front of me." She returned to him and laid her arms around his neck.

"This tour was a stupid idea." It took him a moment to return the embrace. "It's too early for you, the stress is insane, and we have only just started. We should have canceled the whole bloody thing and retired to Halmar, where you could heal in peace and regain your strength."

For a moment she was tempted to agree, but then she replied, "No. No, Jon, we can't do that. We need to step forward. I need to step forward. This is our life now, this here, you…" Her words trailed off into an exhausted silence.

"You know what?" Jon knew exactly what to do. "I think you need to lie down and sleep some more. All this stepping forward stuff is well and good, but it will be so much easier if you're rested and not jet-lagged and tired. I promise, I'll wake you for tea."

She complained some more, mumbled how she wanted to go out for lunch later and enjoy the sunshine on the Embankment, take a walk down Regent Street and watch the bustle on Oxford for a while, but she did as he suggested.

Jon watched how she peeled off the skirt and blouse and kicked off her shoes, how she pulled the clips out of her hair and then curled up under the blanket, her eyes closing while she was still muttering about the things she would miss. Carefully he closed the curtains until only a small sliver of light remained, an arrow pointing toward her like an invitation, and left her to sleep.

chapter 6

IT WASN'T WHAT Parker had hoped for.

In the more imaginative of his dreams he had envisioned a small table in the corner of a quiet restaurant, a niche where he could stare all he wanted and talk to her in private, dropping the pretense of a newspaper interview, just the two of them, alone.

Walking into the hotel's lobby now though, he realized it had really only been that, a dream, and there was no way for him to make it a reality.

Sal Rosenberg was there to welcome him and lead him to the breakfast room with the beautiful view of the garden.

On the phone, when he had called to ask for the meeting, Parker had been taken aback at how easily it was agreed to. He had been expecting obstacles: requests for credentials, at the worst a security check, but no; Jon Stone's wife had expressed the wish to talk to him, and all those important, powerful people around her bowed to her demands.

Of course they wouldn't let her off their publicity leash, that much became clear as soon as he followed Sal out onto the terrace.

She was there, it was true, and so lovely the sight shook his heart, but an entire posse of men surrounded her.

Parker stopped on the step leading down to where Naomi was sitting like a queen holding court. The table had been set with a shining, heavy silver tea set. There were trays with little cakes and sandwiches, linen napkins and fine porcelain, a bowl of cream and a vase with flowers. It was all so elegant and civilized that he wanted to puke right then and there. She was wearing a dress that seemed made for her, the pale rose giving her skin a soft glow, the thin silk layers of the wide skirt flowing around her legs like water in the dawn. Her hair was not unbound, but she was wearing it in a loose ponytail that at last allowed him to see the glossy curls.

Behind her stood Jon.

The Master, up close, and with the smirk of a pleased cat on his face. His hand rested on her shoulder in a negligently possessive gesture, his posture one of easy pride. He seemed cut from a gentleman's magazine cover: well groomed, well dressed, and so good-looking Parker wanted to slap his face. Grudgingly he had to admit that they were indeed a stunning couple, both with black hair and those dark eyes, setting off each other's attractiveness very well.

There were two other men, the same he had seen with Jon just before the sound check, and they were duly introduced, but he chose to ignore them. She was offering him the seat across the table with a flick of her wrist, rings flashing, making Parker wonder if it was intentional, to remind him of who she was.

His wife, and now Jon was sitting down beside her, as was Sal, closing the ranks around her in protection.

HE HAD PREPARED his questions so carefully, so well thought out to wheedle all the information he wanted without seeming to pry; and here were these savvy publicity sharks, monitoring every word that came out of his mouth.

He hadn't even taken out his notepad before Sal's eyes narrowed in suspicion and Jon's fingers drummed impatiently on the immaculate tablecloth. Only Naomi, her hands folded patiently in her lap, waited for him to get sorted, a tiny smile on her lips.

"So," Parker asked, "I've always thought if I got a chance to do an interview with you, this would be my most important question." He laid the pen down next to his teacup. "Do you like champagne?"

Her eyelids fluttered. The men surrounding her shifted, but no one interfered.

"I do." A flash of amusement from the corners of her eyes, unnoticed by Jon.

A waiter came to pour their tea and offer cream and lemon. She declined and asked for coffee instead, which was procured instantly.

"You worked with your husband on the movie soundtrack, correct? You wrote the lyrics? I recall there was an album about twenty years back that had your lyrics on it too. How did that come about?"

She took a breath to answer, but before she could say anything Sal replied, "It was a collaboration of young artists. Jon wanted to try something new, and this worked well."

He watched how she took one of the cupcakes and placed it on the dainty plate in front of her, where she pushed it around with the fork.

"How interesting. So how did you meet? You were living in Geneva back then, if I'm informed correctly, and Mr. Stone in LA?"

This time she was faster. "I sent some lyrics I'd written to his office. Sal…"—a small wave of her hand—"Sal contacted me after that. We got together, decided we could work on this, and did."

It was fun to watch the faces around her, and the tension in them. He decided to push a little.

"I'd like to learn a little more about you, and have you confirm my facts. You have a grown son, is that correct?"

Wrong direction, he saw that right away by the shuttering of her expression.

"Mrs. Stone's private life is not the subject of this interview," Sal said.

But this was what he wanted to know. So, carefully, realizing these men were even sharper than he had supposed, Parker formulated his next question. "We were going to talk about the shooting. So may I ask about that now?"

A reluctant nod from her, a tightening in Jon's shoulders.

"How do you feel now? It's been five months, and your injuries were substantial. The tour is only starting out."

"I'm fine." A small smile, a slight softening of demeanor. "I'm looking forward to it, very much."

This, Parker thought, was like plowing stones. "So what exactly happened? We all saw the footage of the shooting, but you have never given a statement yourself."

He could see sadness laying itself over her lovely face like a veil. She seemed lost in her memories, reliving that day, living through the hurt again, feeling the pain. Her hand, the one holding the fork until just now, sank to her lap.

"We were awarded Oscars for the movie soundtrack that night," Naomi said slowly, "Jon and I. We wanted to go out and celebrate. I remember we were standing backstage, debating where to go, and Jon saying to me I should go ahead; he had to do another interview. I remember…" She lowered her head. "I remember kissing my husband and watching him get into the car. And then…" Again she hesitated. "And then I woke up in the hospital, and everything hurt. That's all."

"But you do know who shot you." The moment the words were out of his mouth he could have smacked himself. Her reaction though was interesting. Without moving at all she seemed to gather herself together, removing herself from everyone around her, even from Jon.

"Yes. Of course."

"Your husband is a very famous man. His affairs before he married you were notorious. How do you feel about this? Being shot down by one of his former mistresses?" He knew right away he had overstepped, and the interview would be ended before he ever got a chance to really talk to her. She did not even have to say or do anything; it was as if Jon was so finely tuned to her that he knew exactly what she wanted.

"I think this is over," he said, very calmly and courteously but with finality too, "And you'll have to excuse us."

"We hardly spoke at all!" Parker felt like a fool. "I've hardly asked you anything. This is not enough to write an article!"

"Well, then there won't be an article, right? It's not as if we asked for it." Jon held out his hand to Naomi, who took it without hesitation and rose with him. "Thank you for coming, Mr. Hamilton, and thank you for your interest. I think my wife needs a break now."

They walked away, his arm around her just like the day in the parking lot of the arena, his head bent toward her. She had his complete attention.

Sal gave him a sarcastic glance as he dropped into the chair Naomi had just vacated. He picked up the cupcake she had been playing with, gave the white icing a brief inspection, and then bit into it with relish. "Normally I don't eat this sweet stuff," he said around the cake, "but these are awfully good. You should have one."

"That wasn't an interview. That was a farce."

Sal shrugged. "She really wanted this. She explicitly asked for you. But it seems that in the end she still can't talk about it. You'll just have to live with it."

Resigned, Parker tucked the notepad back into his pocket. Regretfully he gazed at the doorway, wondering if he'd ever see her up close again and wondering, even now, how he could achieve that.

"I would," he confessed, "really have loved to write her story. There's so much more here than meets the eye." He flinched a little at Sal's loud bark of laughter.

THE ROOM WAS dark. Someone had closed the balcony doors against the rush hour traffic; it was cool and dim inside, quiet, peaceful.

Naomi pulled her hair out of the band holding it into a ponytail and shook it, as if that simple act could liberate her from her thoughts and the uncomfortable feeling the brief interview with Parker had left behind. She dropped onto the couch.

Jon had closed the door and was standing in front of her, waiting, but it seemed she couldn't bring herself to talk to him just yet.

"You want too much too fast," he said softly. "Why are you pushing yourself so hard? This friggin' interview was the worst idea ever. For God's sake, Naomi. Why?"

Silently, she shook her head.

"Darling, why can't we just take it easy and have some fun, try to find our footing again? Things aren't what they were before." his words died at the way she looked at him: exhausted, sad, and defeated.

"I remember," Naomi began, her voice so small and broken that Jon wanted her to stop again right away, not take on the terrible task of speaking at all. "I remember how we stood there, backstage, and everyone was there. Russ and Solveigh, Sal, Art and Sue, Joshua…" she broke off again. Her hands knotted tightly in her lap, the fingers white and bony. "Joshua. But he was gone before it happened. He left with Harry and his wife and their kids. They wanted to surf early the next morning." Tears were pooling in her eyes as she looked up at him. "Jon, just think, if he had been there…"

"No, don't even think about that. Don't go there, Naomi; it didn't happen! Baby!" He sank down on the carpet beside her and took her hands in his. "Please. Don't torture yourself like this."

"You kissed me," she went on, undeterred. "You kissed me before going off to that TV interview; and, Jon, I wanted to drown in that kiss." A ghost of a smile slipped across her face. "In that one instant I thought I finally had it all. You, my life with you, and my Oscar."

"Yeah, you really hugged that little guy. Didn't even let go of him to kiss me, as I recall." It was a lame attempt at a joke, but it made her press his fingers slightly in acknowledgment.

"Sean and Sal were with me, and we walked out to the car. Sal asked me something, I don't remember what it was, and I wanted to reply. Only I never got the chance. That's all."

And it was. As easy as that, he had to admit; it was as easy as that. One bullet for her, the other for her bodyguard. She had been hurt; he had died, as if someone had taken a red pen and drawn a final line through their lives, ending everything.

"When I woke up in that hospital room and saw you there, saw you crying and looking as old as the hills in your grief, Jon, all I wanted was to go back to those beautiful places I'd been while I was in a coma and forget everything. And then my father came in..."

"Yes." Even now, months later, he could feel the cold fury churning in his bowels at that scene.

"And then I wanted to die for sure. I know I nearly did. I thought I did. For a while, there was only quiet and peace." Some animation returned to her face. "I was in the loveliest forest, Jon. There was moss under my feet, dark blue ponds like mirrors, and trees...trees like I have never seen in this world. It felt like being on another planet, in a different universe. Someone was with me, walking by my side, someone I knew I could lean on if I faltered, someone who loved me deeply and cared for me; but I could not see him. And I felt safe. I wanted to stay, but he said I couldn't. It wasn't a dream; it was more than that. Somehow I knew if I reached that forest's edge I'd get to a beach, and then I'd be allowed to move onward. Only I couldn't, even though I wanted to very much. They sent me back." She fell silent, lost in her thoughts, far away. There was a soft yearning in her eyes, a distance he knew only too well, one that broke his heart over and over again. No matter how hard he tried, he could never completely grasp her; she always seemed to have one foot in a different dimension.

"But you belong here, with me." Saying it was like plodding up a steep, stony hill. "You can't be anywhere else, not even in another room. Don't you know that? Don't you know how much I need you?"

That brought her back. Gently she touched his face, brushed over his lips with her fingertips. "I know, my love. That's why I'm here; that's why I came to you now. I took all the loneliness I could bear, and for as long as I could. A moment longer would have been terrible torture." A small shrug. "It was torture from the moment the car pulled out of the gate and onto the road, when I could still see you standing in the doorway."

"Ah, you stupid chick," Jon breathed. "Why, then? Three weeks, Naomi, and I nearly died. I was in that house all by myself, and it felt just like it did back when you walked out on me, pregnant with Joshua.

It was like a tomb, no life, no light, no love. Everything left with you."

"Jon."

And with that small word, his name, softly spoken in her gentle voice, something seemed to shift, the universe realigning itself into order.

"Please don't talk of dying or being in a different world anymore, Naomi. I know the burden is mine; my misspent life is the reason for what happened. If I..." He was still holding her hand, and now he pressed it in his anguish. "If I had kept my mind after you left me, when I thought everything had ended, if I hadn't wasted myself on senseless affairs, no love, no feelings..."

"Stop."

"Everything is different now. We're married; you can't just run away every time things get difficult. We have to stick it out together, Naomi; we really do. You allowed me back into your life. You took me back, so many years later. You, Joshua, and I—we're a family. There is no running, and there is no cheating. I'm laying down my soul for you, and in return I want you to come to me and lean on me when life gets hard for you, and not walk away. If this is going to work then that's how it has to be." Jon realized he was on his knees, pleading, but this time she didn't pull away. Her hand was warm, her fingers tightly around his, holding on.

"Jon, I lied to you," Naomi said.

"What?"

The silk of her dress rustled like a brook when she leaned forward to be closer to him. "I lied. I told you I hadn't met that reporter, Parker, before. But I did."

"Yeah, I know you did, at the lounge. That's where all the grief originated, Sal leaving you up there. It's not important." The skin of her throat and cleavage was as pure as a pearl, and he wanted to reach out and touch it; but she was looking at him so earnestly that he resisted.

"Yes, but before that. He was on my plane, and he tried to charm me with champagne. He tried very hard." She touched his face again to make him listen.

Jon shrugged. "So he wanted to wheedle an interview out of you even then. Doesn't surprise me. You didn't have to keep that a secret, darling. That was to be expected."

"No." For an instant she hesitated. "That wasn't it."

"Not it?" A cup of coffee, Jon wanted coffee badly, and he deplored that he had passed on the assortment of sandwiches on the terrace. They had looked very inviting indeed. Wincing a little he got up and brushed off his trousers. Room service it would have to be; at this time of day there could be no idea of walking down the street.

There was no answer from her, so he turned around, phone in hand, to see her blush. Naomi was sitting on her hands awkwardly, almost like a schoolgirl, and for a moment he wanted to grin at her until he saw the contrition on her face.

"Not an interview, Naomi?"

"No. He wanted to…chat. He didn't know who I was."

"Are you saying he was making a pass at you?" It was so funny he had to bite his tongue when she nodded reluctantly.

"And you thought you wouldn't tell me. Seriously, what did you think would happen? I'd have him arrested, gone after him and shot him? So someone has a crush on my wife? Yeah, I can see that happening. I have a crush on you too. It only proves he has good taste." Now he did laugh.

"He invited me to have champagne with him," she said sullenly, the corners of her mouth turned down. "And I did. I drank champagne with him on the plane. He was quite cute. Fun."

"He's a clown." Jon put the phone back on the table and held out his hand. "I've changed my mind. It's too late for coffee; let's be reckless and go out for a drink. Come on. We'll get Alan to drive us. I'm in the mood for a stroll along the Embankment."

chapter 7

"HE BOUGHT YOU champagne?" Jon asked while they were waiting for the elevator. "He chatted you up in the plane and then offered you champagne? Everyone drinks champagne on a long flight. How unoriginal."

He really liked the dress she was wearing. It reminded him, in a way, of the evening gown they had bought for her when they had been in London more than a year ago, when he had asked her to marry him; and he smiled at the memory.

"Maybe not for him." Naomi shrugged. It was the same, small, disdainful movement of her shoulder that had made him wilt so often, and now, seeing it directed at another man, Jon felt a surge of elated pride.

She was searching for something in her purse, not even looking at him, and had said it in an absentminded, negligent way, just as if now that they had talked about it, the entire thing didn't matter anymore.

"Now, if he'd gotten them to serve you fresh oysters with the bubbly, that would have been a feat."

This made her look at him in surprise. "But there were no oysters. I've never heard of oysters on a commercial flight. Do they do that? Really? I would have loved some!"

Jon laughed. "Yeah, I can see how you would have loved that. Come on."

The elevator was opening for them, but just as he was about to usher her in, one of the room doors flew open. Russ stormed out, cell phone in hand, his eyes wide in panic.

"The baby," he stammered, "now. My baby. Now."

"Ah, there goes the drink," Jon mumbled, his hand on Naomi's back. "This sounds like an emergency."

SOLVEIGH'S FATHER HAD called to tell Russ they were taking her to the hospital. Her labor had started, and yes, they all knew it was a couple of weeks early, but what were they supposed to do? The baby was calling the shots, and it wanted to be born, now. And Russ had better move quickly if he wanted to be present for the birth.

"What do I do, what do I do?" Panicked, Russ was pacing the carpet while Naomi tried to calm him. She could see Jon and Sal at the other end of the hallway, consulting, signaling LaGasse to join them, and then Sal taking out his phone. Half the band was there by now, surrounding her and Russ, shouting encouragement, slapping his arms or shoulders, showing him that they were there for him.

Naomi, in the center of it all, looked at the familiar, friendly faces around her and felt the love these people held for one another include her, wrap around her like the softest shawl. There was Art, his Irish accent broad and loud in excitement; Sean, his fine smile like the steady shine of a candle in a dark room; Jones, exuberant and loud as always; the others, a happy, cheering group, nearly as flustered as Russ himself.

She wanted to kiss every one of them, tell them how much she loved them, right then and there.

Jon came over, a wide smile on his face. "Okay, here's the deal. A limo is waiting for you, Russ. The plane is ready at the airport, and it will take you straight to Halmar. We picked a small one that will be able to land at that tiny airport there. Get going! And good luck!"

Confused, Russ looked from one to the other.

"Go!" Jon pushed him forward. "Don't dawdle! Your wife and baby are waiting for you! Don't worry, we'll take care of your stuff. Just go!"

He turned to Naomi. "And you? Aren't you going to go and be with your best friend? Get a jacket and go with Russ! LaGasse will accompany you!"

"But Jon!" She didn't know what to say.

Tenderly he brushed her cheek with his fingers. "Solveigh would never forgive me if I didn't let you go, and I'm really scared of her."

There was a trace of sadness in his eyes. "Go. Don't let her be alone. Go, and have fun. I'll be fine, and we'll meet in Frankfurt."

She couldn't move. Sudden panic pulsed through her, freezing every cell in her body.

The last time he had sent her away in an easy mood, had kissed her good-bye before turning away and leaving her with Sal and Sean, she had nearly died; and now, in the hallway of a London hotel, the memory of that moment came rushing back.

She recalled the terrible, intense, nearly painful love she had felt for Jon as she watched him walk to the waiting car, and only a few breaths later the sensation of being hit right in the center of her body, hit by something brutal and very fast that made her crash backward, cracking her head on the pavement. She could see Sal and Sean bent over her, talking to her, and the shock in their faces; could hear Sal call her endearments he was never supposed to speak aloud; and she could taste the warm, metallic flow of blood in her mouth, choking her, burning in her lungs.

Jon said something but the words did not register; she hardly understood them through the buzzing in her head, and she made a faltering step back. He took hold of her when she stumbled, worry replacing the joy of moments before.

"Naomi?"

She held on to his sleeve, trying to breathe, fighting the fear, until gradually the turmoil subsided and the world around her returned to normal. Sean and Sal had shifted their attention to her; even Russ was staring, his face flushed, the grin dead in his face.

Her hand shaking, she touched her lips to make sure there was not really blood flowing from them; she even gazed down at the front of her dress, expecting to see the red torrent there just like before.

"Baby, are you okay?" Jon asked again.

"I hit my head," she replied, her voice wavering. "I remember I hit my head. It hurt." She looked toward Sal. "You called me 'love.' You cried. And Sean…" A small sob escaped her. "I told you to watch out for Jon."

"Naomi." Sean laid his hand on her shoulder. "It's okay, dear. It's over. You can put it behind you now. Nothing like that will ever happen again."

They were all there, closing ranks around her, murmuring encouragements, all of them, surrounding her like a cocoon.

"It's over now," Sal agreed. "Let it go." And added, even softer, "Let it go, love."

Jon ignored it for once. "You don't want to go with Russ? Would you rather get some rest?"

It was her decision. The fear and pain lay before her like a huge pile of dirt, a vile mess she had to cross, and it was her decision.

"I'm going," Naomi said. Her hands were still clamped around Jon's wrists, her mouth dry and the taste in it bitter, but the moment of panic had passed. "I'm going to Halmar with Russ."

THERE WAS NO time to pack anything.

"Go, go," Jon urged. "Get whatever you need there. The baby won't wait for you to pack!"

Russ was already in the car, but just before she got in Jon caught her in an embrace. "Come back to me. Give me a call when you get there." He kissed her hard. "Come back to me. And give my love to Solveigh."

"I wish you could come." Naomi hugged him tightly. "I hate to leave you."

"That's all I wanted to hear." His breath stroked her cheek. "To hear you say you want me; that's all I need."

The car pulled away and into the night, passed out of the city and westward toward Heathrow.

Wearily, Naomi looked out of the window at the ugly buildings and convoluted roads around it, glad that this time she did not have to pass through the terminals to get to her destination. With disgust she remembered the endless walk a few days before along dingy hallways, around many corners, and up and down confusing, senseless stairs, following exit signs that seemed to lead people in a spiral to nowhere.

Now things were different; with his usual efficiency, Sal had made sure they were taken directly to the hangar where the small jet waited, its engines singing nervously, a hummingbird among airplanes. The lone flight attendant ushered them aboard, and it pulled out and taxied toward the runway almost before they were seated.

The lights of London slipped away beneath them as they circled and flew toward Norway.

It had been dark in London, but the farther north they went, the lighter it got. Homesickness rushed through her, a sudden, hot longing for the quiet beauty of Halmar and for the simple life in her small hotel. She could hardly believe that she would be sleeping in her old bed again, having breakfast in the kitchen with her cook, Andrea, and seeing daily life at the Seaside.

The residue of panic lingered on the back of her tongue, the sudden memory of the shooting had been so strong and immediate. She tried to push it away, but it was there: she could see herself stretched out on that red carpet, the faces of other people hovering over her like balloons from the haunted house on a fairground; and she could remember the feeling of her life flowing away from her, of getting weaker with each beat of her heart.

Scariest of all though, and this she had never shared with anyone, was the memory of the peace.

Even in that moment when she had, blood gurgling in her mouth, implored Sean to look after Jon, there had been no real worry, no concern.

It hadn't mattered. Even then, still conscious, she had embraced the peace of the silence; and even now, healed and well, a small part of her wanted to be back on that black beach of her coma dream and in its solitude.

INCREDIBLY, RUSS HAD dozed off.

Naomi watched him sleep, his mouth open, his hands resting limply in his lap. There hadn't been a lot of sleep for any of them, wouldn't be on the tour with a strange bed every night and many hours spent traveling. They were no longer young. They weren't old either; but in the limbo between the two, and now, on the road, life showed them where they were headed in its cruel and efficient way.

Russ had some gray scattered through his brown hair. It glinted in the light over his seat. There were a few lines around his eyes, fine and clearly put there by laughter, but they were there. She remembered how he had looked when they had first met, more than twenty years ago now: a lanky, awkward young man with curls down his collar and nothing else on his mind but the music. Often enough she had walked in on them working together, shaping a song worth recording out of the fragments Jon had come up with.

"Strings, yes." would have been Russ' argument. "Put some feeling into it, for God's sake!" And Jon, muttering, balking, wanting only the raw, nude sound of a guitar and his voice.

Now, of course, he had filled out. They all had; they seemed taller, more imposing, resting easily in themselves: handsome, mature men, sleek with success, toned by the life they had chosen.

Carefully Naomi laid one of the blankets over him, smiled when he shifted and mumbled a bit, and settled down herself to look out of the window at the glowing sky. It wouldn't be long now before they would reach the Norwegian coast, the fjords and mountains to their right clearly visible in the nightlong sunset. For an insane instant she wished she could open a window to smell the air, find out if even up here the scent of Halmar could be found, if it would guide her home like the geese on their annual wanderings.

She could almost taste Andrea's cinnamon rolls and the crawfish cooked in dill and aquavit, hear the music from the meadow where there would be dancing and partying on such a balmy evening, and feel the weight of the flower wreath she would be wearing in her hair.

She looked down at the clothes she was wearing—an expensive, beautiful designer dress, too nice to be worn on a flight, and the high heels she knew she was going to ruin as soon as she got out of the car on the cobbled street outside her hotel—and, for a brief moment, wondered what had become of her. Her life had been so quiet, so reclusive, in tune with the landscape and the little town, peaceful to the point of boring; and she had loved it that way.

Now, everything was different.

From where she sat she could see LaGasse's blond hair and a part of her black-clad shoulder. The bodyguard was a study in discretion, never in her way, never talking to her if not approached first, an iron shadow always two steps behind her. Naomi had, in an unobserved moment after they had boarded, seen the weapon she carried: a silver monster in a leather holster, a huge, deathly thing that seemed much too sinister for the small woman with the petite hands and dainty face.

There was a chime reminding them they were about to land. Russ woke up and looked around in shock for a moment, disoriented and slightly disheveled, until he realized where he was, and why.

"We're landing," he said, his voice breathless with nervousness. "My baby. I'm having a baby."

Naomi nearly laughed.

THE HOTEL VAN picked them up. Andrea and Christi were waiting for them, both of them waving, cheering, nearly jumping up and down in their excitement to see her again.

"You are too thin." were Andrea's first words. "Those Americans don't feed you enough."

It was such a ludicrous statement that Naomi hiccuped in mirth.

She lowered the window on the drive to let in the cool, tart breeze, happy to be here. They drove straight out of town to the small hospital that lay in its own park beside the road to the next town. They drove uphill, inland, away from the bay; and, looking back, she could see the sun hovering over the hills in the distance, the water calm and red in the late-evening glow, the clouds rose and orange, and the land bathed in that special light only seen up here in the North.

Naomi wanted to get out and walk back down to the shore, dip her feet in the cold water and watch the seagulls, listen to the wind and the stillness of the place, but it was not to be.

They had brought a picnic basket, and while Christi drove, Andrea started unpacking all the delicacies she had made on the spur of the moment, as soon as they had known Naomi would be coming along.

"Jon called," she said, her tone gruff to hide how touched she was by his thoughtfulness, "and told us to get your apartment ready for you and to make you something to eat. He wanted you to feel at home and to enjoy the time you're here. As if we wouldn't have done that anyway." She sniffed, a little indignantly, then added, a little softer, "He takes good care of you."

She had eaten something on the plane, but when Andrea offered her one of her cheese muffins, Naomi bit into it with the hunger of homesickness. The taste brought back memories of impromptu dinners in the hotel kitchen with the girls after all the guests had either retired or left, and sadness washed over her for a second, only to be displaced by laughter when Andrea held out a bottle of aqauvit to her and asked, "Want some?"

Of course she didn't, not now, just before entering the maternity ward and facing Solveigh in labor.

That prospect alone was daunting enough to shake her out of any melancholy and exhaustion.

"SHE'S IN THE labor room," Solveigh's mother said, taking a sip of her coffee. "No need to go into a panic. They just took her in five minutes ago."

She gave Russ a quick hug and pointed him in the right direction, and then turned to Naomi. "As I see it, it won't take her long. She was pacing the lobby up to the last moment, cursing at poor Russ and everyone who got in her way; and she nearly dropped the baby right there. They had to force her into a wheelchair and into the maternity ward. Typical."

A smile softened her features. "I'm going to be a grandmother."

Naomi looked around.

Seventeen years ago it had been, and winter, a bitterly cold night. She had called a taxi and gone by herself, all alone, to have her baby.

So young, so lonely, and even now she could feel the black sadness of those hours when she had lain in that same room, pain washing over her, and her thoughts had flown all the way across oceans and continents to Jon. She had dreamed herself away while she waited for Joshua to be born, dreamed of walking on the sunny Malibu beach and picking up the debris of the warm surf curling around her ankles, with Jon by her side.

While the cramps shook her body she had wished for him to be with her, to hold her and whisper soothing words, as their child made his way into life. She had longed for his cool hand on her brow, and then to see the baby in his arms, father and son, as she rested.

But she had pushed Jon away, left him and vanished, and it had been her own fault that she was alone and desperate that night.

Cell phone in hand, she walked outside and stood in the driveway of the hospital.

Jon did not pick up. There was only the voice mail, and it was not even his own recording but something automated, impersonal, asking her to leave a message. Disappointed, feeling deserted, she returned inside and joined the others who were busy raiding Andrea's provisions. Her appetite had vanished. Naomi watched as they spread out a meal on the low, rickety table in the lounge.

HER LABOR HAD begun late at night, later than Solveigh's, after they had closed the restaurant and everyone but the night clerk had left for home. She had been alone in her apartment, ready to go to bed, when the first streaks of pain had shot through her back and made her double over in shock. Getting dressed again had been such a chore, but she had managed and returned upstairs to the lobby to call the cab. In the driving snow she had waited for the car, the icy gusts whipping around her legs and stinging her eyes, bringing the tears she had held back for so long.

Joshua had been born in the morning, just in time for breakfast, the scent of coffee drifting in every time the doctor came in to check on her. She had asked for some, sweaty and weak as she was from the birth, and got a friendly pat on the shoulder in return and the promise of everything she wanted to eat once she was in her own room, washed, and in a clean bed. A nurse had laid her son in her arms: a tight, tiny bundle with a shock of black hair, tiny fists raised imperiously, screaming for his first meal.

Stunned out of her grief and exhaustion, she had stared at that rosy face and seen the echo of Jon. It had taken all her willpower not to pick up the phone and call him, call Sal or the office and ask for Jon, but she had resisted and instead called her parents.

They arrived later in the day, directly from Geneva, surprised that she had not alerted them earlier, worried. Her mother had lifted the baby from the crib, a gentle smile on her face, and declared that he looked just like her, just like she had looked as an infant, and she was glad this was so.

Her father had not said much at all besides pronouncing himself relieved that she was well and everything was finally over. "Now you can forget this entire ungodly episode."

And she had retired to the solitude and silence of life in Halmar and tried to forget.

chapter 8

RUSS PRESENTED HIS daughter just as the church bells across the valley chimed twice.

"Solveigh wants her name to be Marisol." His voice shook with emotions. "She says it reminds her of the California sun." He smiled at Naomi. She took the newborn from him. She was nothing like Joshua had been. Marisol's little rosebud mouth pursed a little, but she never complained. Her hair was fine-spun like golden candy floss, a promise of wild curls just like her mother's later in life, and she had the face of a precious porcelain doll.

A melancholy yearning pulled at her heart as she cradled the small, warm weight, a feeling of mourning and loss at the way her own life had gone. There would not, she was certain, be another baby for her, ever. She would be forty soon, and her body was badly damaged. The price for her happiness was high.

Naomi handed the child to Solveigh's mother, Marit, who was hovering beside her, and hugged Russ tightly She kissed his stubbly cheek. "I'm so happy for you and Solveigh. How is she?"

Russ, his arm still around her shoulder, launched into a graphic and lengthy description of the birth process until his mother-in-law laid little Marisol back into his arms and said, "Shush. Here, take care of your baby and go look after your wife."

"She's asleep." Russ said. "She fell asleep as soon as they wheeled her into her room. She looked like an angel, my Solveigh, so sweet and innocent; but during the birth she spat curses at me like a New York City cab driver." He gazed at his daughter. "I'm so happy she looks just like her mother and not like me."

"Go," Marit said, "and take the baby back. We're all heading home to sleep now. And you should get some rest too."

"Oh, I can't leave them now!" Russ replied, a wild expression creeping into his face.

It was just too funny, Naomi thought, how Russ' hair always seemed to stand on end when he was agitated.

Marit laughed. "This isn't the Stone Age anymore; you don't have to fear wild beasts. Take Marisol back, and then come home and get some rest."

THE HOTEL WAS unchanged, as if it had held its breath, waiting for her return.

Naomi stood in the lobby—dark and empty at this time of night—and listened. She saw herself and Solveigh, behind the counter, talking to guests, drinking coffee, discussing the menu for the day with Andrea, watching the post ship come up the bay.

Tired now, she slowly made her way down the stairs to her apartment, to the place where she had lived for so long.

Here too everything was as it had always been. On her baby grand, the music sheets still lay where Jon had left them; and she went over to shuffle them around, remembering the quiet days they had spent here before his life had claimed him back.

Her fridge had been stocked with food; everything neatly stored in containers and labeled, her favorite dishes, ready to be popped into the microwave. Andrea had even supplied some bread and butter, and refilled the coffee tin. There was also a note on it saying they expected her to have breakfast with them, up in the kitchen, and that there would be fresh cinnamon rolls.

The bed had been made with fresh sheets. Someone had thought to place a bottle of water by the bedside, had even turned down the blankets; and in the bathroom were towels, soap, everything she might need.

She fell asleep quickly, the scent of lavender from the pillows lulling her into dreams of open meadows and a purple sky, and of running along a beach with white sand and a gentle, light blue surf. Wind was blowing in her hair, the sun warming her skin, and she felt young and whole. There was no pain in her chest, her breath was not short and ragged; she was free again.

Her dream took her into a dark forest where she lay on soft moss, the trees above moving in a breeze, casting dappled light that touched her softly, caressed her skin, kissed her breasts and throat, stroked her naked thighs. Someone was with her, whispering, touching her; and she closed her eyes to listen. Breath tickled her ear, lips brushed her cheek, another body lay down with her on her bed.

"You're mine," the voice said, "and I've come to claim you."

She felt the dream slip and fought to keep it, struggled to stay in that place and play out her fantasy, knowing it was Jon This was just like one of her dreams while they were apart, where he would come to her and say nearly the same words over and over again.

The familiar weight came down on her, the arms she knew so well caught her in an embrace, and she opened her eyes.

"Don't wake up," he said. "Let me be your dream lover."

HE HAD NOT, Jon said later, been able to resist the temptation. She lay in his arms and listened to him with her eyes closed, let the beloved voice lull her into drowsiness.

"I pictured you alone in this bed, asleep, dreaming of me, and I just had to come after you. As soon as you were gone with Russ, it was all I could think of: you, back here, where we spent so many wonderful nights, where we got married. Only two hours on a jet, and it was just too much to bear. I had to come. On the flight I dreamed of waking you up with my kisses, and you, so warm and sweet, so soft, I'd drown in your embrace and fall asleep at your side. After being without you for so long I couldn't stay away."

"But you sent me away," she mumbled. The sun was bright now, its light laying warm fingers on her face, painting designs on the inside of her closed eyelids.

"I did not send you away, you silly chick." His hand tangled in her hair. "I thought you'd like to be here for Solveigh, and you'd never have gone if I hadn't pushed you. But then, as soon as the car took you away, I knew it had been a mistake not to go with you."

Reluctantly, Naomi opened her eyes.

It was just like before. For some many years this had been the first thing she had seen every morning: the slate-gray water of the bay, the mountains in the distance, the trawlers coming back home from their night out on the sea, some yachts getting ready for a day of sailing. Across the little inlet behind the hotel the trucks were even now pulling up to the depot to take on their load of fish and prawns. The gulls escorting the fishing boats, danced around them, screeching, their calls mixing with the voices of the fishermen and the sound of the tart breeze.

Longing pulled at her heart, homesickness, and the wish to gain back at least part of her old life.

The pain of tears stuck in her throat. She tried to speak, but the wordsfelt like marbles in her mouth, cold, smooth stones she couldn't swallow.

Several minutes passed before she could manage an answer. "I thought life would be brighter for us. When we got married I believed our future would be easy and full of laughter. But I was wrong; it was an illusion. For so long my life was small, and bitter, and lonely; and when you found me and…" Gently, she kissed his face. "And made me yours again, I hoped that like in a fairy tale everything would be a 'happily ever after.' Only it wasn't."

"No." There was no way he could deny it.

"When I said I did not want to come back here, that I was done with Halmar, on our wedding night, I really was convinced we'd leave here and sail away into the sunrise or something. And for a brief while it was like that. Only then…" There was no need to finish the sentence, he knew.

Jon, his face in her locks, listened to her breath.

"If you want," he began slowly, "why don't you stay here. You don't have to go with me. The tour has just only started, love. We'll be on the road for months. If you feel better here, then stay. And I'll try to join you as often as I can. It's okay."

Her shoulders shook a little, but there was no reply.

"I'd have Sal send you your stuff," he plodded on, "and you could spend the summer here, get some rest, find your balance. Heal. And then, after the tour, I'd come to you."

"No."

"No, darling? You say that just like that, so sure of yourself? Just no?"

Naomi pushed herself up on her elbows. "No. Do you really think I'll hand you over to all those greedy fans? If I don't watch out they'll be crawling all over you."

"Ah, and would you mind that?" His fingers followed the trail of her spine.

"Indeed I would. I'm the only one allowed to grope you."

OVER BREAKFAST SHE told him she wanted to live in New York, at long last, and not languish in Norway anymore. Andrea had brought down a tray for them, just like after their wedding, with the cinnamon rolls Jon loved so much and pickled herring for Naomi, and set the table for them on the deck outside the apartment, just above the water. The morning air was fragrant with the sea breeze; it was warm and light.

"When we were there," she said, "and I went shopping on my own, when I walked up and down the streets alone, and not only on Park Avenue but also down on Canal and in Soho, I realized that I didn't want to be anywhere else in the whole wide world—and I've seen many places, Jon. But there, right there among the noise and the dust of Manhattan, I felt life sing to me. I want to be there with a yearning that almost hurts."

He stared at her over his coffee cup, speechless.

"I want to hear that hum from the city and walk in the shadow of the skyscrapers. Have lunch at Carnegie's with the tourists and drive over to Flatbush Avenue to buy cheesecake at Junior's, and I want to go to the Met every weekend."

With a sigh, she looked out across the bay. "For the first time in a long while, when I was in New York I felt alive. If I could, I'd live in a tent on Times Square."

"My wife is crazy," Jon stated slowly. "I've married a raving lunatic. Next you'll say you want a house in Jersey City."

Her eyes were bright and curious like a bird. "What's in Jersey City? Do we have to go and see it? Did I miss something?"

That made him laugh. "Ha, totally not. You don't want to go there, baby. Don't even think about it."

Naomi, still in a hotel bathrobe, pursed her lips. "Now that you say it like that, I think I'll have to go and take a look. Is it pretty there?"

Jon, smirking, got up to get more coffee from the kitchen. "Yeah, it's pretty. As pretty as the devil's armpit. Oh, no fear, I'll take you there. I'll even take you all the way to Newark and shock you properly, my dove."

It felt almost like when they had lived here a year ago, but only just.

So often during the long time she had needed to recover from her wounds, Naomi had thought of fleeing and returning here, had dreamed of finding peace and healing in her old life; but now that she was here, she knew she had left in more than one way. She watched Jon as he moved around in the confined space of the apartment, recalling how he had come here to find her and how, for a brief while, they had hidden themselves away from the rest of the world here.She shook herself out of her reverie. It was time to get dressed and visit Solveigh.

In the wardrobe she found some of her old clothes, jeans and a couple of shirts, things she had not thought to take with her when she left for good, things she would not need in her new home in glamorous LA. They were a little loose—she had lost weight during the time she had spent on the roof garden of Jon's mansion recovering—but good enough to wear. In fact they made her feel younger and somehow, as if she had put on a magic cloak, a lot more carefree. Her hair back in its usual braid, in a white cotton blouse and faded jeans, she returned to where Jon was waiting by her Steinway, bent over some music sheets, studying them.

"Hey," he greeted her, "look at these. I forgot all about them. Why in the world did we leave them here?"

Because, Naomi wanted to reply, they were old and sad and had nothing to do with the musical they were working on, because they were from a time in her life she did not want to think back on.

"Those are stupid," she said instead, and took them from his hand. "I don't want them anymore, Jon. Just let them lie here and gather dust."

He snatched them back. "Ah, no, not stupid. Sad, yes, stupid, no. None of your lyrics are stupid. These are lovely."

She had written them, Naomi knew, after a trip to the supermarket, a spur-of-the-moment thing when she wanted ice cream late one evening and did not feel like wrestling with the huge containers in the kitchen. Standing in line to pay, watching the rain beat against the picture window of the store, she had listened with one ear to the music coming over the loudspeakers; and there he had been, the voice she knew only too well, the song he had written with the words she had given him so long ago. The ice cream had ended up on the counter, not bought; and she had driven home, tears and rain blurring her vision, alone.

It had been cold and silent in the apartment, and she had sat down at the desk where she kept a picture of him in a frame and dashed down the lyrics: a plaintive, heartbroken lament, a statement of loss. The next morning, reading her own words, she had been on the point of throwing them away but then stopped. Somewhere in the world, she was sure, there were people feeling the same way, feeling just as deserted; and maybe, someday, they would read them and relate.

"All your songs have this underlying sadness," Jon was saying. "They break my heart, make me want to cry every time I read them. All those songs you wrote while you were alone are a tapestry of loneliness."

"Well, I was alone," she admitted softly, "it was a lonely time."

When he didn't reply she looked up to see him gazing steadily at her, all the regret for the lost time in his eyes.

"Kiss me, Jon," Naomi said, "and then throw away the sad songs."

THEY BOUGHT FLOWERS for Solveigh, a huge bouquet of yellow and pink roses that, Jon thought, looked like the light on sunrise water; and he made the girl at the flower shop tie a big satin bow around them.

"She'll like that," he explained when Naomi raised her brows at him. "It looks like Hollywood. Trust me. Solveigh is a true LA chick now."

He had laughed when Naomi had told him the baby's name. "Spanish. How far away from Norway can that girl get?" had been his comment, "We'll have a hard time convincing Russ to come to New York to work with us."

Inside the hospital lobby though, Jon became serious, and very quiet. "Here, Naomi?"

She nodded, her head lowered.

Slowly he looked around, taking in the stark, simple surroundings. There was not much more than a small reception, an elderly woman sitting behind it doing a crossword puzzle; a few chairs in a row along the white walls, a Munch painting over them. Gratefully Jon noted that at least it wasn't *The Scream* but a Madonna. The image reminded him eerily of Naomi, with the long, black tresses and the shuttered, sad smile.

"Please, Jon." Naomi tugged him forward. "Please, don't dwell."

He didn't budge. She felt his hand clamp around hers, as if even now he wanted to protect her from being alone and scared that night when Joshua was born.

"It wasn't so bad," she said softly. "They took good care of me, and it was an easy birth. Please, Jon."

Gradually, he relented. His arm came up around her shoulder and he pulled her into a tight embrace, his cheek on her hair.

"He started screaming right away." She wanted to stay in that embrace forever, safe and loved. "And he looked just like you. Raised his little hand and waved it in my face and yelled so loud the nurses came running." A smile flitted across her face. "Just like his father. Wants the world to know who is master from moment one. And a killer voice."

"You shouldn't have been alone. I should have been here for you. You should have called me, Naomi, love or not." His grip around her tightened. "I feel bad about it even now."

"Yes, but you can stop. Joshua is seventeen, and we're married. Snap out of it, Jon, and let's go see Solveigh."

Up in the white, short hallway of the maternity ward, Naomi stopped in shock when the nurse told her the room number.

"Here?" Jon asked again, and again she nodded. His hand on the doorknob, he waited until she had gathered herself enough to speak.

"The same room," Naomi whispered. "Jon, I did not mean this to happen. I'm sorry."

He pressed his lips together, hurt in his eyes, but opened the door and stepped in.

Naomi, seeing the tableau that presented itself, sobbed softly and hid behind Jon's back.

This. She had always imagined it to be like this. She tired, happy, content in the bed, and Jon, their baby in his arms, standing by the window, counting his son's fingers in wonder and gazing into his black eyes.

Only it was not Jon now, with a child and the expression of rapture, but Russ; and it was Solveigh in the bed, eating breakfast and laughing at her new family.

Silently, her heart breaking, Naomi fled back to the lobby.

chapter 9

JON FOUND HER outside, on a bench in front of the hospital, where she sat looking out across the bay, nursing a cup of coffee and a cookie.

He didn't go over to her right away but stood in the shade of the entrance for a moment, watching her. She looked so young in the jeans, and he could have sworn the shirt she was wearing was the same one she had worn when they had met for the very first time. It almost seemed as if no time had passed, as if it was that summer day in Geneva and he again a young musician, naive and excited about his blossoming career, overwhelmed by his success and the fact that he was a girls' magazine centerfold.

Naomi, his one and only love, and here she sat, her head bowed, the paper cup between her hands like a candle meant as an offering.

"You should have been here." She made room for him when he sat down beside her. "You had a right to be here and see your son born, and I took that from you. It was my fault."

The old, well-known pain tugged at his soul. "Yes. Should have, could have. We've been over this a million times, Naomi. It's over and past." He thought for a moment before he went on. "When Solveigh told me she was pregnant, when she was on the point of leaving Russ because she was afraid of the future, I told her that it wasn't your fault. It wasn't. You did what you thought was best when you ran from me in LA; you were scared by the life there and of what was to come. I told you I accept that. Please stop breaking your heart, and mine. I'm happy to have you and Joshua in my life now. It's way better than not having you at all."

The wind ruffled his hair. Jon had almost forgotten how beautiful it was here in summer, how every ray of sun seemed like a gift, how the landscape seemed to bloom and blossom with a vengeance in the brief period of warmth. Even the cold waters of the bay looked inviting, frisky, the little white-capped waves like the curls on a baby's head.

"We could have another child." He said it carefully, tasting the words on his lips.

A small, sad laugh shook her shoulders. "It's not as if we are trying to prevent having a baby. It isn't from the lack of trying. I guess I'm just too old, and too hurt." She turned his hand over in hers so she could see his narrow wedding band. "You have the right to see a child of yours grow up, Jon. You're young enough to have another. Maybe…"

"No!" He gripped her fingers hard. "No. Don't even say it. Don't you dare say that, Naomi!"

A tear dropped from her cheek, landing on his thumb.

"I will not set you aside for a younger, healthier woman just because she can give me children. There were many who would have loved to do just that, and you know it. Look at me, Naomi. Look at me!" Gently, he dried her face with his fingertips. "I have exactly what I want. I'm in the place I want to be, with the woman I love and my son—my wonderful, talented, and beloved son. I'm a happy man!" A grin pulled at the corners of his mouth. "And hell yeah, let's try for another baby. If there isn't one, at least I'll have all the pleasure I can think of with you in our bed."

"Oh, Jon, you're never serious." It came out as a tired sigh, a joyless statement.

Jon rose and dusted off his trousers, then held out his hand to her. "Yeah, I'm serious. Can't you see? I rented a bloody jet, again, to come here to you. Sal had a fit, asked me why I couldn't have gone with you in the first place and did I have so much money that I thought I could throw it around like that? And yeah, I do have that much money. But even if it had been the last dollar on my last credit card, I'd have spent it to be with you last night. So there. I'm that serious."

Slowly they walked down the hill toward the dock and the hotel, first along the gravel road that led to the hotel, meadows to the sides, and then when they reached the first houses of the little town, on the cobbled streets.

"I'm so serious about you," Jon went on, "I came here for these few hours with you before I have to go to Frankfurt and then Geneva. I'll have to leave soon."

They stopped outside the little bookshop where Jon had always picked up his *New York Times*, imported especially for him while he lived here, generally two days late but nevertheless presented to him with pride, wrapped in a plastic cover. The owner greeted them with friendly surprise, asking if they had come back to stay, and even offered them a cup of coffee.

Jon remembered enough of the Norwegian he had picked up to thank him and tell him they had to hurry, so no coffee but thanks.

"And I want you to come with me." The entrance door to the hotel stood open, letting in the sun and the fresh air, but in the lobby it still smelled tantalizingly of Andrea's cooking. Jon breathed in. "Ah. She's making those meatballs in brown sauce. God, I think I'll have to stay for lunch; I could kill for those things. Maybe if I ask nicely she'll share the recipe. What do you think?" With a pat on her behind he left Naomi standing by the counter and walked into the kitchen, calling for Andrea, offering her diamond earrings for meatballs.

Naomi smiled, the sad mood gradually leaving her.

The place seemed strange and empty without Solveigh. It was just as well kept, that much was true, but it was no longer her home.

She could see her own shadow standing in the dim spot by the elevator, right beside the stairs that led down to her apartment, holding that tray of plates, and Jon entering the lobby from the snow, come all the way from California to find her. Now she could smile at the spectacle of the crashing dishes, Solveigh's outrage, and Jon looking on as if he had walked into a madhouse.

She could hear his and Andrea's voices from the kitchen, joking, debating, and finally Andrea shouting, "No, no, no, Mr. Jon Stone, you will not get that recipe. Out of my kitchen, now!"

Without waiting for him, Naomi went to pack the few things she wanted to take along.

FRANKFURT GREETED THEM with an overcast sky and a mugginess that reminded Jon a lot of Brooklyn in August. It made him regret for a moment that they were going to move there soon and endure those New York summers. Waiting for their few belongings to be transferred from the plane to the limo, he wondered if someone had thought to install central air in the old house or if they would have to live with the ugly, dripping boxes in every window. Absentmindedly, he stared out toward the runways where a 747 was getting ready for take-off, its wings shuddering with the power of flight. He wondered where it might be headed, homesick and tired of being on the road after only a few days.

This was different from before; then, alone, he'd always been hungry for the stage, for the fans, for the cooing of the girls when he got off the tour bus or gave them three minutes before sound check, and, often enough, for a willing body in his bed after the show.

"I'm failing you," Naomi had said to him during the flight. "I feel as if I'm failing you. You deserve to have this, Jon, a baby, and I'm failing you."

. He had to make her snap out of the depression he could see creeping up on her.

The three weeks she had hidden herself away had been useless.

She could have fooled him as she stood with Sal, chatting, pushing stray locks behind her ears, laughing at something he was saying.

"Oh dear, no," he heard her say when he came closer. "It's not a place anyone ever needs to visit. There is really nothing here, nothing. Frankfurt is the most overstated village in the world, just an appendage of the airport. That's all."

"How unkind," Sal replied, holding the car door for her, "I have a friend who is a publisher; she loves to come here every October for the book fair. And I've heard the opera is really very good."

"Why would I want to come here if I can go to the Met?" Naomi said without even looking at him.

"Will you listen to her, Jon. She's got the Met on her mind. You'll have to buy a box, I think." Sal signaled the driver that they were ready to go.

"I remember," Jon said as the car pulled out onto the highway, "when we were here last time we had those amazing little marzipan thingies. The guy at the hotel told us they were a local specialty, and they really were to die for. And hey, we are in Germany! The beer is really good!"

Naomi threw him a glance so loaded with disdain that he smirked and fell silent.

"I used to go to the book fair with my mother." She looked out at the cityscape as it drew nearer. There was a group of distinctive high-rise buildings, a cluster of them in the center of the town, shiny like icicles. "We came here while I lived with my parents in Geneva. My mother was crazy about the thing. It is open for visitors one weekend, and then everybody goes; it's so crowded and exhausting. And very, very frustrating."

Both gazed at her in surprise, and she shrugged. "You couldn't take any of the books home."

The car left the highway and took them into the city. For a while they drove along a broad road lined with elm trees, old houses on both sides, before office buildings took over.

"The venue is right next to the fair," Sal remarked. "We've been there before."

Naomi smiled at him. "I know. You were here before you came to Geneva, that first time. It was in the papers."

"But you said…" Jon started and then fell silent again.

"I dreamed of being at the book fair during the week, when all the authors and publishers were there," she went on. "And I wanted to be one of them. Not a gawker, not a tourist, but one of the authors. I wanted to sit in my publisher's stall and watch those people walk by, stare at my book, and wonder if I maybe was the writer. It was the only thing I wanted, for a while."

"For a while?" Sal pointed at the hotel. They had arrived.

"Yes, for a while, before I decided I wanted to study music. I couldn't make up my mind. The only thing I knew for certain was that I didn't want to take over my family's hotel business. That I knew for sure." The driver opened the door for her, and she got out.

SHE HAD BEEN here before, she told Jon as they were waiting in the lobby for Sal to check them in; it was one of the best places in Frankfurt and well situated for a walk downtown. Her uncle and father loved it, and she knew they had thought a couple of times about acquiring it; but it was too big for them—they didn't like huge houses like this one, despite the history and the charm. There were so many buildings in this area, she said, that had been built from the red sandstone they seemed to favor here. It looked distinguished, made the city look aristocratic in a way; and yet it was a boring town in the middle of nowhere. There wasn't even any interesting food.

"Except for those marzipan things and the beer," Jon replied absentmindedly. His thoughts were on something else, something she had said without even noticing, and he was determined to dig deeper into it.

Their room looked out onto a terrace where coffee was being served, and the street beyond it. There was a lot of traffic at this time of day, but she was right, it wasn't like other big cities. Everything seemed smaller, provincial, in a way striving to be cosmopolitan but failing. He had never noticed before, never cared to notice; but with Naomi at his side, the world was a different place.

"So you knew." Jon watched her open the luggage that had been brought from London and pick out clean clothing. "You knew I was in Europe, even before we met. You never said."

Surprised, she let the skirt she was holding sink. "Of course, what made you think I didn't? I sent you the lyrics, Jon. I knew who you were. I had a ticket for your show."

So strange, and he had always thought he had been as much of a surprise to her as she had been to him, and he found himself wishing it had been so. This gave her an advantage in a weird way, as if she had known what she was getting into and he not.

"After I sent those lyrics to your office," Naomi was saying, "I had this fantasy of you coming to me. I used to lie in bed at night and dream of you showing up out of nowhere at our door, just standing there and asking for me, because you wanted to know who had sent you these lyrics. One day…"—her eyes sparkled at him—"one day I was sick, lazing around on the couch with the flu and all alone in the apartment. My mother had made me tea and left me there to go to work, and I was feeling so sorry for myself. So bored. That was a couple of weeks after I had sent the lyrics. And I lay there in a doze, and imagined you getting out of a plane at the Geneva airport, taking a taxi, and coming to our house. I saw you walking to the entrance, asking the doorman for our apartment, and him letting you in. You took the elevator, and then you stood outside our door. I was excited. I really had spun myself into that reverie. And then the bell rang."

"And?" It was silly, but he was entranced, could even see himself standing there; and now, so many years later, he wondered why he had not indeed done just that. He had wanted those lyrics as badly as anything, ever.

"It was the cleaning woman. She had forgotten her key." From the suitcase, she took a white cotton blouse, much like the one she was wearing just now, much like the one she had worn when they had first met; and for a minute he wondered if she had a secret stash of them, or a seamstress who made them especially for her.

"And if it had been me, then what?" The fantasy was too delicious to drop.

"Oh." Naomi sat down on the edge of the bed. "I don't know. I think it would have been very embarrassing. I was in jogging pants and a sweater, and I had a red nose from all the sniffling. You would have walked away, disappointed."

"Ah, no, I don't think so." She crept away, farther up on the bed, when he came closer. "I don't think I'd have left, drippy nose or not. I think I'd have whisked you away despite the flu and the jogging pants. I think I'd have fallen in love with you anyway, no matter how red your nose was that day. I would have wanted you, sweatshirt and all, just like always."

"You're getting maudlin again." She giggled softly as he bent over her.

"Nah, not maudlin, just seeing that picture all too well, my dove. I can see you wiping your nose and tugging at your silly pants, trying to collect yourself into a semblance of respectability, and me, staring at your navel, at your stomach because your sweater is really too short; it's one you've been wearing since you were a kid, with Winnie the Pooh on it, in pink, too."

"Don't care for Winnie," she mumbled, and he laughed.

"Yeah, it's Winnie all right. You're pulling him down to hide your skin, and he looks like a yellow giraffe when you do that. And me, lyrics forgotten, jet lag forgotten, I want to touch that smooth stretch of belly and run my hand along your waist; and I want to kiss you right there in that posh hallway, and to hell with who might see us." His lips were close to hers, close enough to feel the caress of her breath on them. "I take your hand and pull you into my arms, and there is no resistance. You just come into my arms, just like that. As if you'd been waiting for that to happen. As if, opening the door to me, you knew exactly what the outcome would be, flu or not."

"And you catch the flu from me, and there goes the tour. No more singing." She kissed him lightly.

"Yeah, who cares? Why would I want to sing when I can make love to you instead? Which, of course, I'd want to, after that first embrace. Oh yeah, that's what I want. And so I whisk you away to the hotel, and you're mine, no excuses, no delay. It's all that matters, you and me."

Jon wanted to drown in that embrace, over and over again, feel the shape of her body against his, her fingers playing in his hair. For a blessed moment, all the worries and fears dropped away and they were once again young lovers, enchanted by each other, locking the world out of their intimacy.

"You have the worst timing," Naomi whispered. "You know you have to be at the venue, and do the sound check. You know there's a concert in a couple of hours. Again."

"Yeah, baby, let the Germans wait. I want to be here with you now." His hand slid under the blouse.

"They won't give you marzipan if you're late. They love things to be on time here," Naomi said, laughter in her voice.

"To hell with the bloody marzipan," Jon replied.

STANDING BEHIND SAL, she watched the meeting with the fan club just before the concert, grinned at the huge package of sweets he was given, lovingly decorated with a white bow, and the stuffed animals. There was a pink elephant, and, of all things, a crocodile.

"I think it's a hint," Sal mumbled toward Art; "they want us to go on a tour in Africa," to which Art snickered and replied, "Only over my dead body. I'm not good with lions and snakes."

Naomi was fascinated by the rapture in the women's faces, as if they were not facing a real person at all, not a normal man, but something more, as if he had come down from some kind of Olympus to hold court among his mortal followers. She wished they could see him, just once, early in the morning before his first cup of coffee, unshaven, grumpy, not a star at all.

There was a rigid protocol for these events, one she always observed with a mix of relief and melancholy. The army of security men, the careful screening of the fans, the rope that separated them from Jon—these all were necessary, she knew, but they also felt like a border between real life and theirs.

Jon was all graciousness and charm, accepting the smiles and adoration with kind words and small jokes that sent ripples of giggles through the group. He allowed one of them, and Naomi was sure she had been carefully selected by Sal before, to kiss his cheek and stand beside him for a few photos before he autographed tour books, CD covers, shirts, and even one bare shoulder.

"You may not want to take a shower too soon," he drawled at the blond, blushing girl, "or all your lovely memories will wash away."

Naomi had gone up on the stage during a break in the sound check and stared out at the huge, empty hall—the round cupola and the iron rafters like the ribs of a large animal, the many rows of seats—and wondered how it would feel to stand up there when it was packed with people, their attention directed at Jon and his musicians, singing with him, cheering. It had to be the headiest feeling, to look down at all those faces and see the adoration in them.

"It's like sex," Jon had told her when she'd asked. "It's just like that. Only it's over as soon as you leave the stage, and the silence and emptiness afterward are like the worst hangover in the world. There's nothing worse than sitting alone in the dressing room after a really good show; you know the audience has floated back home, and all you have is a sweaty back and a sore throat. There is no loneliness like that. It's the loudest, most silent, loneliness you can imagine."

He had handed her his guitar to hold and added, "And no, it's not like sex with you. After loving you I feel whole, and entranced, and terribly hungry for more."

Sal stirred. "All right, enough smooching and fondling, Art. Let's get him out of there."

THE CONCERT WAS sold out, as always, and it went as well, as always. This time Naomi did sit in the front row, right among his biggest fans, LaGasse beside her and Alan, his back to the stage, right in front of her, in a row with the other guards. She could see Sal and Art looking her way every so often, anxious, but she wasn't recognized. The people around her were too busy listening to Jon to even look at her.

There were some reporters around, mostly to the side and under close observation by security, but a couple of them had made their way to the edge of the stage where they could shoot some close-ups. One of them turned around and pointed his camera at her. Alan was beside him instantly, nearly slapping it out of his hands, while LaGasse stood in front of her, shielding her.

Barely anyone else reacted. From the corner of her eye Naomi could see Jon move closer to see what was going on, guitar held tightly, and relax again when he saw Sal rush forward.

The photographer was Parker, a contrite grin on his face and a shrug in her direction when Alan let go of him to hand him over to the local guards. He looked slightly scruffy, his dark blond hair a wild mess, the shirt hanging out of his jeans. He didn't seem too concerned; but, she had to admit, he was still a handsome devil with a charming smile.

Naomi took a step in his direction, and he stopped to wait for her.

"Why?" she asked against the noise of the music. "Why do you keep following me?"

"You're beautiful," Parker shouted back, and walked away with the hovering guards.

"What was that all about?" Sal was there, his hand on her arm, ready to take her backstage to safety. "Is he stalking you? Do we have a problem here?"

"No, no. Everything's okay." She had no idea why she was saying that. Jon, guitar laid aside, was about to launch into *Secret Garden*, his voice soft and mellow, pouring over her shoulders like warm maple syrup. She turned to see him standing right above her, singing down at her, a small smile on his face. She smiled back, threw him a kiss, and fled to the safety of the backstage area.

chapter 10

IT WAS RAINING.

Parker stood outside the concert hall, the red sandstone walls rising up behind him like a fortress from the Middle Ages, all alone in the open space. There were a couple of taxis lined up, waiting for the show to end and for people wanting a ride. On the street outside the compound, the evening traffic went by as if nothing at all had happened, the cars mindless of his turmoil and loneliness.

They had not taken the camera from him, nor checked for pictures—a mistake, an oversight—and he cradled it to his chest gleefully, impatient to see what he had gotten.

There she was, in a couple of snapshots he had managed to take before they'd noticed him. She was looking up at the stage, her hands raised to applaud, a soft smile on her face, caught in a blue spotlight. He could not get enough of looking at her, at the fine profile and the curve of her neck, that braid, the slender shape of her shoulder. Everything about her screamed class and breeding, and for the life of him he couldn't understand why she would be married to someone like Jon Stone, a rock star, a cheap self-taught songwriter, famous for his many affairs and, earlier, even drugs. Now he might run around in silk shirts and hand-tailored suits, but Parker remembered only too well the photos of him at one or another LA party, a girl in one arm and a bottle of whiskey in the other, drunk, laughing, not giving a damn about anything.

And her, by now he knew everything about her, about her wealthy family and their hotel empire; her old, European ancestry and the role she had refused for Jon's sake. Parker couldn't understand why she had left that huge inheritance behind just to play groupie to this man and his band, how she preferred to travel with him when she had that incredible family estate waiting for her in Toronto and the ownership of all those hotels at her fingertips.

Jon Stone—Parker shook himself in disgust. So famous, so celebrated, so good-looking and successful, and as powerful as a Mafia boss. He had managed to lure her away from her life, drag her down into his sordid Hollywood existence, and she seemed happy about it.

There was their son; he had used all his influence to find out about him. So well had they hidden the boy, tucked him away with his grandmother in Brooklyn, and yet Parker now knew everything about Joshua. Their love child from long ago, from when Jon had only just started his career and Naomi had been barely more than a teenager. Supposedly, he was even more talented than his notorious father.

Parker had been about to go to New York and find him and then stopped. He didn't want to risk being found out and thrown into jail at the wave of Jon Stone's finger.

With a sigh and a shudder, Parker made his way toward the line of cabs. They would be going to Geneva next, and he wouldn't follow her there. But he would wait for her in Hamburg, and then he'd try to get her alone.

"YOU DON'T HAVE to come," Jon said at the last minute, just before they were about to leave for the airport. "If you don't want to go to Geneva, you don't have to come. You could always go ahead to New York and wait there for me. It's only a few more stops here in Europe. I'd be with you in a couple of weeks." And added, with a mischievous grin, "You could get the house ready for us. Do all the shopping you want, baby, right there in your dream city."

She just shook her head and finished packing her few belongings.

"Your parents will be in Geneva, your father." He said it gently, as if he was breaking some dire news to her, and it made her look up.

"You don't have to see him if you don't want to," Jon went on. "It's no big deal. Security will keep him away."

He saw her touch her side where the scar was and fell silent.

The hotel suite they were in was nothing like what he was used to; everything seemed just a bit shabby, worn by time, though the furniture must have been nice when it was first placed here. Always, through all the years he had been traveling the world, he had hated the German feather pillows and the too-warm duvets. There was something terribly provincial about the beds.

"I liked the sheets at the Seaside, in Halmar."

Confused by this remark, so completely out of context, Naomi stared at him.

Jon shrugged. "Yeah, I did. Nothing fancy or colorful." He gestured at the bed with disgust. "I hate patterned sheets and covers. I want my bed white, or cream, or if you're in it, rose for all I care. But that's the limit of my color endurance."

"I'm going with you to Geneva," she replied.

THIS WAS DIFFERENT, and for the first time Naomi felt the excitement of being on a tour.

They were all in the lobby to check out and get on the bus, the entire band, Sal, and Art. Security was heavy, the entrance blocked off, and from where she stood by the counter, she could see the fans on both sides of the roped-off path. They were shouting for Jon, brandishing posters with his name on them, waving scarves and shirts bought at the concert.

"You could," Sal said from behind her, "walk with the band. Or we could smuggle you out the back entrance and pick you up there. You don't have to do this."

"It's a bit late for that, Sal, isn't it?" There was a bowl of apples right beside her, and she took one. It was a beautiful apple, red and shiny, as if it had been grown as a decoration piece. "I'll deal. It's time I did."

"No, you don't have to, ever again."

Surprised, she tilted her head at him.

"You don't have to walk into public ever again, darling. I'll see to it, and protect you in every way." His voice was as gentle as she had ever heard it and the words so strange, coming from Sal, that she couldn't reply.

"I'll see to it you have a private and protected life, Naomi, as private and secluded as I can manage."

Jon, standing with Sean and Art at the other end of the lobby, smoking a cigarette with them and idly chatting, had his back turned to her.

"I'll never forget that moment when you fell, shot down, and I unable to help you, afraid you would die. It was my fault, and I'll do anything I can to keep harm away from you."

She listened, her head bowed, fighting tears, again drawn back to that day in her life, and to the pain. Once more she felt the needles in her body, the tube down her throat, and the burning of her wounds, and heard the remorseless beeping of the monitors beside her hospital bed. It was almost as if it was a parallel world waiting just a breath away, and any little trigger pushed her over the brink into it. It was a world where her body was always hurting and she choked on blood again; and always, always she felt the lure of that peaceful, silent shore she had seen in her coma dreams.

"Naomi." Jon was there, his arm around her waist, supporting her, glaring at Sal. "What did you say; what did you do, Sal?"

"He didn't do anything, Jon." She leaned into him, shaking. "Everything is okay, don't yell at Sal again. It's not his fault when I feel faint, for crying out loud."

Jon saw how she pressed her hand against her side where the bullet had hit her and how she struggled to breathe, her tongue brushing over her lips as if she was trying to lick something off them, and it broke his heart.

"Come, baby," he said gently. "I'll take you the back way. Let them wait out there until tonight." He couldn't understand why that offer put the hint of a smile on her face and made her glance at Sal.

SAL CAME TO her in the bus, and, leaning on the back of the seat in front of her, asked, "Are you okay? For a moment I thought you were going to faint."

Jon looked up from his newspaper but said nothing.

Naomi pulled the jacket she was wearing tighter around her body. "I'm fine, Sal. I just felt sick for a moment. It was…" She gazed out at the highway, for a moment lost in thought. "I guess I'm just tired. The past few days were a little bit much."

Sal rubbed his forehead. "I know. It's always like that at the start of a tour. The routine will settle in once we're back in the States, don't worry. Europe is always a hassle. The languages and everything. Strange food, strange customs." He waved at the road outside. "Even different traffic. You'll feel better once you're back on home ground."

That made her smile. "But I'm not American, Sal. I've lived all over the world."

"Yeah."

"I'll be all right, don't worry. Thanks." She closed her eyes and rested her head against the window, and Sal left her to return to his seat behind the driver.

THE PLANE WAS waiting for them in a hangar, in an obscure corner of the airport well away from the regular traffic. It was a larger one this time to accommodate all of them: the band, Jon and herself, and the rest of the entourage that had not gone ahead with the trucks during the night.

Someone had provided coffee for them while they waited for their luggage to be loaded. There was even a tray of sandwiches—not the American kind with soft, white bread, but crisp rolls liberally spread with butter and good German sausage and ham, cheeses Naomi had badly missed in Canada and the US, even some pickled herring. She let the raw, tender fish melt on her tongue, savoring the salt and the flavor of dill and juniper, trying to knit it into her memory so she wouldn't forget it once they were gone. Some things she missed terribly. This was the taste of Norway, of the North, and she had never yet found it in LA.

It made her recall how much of it she had eaten during her pregnancy, how she had crept upstairs to the kitchen at night to steal a couple of jars, together with other sour stuff, and then sat on her couch in the dark, watching the beam from the lighthouse pass over the Halmar bay as she picked out the morsels with her fingers, dripping the brine on her nightgown. Once Joshua had been born her appetite had changed radically, and she had wanted sweets, bread, sugar, all the useless carbohydrates, and most of all, Andrea's cinnamon rolls.

"What's this?" Sal had come up beside her and was eyeing one of the rolls critically.

"It's raw meat," she replied, and picked it up. So German, so European. "Not tartare, but pork, finely chopped, seasoned, with raw onion. It's delicious. Try it!"

He walked off again, tossing a disgusted curse at no one in particular. Naomi took a big bite, again thrown back in time. Pastrami was all good and well, but some things could not be replaced.

Jon joined her, eyebrows raised in curiosity. "Sal is pacing across the tarmac like a tiger, telling everybody who wants to hear that you're behaving like a cannibal, eating raw flesh. What's this all about?"

She held out the roll to him, and he grinned. "Ah. I see why he's slightly turned off. I remember Andrea giving you that for breakfast sometimes, and you like the stuff! You'll never be a proper LA vegan, my dear; good thing we'll be living in New York in the future. That's not a trend you're likely to establish in Hollywood." Politely he declined her offer to share but remained with her until they were ready to board.

"You know what makes me sad?" Naomi said just as they were about to get on the plane, while Jon was finishing the coffee he had just picked up. "The most wonderful scent in the world is a newborn's head. I don't know why that is; one would think it would be disgusting, so fresh from the womb, but babies just smell delicious."

"Why does that make you sad?" Jon put down the cup.

"Because you're supposed to smell it on your own baby's head. And you never will." She gathered her purse and jacket from the chair, "And you should have."

HE HAD REFUSED to hold little Marisol when Solveigh offered, afraid of dropping the infant, afraid of crushing her; but he had never in his wildest dreams thought of smelling her. Mesmerized, he had watched Russ handle the baby as if it was the most natural thing in the world, as if the ability to look after her had been delivered to him the same instant she was born. Solveigh, sitting upright in her bed and eating a hearty breakfast of eggs and bacon, had watched her new family with the complacency of a well-fed cat, her face radiant, her blue eyes sparkling. There had been no trace of exhaustion; she was as fresh as a daisy and as healthy as ever. Compared to her, Naomi looked like a ghost, like her own shadow: bloodless, tired, impassive.

Jon wanted to hit somebody. He wanted to feel his fist connect with flesh, break bones, feel something—anything—crumble under his wrath, and for the pain to be transferred from Naomi to that other body. He wanted someone to be guilty, to pay for her hurt, take the burden; only there was no one. If at all, he would have to smash his own face, for of all the people connected with the shooting, he was the most responsible.

Defeated, he climbed the gangway, the last to board.

Their little group didn't fill even half the plane; they had enough room to spread out for the short flight. Naomi had picked a seat in the back, well away from the others.

"You really want me to divorce you just so I can smell a baby's head?" He dropped into the seat beside her. "Or are you thinking of becoming a Mormon so I can have more than one wife?"

"I think you would have to become a Mormon for that; besides, they don't allow that anyway, Jon. No, I don't want you to have any other wife but me." Her seat belt was tangled, and she pulled impatiently to close it.

"Ah. So no other wife. That leaves only one option. Divorce. Well then. Let's get a divorce." It had been said so calmly that it took a while for the words to register with her. Her face paled as if all the blood had dropped from it with one breath, and her eyes closed for an instant. Jon was almost sure he could see her lashes tremble.

"All right," Naomi said.

The softly spoken word felt like a long, hot needle pushed into his throat.

The plane was moving, taxiing toward the runway. A flight attendant came to check on them, nodded, and left again.

"You would really do that, wouldn't you? You would jump off this plane just to atone for something that's not your fault." Jon gripped her hand hard, probably hurting her, but he didn't care. "You would divorce me. And what do you think would happen then, huh? Do you really believe for one second that I'd ride off into the sunset with a young nubile maiden and get her pregnant within the next twenty-four hours just so I could hold a baby in my arms? Don't you understand anything?"

She didn't react.

"Look at me, damn you. Don't sit there like a dying swan. I will never divorce you, so you can stop hoping for that. I don't give a shit about a baby's head, and you have to stop punishing yourself." He drew a deep breath. "You can't go on like this, my love; it will destroy you. You're torturing yourself every day; you wallow in the pain."

That shook her out of her distress. Furiously, she pulled her hand out of his to tug at her clothes. "Do you want to see my scar? Do you want to see where they cut me open from top to bottom; do you want another look at the X-rays with the black hole where my lung should be? Would you like to watch the video again, of the shooting, when you were not there, and…"

Jon caught her against his chest when she started sobbing, fighting for breath, cradling her head, just as the plane took off. The land slipped away beneath them, just like his anger; and he wondered, miserable now, why he had felt the need to lash out at her, dump something as stupid and painful as the prospect of divorce on her, when he wanted nothing of the kind.

chapter 11

SHE REFUSED TO talk to him, even changed places as soon as the seat belt light went out, scrambling over his lap because he refused to get up and let her pass. He went over to her once and tried to apologize, but she turned her head away and leaned her cheek against the window, her arms wrapped tightly around her body in an attitude of rejection.

"There's nothing out there but clouds," Jon said in an attempt to lighten the mood. "Look at me instead. Look at me, and talk to me." He could have slapped himself for his outbreak, seeing her cry now. "You were driving me crazy with this baby talk, Naomi. Can't you just let it go and forget the whole issue? Hurting yourself like this doesn't help at all. It doesn't help! It won't give you a baby. For that we need to do different things, loving things."

But for once she didn't listen to him and his lame attempt at bantering. Jon felt like an idiot standing in the airplane aisle, in the way of the flight attendant when she came around with coffee and drinks. He had to squeeze himself into the row next to her and wait there until the serving cart was past. The band and everyone else was farther up front, most of them dozing or reading and not paying attention to them.

"You know I'd never divorce you. I was just..." Exhaustion crept up on him as he looked up the aisle to where his friends were, accepting the offered beverages, stirring, beginning to chat over their plastic cups. An insane longing to be up there with them, have an orange juice with a hint of vodka, crack a couple of stupid jokes, and relax, overwhelmed him. "It was a stupid, senseless joke, okay? I thought I'd be able to shock you out of your sadness, but it didn't work. Can this please be over now? Can we have a cup of coffee and forget this whole thing?"

She barely glanced at him. "Go and have your coffee. I don't want any." Naomi turned even farther away, her face shuttered, lips tightly closed.

Art was calling him, asking why he was standing around in the aisle, if he wanted something, and why they were hiding in the back anyway. He held up a glass of tomato juice. "Come here; we're discussing where to live in New York; you should be able to make some suggestions."

For a moment longer Jon looked down at her, waiting for a response, then he left and joined Art and Sal.

THE CLOUDS BROKE when they crossed the Alps, the white-capped peaks gleaming below the plane in the sunlight, the meadows and forests in the valley sparkling like jewels, the rivers blue ribbons outlining the landscape. Naomi nearly cried again when they approached Geneva and she could see the huge plume of the fountain in the distance and the rainbows its haze cast. She remembered being a young girl, enjoying the easy life of a teenager without a worry in the world but which dress to wear for the party that night or which invitation to accept for a cruise on the lake. She had been so free, like a moth dancing in the warm air. For a short while she had been carefree, happy, the burden of her family's business forgotten. Sometimes she had even been able to pretend she was someone else, just one of the girls who were the butterflies on the promenade, eating ice cream, dipping their bare feet into the small waves of the lake that kissed the pier with little smacks while they laughed at the boys slowly passing by and ogling them. They had been so sassy, hitching up their short skirts to show off tanned, sleek legs and confuse the young men. Young queens, trying out their power on everything in trousers; and when one of them dared to come forward, they quickly closed ranks and retreated, their silver giggles like a trail of perfume, fading.

Wiping her eyes with the back of her hand, she raised her head to look for Jon, but he had sat down somewhere with the others and she couldn't see him.

None of those boys had appealed to her despite her friends' attempts to set her up and their constant questions about why she didn't pick one, even if only for the fun of it. She had not wanted a boyfriend. In her dreams, there had always been someone else, someone who wouldn't blush and stammer when she batted her lashes at him and who would wipe away all the silliness and play with one glance.

She wanted, she had told the other girls, a man. Not one of the kids. It was not the entire truth; but it made them stop matchmaking and look at her with a new attitude, something like respect, and envy.

The warning lights for the seat belts blinked.

Naomi rose from her isolated seat and wandered up to the others. Jon was sitting beside Sean, listening to something on his headphones, but when he noticed her he jumped up.

"If the plane crashes during landing," she said, "I want you beside me. I don't want to die alone."

HER HAND WAS in his again. They hadn't spoken yet, but her body had relaxed against his when they sat down on the bus, side by side, the way he wanted them to be every moment of their lives.

Jon recalled only too well the one time he had been in Geneva before. He had never returned there on tour, despite the many requests and invitations, even once by the mayor himself, saying his wife was a great fan and they wanted to show him a great time in their lovely city by the lake.

Without Naomi he couldn't. He couldn't stand the thought of entering that hotel lobby again and not see her standing in the entrance, looking at him across that space, or taking a walk down the promenade along the lakeside and thinking of that first kiss, that enchanted moment, and not having her there, beside him.

Out of sheer sentimentality he had insisted on the same hotel they had stayed in back then. Sal had given him the eye and asked, his voice dripping with sarcasm, if he hadn't been able to find a more expensive or exclusive one; and Jon, with a shrug, had replied that he didn't care. They had been able to afford it back then and no one had complained, and now they were wealthier than they were then.

"You want to repeat that moment with her," Sal had said, and earned himself a withering look in reply. "You think it will be just as magical. Dude, I have news for you. That's not how it works."

Jon had nearly choked on his coffee.

"Oh," Naomi sighed softly, and he woke from his reverie. Her fingers were curling around his as she looked out at the promenade and the old buildings, at the grand facade of the hotel. "We're here. Jon, we're back where..."

"Yes." It was a moment he had dreamed of for many years, being back. During the time they had been apart he had resisted the temptation to come back, to once again sit on that sofa in the lobby of this hotel, sit there and wait and look toward the entrance; and maybe, if the gods were kind, she would walk in and stand there, bathed in sunlight.

"Please, baby," Jon said as the bus stopped, "please stop punishing yourself for things that aren't your fault. Isn't it part of marriage, to bear the bad stuff together and enjoy the good? You'd never leave me if I lost my voice, would you? You wouldn't have turned away from me that day when I came to find you in Halmar if I hadn't been famous, successful, wealthy anymore, would you? If I had told you I sold vacuum cleaners door-to-door now? Would you?"

She shook her head, a small smile tugging at the corners of her mouth.

"Or…"—dramatically Jon spread his arms, right there outside the impressive entrance of the most exclusive hotel in Geneva, ignoring the stares of the passersby—"if I had lost a leg, or I was bald and fat. You'd still want me, right?"

"I'm not sure about the bald and fat."

He laughed when he saw her turn her head to hide the grin from him. "Yeah, I'd think about that twice too. Come on. This is our day, and we'll play this out. Let Sal think we're maudlin fools. I don't care."

But she didn't budge. "Jon, this is different, serious. You're throwing away the chance of having another child."

On the point of walking up the stairs after the others, Jon stopped. She was still down on the pavement, amid the piles of luggage the driver and the hotel attendants were beginning to take inside, her purse clamped in her hands, waiting for his reply.

"Yeah." Slowly, nodding, he took the two steps back to her. "Yeah, I'm throwing it away. I'm very deliberately throwing this away. I'm cutting the thought of ever having another kid out of my heart. And yes, I wanted it very much. But, Naomi, I don't want it as much as I want you. I have this choice and it's mine alone to make. You have no say in this. It's either you, or some other woman and a baby. Well, I choose you and no child. I can't imagine my life without you. But I can well imagine it without another child. It's that easy. My choice. Now will you please come inside and let me see you in that lobby, and relive that sweet moment when I first saw you? Please?"

Naomi gazed at his outstretched hand for a moment and then took it to follow him inside.

SAL WATCHED THEM enter the lobby, her arm through Jon's, like a bride walking into a church. The picture was like a heartbreaking déjà vu, like a painting of that moment when he had first seen them together, right here in this spot. Only then they had not come toward him like royalty, their faces serene. Back then she had been a schoolgirl in jeans:

now she was everything he wanted her to be: a beautiful, elegant woman with jewels gleaming on her skin.

He remembered that moment only too well, when he had stepped out of the elevator and into the tableau of love at first sight: Jon, the hot young rock star, holding the hand of a stranger, lost to the world; and Naomi, her head tilted up at him, so lovely it had made him forget to breathe.

It had been like looking at one of those cheap postcards that could be bought at tourist stands, the ones that when tilted showed a second, hidden image, as if by looking from a different angle at them he would be able to see the kiss they were both longing for.

"The rooms, Sal?" Jon asked, breaking into his reverie, and Sal nodded. He had the key Jon had requested, of course requested, to the same suite he had occupied all those years ago.

He had watched them leave the venue all those years ago, vanish into the limousine before anyone even understood where they had gone, and known Jon was taking her here, to his room, to his bed, claiming her before any other had the chance, putting his mark on her so no one else would dare approach her, ever. This had been different, Sal had realized. This was not a tour flirt, a fling along the way; this was serious, magical, final, and it had broken his heart. He would never have a chance.

Naomi glanced down at the key. "The same room?"

Her softly spoken words felt like drops of molten lead on his soul. And when Jon replied "Of course. I can't wait," he turned away, pretending to be busy with the other keys he was still holding in his hand, so he did not have to see them go upstairs, did not have to imagine the door of the suite closing behind them and her in his arms, just like then, lost forever.

SAL STAYED BEHIND after everyone else had left, the lobby suddenly eerily quiet and empty. There were a couple of guests sitting in the far corner, a map spread out on the table between them, discussing the day's adventures, and some liveried hotel employees hurrying past; but he was alone.

Slowly, almost surreptitiously, he strolled over to the couch where Jon had waited for that writer he wanted to meet so badly, the one who had sent the lyrics to them from here, not knowing she would be the love of his life. He sat down, his hands on his knees, and tried to feel what

Jon had felt then, seeing her come in. She hadn't been at all what they had expected—not a seasoned professional, someone who wanted to sell them something and strike a deal with the Hollywood star, but a mere girl.

And how she had changed all their lives, had turned everything upside down that day.

Out on the terrace, where the three of them had sat down together, he had watched them stare at each other, ignoring the ice cream and cake that were offered, the air between them simmering; and he had felt old, left out, lonely. For the first time he had been envious of Jon, of his good looks, his intense dark eyes, his voice, the power he had over women, the talent, the success.

A pretty young waitress came over to him and asked if he wanted anything, and he gave her a tired, lopsided grin as he asked for a whiskey, make that a double, and the best they had. Bourbon, if possible. She rattled off a list of brands; and he waved at her, picking one, not really interested, just craving the solace of the familiar burn in his throat and the moment of ease when it went to his head.

It was still early afternoon, and the show was not until the following night.

Sal wondered if they were in bed yet, she in Jon's arms, sighing, softly whispering his name, her arms around him, her skin white and silken, her lips open to his. The same room, the same bed; and he could just see Jon, overcome by his memories, wanting her right away, intent on reliving that first night, wanting to make love to her.

Sadness settled on his shoulders like a big, black bird as he raised his hand to order another drink.

THE ICE CREAM truck was no longer there. Instead, there was a pavilion with tables and chairs around it. They sold beverages and sweets, souvenirs and newspapers. The trees were the same, and the place that rented out boats; even the swings on the playground along the promenade looked much like they had twenty years ago.

"I remember the exact spot where I kissed you," Jon said. "It was right here." He stopped and pointed at a red bench. "I recall that bench. It was here back then."

"It might be a new bench. I don't think they last that long." She went over to read the plaque on the backrest. "See, it says it was put here in memory of one Madame Madeleine Grisson, who loved to come and feed the swans and sit here. She must be dead. What a sweet, sentimental thing to do, to put a bench here in her memory."

"I think it's perfectly good taste to put it right here. In fact, we should put up our own bench and plaque." He joined her. "It would say, 'Here, the universe shifted and made room for lovers. It will never be the same again.' Or something in that vein. Absolutely."

They were, he knew only too well, drifting toward her parents' apartment. It was not far away, right there in one of the palatial houses along the shore. He had only been there once, after she had left him, in a vain attempt to find her. What a nightmarish experience that had been. Never before had he run into European snobbery in quite that manner, and he had not been in a mood for an overseas tour for a long while after.

Now, looking up at the elaborate facades of the buildings on the other side of the street, the memory of that day crept up on him.

It had rained, and an ugly wind had blown down the elegant avenue, whipping the lake into a white-capped frenzy, hiding the mountains behind a curtain of water. That French-speaking doorman had treated him like a street vendor, a beggar, someone who was not worth the dirt under his nails, and had sent him on his way with a look of utter disgust. Soaked, the collar of his jacket turned up against the foul weather, he had stood and stared, his hope washing away with the torrent gushing down into the gutter.

SHE HAD NOT mentioned with one word where she wanted to go when she had suggested a walk, but he had seen. Shortly after they had been shown to their rooms, she had gone out on the balcony and stood there, her shoulders drawn together, lost in thought.

Meeting her parents was not something he was keen on. Jon could well have done without ever confronting her father, Olaf, again. If there was one person in the world he hated with all his heart, it was he.

"Sure." had been his reply. "Let's go and find the spot where we first kissed. And I'll kiss you again."

So here they were, and he could see by the way she turned away from the bench and toward the street that the moment had come.

The thought of ringing that doorbell made him heavy hearted. He could not figure out why she wanted to give herself the additional pain of facing her parents after that terrible scene with her father when she had just woken from her coma, so weak and ill, and he had dumped all his anger about her marriage on her. Jon recalled well how he had wanted to pack his fist into the man's face right then and there in the hallway of the hospital while the doctors were fighting to bring her back to life. He'd not often wielded the power his fame and wealth gave him in this manner, but that day he had used it to lock her family out of their life with a court order.

Naomi took his arm. "They love me, Jon. And I love them, despite everything. I want to see my mom."

"Of course." This, he could understand.

Together they waited for a break in the stream of cars to cross the road.

chapter 12

AT LEAST THIS time he made it into the lobby of the house. Curious, Jon took in the marble floors and stucco walls, the highly polished brass mailboxes and the elaborately carved banister. The elevator at the back of the hall had art deco doors, a veritable upright garden of iron leaves and flowers. He could have sworn there was a nymph hiding amid the foliage.

"They're not here?"

The tone in Naomi's voice made him turn around.

"No, madame," the concierge replied with a shrug. "Your parents moved out last month. Monsieur Carlsson told me it was time for him to retire."

"And where…" She stopped and bit her lip.

Jon laid his hand on her shoulder. "Come on. Let's go." He led her out to the sidewalk, where she stopped to look back.

"They can't be gone," Naomi said. "They can't have just moved away. Why wouldn't they tell me, Jon? And where are they?"

"Come on," he repeated, and waved to stop a taxi. "There's no use in standing around here. Let's go back to the hotel."

She didn't talk during the short drive, and he didn't push her. Once again anger at the sheer thoughtlessness of her father blossomed in his belly.

They had to have known they would be coming to Geneva, known Naomi would try to see them. Looking at her profile, at her lowered head and folded hands, he tried to imagine a scenario in which he would desert Joshua, show him disapproval in such an unforgiving, final manner, and couldn't. He couldn't imagine moving without informing his son, telling him when and where he was going. Even now, on tour, even while Naomi had been away, he had called him every night, sometimes just for a minute, just to hear his voice; but mostly they chatted for a while, Joshua telling him about school and the girls he liked. Jon would listen, seeing him in his mind, wishing he was closer. But Joshua had no interest in traveling with them and no interest in the tour; he wanted to be in New York, at Juilliard. In a way, this pleased Jon, the passion he had for his studies, but it also saddened him. He would have loved to have him along.

"I'm sure they're back in Toronto," he said. "Where else would your father go?" Immediately he was sorry for the spite in his statement, and he added, softer, "Call your uncle Carl from the hotel. He'll know."

She nodded.

"You did talk to your uncle, didn't you?" Jon continued. "You told him you were going to that hotel on the Eastern Shore; he knew you were there?"

Yes, she admitted, she had spoken to him, and he had known she was staying there for a while. He had even instructed the staff on how to treat her and not to let her do any work while she was there. Naomi smiled sadly. "But we never spoke about my parents. It was only a brief conversation. I think he was too afraid to say much, in case he might offend or scare me off."

"Your father in his senseless hatred nearly killed you, my love." He had to say it even though he knew it would hurt her. "He didn't give a damn about your health, about your condition; he just wanted to vent his fury somewhere, and you were there."

"He was scared and worried, Jon."

The drive was short. Jon realized he didn't have any Swiss francs with him. He had forgotten to get some from Sal before they had left the hotel. Naomi got some bills out of her purse and paid wordlessly.

"I never take cabs." he protested. "Why in the world do we book limousines if we're going to use taxis?"

She waved him away and went inside.

"He never meant to hurt me," Naomi went on when they reached their rooms. "Only I didn't lead the life he wanted for me. It's not his fault. But it's also not mine. We just disagreed."

"Yes, and it was his job to let you lead your own life, Naomi. Children can't live the lives their parents want for them; they have to pick their own way, whether it hurts or not. And you, dear, didn't exactly pick the life of a striptease dancer. You're an artist, a writer; you made a very nice career for yourself."

It was the middle of the afternoon, the sluggish, hazy time of rest in this nearly Mediterranean climate. Jon imagined lounging in a café along the lake, with espresso and brandy and a good cigar, whiling away the hours until it was time for dinner and a stroll through the old part of the town, maybe some leisurely shopping and a drink with the group on the hotel terrace before retiring.

"I'm only a writer because you decided you liked my little rhymes, Jon." She tossed her purse on the couch.

"You crazy chick, it wasn't me who gave you that Oscar. And you sure weren't picked because you're my wife. You got that award for your work. I'm the lucky one here; you chose me to send your lyrics to. I'm so glad you fell in love with me and not Mick Jagger. Or that Neil Diamond, God forbid."

That made her laugh. "You share a love for funny shirts."

"Yeah, so did Elvis. What the hell. Don't change the subject. We're not talking about my stage shirts; we're talking about your father." Jon sat down and pulled her onto his lap. "Baby, he's a brute. He doesn't give a damn about your feelings. If I could..." He stopped. This he could not say to her, but right at that moment he wished he had his hands around that old man's throat or his fist connecting with his chin.

Her hands were on his face, touching his cheeks gently. "If you could, you would go to Toronto right now and bring him back, I know, just like you did last year in Halmar. But that's not how it works, Jon. Let it rest."

"Yeah." That hadn't been what he was thinking,but if it was what she wanted to believe, he was willing to let it pass.

JON WOULD HAVE loved to spend the evening alone with her, in private, but there was a dinner invitation, one Sal insisted he accept.

Grumbling, complaining, he changed into a tux while Naomi watched him from the corner of the bed.

"I wonder why everyone wants me in a bow tie," Jon said, "when I really feel best in jeans and a t-shirt."

It was a lie, and he could see she knew by the way her lips twitched.

"These things are uncomfortable. I hate them. They make me look old," he added for good measure, but she didn't rise to the bait.

The last time he had worn formal attire had been at the Oscars. He hadn't taken it off for two days, sitting by her hospital bed, praying for her. When at last he had showered and changed, more or less forced to do so by Sal, he had thrown it away. He was sure he never wanted to wear it again.

"You look sexy in a tux," Naomi said interrupting his thoughts. "And you know it. If there ever was a man made to wear one it's you."

Jon finished tying his tie; he gave his sleeves one last tug before he straightened and turned to her. "Well? Happy?"

She was indeed pleased; he could see it in the faint blush that crept up her throat.

"You look wonderful. I'm afraid to take you out like that and have you meet the Swiss aristocracy. There'll surely be someone with a yacht and a castle in the mountains who will try to entice you away. Can't let that happen," he said.

That made her smile. "I had that chance, Jon, and I didn't take it. You needn't worry."

He loved her new dress. She had bought it that afternoon, right here in Geneva when they had gone out for a stroll in the old part of the city.

"Show me," Jon had said, "where you used to go shopping, where you used to hang out with your friends," and he had pictured her on those old, cobbled streets, arm in arm with other sweet young girls, carefree and beautiful.

"I'd have picked you out right away," he had told her as they'd stopped in front of a boutique where a black dress was displayed in the window. "I'm sure, had I met you here somewhere that day, even without the lyrics, without our appointment, I'd have picked you out anyway; and you'd have been mine. I know it."

She had thrown him a cool glance over her shoulder, on the point of entering the store, and replied, "Not so. I'd have seen you first and then quickly made sure none of the others had a chance with you."

He had never liked black on her, but when she stepped out of the changing room, he'd nearly jumped up off the couch where he had been sitting. The satin hugged her body like a sheath, and with every step she took, the long slit revealed her leg nearly to her hip. Thin straps crossed her bare back, a startling contrast to her white skin, and very inviting.

"You can't go out like that." had been his first startled reaction. "I'm not taking you out like that," but Naomi had only smiled and paid for the gown.

NOW, AS SHE rose from the bed and raised her arms in a fluid moment to check the tight coil of hair at the back of her head, his breath caught, all the grief and pain forgotten.

"You're so beautiful," Jon said softly. He wanted to run his hands over the sleek material, feel her body under it, and then slide his fingers up that stretch of leg, all the way up, and find out what she might be wearing underneath; wanted to lay her down and feel the warmth of her skin through the silk, the movement of her breathing. "You give me fantasies. I'll be thinking of making love to you all evening long, and then I have to bear others seeing you, wanting the same thing."

That made her laugh. "Jon, no one but you thinks like that. You have a dirty mind. You're always thinking about sex. Always."

"Nah, I'm not." He held the door for her, his eyes firmly on that naked leg and the high heels of the black sandals she was wearing. "I'm always thinking of sex with you. Big difference."

In the elevator, alone, in a moment of unexpected eroticism, she leaned against the mirrored wall behind her and shifted her hip so the dress fell open, and gave him an inviting, sultry glance.

"Is that what you want," Jon growled. "You want to be ravished in the elevator? There's a camera here; you know that, right? I'll do it. I'm the rock star, I have a reputation to keep up, and doing it in an elevator won't hurt it one bit. Come here, then."

"You're too much of a wimp to try it."

She was wearing the dark red lipstick she had bought in London, a luxurious, impertinent splash of color.

"I'm no wimp. You are an outrage in that dress. People will talk. We can't go out. You're coming back to the room with me, now, and to my bed." His heart soared; at last, at long last, they were playing again, enjoying life.

"I'll come to your bed if there's no one else who seems more inviting," Naomi tossed at him as the doors opened, and stepped out to where Sal and Art were waiting.

NAOMI MISSED SOLVEIGH more than she could say.

Getting out of the limousine that had been sent for them, she could just hear her comments on the place and the people, the cars parked along the gravel driveway, even the yachts lined up at the dock.

They had gone a little way out of town, driven along the shore and then entered the forested estate through a wrought-iron gate, guarded by two liveried men.

She remembered the villa on the water all too well. Nothing had changed over the years; there was the same deep porch, the white lawn chairs lined up along the beach, the torches stuck into the sand with their reflections flickering on the water, the same kind of music drifting toward them from inside.

The last time she had been here she had worn a yellow chiffon gown, and she had come with her parents. On the way, her father had once again implored her to at least dance with some of the boys; they were coming here for her sake so she could meet someone since she didn't want the man her family had chosen for her. And she, an impetuous teenager of seventeen, had told him to leave her alone and stop treating her as if she was his favorite mare, which had made him launch into one of his well-worn lectures, the one about the importance of picking the right husband, one who would contribute to their business and not marry her only for her money. That night he had spoken the fatal words that she had never forgotten.

"You are an asset, Naomi. With your looks and your education, you'll be able to bring someone important into the family," he had said. "I'm looking for a union with one of the other big hotel owners. If you don't want Seth then that is the next best choice."

Seth. She had never cared for him, or for any of the others her father presented to her. That evening had been no different.

"You're dreaming of a knight in shining armor." Her father had caught her hiding in a corner of the porch, a large bowl of ice cream in her lap. "He will not come, Naomi. You are who you are; your marriage will be a business arrangement. And I'll see to it that it will be a good one."

"He will come" had been her obstinate reply;. "Someday he'll come and rescue me, and then I'll be gone and you'll never see me again."

Olaf had thrown his hands up in defeat and returned inside to his talk about money, and her tears had dropped into the strawberry sorbet.

"DREAMING, BABY? DON'T you want to go inside?" Gently, Jon touched her bare shoulder. "It's a beautiful place, isn't it? I love how the air smells. Lavender, isn't it?"

"Flowerpots" was her absentminded response.

The only invitations Jon ever accepted while he was on tour were the ones he could not decline, such as this one, extended by the mayor and a group of bankers too influential to ignore. As always he knew it was not really the men who wanted to meet him, but more likely their wives and daughters. There had been many of these dinners, and often enough one of the ladies had gone back with him to his hotel room for another bottle of champagne, a quick tussle, and a good-bye. The mornings had been the worst, waking up alone, the trace of unfamiliar perfume still on his pillow, the sheets crumpled and the wine all gone.

He took Naomi's arm in his and led her up the stairs and into the building, a sudden pride swelling in his chest at having her by his side. She was stunning in that gown, as slim as a young girl, her skin flawless, just the way she had been when they had met.

"Love you," he whispered just as one of the men came forward to greet them. "You're the loveliest woman in this room tonight." And grinned at her pert response. "Thank you, but just tonight?"

chapter 13

"THE SWISS REALLY know how to throw a party." Art remarked. Sal, eyeing the dessert being set down in front of him, replied, "Europeans have class. That's simply a fact of life. They are the better fans, too."

"They are more polite fans, big difference." There was some very fine wine in their glasses, and there had been some very fine food too.

Their hosts had placed Jon and Naomi at the head of the banquet table like a wedding couple, the guests of honor, where everyone would be able to see Jon.

No one had the bad taste to take pictures without asking, much less ask for an autograph; and the talk never touched on his work or his private life. It was always polite, friendly and well mannered.

Sal, watching them, recalled that day at the open-air venue here in Geneva when Naomi had sat with him during the sound check and he had asked her about her life. Even then she had been different, like a clear flame, as if a light shone in her and spilled out onto her surroundings. He had hardly been able to look at her, she was so beautiful. And Jon, up on the stage in the sun, had glared down at them, his mouth set in a thin line of disapproval, his fingers on the guitar missing more than one beat while she told him of summers on the lake, boating and swimming, water-skiing, attending dances at yacht clubs, and winters in the mountains. With a graceful wave of her hand she had pointed at the white peaks in the distance, on the other side of Lac Léman, and told him that Mont Blanc wasn't too far away, just over there, to the south, and Chamonix was really very pretty in the snow.

He had listened as she told him about trips to Montreux for music festivals and lazy afternoons with friends eating ice cream and tossing their crumbled wafers to the swans, and evening strolls along the shore. She loved going to Lausanne for shopping trips; it was such a nice little city. The names of those towns had blurred past him, names he had only heard in old Technicolor movies of places never on their tour plan.

For a brief moment he had seen their lives as a long train ride with a few stops, while in the distance other places, barely seen, beckoned, places they would never visit, that would ever only remain legends. He had made a vow to himself then and there to visit Montreux someday, even if it was only to have a cup of coffee in a restaurant on the lake, just so he could say he'd been there.

Jon had broken into this magical moment when he had jumped from the stage and come over to them. She had turned toward him, Sal forgotten, everything else forgotten; and he had given up and left.

HIS BRANDY GLASS refilled, Sal settled back. Dinner was over; it was time to pay for it. He didn't envy Jon in these moments, when the music and the dancing started and every woman in the room quivered with anticipation, dreaming of being in those arms even if only once, if only for a heartbeat or two.

Jon leaned toward Naomi and whispered to her, his hand caressing her naked shoulder; and she listened, her head tilted toward him, eyes cast down and mouth soft in a small smile. Sal wondered if they did it intentionally, if maybe they took the time to rehearse just the right angle and timing in front of a big mirror, if they had ordered the candles and flowers to be placed just so, the bottle of champagne in the silver cooler and the crystal glasses, to present this perfect tableau to their enraptured audience.

"They look like they are one being, don't they?" Art said from behind him, admiration in his voice. "It's really interesting to watch. Like two puzzle pieces that fit together perfectly. Or maybe like an Oreo cookie: two halves of the same thing, stuck together with love instead of cream…"

"Stop being so disgusting," Sal interrupted him. "I get your point. And yeah, you're right." He needed another brandy.

Jon was rising now, buttoning his jacket and doing it in a way that made all eyes turn to him. There was more than interest in some of the men's faces as always, and as always this made Sal grin. Desires and dreams, fueled by a simple gesture. If anyone could do it, it would be Jon.

The city's mayor, the host for the evening, asked Naomi for a dance; and with a last, slight touch on Jon's sleeve, she followed him.

"Come on." Art sighed. "Let's do our bit. Dancing with us is nearly as good as dancing with the Master himself."

Sal wondered if there were any among these people who knew Naomi from before, who had been to school with her or danced with her here in this same spot twenty years ago. She did seem rather friendly with the mayor, a tall, slim man who had introduced himself as Walter. He was too old to have been a classmate and yet not old enough to be of her parents' generation.

Sal had asked his wife to dance, a petite blonde in a flaming red dress, a lively, chatty woman in her late forties who did not stop telling him how excited she was about Jon having accepted the invitation and how much she was looking forward to the concert the following night.

"You have backstage passes, of course," Sal murmured, looking at Naomi over her head.

Yes, they did, she nodded, and she could hardly wait; she'd been backstage to a number of shows, but none like this, of course. "It took you so long to come back here," she said. "Many years. I went to see Jon in Zürich a couple of times; but you never returned to Geneva, even though his wife used to live here. So strange." She had the cutest French accent, Sal noted, and asked her name.

Pauline, she replied, and moved a little closer to him; her name was Pauline, and she was enchanted to make his acquaintance. The words sounded charming with that accent, Sal had to admit. He turned his attention to her, away from Naomi's bare back and Walter's hand on it, right where the straps of her dress crossed below her shoulder blades, a strange man's hand touching her skin.

"We used to see her when we had a party here, or at our house. She was such a sweet young girl, always so quiet. My brother was madly in love with her," Pauline was saying, and he made himself listen. "But she never cared for him. I always thought she was listening to something, some other tune, as if she was not even here."

"I love the way you say that," Sal answered, holding her tighter. "Your English is very cute."

This made her blush; it was not very becoming and clashed with the red of her dress, but Sal found it enticing anyway. She didn't look too bad for her age, and she was a good dancer.

"Anyway," Pauline went on, slightly flustered. "Naomi, she was always different. I had a feeling her father would really have liked her to date Pierre, but she wouldn't even go to the movies with him or with any of the others." She shrugged. "Pierre now works at CERN. He's a scientist. I don't think they would have fit well together."

He didn't say it, but Sal agreed. If there was something he could not envision, it was Naomi as the wife of a scientist, bogged down in Geneva.

"I remember when Jon came here for those two concerts, way back then. Naomi and I were not really friends; I am so much older than she is. But she was somehow always there, like a fairy dancing in the corner of your eye. She was so excited about that concert, it was very amusing. We were all supposed to go together to the show, the entire group of young people, but somehow she was gone when we were supposed to leave. No one ever knew where she was." Her lips twitched. "But I have an idea now. No wonder he picked her; she was so lovely."

"She still is."

He could have slapped himself, but Pauline nodded. "Yes, a beautiful woman." Another shrug, then: "But she would have to be, to catch Jon Stone, *non?*"

JON FOUND HER on the lawn down by the water, her shoes in her hand, looking up at the full moon hovering over the distant mountains.

The air was balmy, soft and fragrant in a totally different way from LA, from any place at all he knew. He wondered if he had noticed when he had been in Geneva the first time, but he was almost certain he hadn't.

"You turned my head so completely."

Surprised, she looked around.

"I didn't give a damn about the concert that day. All I wanted was to be with you." There was a single tendril that had freed itself from the coil of hair, floating on the back of her neck in the breeze, and he caught it between his fingers.

"I know. You are easily distracted." She turned into his arms. "You didn't dance with me at all. All those ladies, they're probably still dreaming of you, and I get nothing."

"You get everything. You get all of me." The skin of her throat tasted of roses, of the perfume she always wore. It hadn't changed since they had first met; and everywhere, whenever he had smelled roses, he thought of her. "We could dance right here, where no one can see us. We could pretend you are my mermaid again, the sweet young thing I caught here on this lakeshore."

She swayed in his embrace. He pulled her closer to feel her body against his.

"I'm no lake selkie. I want to be from the cold waters, the dark, gray ocean, not this tepid puddle here." It was the gentlest whisper, like the touch of soft wind on his cheek.

"But your lips are warm. You can't be from the cold." His hands wandered down over the smooth silk, exploring the shape of her hips. "You're warm and supple, and you smell of flowers, not kelp or seaweed."

"I have my secrets."

"You want a kiss. I know it. But this is a dangerous place, my pretty mermaid, right by the water's edge. You might drag me under," he said into her mouth, inhaling her breath, savoring how she moved closer and her arms tightened around his neck.

"I will steal you away, oh yes." Naomi pulled back when he tried to kiss her. "I will tease and torment you until you come away with me and live with me in my underwater castle. We've had this discussion before, remember? You can't win."

Jon remembered only too well. "We made love in the shower. I think I won. You begged for mercy."

She gasped when he rocked his hips against hers suggestively but replied, "You did not win. I wore you out and had to help you to bed. Like an old man."

That made him laugh out loud. "Like hell you did. I recall I had to shake you awake when we were in bed at last; you dropped off like a baby. And now let me kiss you or I'll have to go inside and ask that blonde in the red dress. She's the youngest one here tonight, except for you. So if I want a kiss and you won't, it will have to be her."

"Pauline," Naomi said softly. "Her brother wanted to date me. Their parents had a nice yacht. We used to come here for summer balls and sit on the lawn to watch the moon, just like now."

His grip around her waist tightened. "You watched the moon with someone else? Right here? And you kissed him like you're going to kiss me now?"

She surrendered nicely, her lips coming open under his, melting into his embrace, just the way he liked it.

"I never kissed anyone like I kiss you, Jon. No one else had the magic," she said when he let her go.

"Why is kissing you so different?" Jon asked. "Why is it so magical with you? I don't want to stop, ever."

Instead of an answer she kissed him again, holding his face between her hands, standing on her toes to reach him.

"THEY JUST LEFT," Naomi said as they strolled back to the house. She hadn't put her sandals back on and had to hold up her dress so she wouldn't trip on it. With every step she took, Jon could see a glimpse of leg, the white skin shining in the moonlight. Again he thought of that mermaid they had made up and how she would wander this garden at night to watch the people inside the building while they danced and ate, humming along to the music and wondering what the golden, bubbling liquid in their glasses was.

"They just left, and nobody bothered to tell me." She stopped at the bottom of the stairs to the terrace. "I've been trying to think, Jon; what if we decided to move somewhere, even if we only went back to live in Halmar. Can you imagine us doing that without asking Joshua to come along? Without even letting him know? I mean, if something happens, he would need to know where to find us."

It seemed uncanny how her words echoed his earlier thoughts; only he had been furious, and Naomi was sad, withdrawing into that stillness he had come to hate. He didn't know what to say. No friendly or comforting words that he could come up with; everything would have been full of the anger and hate he felt for her father.

"I thought..."—a small shrug, the attempt at a smile that failed—"I thought we would bury what had happened, maybe get him to accept our marriage, and then we could have peace." Her words trailed off as she gazed back at the lake. "If I can live with what happened, then my father should be able to. I'm the one who got hurt."

Jon hated that he couldn't rip the memory of that day from the fabric of time or turn back time so it had never happened, make her healthy again and their life together the bright and shiny gem it should be instead of this constant struggle for a little happiness.

"It wasn't your fault, love." The curve of her shoulder fit into his hand like a silky peach. "If anything it was mine, and you know it. We've talked about it a million times. I'll bear the guilt."

She shook herself out of her moodiness. "It wasn't, Jon Stone. It wasn't your fault, so stop saying that. So you broke up with a girlfriend. That doesn't give her the right to shoot me, or anyone else." Holding on to his arm, she bent down to put on her sandals. "She could have written a book about how you look like a monster when you crawl out of bed in the morning, or how you leave your dirty clothes lying around on the floor. That would've had style." On the point of walking up the stairs she turned and added, "Or gone on every talk show in Hollywood and told the world that you had really nasty sexual habits. There are so many ways to hurt you that are far worse than aiming a gun at me."

"Oh no," Jon replied hotly. "That's not so. Nothing could be worse than that. Nothing. You're wrong, Naomi."

For a moment she looked at him. "Well, I could be dead. Now that would really be worse."

WALTER ESCORTED THEM to their car, saying what a great honor it had been to have Jon attend their dinner and how much his wife had enjoyed dancing with him. They were so looking forward to his concert.

"Your parents picked an awkward moment to move," he went on, addressing Naomi. "They missed meeting you here. But then, of course, you'll be seeing a lot of each other in the future. It must be nice to know they are close by. I envy them a little, I have to admit. Retiring to New York seems like a terribly exciting thing to do. Compared to that, Geneva feels like a village in the mountains." He laughed. "Which it is, of course."

Jon felt her fingers go cold, just like that, in an instant; and her body became rigid.

"Yes, we agree," he said, grateful for the years of practice he had lying to the press and fans. "It was a great surprise, but wonderful." Smoothly he bade him good night and ushered Naomi into the limousine.

"What," Sal asked, his eyes wide with suspicion. "What did he just say? Did I hear that right? Jon, the restraining order…" He shut up when Jon raised his hand.

"Joshua."

They all turned toward her: Art, Sal, Sean, Jon.

"Jon, he'll take Joshua away." Naomi, shaking, held on to him.

"No, no, baby, no one will harm Joshua." Jon laid his arm around her. "Don't worry about him. He's well protected." Even while he said it he threw Sal a sharp glance, and Sal nodded.

"What does this mean?" Her voice wavered. "Why would they do that? Of all places, New York?"

Sean bent forward. "Maybe, Naomi, maybe they are trying to find a way to make peace with you. I'm sure you'll find out soon enough, in a few weeks when we go back."

She didn't want to hear that, and she didn't want to see the careful glances between Jon and Sal, or how Sal got his cell phone out as soon as they arrived at the hotel, taking a few steps away from them to bark instructions into it.

"I want to call Joshua." She held out her hand for Jon's cell, but he shook his head. "You'll only upset him. Let's wait until we see what Sal finds out," and added, when he saw the worry in her face, "patience."

Jon stood, his hands in his pockets, lips slightly pursed, listening to Sal's conversation. Naomi could feel the tension in him, so well disguised by his easy stance; but there was something else, a hard, calculating attitude, the willingness to take on this problem and deal with it. He didn't show her this side of his personality often; but when he did, when he took command, she got an idea why those working for him liked to call him Master.

Sal hung up and came back over to them. "Nothing," he said. "Joshua just left school, and he's in the car now. Kurt says the surveillance was not broken for a moment, not since you were there. They can account for every minute. There's no reason to worry."

"Good." Jon took her arm with a grim nod toward Sal. "Let's call it a day then, Sal." On the point of entering the hotel he added, "Two more guards," and Sal nodded, opening his phone once again.

chapter 14

ONCE THEY WERE inside their suite he called Joshua, anxiously watched by Naomi. Hearing his young, clear voice and the impetuous tone in it, tugged at his heart, so much that he used any excuse to talk to him. Joshua's impatient, off-handed reply that yes, he had just returned from school and his grandmother was making dinner, and no, he had not gone anywhere else, made him breathe a little easier. "Take care," he told his son, and handed the phone to Naomi, who sat down on the couch and kicked off her sandals. She seemed to have forgotten he was in the room at all, chatting with Joshua, pulling out the pins that held up her hair. Barefoot, her hand full of pins, she reclined onto the cushions to ask him about the girl he had met the other day, yes, the one he had taken out for lunch, and where had they gone? Oh, Syrian, what an exciting choice, and she laughed at his reply. The black satin slipped on her thighs when she pulled up her legs to massage her toes as she ended her conversation with Joshua.

His wife, his son. Jon was certain he would never let anything change that, ever again: no other woman, no stalker, and least of all her father.

Naomi looked up at him. "What?"

"Nothing." Jon did not feel like talking about it. "Nothing at all. I like your dress. It's totally outrageous, and I love it. You were the loveliest woman at that party tonight."

She shrugged. "Easy. I was the youngest. Your fans are getting old."

Nodding slowly, Jon dropped his jacket and loosened the tie. "Get in bed. I'll show you old. You don't think there'll be any sleep tonight, do you?"

But when he came back from the shower she lay curled up under the sheet, shivering, her lips gray and her face bloodless.

"I'm so tired, Jon." Her voice was barely audible, it was so low and brittle.

All thoughts of wild, sweet moments were blown away, seeing her like that, seeing once again that she was not well by a long shot, no matter how much they tried to ignore it. Carefully he slipped into bed beside her and drew her into his arms, startled by how cold she was despite the warm summer night, and how weak. Her fingers gripping his wrist were shaky, nearly lifeless.

"I'm just tired," she repeated when he asked, scared now, if she needed a doctor. "I just need sleep." And added, snuggling up against him, "Could you hold me? You're so warm."

Jon held her against his chest, listening to her breathing, feeling her heartbeat, feeling her gradually relax and go soft with slumber as outside the birds started their early-morning song and the sun crept over the mountains.

"HERE," JON SAID.

Naomi leaned against the white-washed wall. "I know."

She was back in jeans and one of the white shirts, her hair in a braid, and she looked just as she had back then, all traces of the bitter, exhausting night gone.

"This was the spot where you told me you would not be in my bed that night." Jon, standing before her, rested his hand against the bricks, right next to her shoulder. "You told me that was not the way things worked, and you let me stand here with all my need for you, a little thing of nineteen telling me off."

"You deserved it."

The moment was so much like a déjà vu, he caught his breath. "Stop saying things like that. You drive me crazy. I'm trying to re-create a romantic moment, back with you here after all these years, and you say nearly the same things you did then. Can't I just live in my memories for a minute?"

"You don't have to." Her blouse slipped and revealed her shoulder when she moved to kiss him. "I recall quite vividly waking up in your bed this morning. Stop wallowing."

His eyes sparkled at her. "Yeah, that was good. That was how I wanted it when we stood here for the first time. I dreamed of finding you beside me when I woke up, just like today: so warm and sweet, your hair tousled, and you curled up against me, mine. My selkie, finally caught."

"Jon." No more than a whisper, barely audible over the noise of the loudspeakers from the stage where the band was still rehearsing.

"I want this tour over so badly." The playful mood gone, he wrapped his arms around her. "What a stupid idea this was; there's hardly any time for us to be alone. I want to regain what we had, the happy times, the carefree and easy days before…before." He broke off, his lips on her hair, her breath on his throat.

There was no answer, but she did not pull away and did not stiffen. He could feel her hands on his back, her fingers exploring the contours of his muscles, tracing a line down his spine.

"Careful," Jon growled, "no teasing. Bad timing, my sweet, very bad timing. Or are you thinking of that dressing room table again? Ah, you are one crazy chick, Naomi."

She laughed softly.

They could hear Sal's voice from the end of the hallway calling something toward the stage, and Jon let her go, running his fingers through his hair. "All right then, let's check out the dressing room."

She had not come in the last time. He recalled only too well how she had stopped outside the door and shook her head at him, offering no explanation, and how he had nodded unwillingly, afraid she would leave for good if he didn't prevent it.

"But I have to change" had been his plea, "and get ready for the show. What do I do if you're gone when I come back out?"

And he remembered her cool shrug and the simple statement, "You'll just have to wait and find out, right?"

No one, no girl, had ever treated him like that before, not since he had become famous and adored. They had all offered to entertain him in any way possible, had allowed him to use them in the hope of being the one, the woman he would take back home. She, Naomi, had turned away outside the door and, walking away, tossed at him, "I'll find someone to keep me company while they fuss over you. No worries." He had watched her wave to Sean, who had waited for her to catch up and, her arm through his, had vanished into the hospitality area and out of his sight.

This time, though, she did not hesitate and when he threw her a doubtful glance, said, "What? I'm your wife, I'm entitled to be here with you."

He loved the way she sat on the table, her back to the large, illuminated mirror, and examined the makeup tools, once more fiddling with the silly eyeliner. Today she swiveled around and applied it to herself, blinking at her image.

"This is good stuff," she declared. "No wonder your eyes look so sultry and dark on stage. I'm stealing it!"

Jon laughed. "No you're not. I'm not sure there's another one."

With a pout, she hid the pencil behind her back when he tried to take it from her. "Those fans of yours are not supposed to swoon at you anyway. You can't have prettier eyes than I have."

"You're impossible." But he smiled, seeing her in good spirits, seeing her laugh. "Do you feel up to another long night, baby? You could rest at the hotel, and…" Again he had been about to offer her an early return to New York, to their house in LA, even Halmar, anywhere but here on the road, but stopped when she shook her head.

"Here, and now, Jon. Stop trying to send me away or I'll start thinking you have someone else you want to meet, and you want to get me out of the way. Do you? Do you have someone else hidden away, a young, blond thing, someone with…" Naomi choked on her own words. Slowly, deliberately, she put the eyeliner back in its spot next to the powder and slipped from the table in an attempt to get past him and leave, but Jon blocked her way.

"You're not going anywhere," he said, his tone harsh with hurt. "This has to stop, and now. I know what you were going to say, Naomi. You were going to go into the baby thing again, right?"

"Yes, but not intentionally." Her fists were balled at her sides. "I didn't mean to say that! It just happened; it just popped out!"

"Hell yeah, it just popped out; but it could only pop because it was in your head, right? That thought is stuck in there, and no matter what I say you're not going to let go of it; I just know it!" He was, Jon realized, nearly shouting, her words had cut that deep. "I'm not going to leave you for another woman; you've got to accept that. If you are looking for a way to get rid of me, well, I'll tell you; you don't need all that female crap talk. Just tell me and be done with it, but for crying out loud, stop torturing me with this baby talk!"

Softly, silently, the tears spilled over her lashes and dropped on her cheeks, where she wiped them away with the back of her hand.

From the hallway they could hear laughter and voices, the background noises of an approaching show, Sal's and Art's among them, coming closer. Jon cast a furtive glance at his watch. One hour, and he had not yet showered, not changed; and beside the press and the fans, he would have to welcome the mayor and his blond Pauline. He took a couple of calming breaths. "I don't have time for another drama now. If you want to leave, go. I'm out of arguments."

"But I never meant to say anything!" She threw her hands up, exasperated. "You're trying to send me back to bed or the hospital or wherever all the time! It's you who wants to get rid of me!"

"That's just not true!" Jon's head was spinning. He couldn't figure out why they were suddenly back in one of their bitter discussions when only moments before they had been flirting and joking.

"I know I'm an invalid," she tossed at him. "I know I'm useless now, weak, and…useless." The fight went out of her. "Useless. That's what I am, yes. Like a broken cup, that's how I feel." Sad, her eyes tired, she looked up at him. "And you, Jon, you're trying to hold together the pieces, but it's not working. I'm just damaged goods."

"I want to slap you for saying that. You deserve to be slapped for calling yourself damaged and useless." He turned away from her and began taking off his shirt to get ready for the stage. "I'm not even going to try and talk sensibly to you now. You are not useless, and you are not damaged." Furious, he tossed the shirt into the corner of the room. "Do you even realize what you're saying? You're throwing your life away. Yeah, you were badly hurt, and in a totally senseless way. But Naomi—" he gripped her shoulders, ready to shake her—"you're alive. You're cared for and loved, you are on your own two feet, and you have enough life in you to give me hell. I love you. I love you more than anything or anyone else, and yet it's not good enough for you."

"But that's so not true!" She tried to free herself, but he did not allow it. "I'm a burden now, Jon, and our life is not going at all the way it should! We should be happy, and we should have another baby, and you should not have to worry all the time about my health."

Defeated, Jon sat down in the chair in front of the dressing table, her hands in his so that she had to perch on the corner of the table again. "Yes," he said, "you are right. Your health is a burden. I worry about you all the time, but not for the reasons you name. I worry because I want you with me, and I can see how you walk on the edge of life, how you sometimes even step away from it, as if you're testing how death might feel. Seeing you in those black, weak moments scares me more than I can say. I want to fight them, drive them out of you, only I don't know how." The exhaustion and defeat crept up his shoulders and settled behind his eyes.

"I can't follow you there, Naomi. I'm not ready to head into the abyss.

And I'll do my damnedest to keep you from falling in too. You belong here, on this side of the wall, with the living. With me."

For a moment there was silence. She did not pull away but looked down at their hands, at the watch on his wrist, the time ticking away, running from them.

"But I don't want to die." It came out so softly that Jon glanced up. "I don't want to die, Jon. All I want is to be with you. Only…" She leaned forward to brush her fingers through his hair and gently stroke his temples. "Only, I want to give you everything, because you deserve that, you're entitled to it, and I can't. And that makes me so sad."

"Stupid chick." Jon, his arms around her hips, buried his face against her breasts. "When will you realize I have everything I want? When will you realize I don't want anything else, nothing, not a thing, only you? Please?" He felt her hands on his face, a cool, gentle touch, and he looked up. Her eyes were large and dark in her pale face, her mouth the loveliest shape he could imagine. "Don't you know what a miracle you are? You're as beautiful as the dawn, and the only writer I want to work with. You're the one woman I want to make love to all the time, who can turn me around with a simple glance. You are my treasure, my beloved, and I can't bear to see all this pain and darkness in you." He felt drained, out of words, overwhelmed by sorrow.

"As beautiful as the dawn?" Naomi asked thoughtfully.

Jon smiled sadly. "Yes. Dazzling, like a sunrise on a clear day, like light skipping over water. A perfect rose."

There was a knock on the door. It was Ralph, asking if he could come in. Jon didn't bother to answer, intent on Naomi, waiting for her response.

"You are so perfect," she said gently, still caressing his cheeks. "You are the man every woman wants, dreams of; you are my dream. You do everything right, and you always say the right things. I can never wait to be in your arms. I love you beyond words; you are the only one. I want to give you all the happiness and joy life can give, Jon. It's what I want most, to see you content."

Her words were like the key to the chain of dread around his heart. "Come here." He pulled her down to straddle his knees, bodies touching, her arms around him.

"What would you do if I walked out on you, Naomi? If I left you?

How would you live then?"

Her lips opened in shock; Jon could feel a shiver running through her.

"Nothing." It sounded like a dying breeze. "There would be nothing. Life would end. How can you ask?"

"Because…" Those lips were so close, so tantalizing, and Jon wanted to kiss them and stop talking. "Because you keep offering that to me. And now think again and ask yourself how that makes me feel. I don't want to be without you either."

At last she softened against him and allowed the kiss.

chapter 15

JON TOOK THE eyeliner from the table, saying she would not get it again and, hey, maybe he wouldn't even use it himself anymore and to hell with the good looks onstage; he didn't care one way or the other anyway.

"Then give it to me," Naomi said, and held out her hand; but he shook his head and tossed it into the trash.

"No. You'll get stupid ideas again, and I'm done with these scenes. Go buy your own."

Ralph had wrapped a towel around Jon's neck to get him ready, while Naomi sat on the table and Sal lounged in the doorway, smoking a cigarette and telling them how things looked outside.

"I don't get it," Naomi interrupted his stream. "Why do you have to wear makeup onstage. I understand why it has to be done for the camera, but for the stage? I've always wondered."

They all stared at her, distracted from their tasks, until Ralph told her how the spotlights made everyone pale and how the distance blurred features, making it necessary to enhance a face, even a male one. She shrugged. It looked fake, even unreal.

Jon grinned at her from his chair, his teeth white and shiny against the powdered skin. "Even the girls in the last row want me to look good for them, sweetheart. It's not for you. It's for my other lovers."

She had used his dressing room to change into an elegant dress and matching high heels, both in an understated cream, explaining that she would not sit beside the stage dressed like a teenager. She had worn that outfit just for him and his sentimental memories. But she would not present herself to old friends and the Geneva audience as if he could not afford to take her shopping.

"Those discussions have to stop," he had told her, watching her pin up her hair and put on lipstick. "I'm completely worn-out, as drained as a dishrag, and I have to go on and perform in an hour. Can't you please stop wanting to leave or die or anything like that? Can't we just live day by day, enjoy what we have, and love each other?"

She had promised she would try, but it had sounded brittle, half-hearted, and he hadn't pushed any further.

"Your other lovers," Naomi now repeated softly, "yes. But they don't know you the way I do. They don't know the sloppy weekend you."

Strangely, with these words Jon felt a yearning rise in him, pulling, nearly hurting, for the quiet of the Malibu garden and the clutter of his studio, the sun on the dark wood of their bedroom floor, and even the coffee maker in the kitchen. Never before on one of his tours had he felt anything like homesickness, but here it was: he wanted to be back there, and right now. He wanted to wander through the cedar grove, through the gate in the fence out onto the beach, wanted to sleep in his own bed with the sound of the Pacific in his ears and breathe in the jasmine scent from the bushes below the window. They had been traveling for three weeks, had given only a handful of concerts, and yet he was tired of it.

From somewhere down below his heart, from a spot right at its tip, Jon could sense a familiar tugging. He knew it only too well. Once, in a drunken, maudlin moment, he had told Art about it. It was, he had said, as if a tiny hand reached into his body, an unseen and very strong hand from another dimension; and it was there to pull all the melodies out of him, right out of his heartstrings, blood and everything attached. The only strange thing about it was that it did not hurt, and it did not make him weaker. Rather it was as if, by taking them from him, it had lightened his soul. Yes, by ripping the music from him, the same hand poured light into his soul. And Art had stared at him over the rim of his glass and asked if he had eaten some magic mushrooms; he had never before sounded so delusional.

THERE WAS MOVEMENT by the door, Sal turning to look down the hallway over his shoulder; and Art appearing behind him. Jon stood with his hands pushed into his jeans pockets, and looked at Naomi.

Ralph removed the towel from Jon's neck and began brushing Jon's hair.

"There are some people to see you," Art said to Naomi. "They're waiting in the arena."

With a sigh, Naomi left her seat on the table. "To see me? Not Jon? No one wants to see me."

When there was no immediate reply, Jon swiveled in his chair expectantly, and Art shrugged. "Yeah, kill the messenger. Your parents are here, Naomi. They asked to see you."

She took a small step back, bumping into Jon's chair, her hand coming out to find some support; and he grabbed it and held it tightly.

"But they weren't here," Naomi said, her voice shaking. "They aren't here. They don't live here anymore. How can they be here now?"

"How am I supposed to know?" Art threw his hands up. "They are out there, and they are asking for you. Guess they must have bought tickets. Do you want me to bring them in now or what?"

"Baby, your parents know quite well how to use a plane," Jon murmured. "What do you want to do? You wanted to see them, remember? Now they are here." He did not look at her. The old anger at Olaf boiled in his gut, spiced by new fury at their surprise visit now. Silently he cursed at Art, wishing he had told him in private first so there would have been a chance to send them away or, even better, have them taken out of the venue altogether. But now, like this, he could do nothing. It was her decision. "You want them here, backstage, with us? Or do you want to go out and say hello and come right back? Or give Art a note to tell them to meet us later, at the hotel? You know I won't let you go anywhere alone with them. I'm way too afraid your father would abduct you and I'd never see you again."

She had paled visibly, so much that the light cream of her dress looked nearly tan against her skin. Jon loved this narrow cut on her, loved how it followed the shape of her body like a sheath of silk. It was graceful and elegant, and it made him proud of her beauty.

"You have to come." Her fingers clasped his tightly.

"Baby…" Jon began, but stopped when he saw her expression. There was no way he could go with her, and she knew it. Half an hour before the show, and the arena would be packed with people, the audience waiting for the concert to begin. He couldn't show his face. "Well, bring them in. I'll meet you in hospitality."

This was just what he needed after their murderous discussion, another problem. "And if you don't want to face them out there at the entrance with Art and Sal, stay here with me and we'll meet them together." He did not add that he thought it was a masterful provocation, and actually very well timed.

"I'll go with you," Sal said, and she looked up at him. "Come on, Naomi, they are your parents. Jon, you get ready. It's time to welcome the mayor. Art will do the press meeting with you. I'll take care of this."

It was so unusual for Sal to give orders to Jon that everything stopped for a moment. Everyone's attention turned to Jon, waiting for his reaction.

"Yes." Jon's verdict came slowly, thoughtfully. "Yes, that's how we will handle this. Sal, you and LaGasse, not one yard away from Naomi."

Sal snorted and stepped from the door to make room for her.

HE FOLLOWED HER along the hallway toward the arena. She seemed so small, so fragile, her shoulders narrow like a child's, her neck a slender stem, too frail to carry the heavy coil of hair. Sal wondered how her injury looked now, nearly half a year later, how much it disfigured her, or hurt. In the dress she was wearing she looked like a model, a rather short one but still a model, she was that thin.

"Do I look okay?"

Her question made him stop walking. "Yes. Yes. You look beautiful, stunning." He could have slapped himself, seeing her blush and bite her lip.

"I mean," he added, "you look the way you're supposed to look, as Jon Stone's wife." For good measure, he threw in a shrug. "It's part of the job. I remember you saying much the same thing before the Grammys."

She gazed at him from those big, dark eyes that always reminded him of shadowy forest ponds, her mouth that soft, curved invitation he adored, her hands folded, waiting.

"You said you would take care to look your best, if only for his sake." Again Sal shrugged. "And you did. You do." Tentatively, he reached out to touch her arm. "They are your parents, Naomi. They love you. No matter what you did, no matter how much you disappoint them, they still love you. They are here, aren't they?"

"I know."

He could feel the shiver that ran through her.

"But my father, he hates Jon, he hates what Jon is; and Jon, he can get so furious and…" Her voice sounded quite unsteady.

"Yeah." He did not need to look at his watch to know time was running. Over the years Sal had developed a very fine instinct for the flow of the last minutes before the show. Right now, in this very moment, Jon would be entering the dressing room of the band for a last word with them, a short pep talk, maybe a joke or two, and then everyone but him would take their places on the stage.

"We have to hurry," Naomi said into his thoughts. "It's almost time, and I want to be there for Jon."

A few more steps and they had reached the curtain that led out into the open.

Jon didn't want the audience to see even a little bit of what went on backstage, not even the band's or his approach, ever since they had started out, saying that it was no one's business how they hitched up their pants at the last moment or fiddled with their in-ear monitors. He wanted the glamour to be perfect. For the open air venues where there were no doors they brought along stage curtains to insure that privacy.

A burly security man held the heavy cloth to open a path for them.

Stepping out into the warm night air, Sal breathed in the scent of pine trees and freshly trodden grass. He loved this. He loved these moments best before a show; they were the culmination of everything he worked for, these seconds of excitement, of joy, when the air vibrated with the expectation of Jon's music. So far, the stage looked serene, empty, waiting for the band. He noted that everything was in place: the guitars polished and in the right order, the little dish with the picks next to them, a towel, a glass of water. The microphone stand at just the right angle, just the right height; the lighting dimmed a dark blue, very male, very cool. They were good to go.

At the point where the public area began, just in front of the stage where the security stood in a loose line, her parents were waiting.

Sal fell a step behind, surprised. These were not the same people he had last seen in that hospital hallway where Jon had faced down Naomi's father after that harsh, bitter fight, but an elderly couple, their faces anxious, their eyes searching for their daughter. They seemed lost against the huge backdrop of the arena, the thousands of people waiting for Jon.

Naomi, her shoulders straight and stiff, walked right up to them, the guards making way for her like a forest parting for a ray of sunlight, one of them even smiling at her with a friendly nod. She was not, Sal noted, wearing her backstage pass and yet they deferred to her, knowing who she was. He felt an insane and totally improper pride seeing her like that, and hastened to shake it off and rush to her side.

"Come with me," she said to her parents instead of a greeting, "I need to hurry." And turned away again, back to where Jon was.

JON SAW THEM approaching from where he stood. He had told Sean to wait for his signal, not to begin before he told him to and to hell with starting on time.

"Darling," he greeted her, ignoring her parents. She looked so formidable, cool and collected, not scared at all anymore, and he felt his love for her like a hot flush running from his heart to his limbs. The urge to open his arms and fold her into them was huge, but he stopped, deploring the stage makeup and the cables tucked into his shirt.

Naomi ignored all that and embraced him to plant a careful kiss on his lips. "Take care," she whispered so only he could hear. "I'll watch you. No making out with strange women. No smooching at the edge of the stage unless it's with me."

Surprised, delighted, he hugged her. "Then come to the stage. I dare you, come to the stage, and I swear I'll kiss you, with everyone watching. That'll show them."

She laughed and stepped back. "Maybe. Maybe I'll do just that. Maybe I'll make you kneel and bend down to kiss me, and play the groupie for you. Do you want me to throw my panties too?"

Startled, Jon laughed. He noticed how her father's mouth tightened and how he lowered his head, and replied, "Nah, you can keep them on until later, until we're back in the dressing room and alone. Now let me run and make the girls faint, babe. Be right back." Again he wanted to embrace her, feel her close for a moment, but instead he took his microphone from Ralph and let him put the monitors in his ears. The band walked past, each one of them briefly touching Jon's sleeve, Sean clasping his shoulder for a second and Jon patting his hand.

"Two minutes," Sal said, and left to take his place by the mixing tables next to Art.

At last Jon turned to her parents. "Good evening. I hope you enjoy the concert. We have some seats for guests, if you wish."

Olaf began to reply, but his wife quickly answered, "I'm here to see my daughter, Jon."

"Yes." Jon hated that he had to leave her with them, with her father and his blistering dislike, and most of all on this evening when he had meant to celebrate being here again, on the same stage where he had kissed her twenty years ago and lost his heart so completely. From out in the arena he could hear the applause rising like surf thundering toward the shore, and the first bars of the intro, played softly on Sean's keyboard before Jones joined in on the guitar and Aidan on the bass. His fingers tightened around the microphone, the metal a familiar weight in his hand, his mind wandering away to his music and the stage. He wanted to be there now, wanted to hurry up that narrow stairway and emerge into the blinding light of the beams centering on him, breathe in the soaring sound, be carried away by the cheering, feel the guitar hum from his play.

"She is well protected," he said to Olaf. "There are guards only for her safety. They will remove you if you so much as raise your voice to her. Naomi will not take any more crap from you. She's my wife, and I'll not allow it."

Again it was Lucia, her mother, who was faster. "We're not here to harm anyone, Jon. We are here because we want to make peace with you."

Jon snorted. "You might start by loving your daughter and respecting her decisions instead of drowning her in your disappointment." He reached out to Naomi. "Babe, come here. One more kiss, and I'm off. You know where I am if anything happens."

The last thing he saw before he walked into the darkness of the stairs was Naomi standing in the spot where he had left her a second ago looking after him, her mouth still soft from his kiss, her parents a few steps behind her, wedged between LaGasse and Alan.

Jon liked what he saw.

chapter 16

SHE WANTED TO be out by the stage with Art and Sal, be with the music and Jon, but politely, with a wave of her hand, Naomi offered, "If you would follow me, we can go to hospitality and talk there."

LaGasse shifted, ready to move in that direction.

Smiling, Lucia shook her head. "No, dear, let's go and watch the show. We can always talk later. I want to see your husband perform."

Judging, always judging. Naomi, leading them toward the arena, wondered why it had to be like this, why they couldn't accept her for what she was, why she could never manage to please them.

"It's pretty loud," her father said.

A sudden, sharp spike of fury stabbed her lungs. His first words, the first words he had spoken to her since she had nearly died that day in the hospital, and it was criticism.

"There are twenty thousand people here, Father," Naomi replied, "They paid a lot of money to see Jon. They deserve to hear him too."

Sal jumped from his chair by the computers when he saw her, ready to assist, but she shook her head. The security line opened for them, and LaGasse escorted them to the empty seats in the first row, always kept empty for surprise VIP guests who decided to show up at the last moment, a gallant and generous habit of Jon's, and a constant cause for discussion with Sal and Russ. Pauline and Walter were there, waving when they saw her, rising to greet her parents.

Right behind her, just a few feet away, the first chords hummed from the ebony guitar, calling to her, demanding Naomi's attention, drawing her into the music. She looked around to see Jon at the edge of the stage, his dark red shirt gleaming in the beam of the spotlight. He cast a glance down and smiled to see her and then launched into the first song, a lively, upbeat number to wake up the audience and get them in the mood.

She knew the routine, had heard him preach it often enough to a bored band: you got them with the first two bars or the night was lost. Sean had told her once that it wasn't true, at least not entirely, and Sal always walked out when Jon began talking about how he wanted the shows to go; but she knew. He wanted it perfect. He wanted to connect with his fans the moment he started to sing, not at the end of the concert when he was ready to go home.

"Nice to see you," Walter shouted over the noise of the music. "I thought you'd moved away."

"We came back to see the concert and Naomi. A holiday," Olaf replied, neatly crossing his leg, and straightening the crease of his trousers, "after the stress of moving."

Lucia touched her hand; and when Naomi did not pull away, she held it between hers, softly stroking her fingers like one would do with a baby to calm it. Her touch was warm, comforting, and it took Naomi back to her childhood when her mother sat at the corner of her bed. They would chat for a while, Lucia listening while Naomi told her mother how she would one day be a famous writer, or a singer and composer, how she would travel the world on concert or book tours. Lucia had smiled and nodded, patting her hand just as she did now but never replied. Even then, even when she had been so young, the huge beast of her inheritance had lurked in the shadowy corners of her room, ready to pounce and destroy her dreams.

The questions were burning in her throat, together with anger and a good measure of fear, fueled by the resentment of their intrusion into this moment, this special evening, when she and Jon had wanted to recapture the romance and excitement of their first encounter.

"Why are you here?" It burst out before she could stop herself.

Lucia smiled. "We knew you would expect us to be here, so we came. I did not want to disappoint you."

Naomi bit her lips.

"You never told me you moved. You might have let me know you were moving to New York."

Olaf turned away from Walter. "We wanted to be close to you and Joshua. He can't keep us from living in New York; it's a big city."

Jon had taken the microphone to welcome the audience and introduce the band. "Twenty years ago," Jon was saying, his voice booming through the stadium, "here in your lovely city, I met a girl and fell in love. I'm still in love with her today, so I have a lot to thank you for. Thank you for giving me your beautiful rose, my wife."

Naomi blushed.

"And he can't keep you from meeting us for lunch or coming to visit us if you want," Olaf went on, undeterred. "He's not your jailor, is he?"

"He's my husband." All she needed was to take one step, just get up from her seat, and someone would be by her side, help her escape.

"Yes, we know." A bitter smile crossed Olaf's face. "It's hard to get anywhere near you. He keeps you locked away like a Picasso original behind those Malibu walls."

There were so many things Naomi wanted to say, wanted to fling at him. "I wasn't even in Malibu all the time," she replied instead. "I went on vacation on my own while Jon was practicing for the tour."

"You could have called us." Lucia pressed her hand. "We would have come to you."

Softly, slowly, Sean moved into the *Secret Garden*, the first song she had written for Jon, the reason why he had met her twenty years ago here, in Geneva.

Naomi pushed her parents out of her mind and looked up at the stage, at Jon, who was sipping some water while settling the koa guitar against his body. He gave Sean a short nod and returned to the mike. Applause rippled through the audience as they recognized the melody and hummed along in anticipation.

"This is a nice song." It came out grudgingly, unwilling; and as if to counter his words, Olaf straightened his tie. "I've heard it a number of times on the radio, and it is really very good."

Naomi rose from her seat, which brought LaGasse over. She smiled grimly at him. "This song, Father, this song that you think is very good, I wrote it. I wrote it for Jon."

Sal was on his way to her, but she waved and he stopped to wait for her.

"Don't ask," she said, and sat down on his chair. Art, busy with the computers, gave her a short grin and offered his coffee cup.

Here, right beside the stage, right under the speakers, it was too loud to talk comfortably, so she leaned back to watch Jon and let the music drown her, wash away the black mood and the bitter feelings. She could see her parents, her father, relaxed now, his legs crossed and his long, elegant hands resting on them while he chatted with Walter, and her mother, her lips drawn in a thin line, staring up at Jon.

Jon briefly came over to check on her, and when he saw her surrounded by friends and security blew her a kiss and smiled.

The night was spectacular. There was still enough of the full moon to highlight the mountains, a gentle breeze brought down fresh air from the snowy slopes filled with the scent of pine trees and herbs.

Jon was singing. His voice filled the arena, soared all the way up to the stars sparkling in the sky, enveloping her like a warm shawl, throwing her back in time to that summer day so long ago when she had been in the exact same spot, listening to him, falling in love. Nothing had changed. It was still the same, a heady, hot longing, the desire for his kiss, for his embrace.

"I have," Jon said, "a new song. My wife, who is also my lyricist, came up with these words last summer when we returned to LA from Europe. She has this habit of collecting stones on the beach." He pulled up the stool and sat down. "She puts them in a special corner of our garden, and for the longest time I thought it was a cute but pretty silly habit; but then she wrote this song." The guitar hummed when his fingers touched the strings. "And I knew it had never been about the pebbles. It had always been about love, and about bringing it back home."

Her breath caught. She had not known. He had kept it a secret, to share with her on this special evening.

> *"I'll pick you up; don't be afraid anymore*
> *You have been tossed around and lost your way*
> *A beautiful pebble on a lonely shore…"*

JON SANG THE words thoughtfully, gently, as if he was tasting them on his lips, testing their impact. The band rested, it was only his voice and his guitar, the song a clear, fragile ribbon of melody that wove through the night. Very cleverly they had dimmed the lights until only one bluish-green beam rested on him, serene and cool like an ocean wave, soothing.

Naomi could see her parents, her mother talking to Pauline, and her father, his eyes wandering around, observing the security, assessing the speakers and the stage, the number of people in the audience. Rage blossomed in her chest; it unfolded like a huge, white flower that poured out its poison in a sticky, glistening stream. For an instant she was nearly blinded by it, blinded by the glare of the white petals and their razor-sharp, silvery edges.

She turned her back on her parents, on the hurt and the wrath, and let the music wash her away.

"NAOMI."

The moment he came off the stage, the instant the concert was finally over, he asked for her. Ralph was there to hand him a dry towel, wrap a dressing gown around his shoulders, and hand him a bottle of water; but Jon's eyes traveled over all of them to where she was, a little to the side, to give them space, waiting. His vision seemed to shift when he saw her, mixing the real image and the memory of her, of the girl she had been.

"Baby, did you like it?" he called, his voice cracking, exhausted from the singing. "Did you like the new song?" and grinned when her face softened into a smile.

He wanted to hold her in his arms, but he was soaked, his face a sticky mess of sweat and makeup. The cables itched on his skin; the monitors irritated him.

From the end of the hallway he saw Sal and Art coming toward them, laughing, relaxed now that the concert was over and had gone well, and right behind them, her parents. His good mood wilted. Olaf was a study in politely hidden boredom. He glanced at his watch and then back toward the exit, took his wife's elbow and yawned, hiding it behind his hand.

"So did you enjoy the concert?" Jon asked. He wanted to go to the dressing room and get out of the stage clothes, have a long, hot shower and feel human again; but he realized it would have to wait.

Naomi took a step toward him, close enough to bring her to his side and clasp his hand.

"Enjoy is not the right word," Olaf replied. "But yes, it was quite impressive. You do draw a crowd, I have to say. I bet your revenues are quite satisfactory."

A crease appeared between Lucia's eyes. "That was a beautiful song, Jon." Her tone was friendly, conciliatory, and she freed herself from Olaf's grasp. "I liked what you said about the stones and the love."

"Yeah. Thanks." He was beginning to feel cold.

"That's all," Naomi said. "You come all the way from New York or wherever, and all you can say is it was nice.." She was shaking. "You come here and say you want to make peace, and that's all you have to offer?"

"Baby…" Jon laid his arm around her shoulder, but she did not react.

"My whole life," she went on, "I've never been able to do anything to please you. Nothing I did was good enough, was it? I'm not really your daughter at all; I'm something you produced to keep your precious company going. I bet you cried, Father, when you found out I was a girl."

Jon realized they were standing in the middle of the hallway, the technicians streaming around them on the way to the arena to take down the stage; Sal, Art, everyone else, listening to Naomi's bitter words. It was Sal though who reacted even faster. Without much ado he took Naomi's arm and pulled her with him, saying, "Not here. Let Jon get out of his sweaty clothes; and if you need to have it out with your old man, go into the press room, please, where no one will hear. Please, darling."

Impatiently, she shook him off when they had reached the dressing room. "I'm not going anywhere, Sal. My place is right here, with my husband. He worked his ass off tonight to please his audience, and me, and I'm going to take care of him now and not waste my time arguing with my father."

"I beg you, Naomi." Olaf sighed. "This is so useless. We came all the way from the US to see you, knowing we would maybe get a chance to see you here, where he could not keep us away; and you start another of these stupid discussions. Yes, I'm sorry you don't want to take over the business. Yes, I'm not pleased…" He broke off when Jon moved toward him.

"Careful," Jon said softly, "careful with what you're going to say next. Don't overstep your boundaries. You might scare your daughter and intimidate your wife, but not me. Naomi went to see you yesterday; she went to your house, wanting to see you. We didn't know you had moved away." Impatiently, he tore the monitor cable from his shirt collar, ignoring Sal's yelp of protest. "I'm not going to explain to you again how amazing Naomi is as a songwriter and what a waste it would be if she did anything else, but that's not the point. The point is that you're unable to love your only daughter the way she is, the way every child should be loved by their parents, without condition. She's right, you know. You didn't want a daughter; you wanted someone to inherit your bloody damned hotel empire. Well, she ain't it. She's a writer, an artist. Find someone else to run your hotels." He took a deep breath.

"This is impossible. I'm exhausted, and I need a shower and something to eat. I'm not going to leave Naomi out here with you on her own for a moment. She's taken all the crap she has to from you." On the point of walking into his dressing room, he turned around. "I have not forgotten, Olaf, what you did in that hospital, how you twisted the truth to convince Naomi to leave me and nearly killed her with the sorrow. You laid the blame of those deaths at the Oscars on her, just to get her to go back to Canada with you. I wonder what else you would have done?"

"This is totally insane." Olaf, his face flushed, stepped back from Jon's glare. "I never wanted to harm her, for God's sake. I truly believed she would be safer, better off at home in Toronto! The fact that she is your wife is what put her in danger in the first place!"

"Yes." The same old guilt, the same old sadness. "Yes, it was my fault. So maybe you should have tried to kill me instead of her." Exhaustion threatened to overwhelm Jon. The joy had gone out of the evening, his expectations of a romantic night drowned in bitter memories.

"No." They all turned toward Naomi, who was still standing beside Sal, pale now, her mouth a tired line. "No. Not you, Jon, not your fault. Not yours, not mine." A ragged sob escaped her. "So this is what you call making peace, Father? Coming here, telling me all over again how bad my choices are, how useless my life is? Why did you and Mom really move to New York? Did you really move there?"

"Because Joshua is there, Naomi," Olaf answered for Lucia, "and he is our only grandchild. I know you're raising him to be like…" He waved in Jon's direction. "Like his father. A musician. But that boy is as bright as gold, and he has more in him that writing little songs; and someone has to show him there's more to life than this."

Sal grabbed Naomi's arms when she was about to lunge at her father, shouting, "You're not going anywhere near Joshua! You're not even going to see him! If I have to I'll hide him from you, have him escorted by guards all the time; but you will not lure him into your infernal business!"

Olaf nodded slowly, unimpressed. "And what, my dear, if he wants to? It's his birthright; you can't take it away from him. What if he tells you he wants his part of it, wants to go to business school and join the family company?"

Jon moved toward her and took her into his arms. She was shaking badly now, swaying on her feet, her breath short and painful.

"Then," he said, "it will be Joshua's choice. We will not force anything on him. If he decides he wants to join you, then he can. But..." He grinned evilly at Olaf, "I doubt it. I doubt he wants to give up his music. You'll have to find someone else to run your hotels for you."

With that they entered the dressing room and slammed the door.

chapter 17

"I THINK," SAL said carefully, "you should go." He had never been this grateful for a closed door between himself and Jon. He gazed at Lucia, at her oval face and the thick, black hair, straight and just touching her shoulders. She was not as frail boned as her daughter but had a beauty all her own: earthier, less elfin. She was a lush, well-shaped woman. Sal wondered how old she had been when Naomi was born and what she had been doing when she met her Viking husband. There was some Italian heritage, he knew, but there had never been any talk about how she and Olaf had met, and where. For a crazy, disoriented moment he saw her serving bowls of pasta in a Neapolitan trattoria and Olaf walking by, seeing her in a low-cut peasant dress, and falling instantly in love. It was such an outlandish vision that he had to literally shake himself out of it.

"I'm not going anywhere." Lucia took a step toward the dressing room. "I've come all the way from New York to see Naomi, and I'll stay right here until she comes out and talks to me. This stupid fight has to end."

Surprised, Olaf stared at her.

"I've had it." Angrily she shrugged him off when he touched her shoulder, her black eyes flashing in a sudden show of temper. "You and your stupid hotels. I've borne this way too long. It's always the business, always the responsibility, the money. Olaf, what good will all that wealth do you if your daughter doesn't talk to you anymore?"

"She's not talking to me now." It came out in an obstinate mumble, and Sal had to hide a grin.

"She's not talking to you because you can't even give her a smile! You can't look at her without seeing your precious family empire floating away, and you can't accept that she has chosen a husband you don't like." Lucia raised her hand to knock on the door, but Sal rushed over to hold her back.

"Oh no." He was ready to break out in a sweat. "Don't. Never. Not after the show, and not when that door is closed. They'll be out soon enough, but don't intrude. Jon needs time to calm down and rest. Leave them alone."

Olaf snorted, his hands in his trouser pockets again, ready to turn away. "Rest. I bet he needs rest after more than two hours of shouting and bashing his guitar."

"Ha!" Sal couldn't help himself; he had to laugh out loud at that. "Hardly shouting. I admit he's a bit harsh on his guitars sometimes, and not the best player on the planet, but who cares. His singing is sublime, Olaf. He's one of the best around, and his songwriting is stellar. Jon's not who he is for nothing!"

Shrugging, he added, "Well, their songwriting. The two of them together, writing songs that are beyond words. You heard that one about the stones and the surf? Hell, I can hear the money rolling into our accounts right now."

Art, who had until now watched the scene in silence, cleared his throat. "This is interesting. Olaf, if that was Placido Domingo behind that door and your daughter with him, how would you feel about that?"

They never, ever did this. Normally, at this point after a show, they would be meeting in the hospitality area to eat something, drink a beer, and talk over the evening; but they would not stand around in a hallway debating their careers. The harsh sounds of the stage being dismantled sounded like a huge percussion set being played by a beginner, like a child trying the drumsticks on every piece of equipment.

There would be a party, either at the hotel or somewhere else, or they would meet in one of their rooms for a round of cards and some drinks.

But Jon would never allow fights or discussions until the next day, until they were rested and their minds clear.

"Well, that would be different, yes." Olaf pulled down the corners of his thin lips. "He's a real artist, a wonderful singer."

Art took a step closer, his blue eyes sparkling like marbles. "And Gershwin? Frank Sinatra? Bernstein? Cole Porter?"

Olaf waved him away with a disdainful sigh. "Oh, please. Those were great men, great musicians."

"Yeah," Art breathed, "and with the exception of Domingo, they are also all dead. Jon, he is what they were in their time. It's that easy, Olaf. You want to see only the man on the stage, the one with the mike in his hand, and the guitar and the flashy shirts; but you refuse to look deeper and see the creativity. This…"—he pointed back at the stage—"this is only a very small part, the moment of glory. If you judge Jon by this, then you are not as savvy as I thought. Who do you think writes all these songs? Your daughter and your son-in-law. They write songs that make the world cry with joy and yearning; they break hearts and make people fall in love. Every time they put something on paper you can rely on them earning a new fortune, and it's that way because they think and feel as one person in this." He drew a deep breath and rubbed his hand across his forehead. "Makes me want to go all lyrical and sentimental. But then I'm Irish, and we get sentimental easily."

"Well, I don't know." Olaf looked at the closed door again, his brow drawn in doubt. "Is this really how you see him?"

"Hell, yes." The red curls on Art's head seemed like extensions of his mirth. "But not only us, the world does! We are lucky to be able to work for him, be along on the ride! Jon may seem like the glittering beast of show biz to you; but he's the Master, the one who pulls the music from the spheres and shapes it into song, Olaf."

Sal stared at him, but Art shrugged. "What? I'm Irish; we tend to get lyrical. Or sentimental. Whatever fits."

From inside, they could hear Jon's voice raised in laughter, and Naomi's, responding sounding like a silver tinkle.

"Maybe we should move." Sal had no idea where to take them, if they would even agree to leave; but he was certain it would not be a good idea to still be here when Jon came out. "Why don't we go and find some coffee or something. Which hotel are you staying at?"

"The same as you, obviously," Olaf replied.

JON REMEMBERED HOW he had stood in this shower those twenty years ago, the water running over his shoulders and down his back, the shower curtain sticking to the tiles, his eyes closed; and he remembered thinking of the girl waiting for him somewhere with Sean and Sal. He had been almost angry at her for letting him stew, for not coming into the dressing room with him and letting him have her when there was nothing that he wanted more. But she had waved to him merrily and walked away, and he had stared after her like the last idiot in the world, speechless, stunned.

She was sitting on the couch when he stepped out, his hair dripping, a towel wrapped around his hips.

"Now that I know better," Naomi said, "I can see that you're wearing makeup even in these photos. I'm not sure I like it."

Jon shrugged. Ralph had laid out fresh clothes for him, comfortable jeans and a soft shirt, nothing fancy. He loved this moment when he returned to being himself, no cables, no powder on his face, no false smiles for the press.

There were no ghosts of loneliness waiting in the shadows of the corners either. Naomi was here.

"Babe."

She did not look up but leafed through the tour book she had picked up from a box beside her.

"Baby, listen to me." He dropped the towel, but not even that made her glance up. "Naomi, we need to talk. We have to decide how to handle this."

Furiously, she flung the book away, which made Jon raise his eyebrows and mumble, "Careful. Those things are expensive."

"They came here to tell us they want to take Joshua away, Jon. There was never any thought of making peace with me, or accepting you. It's always and again about the stupid business." Her hand trembled as she wiped away her tears. "And I thought…really, I thought I'd come back here and see them, and everything would be different. I'm so stupid. I really wanted to see them, and tell them I'm sorry."

His stomach was growling. There had not been a chance to eat anything before the concert, not even the banana he normally had. "Tell them you're sorry? For what?"

Her fingers knotted around the hem of her dress. "Well, for shutting them out, for not calling, for not letting them know I'm okay."

"Yeah." The idea was disgusting enough. Jon envisioned her picking up the phone in their Malibu home and calling her father, letting him intrude into their lives, allowing him to make her miserable all over again.

"Would they have cared? Would your father have cared?" Something new occurred to him. "Why does your mother tolerate all his shit, I want to know? She's not stupid, and I know she has something like an opinion; there are moments when it shines through."

Surprised, Naomi blinked at him. "Yes. Yes, she does have her own opinion. But she loves my father. I think she loves him a whole lot."

Jon felt laughter bubble up in his chest despite the dire prospect of having to see Olaf again in a few moments, and he decided to change the subject. "Tonight is not at all what I thought it would be. I thought we would have a romantic dinner, and then I'd take you to bed, make love to you like I dreamed of doing back then. Instead we have your parents to deal with." He sighed. "Oh well, can't be helped. What do you think; are they still out there somewhere?"

Naomi rose from the couch and straightened her dress. "I don't know, and I don't care. Jon…" Her tone made him turn and look at her. "Jon, they want to take Joshua from us. My father, now that he realizes he can't have me, he wants Joshua; and I can't let that happen! I can't let him snare Joshua away from what he's really supposed to do! I can't allow that to happen."

Carefully, slowly, Jon buttoned his cuffs.

"Joshua was born to be a musician like you, Jon. Not to run a hotel business. That can't happen, not ever. It's the worst nightmare I can think of!" She stood before him, her hands in a tight knot, and gave him such a sad, imploring look that he hesitated for a moment before speaking; but then Jon replied, "Joshua will have to decide for himself what he wants for his life, my love." He said it as gently as he could. "It's his choice. We can ease his path and pay for his education. We can show him the possibilities he has and encourage him, but in the end it's up to him."

Relieved, she nodded, a tentative smile playing on her lips.

"But, Naomi, if he decides to go into your family business and work for your father, then that's his choice too. And it's his right. What your father says is true, darling. You may refuse it, but it's Joshua's heritage. It's his birthright." He shrugged. "It would break my heart to see him give up music, but if he wanted to go to business school instead, well…"

"I don't want to hear this!" Her shoulders came up in that gesture of denial he knew so well by now.

"Yeah, I know you don't. Come here." It felt good to hold her in his arms, even though she was still bristling, unwilling to soften into the embrace. "It's like this, Naomi. If we keep Joshua away from your parents, if we don't let him make his own choices, we'll be no better than your father. We'll put the same pressure on our son that he put on you. He hates that you picked me and music. We would hate for Joshua to go into the hotel business, but don't you think we love him enough to let him go and be happy with whatever he chooses? I know I do. I know

I can put my own dreams for him away to see him live his. Can you?"

She didn't reply for the longest time, just rested her brow against his chest. Jon mulled over his own words, thought about the cool sanity in them. It made his stomach churn. The idea of Joshua leaving Juilliard made him sick with dread. All the hopes he had harbored of some day working with his son, of composing wonderful songs with him, performing them, even touring together, seemed to wash away.

"But it's so not what I want for him. I want him with us, sharing our life." Her voice sounded muted, defeated.

"I know, baby. Just like your father wanted you to share his life." Lovingly, he ran his hand down her back to cup it around her hip. "I know. Only your father chose to use pressure to get you there, and you ran. We won't make the same mistake."

Tired, he was so tired, drained from hours on the stage. There was nothing he wanted more than a hot dinner and a nice, warm bed. In a way it was ironic; during all the years they had been apart he had lamented the loneliness after the concert, and now it was nearly too much excitement.

"I'm not worried about Joshua," Jon said. "He'll be fine. We'll see to it, and let him make his choices. It's you I'm worried about." Over her head, he looked around in the room. There was a stuffy smell to it, the vent in the shower did not work properly, and his stage clothes were lying around on the floor. The dressing table was a mess, littered with the tissues he had used to remove the mix of sweat and makeup from him face. Wryly, Jon wondered how many of his fans would really care to see the realities of his life, the unglamorous backstage hours, the exhaustion.

"Me?" Her fingers were in his hair, stroking down the back of his neck, her face upraised to look at him, her eyes dark and troubled.

"Yes, you, because you permit your father to hurt you, because you carry around those old hurts like a ball. I want you to let go. Drop it. Give it a kick and tell it to go to hell. He can't harm you anymore, love. He can't harm you because you owe him nothing. He can't do a thing, Naomi, and if you're smarting it's only because you allow it. Just let it go." He kissed her, prying her lips open with his tongue, gently forcing her to yield until she relented, at last melting into the embrace. "There, much better," Jon breathed.

As if someone had pulled back a curtain, as if a sound or a scent had triggered the memory, he saw that hotel room before him and the young girl she had been then in his bed, the sheet pulled up to hide her body. The middle of the night it had been, and he had gone to get some champagne from the fridge. Returning, he had looked at her, at the sweet curve of her mouth, the curtain of black hair falling over her pale shoulder, and he had nearly dropped the bottle. His heart had been ready to burst with love that first night, and it still was.

"Babe, let's just go to the hotel, shall we?" The skin of her throat was warm and soft; a hint of her rose perfume still clung to it. "Let's go to our room and hide. Let me take you to bed and love you, and we'll just forget your parents."

"Yes." No more than a breath on his cheek. "Yes, yes, Jon. We'll worry about them tomorrow."

He laughed at her words. "You said it, Miss Scarlett."

Chapter 18

A GROUP OF fans was waiting outside the hotel when they drove up. The driver cast a questioning glance at Jon through the rearview mirror, but Jon shrugged. "We'll get out. It's a quiet and disciplined crowd." He chuckled. "Hey, we're in Switzerland. They don't even know how to make an uproar."

Naomi threw him a disdainful glance. "You have no idea. If you hadn't stolen me away that day, I'd have been standing here that evening after the show."

On the point of getting out of the car, he turned back. "I stole you? I don't think there was a lot of stealing involved. You came quite willingly. You came to my bed willingly the next night. Didn't take lot of persuasion to get you there, you wild hussy."

"Jon." It was hardly more than a sigh, and he took her hand.

"Come on, then. A couple minutes giving autographs, and then I'm all yours." His mind on more exciting things, he led her up the stairs and toward the hotel lobby. Sal and Art were there to greet them, a number of guards to keep the fans in check, but it was an orderly, polite thing.

Sal handed him a pen, and he signed the tour books and CDs, chatted, even allowed a few photographs. Naomi had not, to his surprise, gone inside ahead of him but remained by his side, even smiled and talked when she was addressed, most of the time very close to him but once or twice talking to someone on her own. Sal hovered close behind her, and LaGasse watched every movement.

"No," he heard her say at one point, "I think I want to settle down after this tour. There is so much writing still to be done," and wondered if she had something special in mind, something he knew nothing about yet; and it made him want to wander over to her and ask right away. With that simple sentence, spoken to a stranger, another piece of the universe seemed to fall into place, putting the world back in the shape it was supposed to be.

Pen in hand, Jon stared out at the lake over the head of the woman in front of him, an elderly blonde; and for an instant he saw the vista of winter days in Brooklyn, in their new house, writing, composing, living their life. He even thought he could smell the snow despite the mild summer night.

Mindlessly he put his name on the cover of the book, right across his own face, his heart filled with the sudden hope that they could indeed find peace, put away the dark ghosts of the shooting, the sadness.

"Darling." She was right behind him, her hand sliding up his back. "Are you done yet? Can we go?"

"Yes. Yes." It was as if she had read his mind, as if she knew what he wanted more than anything right now, more than food, even more than a drink. He put his arm around her waist to feel her warmth, the curve of her body, the promise of love. "Let's go."

"I THOUGHT I should tell you," Art said diffidently as they entered the lobby, "your parents are waiting for you in the bar. It was either that or they would still be standing outside your dressing room, Jon. I couldn't very well have them arrested for stalking, could I?"

Naomi stopped walking, but Art shrugged. "It's your family, my dear. No matter how much you fight it, they're still your family. Blood is thicker than water and all that crap." He grinned. "In fact, I think there is hope. Your father does like music; he just doesn't understood yet that Jon's is just as good as Bernstein's or Mozart's, just…more modern."

"You're talking garbage, Art." Jon had the urge to throw something, preferably something big like the crystal vase with the thick gladiola bouquet in the lobby. "Why are they here, for crying out loud? Why did you bring them to our hotel?"

Again Art shrugged. "They're staying here too. What am I supposed to do: have the management throw them out? Put them in another hotel?"

There was a juicy curse forming on Jon's tongue, but he swallowed it and sighed. "All right then, the bar it is."

"Isn't anyone going to ask me what I want?" Her fists on her hips, Naomi glared at them. "I don't want to talk to them. I want to go to bed, and I want my husband to go with me. I want champagne and strawberries, and I sure don't want them with my parents."

Delighted, Jon laughed. Art was trying to hide a grin, but it wasn't easy. "Right on, honey," he replied, trying to be serious. "I know what you mean. But honestly, you can't just walk away. Also, I think this is a good moment. Your father seems…willing to talk. As far as he can be willing, that is."

Naomi threw her hands up.

"Come on, babe." Jon looked at his watch. "We'll give them ten minutes, and then it's you, me, and the champagne, all right?" He added when she hesitated, "You know it would just gnaw at you all night if you walked away now. Come on, I'll buy you a drink while we talk to them."

She was so lovely when she was angry. It put some color into her cheeks and gave her eyes a wild sparkle. Jon loved how a few locks had loosened from the tight chignon and floated around her face, little statements of freedom, tiny flaws in her perfect appearance.

"A double," she said, "make it a double Scotch. All right then," and stalked off ahead of them.

"Man, Jon." Art rubbed his now stubbly cheeks. "You really must have the guts of a lion. I wouldn't want to get into a fight with her, ever."

"It's not that bad." Smiling, Jon clapped his shoulder. "She's easy to appease. "

SHE SAT WITH her legs crossed, leaning back so her face was in the shadows, as if she had calculated the effect. Jon thought she looked very dramatic with only her mouth highlighted by the candle on the table, and it painted that dark, luscious red, a stark contrast to her light skin. It was interesting to see her with her mother again. Lucia looked like life itself in comparison, a generous, mature version of her fragile daughter; and it made him worry about Naomi's health. She was holding up, traveling well, never complaining; but Jon had a suspicion she was more exhausted than she let on.

Sal and Art were with them. They had picked a booth in a far corner of the nearly empty bar. There was no Scotch. Olaf had ordered champagne, and he served it to them himself, mixing a dollop of peach brandy into every glass.

"My wife," he said, without looking at any of them, "loves her bubbly this way. When she was younger, Naomi liked it too. Of course, her tastes may have changed now."

Naomi's lips tightened briefly, but she took the glass her father offered her with a nod of thanks.

"And I thought I'd better indulge my wife tonight," Olaf went on, "because she's really angry at me, and I can't live with that."

Surprise washed over Jon. The exhaustion that had threatened to drown him vanished, and he sat up straight.

Olaf's blue eyes flashed at him. "There's nothing worse than an incensed Carlsson female. You should know by now."

"Yes." Carefully, very cautiously, Jon looked at his father-in-law, but Olaf was busy handing Lucia her glass, and she was smiling at him.

For the life of him Jon could not understand how anyone would want to smile at Olaf. It seemed a bit like smiling at a wolf. Heat prickled between his shoulder blades, watching them. They were such an unlikely pair, Lucia as lush as a tropical garden, Olaf as stern and cool as an iceberg.

"Your man Arthur here," Olaf said into his wild thoughts, "says you are the new Leonard Bernstein."

"Uhm." Jon felt he needed a stronger drink, and badly. The situation was as unreal as a dream during an overnight flight.

"I love Cole Porter." Olaf took one of the cigars offered by the waiter and sniffed it before lighting it. "Perhaps my taste in music is old-fashioned."

Naomi didn't move.

"Jon did a recording of Cole Porter songs a few years back," Art replied, holding out his glass for a refill. "It was quite a success. For a while we thought about going on tour with a big band, but Jon didn't want to." He grinned at Jon. "Said it was too hot onstage for a tux."

Jon shrugged. "My wife makes me wear one often enough, I don't need to go to work in a tux too." He saw Olaf's eyes travel to Naomi, but she didn't react.

Lucia leaned forward, her hair falling over her shoulders in a thick, straight curtain. She was elegantly dressed in a caramel linen suit, a thin, cream silk blouse under it, with a beautiful triple string of pearls and some rings on her fingers that rivaled Naomi's. For a quirky moment Jon felt an insane satisfaction at having won Naomi as his wife, a woman as well-bred and sophisticated as she was, marrying him a mere Brooklyn boy. He took one of the cigars and let Sal light it for him.

"It is hard." Olaf had folded his hands on his knees as he slowly picked his words. "It is hard to see well-laid plans come to nothing. I was raised to take over the business, and it was a matter of course for me that my child would do it after me. The hotels have been in this family for centuries; and now, with Naomi, it ends." Sadly, he smiled at Lucia. "My beloved wife has put the dagger to my throat. She is forcing me to choose." His shoulders came up in a gesture Jon knew only too well, and he bit down on his cigar. "How can I not choose Lucia? How would I live without her?"

Jon was sure he could see Sal's jaw drop. A smirk appeared on Art's face, and he hurried to hide it behind a cigarette.

"I still believe Naomi was cut out for this task. She ran the hotel in Halmar superbly, with love and dedication; and I had the feeling she enjoyed it. She managed to hire excellent staff, had the house full almost all year long. We were very impressed, and very hopeful. But..." Again he shrugged. His hand crept out to Lucia, and she took it. "I don't understand your life, Jon. From where I stand it looks shallow, glitzy, the epitome of jet-set."

"Yes..." Only someone who didn't even try to look properly would see him like that, Jon realized. Most of his fans knew how much he liked to keep his private life hidden, how carefully he decided what the public knew about him.

Before he could reply, Naomi stirred. "Our life is dictated by what we do." Her voice sounded distant, disinterested.

Jon stared at her, fascinated by her cool attitude and the utter elegance of her posture. She looked like a model posing for lipstick, or maybe champagne, her face and her body half hidden in shade but her hands and legs well visible.

"What you see here, now, is only a small part of the work," Art added. He signaled for the waiter and ordered whiskey. "This is the marketing part, if you want. But it would not happen if there wasn't the creative part first."

"I love this part of your job." Lucia gave Jon a gentle, slow smile that made him feel quite warm; there was such an eerie echo of Naomi in it. "The concert was great fun; you and your band are well tuned to each other, and your sound is quite full, quite orchestral." A trace of irony sparkled in her eyes. "And you are quite...sexy onstage. In a classy way, of course." Her glance flitted over to Naomi. "The ladies were quite taken."

"I want to say this," Olaf interrupted. To soften his rudeness he brushed his hand over her cheek, which made Sal cough on his drink and quickly wipe his chin.

"I know I tend to be single-minded. Lucia has told me often enough. But I never wanted Naomi to be unhappy."

There was a second of silence, a moment when they all looked at him and no one had anything to say. Jon noted that the bar had emptied but for them, and the only waiter left was looking at his watch.

"You never thought I was able to decide for myself what would make me happy." Naomi put her glass down on the table. "You never cared to find out either. For you it was clear that I would go to business school, marry Seth or someone else you would pick for me, and dissolve into the oblivion of the family's business. Oh, I forgot—and produce heirs, of course, preferably male ones. What a disgrace; you, the owner, the capo of Carlsson hotels, and no son; and your only daughter has other plans." She rose. "All this talk of peace and love and flowers, Father, won't lull me into believing you mean a single word of what you're saying. You still want the same thing: me and, if possible, Joshua too." With a flick of her wrist she indicated her mother. "I'm surprised you are still married to each other. You could easily have divorced Mom, paid her off and found someone else to give you the children you needed. Too late, isn't it?"

"Sit down." Calmly, her tone soft and melodious, Lucia pointed at Naomi's chair. "You're just like your father. Both so stubborn, both so easy to flare up. I wonder why, when I'm the Italian and should have the hot temper."

Jon watched with interest how Naomi's mouth turned down obstinately, how she dropped back into her seat, no longer cool and collected but in a visible sulk.

"I want you to talk to each other, for crying out loud," Lucia said, just a little louder than necessary. "I've had enough of these icy silences and the animosity and... whatever." In a truly Italian gesture she shook her fingers at them, reticence and good manners gone. "I've so had it. Olaf, you stop being such a bastard right now. I want my daughter in my life, and my grandson, and any other possible grandchildren too. I want to get to know my son-in-law. And you!" She rounded on Naomi. "You stop treating your father like he's the devil incarnate, as if he wanted to lock you away in a convent or something. He meant well, both for you and for the business. He is right, you know; you do have a talent for it. You did run the Seaside very well. With you running the entire estate, we would all be much easier." She took a deep, calming breath and settled back into the black leather chair. "You have made it abundantly clear you don't want anything to do with your inheritance. You refused to touch your money; you even raised Joshua on your small income from the Seaside. For God's sake, Naomi, he could have gone to the best schools in the world instead of attending that village school in Halmar."

"He did." It came out a little sullenly. "I did send him to you to attend boarding school."

"Yes." Lucia pushed her hair behind her ear and took a deep drink from her glass. "Yes. So you did." A fine layer of thoughtful sadness settled over her words. "You sent him to us."

Jon recalled the day they had gone to Bergen, soon after he had found her, when she had told him Joshua was at Oxford, studying music, and how sad and lonely she had seemed talking about their son.

"I did whatever it took to educate Joshua and let him develop his talents." Naomi sat, her eyes lowered to her folded hands. "I wanted him to turn into the fine musician he could be."

"Just like us." Olaf said it so softly, so thoughtfully that they all looked at him. "Just like me. I wanted to give you the best education to turn you into the fine businesswoman I could see developing in you. You know you have the instincts and the talent for it. You know you do."

Naomi shrugged.

"You do," he insisted. "And I still think you would have been happy, eventually, running the estate. It's not a bad place to be in this world, owning and managing our hotels." Again his hand took hold of Lucia's, who held it between hers.

Slowly, sadly, Naomi raised her eyes to him. "But I never wanted to. I always wanted to be free, to write, to travel, by myself. And then…" A small flutter of her wrist in Jon's direction. "And when I heard Jon sing, I knew where I belonged. It felt as if he was telling me what I had to do. I don't want to be anywhere else." She sighed. "This is the most useless discussion ever. Nothing will change."

"Maybe." Jon cleared his throat before he went on. "Maybe this is the way of world, and you just feel it more than others because so much is at stake, Olaf." Enviously, he eyed Art's tumbler of whiskey. Olaf noticed and, with a lopsided grin, waved the waiter over.

"My parents were deeply disappointed when I quit college; they threw me out of the house," Jon went on. "I had to fend for myself, and those were hard times. Sean, my band leader, and I, we shared a small apartment in Manhattan; and often enough we went hungry. But I was just as stubborn as Naomi. It was the music or nothing for me. I have a feeling this is how it has to be. Joshua…" He took a glass of bourbon when it was offered. "Right now he's happy at Juilliard. No one knows what he'll want to do in a couple of years, and I'm bracing myself for surprises. But I can tell you this, Olaf: if he decides to drop the music and join you instead, we will not stop him. I've learned my lesson. You can't control your children. They are not made in our image. They have their own lives, and those may be very different from what we wanted. And I've also learned this, seeing you and Naomi: you accept it or you lose your children, and I'll be damned if I'm going to lose my son. That's not going to happen. I love Joshua more than my life, and I want him happy more than anything else. That's all that matters." He felt a stab of sadness at his own words, but there was a sweet taste of truth to them too. Exhaustion was finally creeping up on him, and he realized they hadn't eaten yet. It was well after midnight, and he had no idea if any restaurants would be open. With a sigh, Jon looked at his watch. It would have to be room service.

"We should move." Olaf signed the check and handed it back to the waiter. "I don't know about you, but I'm hungry. There's a fabulous little Italian restaurant in the old part of town. I think we should all go there."

Chapter 19

THEY HADN'T BOUGHT a penthouse, Lucia told them over the antipasti; that was a joke. In fact—she threw a sidelong glance at Naomi—they had moved into the private apartment at their New York hotel. It had a roof garden and a view of Central Park. It was very close to Lincoln Center, and they liked to go out for breakfast to a small café across the street, where they could look at the facade of the opera house and the fountain. They often went for a morning stroll down Broadway, sometimes all the way down to Times Square, once all the way to Chinatown where they had lunch and then took a cab back.

"I love living there," Lucia said; "it reminds me of home. Manhattan is as lively as Naples," which made Olaf laugh.

Jon still thought it was quite sinister to see him do that, see the stern, narrow, nordic face brighten up, his teeth blindingly white and quite large, his nose as long and sharp as an eagle's.

"We know you're Italian." Sal toasted her with his glass of red wine. "How did you get to meet your husband? A Canadian? May I ask?"

Lucia speared a tiny tomato with her fork and looked at it critically before popping it into her mouth. "I was visiting friends in Toronto over the summer. At the time, I dreamed of being a journalist and living in Canada. I had this obsession with the English language, and so my parents sent me there for a while. The family I was staying with took me to Kleinburg to see the McMichael Collection." She paused to pick one of the breadsticks from the breadbasket. "God, I fell in love with that place instantly. It was magical, wonderful. I walked down those halls built into the hillside, the silhouette of Toronto in the distance, forest all around me, and those paintings! I remember being spellbound by Lawren Harris and his icebergs and dark conifers, I wanted to travel North and see that landscape for real. They had to pry me out of the museum."

The heady aroma of garlic and fresh herbs wafted from the platters as the next course was served. Instantly Jon's stomach began to growl. He could hardly wait until the waiter ladled some of the golden pasta onto his plate.

"We went to lunch at a restaurant in Kleinburg, The Doctor's House and Livery. I recall the celery soup was excellent, and the apple pie; but I have no memory of the main course because just then this blond young man came in, in riding breeches mind you! My, was he dashing! I fell in love instantly."

"That's not how it was," Olaf interrupted. "She was as aloof as you can imagine, turning her back on me, ignoring me completely. And she, she was dazzling, like a star—the first thing I saw when I walked in, and the only thing I wanted to see. That long, black hair and those velvet eyes, incredible."

"So what did you do?" Art pushed away his plate to lean forward.

"Oh, I went over to her and asked her to go out with me." Olaf poked at the pasta on his plate. "And she agreed. We went for dinner downtown and then walked along the lakeshore, and we kissed. I took her home, and we met again the next day. Lucia had to go back to Italy a few weeks later, and I went with her. We got married, right there in their church. I wanted her in my life, and I didn't care about anything else. End of story."

Jon's hand, still holding the fork, sank onto the table. Hunger forgotten, he listened to Olaf and Lucia, the echo of his own life ringing in his ears. He looked at Naomi, who was sitting quietly between him and Sal, not eating, as distant as she could be without getting up and leaving, a cloud of stillness gathered around her like a cloak.

"But…" He did not know how to say it. "Then you know. Then you know how terrible falling in love can be. That's just what happened to me, with Naomi. When I saw her that day, in that hotel lobby, I knew my fate was sealed. It was final, like a door falling shut, like sudden silence where before there was turmoil and uncertainty."

"Yes. Yes." Olaf stared right back at him across the wine bottles and food between them. "You have a good way of putting it. Silence after the turmoil. Yes."

"It's my job to put feelings into words and music. That's what I'm good at; it's what made me rich." The meat melted in Jon's mouth, well doused in cream and cheese. For some quirky reason it made him think of his walk along the lake with Naomi all those years ago, right here in Geneva, and how they had talked about lunch and his disappointment at not being served chocolate for breakfast. "But I'm not nearly as good a writer as Naomi, not by a long shot . The melodies come easily, but I have to wrestle with the words. And she…" He smiled her way. "She just plucks them out of the air. It seems as if they are floating around her, and she just needs to put them together in the right order."

Music was playing in the background, a tenor singing an Italian song, one Jon had hummed a million times. He had never understood the words or wondered what they meant, and it had never occurred to him to ask Naomi. Once, only once had he heard her speak Italian, and then it had been in London, the day he had asked her to marry him.

"What's he singing about?" he asked now, but she did not answer.

"Pavarotti," Lucia said instead. "The way he sings you might have believed he was from Naples. But in fact he is from northern Italy." She smiled maliciously. "A butter eater. We in the south use olive oil. He's singing about an ungrateful heart, about his girl, Catharina, who does not listen to his pleas of love and even ignores him in church."

"She must have been from Naples too," Olaf threw in, and mopped his plate with a good-size chunk of bread. "Beautiful, cruel women who walk over men's hearts."

Naomi dropped her napkin on the table and rose, pushing her chair back rather forcefully. "I'm tired. I'll go to the hotel. Don't worry, I'll take a cab. You…"—she placed a brief, dry kiss on Jon's hair—"stay here and enjoy the canolli. You'll love them, I promise. Good night." She walked away before anyone could react.

SHE WAS ALREADY in bed when he got back to the hotel, the sheet drawn up over her head, but Jon was sure she was still awake.

It was dark in the room; the only light came from the streetlamps casting a bluish glow on the ceiling and the walls. He could smell the lake, so different from the ocean—sweet, brackish, almost tepid—and hear the little waves smack against the quay. Even at this hour there was traffic outside; life was going on in the warmth of the summer night. Jon wondered how it must have been for Naomi to actually live here, a young girl of eighteen.

"I know what's eating you," he said, unbuttoning his shirt, "and yeah, I agree. Come on, look at me."

There was no response so he went on. "This was the most unreal evening of my life. I never thought I'd sit down to dinner with your father again, let alone actually enjoy it. Did you know he could be this charming, this outgoing?"

The sheet flew back, and she sat up. Jon's breath caught at seeing her like that, her hair in a wild tumble and her nightgown straps slipping from her shoulders. The words he had meant to say, every thought of Olaf, drifted from his mind. "You're so beautiful. You look just like you did that night when we first were here, when you became mine."

"Don't change the subject, you miserable man!" Furiously, Naomi slapped the sheet. "You sat there and chatted as if he was your oldest friend, as if nothing ever happened! I felt as stupid as a schoolgirl!"

Jon dropped the shirt on a chair, grinning. "You looked the part too. There was steam coming out of your ears!"

She looked ready to throw something at him, so he raised his hand in capitulation and sat down next to her on the edge of the bed. "God, if there was ever a night I wanted to go differently, it was this one. But here we are, discussing your father. Again, again, when we should be making love, when you should be in my arms, sighing, sobbing with longing, yielding to me, mine."

Her lips parted in a soft invitation. Jon reached out to touch them, tracing the fine curve with the tips of his fingers. "Since I woke up this morning I have thought of nothing but tonight, of reliving that night when I first loved you, right here in this room. My miracle, my love."

Gently, with a small smile, Naomi laid her hand over his mouth. "We have to talk about this first, Jon. I'm spooked, both by my father and by you, sitting over the manicotti as if you were Mafia dons, chatting like old friends. You had a restraining order placed against him only a few months ago, and now this?"

Jon took her hand in his and kissed the palm. "If it was me, I'd never face the old bastard again, believe me, Naomi. There's no one in the whole world I care for less than your father. But baby…" That slipped strap was badly distracting. He wanted to slide his finger under it and pull it down, feel the warm, silken skin, lay his head on her chest and listen to her heartbeat. "You even wanted to go to their house, meet them; you told me they were your parents after all was said and done, and they only meant well. Okay, so they showed up when and where you never expected them. But honestly, I think Olaf really, really went out of his way to be nice tonight."

It took her a moment to respond, her voice sad and small. "Jon, he knows he won't get anywhere by fighting you and so he's trying to charm you. Nothing has changed. He will never change. All he cares about are his bloody hotels."

"Maybe." He caught her around the waist and picked her up, settling her on his lap, facing him. "Maybe, I don't care. The food was great, the restaurant was nice, and I'm quite taken with your mother. I wonder if you'll look like her in thirty years? I wouldn't mind that one bit."

"You didn't do this the last time we were here." Her arms came up around his neck.

"Because you were an innocent young thing; you had no idea what sex would be like." The long mane tangled around his hands like seaweed. "You had no idea what was in store for you, did you? Did you get from me what you'd expected that first night?"

"Oh yes." Whispered against his lips, her body a sweet curve against his. "Yes, you were everything I had dreamed of seeing those photos of you in the magazines. How I used to stare at them, at that centerfold; how I wished to take off your shirt and touch you."

"You were in love with my voice on the radio, with my picture in the magazines; you really fell in love with the rock star?" He cupped her buttocks to pull her closer. "You really are a groupie. Your father was right for once; you are my groupie. How I love it. All right then, let me love you, my sweet little fan."

IN THE LAST dark hour before dawn Naomi was woken by the sound of the street cleaner passing below their open balcony door. She rose quietly from the bed to step outside. It was quite cool now, the wind bringing chilly air from the mountains and mixing it with the spray from the big fountain out on the lake.

Naomi stood, her arms wrapped around herself, listening to the sounds of night. There was a café not too far away, one that served breakfast very early in the day, where they were even now setting out the chairs and opening the blinds. She thought she could smell coffee, fresh French bread, even cinnamon rolls.

The scent made her long for Halmar, for the still, peaceful life that passed in small, orderly steps, for the life that she had been able to control and direct.

There, nothing had touched her, no one had been close enough to hurt her, and she had always been able to retreat into the solitude of her apartment. She had never been exposed, never threatened.

There had been one man, only one she had ever allowed to get to know her a little. He had been a doctor from Bergen who had stayed at her hotel over a weekend to, as he had told her, rest. His unassuming, friendly manner had drawn her toward him. At first it had only been a cup of coffee, taken together outside the hotel door in the sunshine sitting on the low wall of the quay, then a dinner, then a visit to the theater in Bergen. She had broken off the budding affair after that, telling him she loved someone else, an American songwriter, and actually she was committed to him. The doctor had been bitter, accusing her of using her adoration for some rock star to break it off, telling her she was being childish and naive. He had abandoned her at the restaurant where they had been having dinner. She had caught the last ferry back to Halmar and stood out on the deck in the blustery wind, listening to the seagulls and the song of the ocean and imagined hearing Jon's voice in it, calling to her.

Naomi turned around to look at him where he lay sleeping, sprawled out as always, his arms flung across the bed. No curling up for Jon, no hiding under covers.

A wave of bitter sadness threatened to drown her. Her body was still humming from their lovemaking, her lips tingling from his kisses. She let her hand glide over her scar and come to rest on her lower belly, feeling for life, wishing for it with every fiber of her soul. A girl, a little baby girl with Jon's eyes, his love for music, his easy sense of humor. She could see them together: Jon at the piano with his daughter on his knee, teaching her a few first, simple melodies, teaching her to sing, while outside the snow fell on the Promenade. Naomi had no idea why, but she saw them in that parlor of the Brooklyn house, the big room with the bay windows looking out on the river where she placed the Steinway grand. That was the place she had picked for him. Just like in LA where she put his studio below her bedroom so she could listen to him when he chose to work late at night, listen to the soft, hesitant playing as a new song grew. His voice when he tried the lyrics. She would, she decided, buy a very comfortable, very cozy couch to put in the bedroom and put it right in front of the balcony door so she could sit there and look out at the skyline of Manhattan and the bridge. And again she envisioned snow, the peacefulness of a winter afternoon, the quiet of the white blanket muting the traffic, mellowing the contours of New York.

Carefully she crept back into bed. Jon didn't wake but turned and put his arms around her, muttering in his sleep, burying his face in her hair.

Naomi pulled up the covers and drifted off, the image of falling snow following her into her dreams.

chapter 20

IN A STRANGE way, Hamburg reminded her of New York. Naomi thought it was the weather. They had last been in Brooklyn for Christmas, and it had been gray and dark too. She recalled walking along the Promenade with Jon, a day after they had arrived from Halmar, to buy a Christmas tree for his mother's house. It had been so miserable that her love for the place had considerably weakened for a moment.

Getting off the plane and standing on the tarmac of the small airport, she glanced up at the gray sky. Fine, misty rain settled on her face like a thin veil and made her hair instantly spring into curls.

A line of limousines and vans was waiting for them right next to the hangar, all of them with tinted panes, all of them in discreet, sober black, their drivers in immaculate uniforms.

She hadn't been to Germany often. Her mother loved opera, and she loved Placido Domingo. They had come to Hamburg to see him a number of times, and her father had even debated acquiring a hotel here, stating that he kind of liked the town: it had the charm of an English place combined with the typical cleanliness and efficiency of Germany, and it was quite pretty. They had always stayed at a hotel overlooking the lake in the center of town. It had reminded her of Geneva, with the fountain and the panorama of the city surrounding the water; but there were no mountains in the distance, no landscape at all worth mentioning, only the big harbor with the huge overseas container ships. She remembered the narrow shopping streets fondly, similar to Bond Street in London or the old part of Geneva, but there were no outdoor restaurants and cafés; everything was turned inward, hiding from the cold.

It was July, and it still was cold and drizzly.

Shivering a little in her thin jacket, still used to the milder climate of Zürich and Munich, where they had stopped after Geneva, Naomi watched as the instruments were loaded carefully into the vans, Sal himself supervising the handling of Jon's guitars, while Jon and Art greeted the local promoter and a couple of people from the record company who had come out to welcome him and the band.

THEY HAD PARTED from her parents in the lobby of the Geneva hotel while the bus was waiting for them, Sal standing in the door, nervously glancing at his watch.

"So when will you return to New York?" Olaf had asked, turned more toward Jon than her. "When will we see you there?" Jon, in a pleasant, easy tone, had replied that it would be another couple of weeks or maybe more, he could not tell. It depended on what Naomi wanted. Perhaps her heart was set on visiting some other places in Europe? Smiling at her, he had slung his arm around her shoulders. "Naples, babe? I haven't been that far south in Italy yet. What do you think; would you like to go there? See your roots? We could take a vacation in the sun; I'd learn how to order my food in Italian from you. We could even hire a yacht to sail to Capri. We have some time before the US leg of the tour starts; we could take a vacation and get some rest."

To which Lucia—a fine smile on her lips—added, "Or visit your family in Positano. Your uncles and aunts would be delighted to see you."

Blushing, Naomi had mumbled that she'd been there, thank you, and yes, it was pretty, but no, not right now, and waved after her parents halfheartedly when they got into their cab. The thought of living in the same town with them seemed dire beyond all imagination.

Now, on the rainy Hamburg tarmac, Naomi thought that Naples would be just fine. It would be blistering hot, stinking of garbage, noisy, and filled with the exhaust fumes of Vespas; but it would also be full of flowers, sunshine, and good spirits. A wild, romantic longing for Ischia gripped her, for the narrow, winding roads around the island and the beach of Sant'Angelo, for a dinner of mussels in one of the little trattorias along the pier in Porto. She even thought she could hear a silly, Italian song playing somewhere in the back of her mind.

Or Positano, and how long since she had been there. The scent of gorse and bougainvillea crept into her memory, the soft sound of the Mediterranean breeze rustling in the wisteria canopy of the patio, the whisper of the surf.

"We used to pick figs from the tree on the patio," she said when Jon came over to her, "and eat them for breakfast. Then we climbed down those long, long stone steps to the beach and lazed away the day. There was a small restaurant right on the water, barely more than a deck and a kitchen; and two old women would cook whatever the fishermen brought home in their boats—shrimps, mussels, tiny fish—and toss them on a plate of pasta doused in olive oil, parsley, and garlic."

He waited, his hands in his pockets, the collar of his leather jacket turned up to keep the rain away, wind blowing his hair into his eyes.

"I was as brown as a nut. And in the evening my uncles grilled fish for us, and there would be salad and fresh bread and lots of red wine." Thoughtfully, she paused and tapped the tip of her shoe into the puddle that had formed at her feet. "It was really nice. We used to spend the summers there before I ran away with you."

"Where? In Naples?"

She shook her head. "In Positano, on the other side of the Sorrento peninsula. Most of my mother's family lives there. They only say they are from Naples because people overseas don't know Positano."

"Do you want to go?" Jon felt a crazy, wild impulse to see this place, to stand on that patio and look down at the gentle Mediterranean in the dusk of a warm summer night. He wondered if the stars looked different down there too, until he realized that Naples and DC were almost on the same latitude.

"We should go. I think we should go, Naomi. It would be lovely to see where your mother comes from." He drew her into his arms. "And you. I'd finally find out if there are more girls with your looks and temper. Is it pretty down there, in… Positano?"

"Pretty?" Naomi drew a deep breath and slowly let it out. "It's not pretty, Jon. It's stunning, beautiful. If you drive there from Naples you have to cross the mountains, the peninsula, and then, well below, you see the little town, the colorful houses clinging to the hillside, all the way down to the shore. There's only a small beach—the rest is steep cliffs and stone—and there are flowers everywhere, wonderful, wild flowers, and the scent mingles with the aroma of the sea; and at dusk you can watch the swallows flit along the rocks, hear their calls…" She sighed. "The water is so warm and soft, so gentle, dark blue, much darker than the Pacific, totally different from the North Atlantic. Everything is… kind, gentle, soft, just, lovely."

"You're homesick!" Surprised, Jon let go of her and took a step back so he could look at her. "You're homesick for that place! Why in the world is this another secret I have to pry out of you, and again after a confrontation with your parents? Why do you make life so hard for yourself, my love? Why do you deny yourself all this: your family, your home? What is wrong with all that, Naomi?" He raised his hands in a gesture of supplication. "You come with me to see my family, you even buy a house in Brooklyn so we can live close to my mother and sister and brother, and yet you refuse your own, even those in Italy?"

She pulled up her shoulders in that well-known gesture of denial but did not reply.

"So do you want to go?" Jon repeated. "Do you want to go to Naples and Positano?"

A sudden, painful yearning filled Naomi. "Yes," she said. "Yes, Jon, I want to go. I want to go very much, as soon as we have the time. Please, yes."

PARKER SAW THE cavalcade of limousines come up the road, but they turned into the small back street that led into the garage of the hotel and vanished.

Silently cursing, he crossed the pavement to get from the tree-lined sidewalk along the lake to the hotel entrance and walked inside past the liveried doormen.

No one stopped him from sitting in one of the couches and ordering coffee from the bar, but he could see there were security guards standing by the elevators and a couple of very stern men denying a small group of women access to the doors leading to the stairway.

Fans, they were the best indicator that someone had arrived who was not keen on publicity. He imagined he could hear commotion behind those thick walls, feel the hum of the elevators as they ran up and down with the luggage of the illustrious guests, and finally, with her, taking her into one of the suites on the locked-off floor where no one had access except the most trusted personnel, and even those were accompanied by security.

There was no way to get to her except to lie in wait here for hours and hours, hoping she would venture out on her own for a shopping or sightseeing trip and her husband would choose to stay in hiding.

The thought alone made Parker swallow bile. He had seen the press releases from the other cities, read the raving review of the Munich concert and seen the photos of Jon leaving the venue after the show, walking through a throng of fans with her by his side, one arm around him, laughing. She had looked so pretty in that rose silk dress, the same one she had worn for their interview, her braid falling over her shoulder. Seeing that picture, Parker had made one of his editors call the newspaper where it had been issued and ask for a copy. Once printed, he had hidden it away in his desk drawer, peering at it every ten minutes to stare at that smile, at the dark eyes gazing up at Jon, wishing with a gutwrenching fervor that it was meant for him.

In a moment of sanity, while navigating the hallways of Heathrow, Parker had realized he was about to fly to Hamburg, where he would lurk in hotel lobbies, on sidewalks, and in backstage entrances, all in the wild hope of catching her alone, of having her to himself.

Dazed and despite the early-morning hour, he had made his way to one of the bars and ordered a stiff drink. He was stalking Jonathan Stone's wife. He couldn't help himself. Drink downed, he had hastened to the gate when his flight was called. He could not help but wish that the plane would fly a little faster, cross the Channel with lighting speed and take him to Hamburg, take him closer to where Naomi was.

"WE COULD GO after the European leg of the tour." Jon said, tossing his jacket on the couch. We would have six weeks before the tour starts again in the US. Why not put that time to good use, lazing in Italy. I really like the idea!"

Carefully, just peeking, Naomi pushed the curtains aside and looked out of the window at the steady drizzle of rain. Right across the street was the lake with the fountain, more of a large pond compared to Lac Léman in Geneva; but there were cruise boats on it, going toward a bridge at the far end, crossing under it into a larger body of water. Just to the right, around the curve of the lake, she could see the facades of the old buildings, shops on the ground floor, the inviting side streets with the expensive flagship stores.

"I really wanted to use the time to get some work on the Brooklyn house done." She remembered walking down those streets with her mother one day and buying a purse. They had searched for a nice place to have lunch but had found only a steak house, which had made them return to the hotel, slightly disgruntled. Her father had laughed at them and taken them back across the street, up a flight of stairs in one of the massive buildings, and ordered one of the best oyster meals she'd ever had. There had even been champagne. Olaf had poured for her, stating how he enjoyed taking out his wife and daughter, he was so proud of them, the beautiful women in his life.

"I wanted him to love me because I'm his daughter, not because I'd be important to the business someday. Love me just for me." It came out of nowhere, a sudden, bitter outburst; and it made Jon stop and listen to her.

"All the while," Naomi said softly, "all the time he was scheming and plotting and thinking of me as a pawn." She turned around. "There were stories, Jon, in my head. Sometimes I felt like I had one foot in another world, listening to other people's lives. I wanted to write it all down so badly, but there was never the time nor space for it. I would go to a party or dinner with my parents, and in my head this scene was humming that wanted out so badly." Her hands fluttered nervously with the need to explain. "Like a bubble growing inside my chest, something that has to be poured out, brought to life. And I tried to stop it, tried to suffocate it; and it made me sad, silent, and angry." With a little shrug, embarrassed at her outbreak, she added, "And then, one day, there was you; and I knew where I had to take that need to write. When I heard you on the radio, everything made sense. Everything else became meaningless." The old pain tore her spirit. "I wanted him to be proud of me for what I am, not for what he wanted me to be."

Holding her breath, she waited for a response, but Jon just looked at her, waiting.

"You..." Her heart skipped, and she had to hold on to the table beside her. "I'm married to you! I don't have to spend a single moment of my day thinking about my father if I don't want to. I can sit down and write a novel, and no one will tell me it's a waste of time, worse, nonsense."

Jon shook his head. "To be yourself, Naomi, to do what you want, for that you don't have to be married to me." He grinned and moved toward her. "I like it way better like this, of course, but you doing what you want to do with your life has nothing to do with me. For crying out loud, babe, let's go out right now and buy you a new laptop, and you can sit down here in this hotel room and start writing that novel that's clearly waiting in your head! You're way beyond song lyrics, Naomi, and way beyond writing plays. You need to start your real work. Let's go!"

Stunned, she took a step back.

"Don't you see?" Jon didn't touch her, didn't even come close enough for it. "The only one holding you back is yourself. I've been telling you over and over. You don't have to keep yourself small and hidden, or live in my shadow!" He pointed in the general direction of the hotel telephone. "Go ahead, call Harry. Tell him you're ready to finally write that movie script he wants from you; make his day! Lock yourself in and write the great American novel!"

A small giggle escaped her at his dramatic gesture, and she hid it behind her hand.

"Stop laughing, you silly chick. I'm trying to make a point here," Jon said, but he smiled. "You can do whatever you want, and you can do it now. Like, let's go out for lunch and buy you a computer, and then let's think about going to Italy. It's time we started to seriously enjoy our lives. I've had it with the sorrow and the pain."

With a shaking finger Naomi pointed at the building where Olaf had taken them out for lunch. "Over there, we sat in that restaurant, and I remembered just now what a blast we had, my parents and I. That was such a carefree, easy day; and for once there was no pressure, no looming future. I was happy that day, Jon! I was happy with my family, and I loved being who I was. For that one day."

"Come here." Gently he pried her from her corner. "We'll go out now. We'll go out and enjoy the day, and I'll buy you the best laptop this town has to offer. Then tomorrow we'll do the show, and then we're off to Italy. What do you say?"

Her body was stiff in his embrace.

"What? What now?"

Uneasily, her face leaned against his chest, Naomi mumbled, "If we really want to go to Positano, I'll have to call my mother and have her arrange it. I haven't been there for ages, Jon. I don't even know if I'd recognize my relatives." Slowly, her brow wrinkled, she looked up at him. "I think if we decide to go, my parents will want to come. And, well, Joshua…he hasn't met his family there."

That made him let go of her in surprise. "Never? You've never taken Joshua to meet your mother's family? Why? Why, Naomi?"

"It just never happened." Again she shrugged. "We were in Halmar.

My life was small, hidden, quiet. I didn't travel. I did nothing but raise Joshua and work and write sad songs." Slowly, with a small sigh, she gave up. "I guess it's time, yes?"

Jon nodded.

chapter 21

"THEY LET PEOPLE come all the way to the back entrance," Sal said on the bus, uneasily glancing out at the highway on which they were traveling. "That's one thing I've never liked about Hamburg. They think security is a courtesy and not something vital. These Germans, they have no concept of danger."

"Maybe they just don't treat their celebrities the way we do." Sean leaned back in his seat and drew his baseball cap down over his eyes. "Maybe they still see them as people and not as public property or someone to be stalked."

Jon, sitting by himself a few rows behind them, snorted, but didn't comment. He had closed his eyes and folded his hands on his stomach, legs stretched into the aisle, snatching a few last moments of rest before they arrived and the routine of a show night took over.

"Europeans are easier about these things." Art turned around from where he was sitting right behind the driver. "But as long as it's this civilized, who cares."

Jon opened his eyes. "I do. I want safe in addition to civilized, especially now that Naomi is on the road with us." He exchanged a glance with Sal.

They had both seen the blond, tall man in the lobby when they had gone down to give a few autographs just before they had left for the sound check. He had kept his distance, mingling with some other reporters, chatting, exchanging business cards, commenting on their cameras; but his eyes had darted back to them. Naomi had not been there; she had chosen to stay behind and play with the laptop he had bought for her at the department store next door to the hotel. When he left, she had been sitting on the couch, legs drawn up, fingers gliding over the smooth, black surface of the thing, hesitant, as if she was afraid to open it, as if opening it meant altering the fabric of reality; and she had barely looked up when he said he would be right back.

NOW, ON THE bus, he wondered how it was for her, if owning this one piece of technology really made that much of a difference, if it felt to her like a new, custom-made guitar felt to him when he made it hum for the first time. His gaze wandered back toward Jones, who was seldom without his favorite instrument. Even on this short ride from downtown Hamburg to the venue he had it on his lap, his hand resting on the strings, singing softly under his breath. Jon thought he recognized the melody but he wasn't sure. The bus left the highway and entered a narrower road leading through a stretch of forest. They passed a huge garbage facility with a line of trucks waiting to dump their loads. The chimneys rose up into the sky above it, but there was hardly any smoke, and no smell at all. Everything was clean, neat, efficient. Right outside the fence a trailer had parked, its side windows open, with a woman selling sandwiches and sodas to the workers who had come out for a break. They too did not look as if they handled muck; their orange work suits were spotless.

"They don't do gritty in Germany," Sean remarked. "Isn't it amazing? I think these people clean their waste before they put it in the garbage."

For some reason this made Jon think of his promise to take Naomi to Newark someday, and it made him grin.

"Naomi wants to see New Jersey," he said.

Sean nodded. "Yes, I've been thinking of getting a house somewhere there. Maybe down by the shore. If it's not too much hassle to drive into town every day." Laughing, he slapped the armrest of his seat. "Look at us; we're going to be New York City commuters soon!"

"Yes." It seemed right. It felt right, this prospect of settling down and starting something new, going in a different direction. "But New Jersey, Sean? Really? I mean, everything I've seen of it is…" Jon sought for a word. "Dismal?"

They had stopped at a red light, ready to turn onto the street leading to the venue. There were police cars, ready to close off the road behind them and keep other traffic away. *What a strange place*, Jon thought, looking out, with the concert hall on one side of the narrow driveway and the football stadium on the other. It seemed displaced, so removed from any kind of neighborhood, planted in the middle of empty land. A plane crossed overhead, so low that he knew the airport must not be too far away, and he could see a highway overpass in the distance. But close by there was only industrial land and greenery.

"Are you sure we're in the right spot?" he asked when the bus pulled up at the back entrance of the ugly concrete building, "Looks more like a prison."

But he knew. He had seen the tour posters glued to the gray walls and the announcement on the billboard over the entrance. It made him wonder who would come all the way out here to see them.

There was a small group of fans waiting, maybe fifteen, nothing compared to the throngs he was used to; and they kept their distance, quietly obeying the guards' orders. There was no press. They waved his way when he got out, but no one even tried to approach.

"I'm going to say hello." Sean hitched up his jeans and sauntered over to the waiting group, where he was greeted with pleasure and surprise.

"And you?" Autograph cards in hand, Sal waited for Jon's answer.

"Yeah. What the hell." Jon took them and followed Sean. The cheers got considerably louder.

IT WAS HOT behind the venue. There was little shade, and the pavement smelled of gasoline and molten tar. From where she stood, cell phone in hand, she could see the row of container trucks parked neatly along the fence, fourteen of them now. One was still open, with some of the tour technicians climbing in and out.

Joshua told her, quite simply, that he had no interest in traveling to Italy in the heat of summer; and anyway, he had an invitation from Harry to spend a few days at his home in LA with him and his wife, Grace, and their daughters. They were going to surf and have parties, maybe drive along the coast and have some fun. And sure, he added, he was pleased for them; Naples was going to be exciting, but not for him. His Italian was shaky at best; and right now, with his grandparents in NYC and spoiling him rotten, why should he leave.

Naomi's heart stopped for a second. "Your grandparents?"

"Yeah, they live here now, don't you know? You with all your traveling and never being at home; of course you miss everything. Grandma is all crazy with the idea of you going to Naples; they took me out to some Italian restaurant yesterday, and she talked to the waiters in Italian the entire time. Grandfather laughed his head off at her, said it was high time for a visit with her family. Seems they haven't been down there in a while too. Strange, eh? We are one weird, spread-out family. I wonder if we'll ever be together in one place, for Christmas or something." He paused to talk to someone else and came back, his voice slightly breathless. "Hey, wouldn't that be something? We could all celebrate

Christmas together this year, at the new house. With all my grandparents
and the rest of the family. Let's do that, Mom." There were street noises
in the background, other voices, a girl's silver laugh, and the siren of a
police car, someone else calling Joshua's name. "I have to go," he said.
"We're having breakfast, a few friends and I. Later, Mom."

Just like that he hung up on her, and she found herself alone in the
parking lot beyond the backstage entrance, with only a couple of
security men wandering across the open space and LaGasse waiting
next to the door, keeping a discreet distance. Even the fans had left,
having wandered around the big building to stand in line, waiting for
the doors to open, waiting for the show to begin. It was eerily quiet
out here. Naomi could hear birds singing in the trees, a couple of cars
passing by on the road beyond the compound, even children's laughter
from nearby; but that was all. From inside, from the auditorium, where
she knew the sound engineers were even now testing the speakers and
the band was rocking the ceiling, there was not a sound.

She knew Jon was singing right now, and she wondered which song it
was. They had never talked about the *Stone Song*; there just had not been
the time for it, and the thought made her angry at her parents all over
again for destroying something so special and precious by turning up in
Geneva. The fury she had felt then was still there, and it had connected
itself to that song and hearing it for the first time.

LaGasse stirred when the door behind her opened and Sal stepped
out, cigarette in hand, ready to light it.

"Oh," he said when he saw her. "All by yourself out here? What's
going on?" A line appeared between his eyes as he gazed at her, worried.

"Nothing." She tucked the cell phone into her jeans pocket. "Nothing,
Sal. Just a quick chat with Joshua, but he's too busy to talk to me." This,
in fact, eased her mood. "He was on his way to breakfast with a group
of classmates. There was a girl's voice in the background." Sal's smile
made her shrug and grin back. "He's growing up! Soon he'll be eighteen,
a grown-up young man. My son. My baby. And now he's living the New
York life and has no time for me. I'm getting old, Sal."

That made him laugh. "Yeah, right. Like hell you are. You're not even
forty; you're a young chick!" Something like a blush crept up his neck.
"And look at you, as lovely as ever; you don't look older than twenty-five.
Nah, you're not old." A new thought occurred to him, and he added,

"Hey, if you are old, then Jon and I are ancient, and I hate that thought."

"Ridiculous." Embarrassed, she pulled up her shoulders. "I was trying to say, Sal, that it's so amazing to see this happen. You have a baby, you raise it, you think all the time that you have a baby: and then one day, quite suddenly, you have to realize you're actually talking to another adult with ideas and plans of his own, and you've lost control." Sadness washed over her, and she wrapped her arms around her body. "Suddenly, you're alone again. There's a new freedom, but it hurts."

Sal lit his cigarette. "But you let Joshua go quite early, didn't you? Didn't you send him off to Geneva to live with your parents and go to that music school or something? And then you let him go to Oxford on his own?"

"Yes." She had no idea where he was going with this. The smoke from the cigarette hung between them in the still summer air, a thin blue veil that seemed to obscure reality.

Before Sal could speak again the door flew open, and Jon appeared. "Baby," he called, "we're taking a break. Want some coffee? There's cake and stuff. You know, those great German pastries." He held out his hand to Sal for the pack of cigarettes and the lighter. "Why are you standing out here? It's hot! Who would have thought the weather would change this much in one day!"

"Joshua doesn't want to come to Italy." It had popped out before she had even found time to think about it, and it showed her how much it mattered to her. Always, always since Jon had returned to her life, Naomi felt as if she was walking on a tightrope, one stretched over a very deep drop indeed.

"He said he's planning to go to LA and spend some time with Harry and his family. And he wants us home for Christmas; he wants to celebrate with the entire family." She paused to draw a breath. "He's meeting my parents, Jon. He wants them there for Christmas too. Didn't you say they couldn't see him? What happened to the restraining order?"

"I had it revoked." Jon turned to look at the line of containers, squinting at them in the sunlight.

"How can you do that without asking me?" Naomi stepped in front of him. "How could you do that without talking to me first?"

With a sigh, Jon laid his arm around her. "Naomi, your father asked. He asked very nicely if I would allow them to take Josh out for lunch, and I agreed. You weren't there, remember? You stalked out of that restaurant in Geneva fuming at the gills, and so I decided on my own. I can't see any harm in it. Well, not anymore. And he's never going out alone; there's always a bodyguard with him. So let them have lunch together!"

"Oh, and now it's my fault?" She didn't even know where to turn with her anger and disappointment. "Now it's me against all of you suddenly? Now I'm the evil one in this story?" A deep, terrible pain was blossoming in her chest, and she had to press her hand against it to keep it in check. "I thought you were on my side, Jon. I thought you wanted to protect me and Joshua more than anything else."

"And so I do." Jon waved at Sal. "Go away. This is private, married people stuff." He waited until they were alone and then said, "I love you more than my life, Naomi. I love you so much it hurts. Every moment of my day centers around you, and you know it. You know you own me body and soul, every fiber of me, every breath." Gently he touched her face, traced the line of her temple and jaw, her lips. "I want to see you happy and free, and I'll do anything in the world to make sure of that." Tears were gathering in her eyes, ready to roll down her cheeks, and he laid his palms around her face. "Part of that is making peace with our past and your family. We can't go on living with this anger. We can't avoid them now that they live in New York. And..." He hesitated. "And as much as I deplore it, we'll just have to let them be part of Joshua's life. It's not as if they are criminals, Naomi. You said it yourself when we were in Geneva and you wanted to visit them. They are your parents, for better or worse."

"But that was before they barged into the concert and messed everything up! Before he threatened to take Joshua away!" Her fingers clasped into his shirt.

"He can't take Joshua away, Naomi. You know that." Jon marveled how it could be that she fit so well into his embrace, as if he was holding a piece of himself, a part that belonged to him and yet lived outside of his body.

"Yes. Yes." She squirmed unhappily, so he let go and took her hand instead to lead her back into the building.

"We're trying to build a new life," Jon said as they entered the hallway, "and part of that is accepting who you are. You've lived with all your secrets and the silence and loneliness for so long. It's time to change that." He waved at their surroundings. "Look, we're traveling we're on tour, going to all these places, meeting all these people, and still you want to live the way you did in Halmar. Only it doesn't work anymore."

From the catering area they could smell hot food, coffee, the sweet scent of fresh bread; hear the voices of the band, a snatch of guitar music.

"We'll be going to Naples in a few days. We'll meet the other half of your family, and I can hardly wait to see if there's a resemblance, see where Lucia is from. Me..."—he shrugged and smiled—"I'm nobody. My family always lived in Brooklyn, and my ancestry vanished somewhere in the back alleys of New York. At some time they must have crossed the Atlantic, but there's nothing to remember, nothing spectacular. But you, you're like a European princess, someone stranded on the distant shores of America, with these clans spread out all over the old continents. You have traveled far and wide, Naomi. You have crossed so many wild oceans in your life, the last of them being the shooting; you need to move into quiet waters with me now. We need to start living. When we move into the Brooklyn house and start working on the musical, I want us to be free and happy, and I know it can be done. If we come to terms with your family and our past, my fame, and turn it all in a direction we want. But the first thing we have to do is accept your father for who he is." Jon paused dramatically, waiting for a reaction, and when none came added lamely, "A stupid old bastard. But he's our stupid old bastard, and we have to deal with him."

For a moment Naomi gazed at him, her hands folded in front her chest as if in supplication, then she sighed.

"I need cake," she said.

chapter 22

IT WASN'T THAT she avoided him, but there was a resigned distance, a silence, floating between them. During the preparations for the show, in the dressing room, Naomi hardly spoke; and as soon as he wanted to touch her she drifted away, pretending to be doing something else.

Jon watched her evade him, watched how she didn't look his way or even pick up the eyeliner to play with it as she normally did. He held up a shirt to her, teasing about the color and the embroidered sleeves; but she just gave him a cursory glance and shrugged, saying it was his choice, he knew his audience best, and to wear what he felt best in. Brushing her hands on her jeans, she rose from the corner of the table and announced she needed coffee, and left.

The door fell shut behind her with a soft, final snap, and he was alone. Once again alone in a dressing room just before a concert, shirt still in hand, the sounds from the hallway muffled and distant. Her presence lingered, like an echo of her voice, displaced air where a moment ago she had been. Slowly he dressed, standing in front of the mirror, careful not to disturb his hair and the cables.

This was his job, the career he had picked, and for a moment he wondered what his life would look like if he had decided to finish college. His brother, Kevin, came to his mind, a surgeon working at one of the big New York City hospitals and living in the suburbs. Every day he rode the subway to his job, returning in the evening. He had dinner with his wife and son and went to bed, day after day, year after year.

Jon, buttoning his shirt, recalled a conversation he'd had with Kevin last Christmas while they walked along the Brooklyn Promenade digesting the duck their mother had served them for dinner. Kevin had leaned on the railing in the falling snow and squinted at the Manhattan skyline, pointed at the glittering towers, and sighed. "I'm a prisoner," he'd muttered, "I envy you. You forged out the life you wanted to lead, ruthless enough to put everything else aside and go where you wanted to go, to shape your career; and what am I? Yeah, a doctor. But in the end it's just a job, a routine, just with more responsibility than some." He'd balled his hand into a fist. "Do you ever feel this urge, Jon, this drive to be more than just alive? To rise above the masses, leave a mark on the world? Put a meaning to life?" He had looked at Jon and then laughed, and added, "Yeah, you know. You know what I'm talking about, because that's where you are, right?"

Stunned by his brother's words, Jon had been about to reply; but Kevin had moved on, shrugging his coat higher up on his neck, talking about baseball and their plans to go to the opera the next day. The moment was over before it had really begun. He remembered going to bed that night at the hotel where he and Naomi had been staying and gazing out at the snow while she was sleeping on his shoulder. For an instant, for a fleeting moment, he had felt that great yearning, the immense pull on his soul, to create something worthwhile, felt the wish to be more than a human, more than one of the horde who went through the daily routine without ever looking up. It was almost like a deep sadness, despair at life itself, a clawing at the fabric of existence, the struggle of a drowning man to rise above the surface. He had to resist the urge to pick up the phone and call Kevin and say, "Yes. I know. It hurts, and it hurts all the time. It feels like being in love, like losing love, like being told you're going to die, like being told there's no life after death, like the blackest night. It's the desire to hold the world in your hand, to take command. And I strive for it all the time."

But he hadn't done it. Instead he had wrapped his arms tightly around Naomi, making her murmur in protest, and gone to sleep himself, his last thought the French toast his mother would serve them for breakfast.

The last button closed, Jon turned from the mirror. He was ready to face the crowd. But first, before he went out on the stage to dazzle his fans, he knew he had to find Naomi and see her smile at him.

JON WOKE TO the sun in his face.

Disoriented, he sat up. The bed was empty, she was gone, and panic surfaced for a moment until he saw her clothes in the open wardrobe, her suitcase in the corner. There was no note, nothing; so often before she had slipped out and left him to fear and wonder where she had gone and whether she would return.

He had been so keen on getting married, convinced that once she wore his ring he would be able to hold on to her, pin her down, make sure she would never run from him again; and here he was on a lovely July day in a Hamburg hotel, and once again he was alone.

He got up and walked over to the window. The sky was a clear blue, the fountain in the lake a white plume against it, and the trees along the street whispered gently in a cool breeze. There wasn't much traffic, just some people strolling along the water, a sightseeing bus much like the ones in London ambling past. The stores were open. He could see customers walking in and out, and the coffee shop at the corner was doing a good business.

The crazy mood to go out on his own overcame Jon. There was the department store, the shopping arcade leading into the older part of town where he had been with Naomi the day before, where she had bought some perfume at a really nice shop while he stood by and listened to her chatting with the shopgirl in German. For once he didn't feel like sitting in a hotel, waiting until she returned from wherever the mood had taken her.

THERE WAS A group of Japanese tourists in the lobby, but no one took any notice of Jon when he walked past and out into the sunshine. For a moment he stood on the steps of the hotel and breathed in the warm yet tart air, wondering where he should go first. A sense of freedom enveloped him, a careless, carefree attitude that made him push his hands into his pockets and saunter across the street right through the traffic, disregarding the pedestrian crossing at the corner and the angry honking of a carhorn.

Standing in line at the coffee shop, searching for German change in his wallet, he noticed how the woman next to him threw him sidelong, puzzled glances. A couple of times she seemed on the point of speaking to him but then stopped and studied the cakes and sandwiches in the display instead. When it was his turn and he stuttered out his order, not sure if his English would be understood, she mumbled, "For God's sake, Jon, just tell them what you want."

Surprised, he turned around, but she didn't look his way and counted her money instead. She was pleasant, a little on the matronly side but dressed in a suit with a computer bag slung over her shoulder, nicely made up, the briskness of a workday in her posture and expression. Her hair was short, hugging her head like a Renaissance helmet, golden and glossy, with a few curls following the curve of her neck.

"Go on," she said. "Pick up your coffee and move."

"You know who I am," Jon replied, and grabbed the paper cup one of the baristas held out to him.

She shrugged. "Yes, but you're holding up the line. I'm in a hurry."

He made room for her, even returned to the sidewalk, but waited until she came out, a paper bag in hand. She stopped when she saw him staring.

"Have a great day," she called; "enjoy Hamburg while you're here. Your concert last night was great; my friends and I had a very good time. I like that new song about the stones. Bye now!" She walked away without looking back, without even a glance.

Never before in his career had he encountered something like this, and it left him feeling stupid, stumped, and speechless. Slowly, sipping his coffee, he began to walk down the broad sidewalk past the stores, enjoying the vista of the lake on the other side of the road, the sunlight dancing on the water. A couple of small boats were out, their white sails like big birds flitting across the surface, gulls circling around them.

The entrance to the department store was to his right. It was a luxurious place, and it would not have looked out of place anywhere on Fifth Avenue with all the marble and brass, the elegant window displays, and the glass cupola at its center, much admired by Naomi. She had pointed out to him that it showed the constellations that were the zodiac. Puzzled, he had stared at it, his neck craned, and wondered how she knew, who had taught her to recognize the stars, and why she knew in the first place. His admiration for her had soared, and once again he had felt the pride at having won her love, his beloved, a wife to show off. Right away shame had flooded him, and he had moved on, asking if she wanted her computer now.

JON PUSHED OPEN the heavy entrance door. A bouquet of scents welcomed him from the cosmetics department on the first floor. He strolled past the colorful counters, glancing at the lipsticks and artful flacons, at the pretty girls in their neat outfits waiting for customers, and made his way toward the escalator. The day before when they had been here, he had noticed a couple of nice sweaters; and now, with nothing better to do, he felt like some shopping.

Going up, his attention was caught by a woman on the escalator going down, and he had to look again. Her face was turned away; she was watching something going on behind her, her hand resting on the rail, purse tucked under her arm. He knew that purse; he knew the shirt she was wearing, every curve and angle of that body, and yet Jon was sure his eyes were playing some cruel prank on him.

"Naomi?" he asked, his voice cracking in disbelief.

She swiveled around, her eyes wide in surprise, and, seeing him, she smiled. "Jon! What are you doing here? You're not looking for me, are you? I was…"

Relentlessly, she was moving away from him; and, like a kid, Jon was on the point of running down the moving stairs to catch up with her. He caught himself just in time. They met on the ground floor, where she stood, waiting for him, smiling at his impatience.

Jon couldn't speak. She looked so different, like someone else, and yet she seemed more like herself than she had in a long time. Her hair, the long braid he had loved so much, was gone. Instead, chin-length curls played around her face. She looked young, like a girl, her eyes even larger and her mouth as fresh as a rose in bloom.

"I'm ready to go to Italy now," Naomi said. "And I bought some swimming suits too. There will be swimming in Positano. Do you have shorts, Jon? You need shorts. You'll love the Mediterranean."

"Last night." The words refused to form in his head. "Last night you hardly spoke to me. I bawled my heart out on that stage, trying to reach you, and you just sat there and stared at the ceiling as if I wasn't even there. You didn't listen to me; you ignored that I was singing just for you. And now you tell me I need shorts?"

Naomi took his arm to pull him back on the escalator going up. "Yes. I was mad as hell at you, Jon. I was so angry because you allowed my father to see Joshua, because I thought it was my choice, my decision. But it isn't. You're Josh's father, and it's just as much your decision. It took me a while to come to terms with it." She was standing above him, their eyes on a level for once, her hands on his shoulders. "I trust you more than I trust myself. I felt this hard, bitter kernel in my heart, all the disappointment and hatred; and then I watched you on the stage, doing what your heart tells you to do, and I realized you will always fight for me, fight for my right to do what my heart tells me, even if it breaks yours. And that was when I decided I had to change, do something that would set me free. I've been somehow liberated with the braid gone. In a symbolic way."

Tentatively, she touched her hair. "Do you like it? Did they cut it too short? Because it feels good! I think it looks good too."

Jon had to swallow a couple of times. "It looks stunning. You look like a fairy; you're so beautiful, I don't know what to say. And no, I don't have swimming trunks."

HE LET HER pick some shorts for him, even bought some polos and those sweaters he had wanted in the first place, and followed her when she drifted back toward the bathing suits, carrying the shopping bags, feeling delightfully foolish.

"Have you ever had this," he asked while she was holding up a short, thin dress in a lovely midnight blue. "Have you ever had the urge…" There was a chair, and he sank down on it. "The need to be more than you are, see more than the world that is around you, to rip apart the texture of being to see what is behind the reality? Have you ever felt the fear, the desolation of dying without having left your mark on the universe? Of being no more than one of the masses, here only to be gone again, unnoticed, unmarked?"

Naomi gazed at him silently, the dress forgotten.

"Have you ever felt this pain of not doing what you're meant to do, what you could do?" The moment the words were out of his mouth Jon realized what he had said, and he took a breath to apologize, tell her he was sorry and of course she would know, having lived her small, hidden life when she should have been a star among writers.

She was faster though.

"It has often driven me into melancholy," Naomi said softly, "and it has made me cry." Her hand came up to rest on her chest. "Sometimes I have the feeling that I'm seeing a different world around me than other people, as if they can't see all the layers there are to the fabric of life, and I want to grasp it all. The only outlet for that…" A small shrug. "The only outlet is the writing. And yes, Jon, I want to make a difference. I want it very badly. I want to soar and fly and sing to the stars, and I want to live forever and never be forgotten."

Jon took the dress from her and dropped it on the counter. "Come along. I'll buy you breakfast somewhere, and while you eat I'll stare at you and think of making love to you, the only woman who understands what I feel, what it's like to live the way we do. I'll take you to Positano tomorrow, and I'll give you the honeymoon we never had and to hell with your parents and everything else. All this shit with the shooting and the pain and guilt, it's going out the window now, Naomi. We've come down to this: you see my soul, and I see yours. Here, in a stupid German department store, we finally understand each other."

chapter 23

SAL TRAILED AFTER them as Jon and Naomi walked across the hangar to the plane that would take them to Naples, the phone pressed to his ear, trying to hear what Russ was saying over the noise of the engines.

"… we're ready to move to New York," he heard. "I'll go ahead and try to find a house or something. Solveigh wants to live somewhere out in the country, and I have no idea where to look. Any ideas?"

"What will Solveigh do out in the country, on her own, all day long?" He was barely listening, staring at Naomi's hair. In a strange, unexplained way he resented the short locks, resented them as if they were a show of independence and he the parent it was aimed at. She looked better too, not as wan and pale as she had when she had arrived in London, as if by losing the braid her energy had returned. Even her legs looked tan; her bare feet in sandals, the toenails painted red, were a provocation he could barely ignore.

"I don't even know what she means," Russ was saying. "The country? It's not like there's anything like Halmar anywhere around New York, not within easy commuting distance."

"You could always move to New Jersey."

Jon was carrying a guitar case. He had asked for the ebony to be brought out of the instrument container; he was taking it along to Italy, slung over his back just like he used to when they were young and had just started out. Seeing him like that—in jeans, with the guitar case—sent a wave of melancholy memories over Sal, and he stopped walking. Nothing had changed. They were older, calmer, well used to their success and their wealth; but deep down they were still the same people, still hungry for the music and the songs. And Naomi—the way she stood beside Jon now, waiting to board the jet, laughing at something he had said, her hand on his arm—she was the same girl too.

He remembered going over to Jon's house a couple of days after they had returned home, back when they had been to Geneva the first time and met her.

She had opened the door, a cup of coffee in her hand, hair loose, wrapped in one of Jon's bathrobes, barefoot, and smiled softly at him, a little embarrassed at being caught like that; and his heart had turned over. So young, barely more than a teenager, and already Jon's.

"Are you out of your freaking mind?" Russ's panicked voice brought him out of his reverie.

"Well, Sean wants to move there," Sal replied. A cart was bringing their luggage, not a lot, just one suitcase for each of them. They were light travelers, careless souls who acquired whatever they wanted or needed along the way. As easy as birds, they were ready to travel south, follow the sun, leave him behind to handle the chore of taking the tour back to the States. All without a second thought.

"Right." Russ snorted. "Sean thinks he's Bruce Springsteen. Oh well, I'll talk to him. Would be nice if we weren't too spread out, right? And you? Are you going to find something in Brooklyn, like the Master and his lady?"

The simple question made Sal quake in his shoes. "Oh crap no! I'll try to find something in Manhattan. You can go and live somewhere in Newark if you feel like it; I'll stick with the real thing. If I have to leave LA, I might as well get the whole deal." He hadn't thought about it yet, had pushed the prospect away to a far corner of his mind. The idea of leaving California for a winter in New York seemed too dire.

Only now did he notice the writing on the side of the plane. It was no more than a single word, tastefully small, the brown matching the cream of the jet; and it made Sal pull back his lips in surprise. "Carlsson," he read, tasting the sound. Her father had sent the family plane, and she was willing to board it.

The pilot was there to greet his passengers, a flight attendant at his elbow.

Naomi turned and smiled at him, raised her hand to wave, and then she was gone.

Sal wanted to go after her, tell her to be safe and come back, not to fall in love with the Italian summer and get lost on those sunny shores; but he stood and watched as the door was closed and the plane moved out onto the tarmac, and then swiftly away toward the runway. In the blink of an eye it was no more than a glint against the blue backdrop of the sky, and then it was gone.

Suddenly lonely, Sal decided to go to the airport terminal for a cup of coffee. Coming here, he had noticed the restaurant with the terrace where you could see the runway; and he felt like standing there, his nose pressed to the fence, smelling the jet fuel and listening to the roar of the engines before returning to the hotel to check out and travel with the band in the other direction, toward home.

He ordered a glass of wine after a quick glance at his watch, reasoning that he was in Europe and it was not unusual to drink around lunchtime. Anyway, he was quite sure Naomi would be having champagne right now aboard her family's Gulfstream while it hurtled toward the Alps.

There were a number of people out on the terrace observing the landing and departing planes. A father was holding up a young child so he could see the big 747 parked right beneath them, the blue crane of the German airline shining on its tail. The luggage was being loaded into it even now, and the catering containers.

In the corner, where the fence met the wall, Sal noticed a figure that seemed familiar, and he squinted against the light to get a better look.

It was that reporter, Parker, busy putting his camera into its bag. His blond hair was blowing in the wind, his jacket flapping around his body. He hadn't seen Sal but kept glancing in the direction of the hangar that Jon and Naomi had left only moments before.

Parker closed the bag and shrugged it onto his shoulder, plucked a boarding card from his pocket, glanced at it, and went back into the terminal.

Slowly Sal followed him all the way to the passport control, where Parker stood in line for a moment and then passed through toward the gates. For an instant Sal felt sorry for Parker and his infatuation.

NAOMI WANTED TO rent a car and drive down to Positano herself, taking the long way. They were traveling for fun, after all, and weren't in a hurry.

The corners of her mouth came down at the thought, as she looked out the plane window at the mountains below. "Unless, of course, my mother has alarmed the entire clan, and they come to pick us up. If that's the case then we won't have much of a choice."

"So tell me." Jon picked up one of the fresh figs from the huge platter of antipasti they had been served. "Tell me more about your mother's family. I have a feeling there's another mystery to unravel here, and I can hardly wait. Is it a big family?"

She pulled up her legs and curled into the wide, comfortable leather seat. "All Italian families are big, Jon." The statement made her smile.

"And everybody knows everything about everyone."

"What I'm not getting..." He didn't know how to say it without steering into deep, dangerous waters. "What I'm not getting is why you've locked yourself away from them. I mean, I can see why you don't care much for your father's family, but your mom's?"

A small shrug, a lowering of her head. "You know why."

He didn't though, and waited patiently for her to go on.

Naomi sighed. "Jon, you ask the most terrible questions." Her shoulders came up, and she tucked her knotted hands between her knees. "There was only one thing I wanted from life, and I couldn't have it. So..." Another shrug. "So I didn't want the rest either. I crawled into hiding in Halmar, and day and night I thought of you, and how I should be with you. Nothing made sense, nothing seemed right, not even breathing or opening my eyes in the morning. You see, I could not allow myself to be anywhere else, do anything else, because I didn't want to forget what it felt like to love you and be loved by you. That was all that mattered, and I wanted to keep it at all costs. If you hadn't come to find me, if Joshua hadn't written to you, I would have gone on like that forever. I would have carried that shining orb of our love around with me until the end of days, and it would have been my only light." She pulled herself together even tighter. "It was the only thing I had, and the only thing I wanted. Loving you, Jon, is terrible. It hurts, it's like the most insistent melody, like a knife in my back that I can't reach and remove. It's all-encompassing and final. There's no way out."

The grainy taste of fig lingered on Jon's tongue like the residue of a summer day. He took a sip of the sweet wine. It tasted like the memory of a kiss in the dusk of a warm night. Her words hummed in him, resonating like a drumbeat.

"So you see," she said, easier now, "how it is. It's either you and the world or nothing at all." Daintily, her fingers hovering over the plate for a moment; she selected a fat green olive and nibbled on it.

"But..." The words he wanted to say seemed so crazy and childish, he had to swallow before he could speak them. "But I love you more. I know I do. If you put it like that then there's no room for me to love you more, and I have to."

"You don't love me more, you silly man." Olive pit discarded, Naomi unfolded from her seat and moved over to sit in his lap.

Jon, his arms around her hips, laid his face on her chest and inhaled the scent of her rose perfume. "Yeah I do. I know so, I wake up at night and stare at you, and I memorize every curve, every part of you so when I go back to sleep I can take you with me into my dreams and never be without you. I want to breathe you in and hold you inside my heart so I'll never have to be without you for a moment."

Slowly, choosing her words carefully, she told him about the big family in Naples and Positano, about the vineyards on the mountainsides, the big house in Positano that overlooked the entire village, nestled into a pine grove. They had not stayed there though, she said, looking away from him, even though her uncle Cesare had wanted it very much.

Her fingers were caressing his neck, playing with his hair, and the soft touch sent shivers down his spine, just like her breath on his temple. "Why not? Where did you stay then?" he asked, and knew the answer even before she could reply. "Don't tell me. Your father bought a hotel there, just because."

"Yes. The story goes that he had a huge fight with Carl over it because he had his heart set on a special one and the old owner was being difficult about selling. I think they paid a lot more than it was actually worth in the end; but my father wanted to own a part of the place where my mother was born, and he wanted that hotel." She shifted so she could look at him. "Now, of course, it's one of the top places in Positano. You will love it. You will love the drama of the setting, the beach, everything." A fine, sardonic smile flitted across her lips. "My family is really good at that. They are really, really good at making money, even if they do something for fun or out of sentimentality." She patted the gray leather of the couch on which they were sitting. "And they really appreciate what they have."

"I can't see anything wrong with that." And he couldn't. As much as he loved her, he couldn't understand this attitude. "I grew up in a middle-class family, Naomi. We weren't poor, but we weren't rich either. My parents could afford to take us away for a week in summer, maybe to Maine or to Florida; but we never traveled the way you do, on a whim, on the spur of a moment, and hell, never in first class let alone a private jet. We couldn't buy whatever we wanted, whenever we wanted; we had to wait for Christmas, and even then it was a *maybe*."

He held up his hand when she drew a breath to reply. "Baby, let me say this. I worked my ass off to be where I am; I worked day and night for many years, and I sold my soul. You know it. You know the dark side of fame and wealth. But I really appreciate what I have. I like being rich, and I like being famous. To me, that's proof that I've achieved something. And yeah, why shouldn't I enjoy it? Why shouldn't I enjoy wearing designer clothes and buying my wife expensive jewelry, driving a Porsche, and owning a couple of beautiful houses? Yeah, I love it! So…" Gently he pushed her short locks behind her ears and ran his finger over the pearl stud she was wearing. "So why act as if it's something shameful? Why not be happy we can have all this, live in ease and luxury, do as we please? There is no reason to be bitter about it."

Naomi gave him a long, thoughtful look.

"Or is there?" Jon pushed. "Is there a reason to be bitter?"

"Well yes," she replied softly. "For me there is. It's part of the package. Using the family jet means accepting that I'm part of them. Taking this gift means owing them something; and Jon, I don't want to owe my father and uncle anything. That's the reason why I never touched my money…" Her words died.

"Your money? What do you mean, 'your money'?" He didn't let her go when she tried to climb out of his lap. "No, no, now I want to know. What do you mean, 'your money'? Are you telling me you have your own fortune sitting somewhere in a bank, and you never touched it, never used it? Not even for Joshua?"

"Well yes, for Joshua." She squirmed. "To send him to school, but only for the fees. I paid for most of it myself. I wanted to."

"Good grief, Naomi."

"It worked! And anyway…" This time he let her rise when she tried to and watched as she straightened her dress with something like regret. "Anyway, I was used to not having a lot of money after the years with you, remember?"

"Oh, don't you go there!" They had been over this a number of time, and it still made him wilt in shame.

"What?" Another olive wandered into her mouth. "I was your little number, the girl you kept in your house. Why should you have…"

"Careful. Be very careful, you little number. Don't you dare say that."

She shrugged at him, but this time it was a saucy, flirty shrug. "Your little lovebird."

"Stop." Jon loved the dress she was wearing, a short, red cotton thing with a halter strap, just right for the beach and summer heat. "You're my lovebird all right, but now I want to know about that hidden treasure of yours."

Naomi pointed out of the window. "Look, the Mediterranean. Look how blue the water is, Jon."

It was true; he had never seen an ocean so cerulean, so gentle. There were no breakers, no waves; it was as smooth and clear as a mirror.

"We are almost there," she said. "Soon you'll see Naples. And then I'll rent a Ferrari and drive you along the coast to Positano."

"Like hell you will. I'm driving that Ferrari. I've always wanted to do that." Once again, and very neatly, she had turned his attention away from the real issue.

Settling back into her seat, putting on the seat belt, Naomi gently said, "If you really want to know, if it matters, I'll tell you. There are some hotels in my name, some houses, a couple of…other things. And yes, there's a trust…" She sighed. "It's a lot. And it scares me."

"You and your Monopoly game life, you scare the crap out of me with this." His glass was empty, and Jon refilled it liberally. "I really wish you would come clean with me so there are no more surprises, and I finally know who I married."

"But…"

He looked up at her.

"But Jon, will you still love me? Will you love me when you know I own a dozen hotels and half a dozen restaurants, and that I want nothing to do with it all?"

She said it so earnestly and full of fear, he wanted to laugh at her. "Baby, I know you better than you know yourself. I don't give a damn about your hotels and restaurants and whatever. To me, you're the poet. My selkie girl. The mermaid I found on my beach and brought home. My muse. Do with your stupid wealth what you want. Just don't leave my life and my bed."

The plane coasted over the water and began to sink toward their destination. The flight attendant came to clear away their meal.

Her lips curled in a smile. "You're so transparent, Jon Stone. It's always about bed with you. I promise, I won't leave yours, ever."

The sound of the engines changed, the pressure popping his ears.

"I'm driving that Ferrari," Jon said.

Her smile widened.

chapter 24

THERE WOULD BE no Ferrari.

Instead, a pair of dark German limousines were waiting for them at the airport. Seeing the two men standing beside them, Jon wondered if he had at last arrived in Naomi's Mafia family and was even now on his way to a sinister abduction scenario in the heat of southern Italy.

"My uncles," Naomi said, "Cesare and Raphaele. My mother's brothers." She smiled. "A great honor. They are here themselves. There is a third one, Lorenzo. They are all older than my mom. Imagine growing up in Italy with three older brothers."

"It was bad enough growing up with Val as my older sister," Jon muttered.

And suddenly, just like that, saying Val's name, he felt homesick for New York and his own family. He wanted to sit at his mother's kitchen table and drink an early-morning coffee with her, run over to the French bakery two blocks down the street and get fresh croissants, watch her do the crossword puzzle while he leafed through the sports section of the newspaper. Sometimes when a tour had taken him to New York he had done this, spent the night at home and slept in his childhood room. Joshua was there now. The thought of his son curled up in his old bed, wrapped in his faded quilt with the stars and his name embroidered along the edge, warmed his heart.

"One should never put away family," he said as the door of the plane opened and the warm air of a Naples afternoon wafted in. "Never. We're doing the right thing."

Naomi threw him a puzzled glance.

"There's no one else. Only your family love you for yourself. With everyone else, you never know."

"But I'm not your family, Jon. Are you unsure of my love too?" She had been on the point of picking up her purse, but now she paused, a troubled look clouding her face.

"Ah, that's different." Jon handed her the bag. "And I wasn't talking about you at all. You know it."

"My father does not love me for what I am."

The flight attendant was waiting for them to leave.

"My father does not love that I'm a woman, and he does not love that I'm a writer. That's not right, Jon. Sometimes there are people outside your family who love you for what you really are and not for what you should be." She turned away, her shoulders slumped, sad once again.

He wanted to kick himself. "That's not what I meant, and you know it!"

"I know." Her smile was wan at best. "I was raised with all these expectations, and now I live with being this enormous failure. There are moments when I understand why my father doesn't love me."

Before he could reply, she had descended the stairs into the noisy welcome of her Italian family.

"I WILL SHOW you the vineyards and let you taste our wines." Cesare said to Jon as they drove along the curvy road.

"We have many vineyards. We make our own grappa, red wine, some spumante. You like grappa?"

He went on to talk about olive groves and their olive mills, the pine trees on the slopes of the mountains, and the honey they produced. "Because, you see, we are farmers. At heart, we are farmers, and there's nothing better than an early-morning walk under the olive trees seeing the fruit ripen."

They were delighted, he rambled on, delighted to see his niece and her husband, the American. Lucia had told them about him, that he was a famous man, very famous, a rock star. Cesare squinted at him. "But I have never heard of you. You are not famous in Italy, are you? Only in America?"

"Not in Italy," Jon conceded. This felt strange. It felt as if he had to defend his success; and once again, just like in Canada visiting her father's family, he felt like her consort, someone of lesser importance and only tolerated because Naomi wished it so. "But nearly everywhere else in Europe," he added, and saw Naomi bite her lip at the bravado in his tone.

"It does not matter." Cesare clapped his shoulder. "We will love you because our niece loves you. You are part of our family." Coming with the brilliant smile and the dark sunglasses, it sounded more like a threat than a welcome.

Jon's breath stopped when they crested the mountains. He leaned forward in the car to take in the view, feeling he had somehow been poured into a painting, into a totally new world.

To their right, the Sorrento peninsula marched away. The mountainside spilled into the sea like a flounce on a silk gown in many shades of green, from the dainty hue of a young leaf to the moody darkness of old jade. The ocean, dipped into the soft light of the late afternoon, shone softly, as opaque as the inside of a shell, melting into the sky in the distance. Nestled around a sickle-shaped beach lay the little town, the pastel houses piled one on top of another, clinging to the slopes, hugging the rocky scarp, their faces turned toward the water and the sun.

Everywhere, clinging to every wall and framing every window, were flowers, most of them in tints of rose or pink.

"Positano," Raphaele announced, his voice full of pride. "Welcome."

The car took them through the town; down narrow, steep streets, back up another hillside to a small road that wound its way through a pine grove toward a big, sprawling house set on its own terrace. The yellow stone shone in the gentle light, its windows glinting a welcome at them.

Jon, looking up at the huge facade, was reminded of her father's family home outside Kleinburg. He had felt equally speechless when they had gone there for New Year's Eve. She had told him her family was rich; he had heard Sal tell him about their business. But only when he had seen that property, after driving through countryside for ten minutes after they entered the estate with no sight of the house, had he grasped the extent of their wealth.

It had made him forget for a moment who he was, and instead he had felt like the Brooklyn boy he still was at heart.

In her world he felt unknown, unimportant; and surprisingly, Jon liked it. He leaned back into the seat, amused by the twists and turns of his life, thinking how much Sal would enjoy this, would appreciate the advantages of the marriage he had made.

Naomi sat beside him as if none of this mattered to her. She was busy with her cell phone, checking it for messages. She hardly looked up when the car stopped.

"Welcome," Raphaele said again, opening the door for them. "Now, at last you are back home."

HE HAD SEEN this in movies, read about it in glossy travel magazines, but Jon had never thought he would one day be part of such a feast.

They had set a long table on the patio, under trellises heavy with wisteria and grapes, in the shade of some old pine trees. The entire bay and the town lay below them. Jon, standing at the edge of the terrace, looked out at the mountains fading into the dusk, at the silvery sheen the sea had taken on now that the sun had set and the light had turned blue. There were fishing boats out on the water, each of them with a lantern on its bow. They moved slowly or not at all. From the gorse growing on the slope just below he could hear the susurration of cicadas, the hum of a bumblebee having a late snack. The whisper of a lazy breeze moved in the trees; and from far, far away there was the sound of Positano, of nightlife on the beach just starting: snatches of music, children's laughter, the hasty, metallic chugging of a Vespa hurtling down the serpentines. A sweet scent lingered in the air. He had smelled it right away when they had gotten out of the car. It reminded him of honey and maybe sherry, mixed with the tart aroma of the pines.

From behind, from the house, there were voices. He turned around.

A group of women came out, carrying bowls and platters of food, Naomi among them. She had a basket with bread sitting on her hip, holding it with one arm as if it was a basket of laundry while nibbling on a piece of pastry. She was talking to a black-haired girl in fast, fluent Italian. With a brief smile at him she placed her load on the table, among the dishes of pasta and sauces, the bowls of salad and ripe tomatoes.

He watched her as she returned inside, her red dress a speck of color against the dimness, highlighted by the candles on the table.

Arriving at the house earlier, he had been stunned into silence when the family came out to greet them. Their names had flowed past him like melodies, like the promise of a summer day: Gemma, Pia, Dorabella, Gloria, and they all looked like Naomi. A little duskier, a little taller or more voluptuous; but the resemblance was so strong that he had stared until they had laughed at him. Her cousins, and at last the mystery was lifted.

Once again, hearing their voices from the depth of the large building, he thought of the mermaid lured away from her natural habitat by a song, caught in a web of love, and forced to live on dry land. To Jon, it seemed as if she had returned, as if he had returned her to her own world and she was swimming at last in familiar waters.

Cesare stepped out of the house and waved to him. "Jon, let us eat. Have you ever had real Italian food?"

"Well." Jon moved toward him and the light, toward the table laden with food, wine, and fruit. It looked like a painting, a still life: colorful, Baroque, and inviting. "I'm from Brooklyn. There are a lot of Italians in Brooklyn."

Cesare waved his hand at him. "That is nothing. We grow our own vegetables. Everything you see on this table, everything, was grown on our own land, even the wheat for the bread. We like it that way; we like to know what we eat. Here!" He took a small dish with green olives from the table and held it out to Jon. "Try. These are from the trees on this estate. I have watched them grow!"

Jon glanced at the mountains rising into the darkness behind them, huge creatures bent over in slumber, motionless and silent. He took one of the olives and inhaled its sour, unique fragrance.

The scent threw him back to the little corner shop on Atlantic where he had gone with his father on Saturday mornings when the whim for a Middle Eastern breakfast had overtaken the family. They had bought pastry filled with minced lamb or feta, humus, and olives. Jon recalled the vats in the corner of the dim store and how the owner had lifted the wooden lids to display the brine, olives swimming in it like glossy brown and green marbles. He had always been given a couple to try by the friendly Syrian man and had taken them to eat on the steps in the sun while his father chatted and paid for their purchases.

He remembered coming home to the aroma of fresh coffee and his mother, Helen, standing in the kitchen slicing tomatoes to go with whatever they had bought.

"Naomi was telling me about a fig tree," Jon said, "and how she used to pick fresh figs for breakfast."

"Yes. It is right over here." Cesare moved toward the corner of the large terrace. There was no rail. Below them, the hillside rolled steeply away. A round table with a marble top and some chairs stood here. "This is where we like to have breakfast. See, there are some lemon trees too." From among the foliage he plucked a couple of ripe figs and handed them to Jon. "She should have come home more often. I know

Lucia was unhappy about it; she always wanted Naomi to come back with her."

"Do they come here often? Olaf and Lucia?" The figs felt strange in his hand, almost alive, human, with their warm, velvety skin and their soft shape.

"Every year. Not in summer though." Cesare laughed. "Most people think it is too hot here in summer. But yes, they come often."

For Jon, hearing these words, the world tilted. It was not so much a new perspective, as it was, looking into a mirror not directed at him and seeing a totally new part of the world that had been invisible to him, hidden in an angle just outside his vision.

"Lucia and my son, Ferro," Cesare went on, "they share a passion. They are the artists in this family. Sadly, Lucia has given up so much for her husband's sake. But she is really a good singer."

He had heard that before. Somewhere it had cropped up, the mention that Lucia sang in an opera chorus, but it had never been talked about again.

"She used to sing in church, you know. All the solos at all the masses, it was always Lucia. We were so proud of her. She stood up there in her white dress and sang like an angel. The clearest voice you can imagine. My little sister."

"And Ferro?" Jon tasted the strange name on his tongue. It sounded harsh, hard, a name for a fighter.

Cesare turned at the sound of female laughter from inside the house. The rest of the family appeared, Raphaele and Lorenzo in the lead, carrying a huge tray with a roast suckling pig between them. They placed it on a side table and began carving the meat, laying the golden crust on a plate one of the women was holding.

Gemma, she was Gemma, Jon was certain, Raphaele's daughter.

There were so many of them. He had counted seven female cousins, one male; and he hadn't even tried to figure out their spouses and children.

"Ferro is my son," Cesare repeated with a smile. "My wife and I, we only had one child, and late in life. He is younger than Naomi even though I'm the oldest in the family."

"Open the wine," Lorenzo called, and Cesare moved away.

Like a lovely painting, Naomi stood with her cousins and watched the men deal with the roast pig. There were four of them in that little group, all roughly the same age, yet they looked like four versions of the same female. Jon wondered, if Naomi had lived here her whole life, would she be like her cousins: lush and tanned, full of loud laughter, her hands brown and strong. He felt a pang of sorrow for her braid. He had loved how it wrapped around them when they made love. It had reminded him of a mermaid, her long tresses dragging him under, while she held him in her arms. Now she looked elegant. Sleek. A city woman, ready to dive into the bustle of New York. For a moment he longed for the quiet days of Halmar, and the simple life, and the easy days that slipped into one another like grains of sand running through fingers. Music had flown out of him there; it had floated in the air, and he had felt it in every breath he took.

"Come, sit," Cesare called. "Dinner is ready."

Naomi sat down beside him and reached for his hand. Hers was warm, her touch firm, without hesitation; and when he looked at her, she gave him the same brilliant smile she had shared with her cousins. "I love it here. Can you smell the flowers, Jon; can you hear the ocean?"

"To be honest, all I can smell is food," Jon replied, and gazed at the table with the many bowls and platters. He could hardly wait to try the pasta with the mussels. "And it's a pretty good smell." He laid the figs he had been holding down beside his plate.

"Ah." Naomi took one of them and broke it open. Little golden seeds lay nestled in the dark pink flesh of the fruit. She offered it to him, but he shook his head. He wanted pasta, and the crackling crust from the pig, the wine, and the bread. Naomi bit into the fig. Juice ran down her chin, and she laughed, wiping it off with the back of her hand like a child.

chapter 25

SOMEWHERE DEEP INSIDE, Jon realized, she did care. As much as she said she didn't want to be part of the family business, she had a way of walking through a hotel with a critical eye, taking note of everything, seeing every dust mote, every little thing that was not perfect and did not meet her standards.

Cesare had taken them down to the hotel after dinner, saying over and over how much he regretted Naomi's decision, but he understood; they wanted privacy, and she was probably curious to see her property.

At this Jon had thrown her a questioning glance, but she had only shrugged and replied that the hotel was her father's hobbyhorse, not hers.

It was not as simple as that, he had seen as soon as they arrived. The manager had been waiting for them, an anxious look on his face. Bemused, walking behind Naomi, Jon had followed them down a flight of stairs from the lobby. The sense of déjà vu was so strong he almost thought he had double vision. It was exactly this way that she had shown him to his room at the hotel in Halmar when he'd first arrived there.

She wandered around in the spacious rooms, opened the sliding doors to the private terrace and stepped outside, inspected everything, and at last declared that it was okay. No more than that, a terse "Okay," and the manager had wilted. With a wave of her hand she had sent him off, ordering breakfast for the next morning, specifying what they would want and when.

"You bossy little thing," Jon said when the door closed behind him at last. "Did you have to make the poor guy feel like dirt?" He was pleased enough with their surroundings. The place was obviously a first-class establishment though less plush than others he had seen. There was a lot of space, the furniture simple and sparse but of good quality. Everything was airy, open, directed toward the outside and the sea. Here, he could hear the ocean and the rustle of the wind in the trees, smell the flowers and the herbs.

Naomi held up a cushion from the couch. "This has not been washed, Jon. You wash the covers before you give rooms to new guests, let alone the owner. Clearly a minus; and here—" she went over to the table where a bowl of fruit stood—"these grapes, they are at least two days old. Impossible." A little gentler she added, "Well, at least at my hotel, it would be. Impossible."

"I think this is pretty nice." He had to take a deep breath to reign in the laughter. "And I think you scared the shit out of the manager. I'm sure he will go to bed now wondering if you're going to complain to the big boss. Your father, I mean."

"My father." She said it thoughtfully and let the word linger in the air. "You know, I've actually never seen him inspect a property. He was always the moneyman, the one who managed the finances. It was always Carl who went and acquired new property. Always." Her lips pursed, she looked around. "In fact, I can't remember my father buying another hotel on his own, or fighting over it with Carl. This must have really meant a lot to him. I wonder if this is the same suite my parents use when they are here?" With a little shake of her shoulders she came out of her reverie. "But it really is a lovely spot, isn't it? Makes me wonder why they offered Halmar to me when I wanted to hide from you and not this. I think I wouldn't have minded living here, and the family so close by. It would have been a little less lonely. Maybe…" A tiny shrug, a brief tightening of her lips. "Maybe, if I'd come here, I would have been able to let you go, find a new life, a new love."

"Oh, very bad idea!" Jon was by her side in two big strides. "Very, very bad idea. I like it a lot better this way. Way better."

Her hair smelled of cooking, her skin of sun; and it was warm and soft, warm from inside, as if her body had come alive again after her long illness, as if at last blood was coursing through her limbs again.

"I could be married to one of my cousins' friends, another landowner, and be running this hotel and living in the sun and the warmth all year long. I could have my own fig tree right here on this terrace. I'd eat pasta every day."

He kissed her hard, holding her tightly when she tried to squirm out of his arms, molding her body to his, inhaling her breath. She moaned a little, but he did not let her go. "I'll feed you pasta if that's what you want, and I'll plant a fig tree for you in Brooklyn and the Malibu garden, but you can forget about marrying a brawny Italian and living here. You're mine; your fate is sealed."

"Yes." A sigh, a gentle capitulation, and the softening into the embrace.

"BUT THERE'S NO reason," Jon said a good while later, "why we shouldn't come back here once a year, just like your parents. Your family is here, after all. I think my mother and Val would love it. We could bring them."

Naomi sighed in reply, but when he raised himself up on his elbow, he saw that she was hardly listening to him.

The moon had risen. It cast a golden path on the calm water, leading toward the horizon and even farther, away into the distance. The fishing boats seemed to dance on it, following the light into another world.

Beyond the terrace doors, hidden somewhere in the bougainvillea, a lonely cicada sang. Her face was turned away; she was gazing at the moon and the few wispy clouds drifting past it.

"I think I've changed my mind, Jon," she softly said.

His heart skipped "About what?"

She looked at him. Her eyes were deep, black pools in her pale face.

"Remember I once told you if I was a selkie I would want to live in the cold, gray waters of the North? I've changed my mind. I'd want to live here. Because then, on a night like this, I'd come ashore. I'd pick flowers and weave a wreath while sitting on the sun-warmed sand of the beach." The sheets rustled when she moved closer to him. "I'd pick figs and oranges, some grapes and peaches, and take them back into the sea with me and eat them down there in my castle and relive the hours in the air." She paused. "But I probably wouldn't eat them. I'd keep them in an empty seashell and smell them, breathe in the aroma of sun and light."

Her skin shone like a pearl. Jon missed her dark tresses, missed digging into them, wrapping them around his hands. The short hair made her face daintier, smaller, more vulnerable.

"I'd lie in wait for you, my selkie," he replied. "I'd lure you out of the water with a basket of flowers. Or no, I'd build a bed of blossoms for you in my garden, and then when you come ashore, I'd take you there and love you, crushing all those petals, releasing their fragrance with your sighs."

Even as he spoke, before she could reply, Jon knew what she was going to say. The *Secret Garden*, he breathed. "Ah, that's what that song was all about. Oh my God, Naomi, I never realized. The image was there all the time; you had that image in your mind all the time."

"Yes." She smiled at him through the darkness. "Yes, that was the image. That was how I felt. Like a mermaid held prisoner in a cold, forbidding world and then, one night, lured into warmth and love by a voice, a smile, the love of a stranger, by someone offering me a fragrant garden, and sunlight."

"You never said!" He tried to remember, tried to recall if this had ever come up.

Naomi shrugged. "It wasn't important. It was good enough that you liked it and could relate to it; what I thought did not matter. I let the song go when you chose to make it yours."

A shiver ran through her when he touched her, let his hand glide down the curve of her waist and hip.

"Yes," Jon said slowly, thoughtfully, "the song is mine, and the poet. And I'll make sure she wants to stay mine."

Her lips were so soft, so warm and welcoming, and her embrace the only thing he wanted.

CESARE CAME TO pick them up while they were having breakfast on the terrace.

He wanted to take them up to the olive groves and show Jon the trees and the mill and introduce him to his son, Ferro.

"Where is he?" Jon asked. The bread was a disappointment. It was nowhere near what they had eaten the night before, at the family home. This was limpid, tasteless; it didn't even seem fresh. He could see, from the deep furrow between Naomi's eyes, that there was trouble in store for the manager.

"He is working up in the hills. I will take you to him." Cesare gazed at their table, his brows raised critically. "Why don't you come and stay at my house? It may be farther from the beach, but I promise, the food will be better. That bread looks very sad."

"Maybe we should." Naomi laid down her knife. "Maybe we really should accept your offer, Uncle. If I stay here I'll end up getting involved. But this is my father's place. If he is okay with the way this hotel is run, then it's his business. I'm glad we haven't unpacked yet."

Her movements when she rose and went inside were sharp and impatient, her steps brisk; and Jon, watching her, had to hide a grin. He knew her so well. He knew that despite her words she would have a talk with the manager, and he would come out of it sweating and unhappy.

"She is just like all the others." Cesare dropped into the chair Naomi had vacated and took one of the apricots from the bowl of fruit. "Just like all the other DeAngelis females. Short-tempered, impetuous, beautiful. Believe me, you are well off. You have only one. I have an entire house full of them to deal with. I have eight nieces, and they are all the same." He bit into the apricot. "Not many boys in this generation. Raul, my brother Lorenzo's son, has quite a bit of responsibility coming his way. But the girls will do their part. They like working for the family business."

"And your son?" The coffee was strange. Jon liked his black and straight, no fuss; and this was only bearable with milk. It had a nutty, bitter taste, not at all like espresso; and he had no idea what to do with it. Italian breakfast, he decided, would never be one of his favorite meals.

"Ah, my son." Cesare smiled. "My son is different. He goes his own way. The farms and the vineyards are not for him."

THEY DROVE UP the winding, narrow roads, the steep, terraced hillsides on both sides, their verdant green luxurious in the bright sunlight. Pastel-colored houses were nestled between the orchards like eggs hidden in the grass, protected by the umbrellas of the pine trees. From time to time a Vespa came dashing down the road, wobbling around the loops of the serpentines like a drunken beast, engine sounding like a dying sewing machine.

"I want one of those!" Naomi pointed when a flaming red one hurtled past them. A young girl was riding it, her skirt hitched up on her thighs, her hair blowing in the wind.

Cesare laughed. "You can use Gemma's, I'm sure. She has one just like that. She is like a devil on it."

The car turned off the road and onto a dirt track that took them up a steep incline under the dense canopy of trees. For a while they drove in the fragrant shadow of the pines until the grove dropped away and they entered a wide meadow sloping gently toward a cliff that dropped dramatically into the ocean. A single building, an old church, stood in the center of this open space. It was more of a chapel, built of the ocher stone so common here, with Gothic windows and a sturdy bell tower.

"Here we are." Cesare held the door open for Naomi. "You will meet my son, Ferro, here."

Naomi took a few steps away from them, into the high grass, and stood looking around, inhaling the sweet scent of the flowers, listening to the hum of bees and the silence surrounding her. Far below, the sea twinkled in the sun, the boats no more than white specks on the azure expanse, the town of Positano a collection of bird's nests plastered to the mountainside. Behind her, the mountains rose into a sky white with heat.

The door to the church was open. After the glare of the sun, it seemed dim and cool inside, the air heavy with the aroma of incense and burning candles and a slight mustiness from the old stone. Motes of dust danced in the sunbeams that fell through the colorful panes onto the mosaic floor.

Behind the altar, a man was sitting on a scaffolding, a lamp by his side, painting. He was so lost in his work that he hadn't noticed them, so they watched for a while as he carefully touched the wall with his brush, adding another dab of light to his work.

Naomi heard Jon beside her breathe out a sigh, and she took his hand.

The girl in the mural was wearing a shawl or cape covering her head and shoulders, flowing over her arms; and she was holding an oil lamp in her hands. Her face was turned away from the spectator, looking toward something or someone unseen, her lips slightly parted, her eyes open. Her entire attitude was one of pause; she was caught in the moment between surprise and acceptance, as if she was listening closely in an attempt to understand.

"The Annunciation," Cesare said softly, but Naomi had already understood.

The Virgin, wrapped in that light blue gown, the clay bowl with the oil like an offering in her palm, shone from the darkness of the surrounding wall like a quiet candle. Ferro was even now applying more of the yellowish white to the flame of the lamp, the only thing to highlight that young, pure face.

"Come, look at this one." Naomi turned to follow Cesare to the side where there was another mural, another image of Mary, this time with the child on her lap. This one made her smile. The infant was no serene and angelic Christ; here was a feisty baby struggling away from his mother, trying to reach for the gifts being presented to him while she had her arms wrapped around his chubby, naked middle and tried to keep him from falling.

"Loretta and her baby were the models for this one. Little Tonio squirmed all the time. To think, he's a teenager now." His low laugh echoed through the vault.

"Ah, Papa!" Ferro climbed down the ladder. "Sorry I could not make it last night, but that color just drove me crazy. I went to Naples to buy something else. See? Now the light shines!" He wiped his hands on a piece of cloth and stuffed it into his belt before he stretched out his hand to Naomi. "Hello, cousin. You have grown into a beautiful woman. You'd make a good model for the Virgin." Critically he looked her up and down. "You have the right figure; the others are all too well fed, too ample. Mary should be ethereal, dainty. Not an Italian peasant wench."

"I've brought you lunch," Cesare interrupted. "Come outside and sit in the sun with us and take a break. How long have you been working?"

Ferro grinned sheepishly at his father. "Oh, you know, after I got the new paint and tried it out, I couldn't just stop. She needed that light in her hands." His gaze wandered back to his painting. "Couldn't leave her alone in the darkness of the night."

chapter 26

"MOST OF THE paintings in the house were done by Ferro," Cesare told them. "He is becoming famous, having exhibitions all over Europe. It is a great gift being so talented, and it is an honor to have an artist in the family."

"An honor?" Naomi took the glass of wine he held out to her.

"Yes, a great honor. An artist, someone with the gift to create, is a blessing, a child kissed by an angel." Carefully, Cesare opened containers with pasta and salad and offered them to his son. "Yes, a blessing. The moment we realized Ferro wanted to do nothing but paint and draw, we saw to it he got the right teachers and the space to develop his talent."

"But the farms? The vineyards, the olive mills?" The wine was sweet and cool, and tasted of almonds and honey.

"What of them? There are others, and even if there wasn't, one can always hire managers. The earth was here before us, and it will outlast us. We can't take any of it with us when we die. The true value…" Cesare patted his chest with the tips of his fingers. "The true value of a person isn't in how much he owns. It's in what he has given to the world, how much joy he has brought to others."

Jon was looking at her, his gaze silent and steady.

"And if you come into the world with a gift, like your mother with her voice or Ferro with his paintings, then you owe it to others to share it, because that is why it was given to you. The arts—music, song, painting, or poetry—these have to be given to others. If you keep them to yourself it's like committing a sin." With a smile, Cesare held out a container to her. "Here, try these. Angelica makes them; they are filled with cheese and herbs."

She held the piece of pastry in her hand but did not eat it.

"So you—" Cesare turned to Jon—"you, I hear, are a great musician. There was some talk about a movie soundtrack?"

"I know who you are." Ferro shook his head at his father. "Everyone knows who you are except my old man. They are only too well mannered to show their excitement. Naomi, how did you catch the famous man? The competition must have been tough."

Ferro was a tall man in his midthirties, with broad shoulders and muscular, deeply tanned arms. His hair was longish; it curled around his shoulders, but he was clean shaven and well groomed, and had the same black eyes as the rest of the family.

"I don't know," she replied, lowering her head. "I didn't catch him. He ran after me from day one."

Jon laughed. "That's true; and after coming here and seeing your family, all these lovely women, I know why. It had to be one of the DeAngelis women or no one at all. And she was the only one I could catch."

"You compose all your music yourself, don't you?" Hungrily, Ferro was taking huge bites of the cold pizza.

"Yes, and I used to write my own lyrics when…while…during my time without Naomi. But she is the writer in this family, and her words are far superior to mine. Now, I don't touch the lyrics anymore." He reached for Naomi's hand. "She says everything that needs to be said."

Embarrassed, she pulled away from him and knotted her fingers in her lap. "It's only writing. There's nothing special about it. Everybody writes in one way or the other. It's nothing."

Cesare squinted at her against the sun. "You think? You think there's nothing special to putting things into words? That painting in there— go on; describe it to me. Tell me what you saw."

"I saw…" Naomi broke off. "You're kidding me, right?"

"No, I'm serious! Tell me what you saw!"

"She is seeing the angel of the Lord," Naomi said. "She is seeing the light of heaven, and she realizes something momentous is about to happen. She's not afraid, not even really surprised. Awed, yes. But there is a stillness to her as if she's listening both to the words the angel is speaking and to her own soul. I think the angel's voice sounds like a mandolin: sweet, mellow, soothing. She is drawn to it, enticed."

A smile on his face, Cesare leaned toward her. "You are a writer," he told her, "because you see. And because you can put into words what you see. If you scrape all the meat from the way you perceive art, it comes down to this: artists are people who look deeper, see more than the upper layer of existence, and who feel a need to communicate that to the world. It's that basic, and that simple. You use words, your husband melodies, and Ferro egg tempera."

Abashed, she settled back against the cool wall of the church and popped the cheese pastry into her mouth and listened to Ferro asking

Jon about life in Hollywood and the music business. She watched Jon as he poured more wine, broke off a piece of the bread, and talked about their life and work, describing a day in the studio, a show night, the quiet hours spent composing.

"And the fans? What about the ladies?" Ferro gave them a dazzling smile, his white teeth flashing.

Jon grinned. "Oh, you know. Many offers, a lot of opportunities." He pursed his lips. "Not all of them bad, some actually quite enticing. But you know how it is. Deep down, you are always searching for the one, the only one, the girl that will make your heart stop every time she walks into the room, the one who holds your heart."

Naomi held out her hand to him. "Give me your handkerchief, please."

Bemused, Jon dug into his jeans pockets and handed it to her. She got up without another word and went into the church. Just as she entered, he could see her unfold the linen, then she vanished into the darkness. With half an ear he listened to Ferro talking about brushes and pigments, about the project he wanted to tackle next, and to Cesare's rumbling voice replying, suggesting they go to Rome and try to find the right stuff there.

Jon, distracted, rose and slowly wandered toward the open door of the chapel.

It took his eyes a moment to adjust to the gloom.

She had covered her hair with the handkerchief, and she was kneeling, facing the Madonna and Child. In her hand was a thin, tall candle that she had taken from a box near the altar, and she was busy lighting it. Slowly, every movement a ritual, Naomi placed the candle in the rack with the others burning there and raised her face to the image. Jon could see her lips move, could hear her soft whisper. Sunbeams, colored from the windows, fell on her and bathed her in an amber glow that made him think of the unfinished painting over the altar, the same woman, the same black eyes and gentle mouth, the same profile.

Careful not to disturb her, Jon retreated.

"I'd like to ask you," he said when Ferro looked up at him. "Would you do a portrait of Naomi? Would you paint her for me?"

SHE COMPLAINED A bit, more about the setting than about having to sit still for the sketches.

Cesare had taken them up along the coast to a small beach that was part of a private property belonging, he said, to a friend who wouldn't mind them using it. Half the family had chosen to join them. They brought along a picnic and spent the day watching Ferro make the sketches for a new painting.

Ferro placed her on a rock with her feet in the surf, the hem of her dress trailing in the water. He emptied baskets of flowers around her, where they floated, slowly swirling, gently clashing against her legs and the stone.

Naomi, startled by the movement, looked down and pulled up her knees, trying to keep her balance by putting her hands on the rock at her side.

"Like that," Ferro said. "Don't move."

And that was how he drew her.

The sun was to her side, pouring golden light over her bare arms, reflecting in her hair, gleaming off the white dress Ferro had asked her to wear. It was borrowed from Gemma and too large, but that, he said, added to the charm of the mermaid image because it looked as if she had nicked it from someone's clothesline. He was, Ferro added judiciously, a bit unhappy about her short hair. Surely there were no mermaids with hair chopped off at chin length. Would it be all right if he played around with that?

Jon smiled sadly at those words, and Naomi, seeing it, agreed.

"It used to come down to my hips until last week," she explained when Ferro drew up his eyebrows in question. "I just had it cut. I swear, Ferro, I can still feel the weight sometimes. But I felt it was time for the braid to go."

"You crazy American girls," Angelica threw in. "Here, her hair is a woman's pride. I would never cut mine. It hasn't been short since I was a small girl, only trimmed." She patted the thick chignon at the back of her head, the deep black liberally mixed with gray, as she peered down at Ferro's work.

"You are too thin, my dear, and he's drawing you even thinner. Ferro, don't make her look like a ghost, for goodness sake!"

Ferro looked up from his sketchbook, first at Naomi, then at his mother, then back at Naomi. "She doesn't look like a ghost. She looks like a mermaid: fragile, pale, and precious. If only her hair was longer.."

Naomi rolled her eyes at him.

"If I work fast I might be able to finish it before you go." His lips pursed, Ferro put some strokes on the paper.

Jon got up from where he had been sitting with Gemma and Gloria and peered over Ferro's shoulder. His face softened into a smile at what he saw, and he looked up at Naom i. "You will look like the selkie in the *Secret Garden*, love."

She blushed and pulled up her shoulders, but he laughed. "I'll put it in my studio, right over the piano where I can always see it. I'm so glad we came."

His heart light, his spirit soaring, Jon gazed at the mountains rising in vineyard terraces behind them, at the clusters of bougainvillea growing over the cliffs like a pink carpet. He couldn't remember when he had last felt this happy, this carefree. He found himself thanking Olaf for putting the idea of coming here in their heads.

Even now he felt he owed Naomi's father thanks for making things easy for once, for sending the jet without conditions and without asking. "Just bring it back when you're done." Jon's eyes had nearly rolled backward in his head at those words. He recalled so well how bitterly they had fought when Naomi had been shot, how he had thrown Olaf out of the hospital, so scared for her life, so mindless of hurting others.

Now his gaze wandered to the water, and at last he allowed those memories to surface. He had come home from the hospital a day after she had woken from her coma, unwillingly and against his instincts, but Solveigh and Sal had insisted. They had pushed him out of the ICU and told him to go home and get some rest, eat a hot meal, and for heaven's sake, shave and take a shower. Dazed, exhausted like never before, he had let Sal drive him home. The house had seemed deserted without her—an echoing, empty cave, no soul, no love, no warmth—and he had crawled into their bed and hugged her pillow, inhaling the elusive scent of her perfume.

"This will be a big painting." Ferro woke him from his thoughts. "I hope you have a fireplace to hang it over. Or better yet, a hallway."

"We have both," Jon replied, easily, "but I want it for myself. Just for me; it will be mine to dream over."

The dress had slipped from Naomi's shoulder, and she tried to pull it up again; but Ferro waved his pencil at her and called, "No. no, that's perfect, leave it," and she did.

"Everyone is allowed to eat and drink," Naomi complained, "and I have to sit here and watch. It's so unfair."

"I will feed you when you're done, "Jon promised. "No worries. I'll take care of you." He bent down to roll up his jeans and waded toward her, water sloshing onto his pants, soaking them. "I saw you yesterday when you went into the church. You prayed," he said softly when he was close to her.

She nodded. From the stone beside her, she picked up a hibiscus blossom that had fallen there.

"You prayed to the Holy Mother. You prayed for a baby, didn't you?" There was no response.

"Naomi, my love," Jon said, but she laid her hand on his arm and shook her head.

"Don't, Jon. It just happened. All of a sudden there was this urge to go inside and light that candle, to say thanks for what we have and to ask, if it isn't too much, and just for your sake, to atone for what I did to you in taking Joshua away, to ask for another child. I came out and back to you, and it felt as if a huge load had been lifted from me. I saw you and Cesare and Ferro sitting under the trees, chatting, drinking wine; and the sea was so beautiful in the distance. For the first time since the shooting I felt at peace." A smile curled her mouth. "I still had that scent of incense in my nose, and the sun was hot and good on my face, and I was happy."

"Good." It sounded stupid and not nearly as enthusiastic as he felt, but it was the best that Jon could come up with. "Well, good." And before he could say more, Ferro told him to go away because he was disturbing the light.

JON WAS LEARNING that things were different here. There wasn't a lot of privacy, but no one seemed to mind. The house was always full of people, always someone coming or going, and somehow it seemed there was always a meal going on or being prepared. Most of life took place outside, on the big terrace, under the trellises, or around the pool, one step farther down the mountainside, in the shade of the pine trees.

Cesare had given him a tour of the house when they got back from the beach. They had strolled through the high-ceilinged rooms with antique furniture and tiled floors, paintings on the walls, beds hung with draperies, flowers on the tables. Everywhere, the windows or doors stood open to let the air flow through the home. Lace curtains were stirring in the warm breeze. Jon could hear the rustling of foliage and the breath of the sea all the time.

There was no air conditioning; the heat was dry and easy to live with, just like in California.

"You are always welcome here," Cesare said when they returned downstairs to search for coffee. "You are part of this family, and very welcome. We are proud to have a musician like you married to one of our women."

Jon blinked. "But you said you didn't even know my music."

Naomi was sitting with her cousins, all of them busy shelling peas at the table in the center of the kitchen, her bare feet propped on the chair next to her. She was still in the dress she had worn for the painting, the wide skirt gathered between her knees; with the bowl in her lap she looked like a peasant girl.

"But I will, soon." Cesare grinned at Jon at he took mocha cups from the shelf. "And anyway, it doesn't matter. Ferro says the world loves you, and if that's so, then you make many people happy with your songs. And that's what matters, isn't it? To bring happiness into the world with what you do. One way or the other, that's what we all have to do."

A happy tune, a summer song, one that would make people want to hum and dance, with words as light and easy as whipped cream, Jon thought. Something about a moonlit night and a meadow warmed from the long hours of sun.

He took the tiny coffee cup from Cesare and wandered away, out onto the terrace to where the breeze from the ocean ruffled his hair and stroked his face.

Like a storm calming, like surf settling after the storm, Jon felt his soul coming to rest at last.

chapter 27

THE PAINTING WASN'T finished before they left. Ferro apologized, saying he needed a little more time for details. He had ordered more pigments—he wanted to get it just right—and no, Naomi could not see it. He took them up to the chapel one more time at her request, and this time she lit a candle in front of the Annunciation picture. She stood gazing at it for a long time, long enough for Ferro to start fussing with his brushes and Jon to return outside into the sun.

Naomi thought it was miraculous how, by just applying the right color, Ferro had brought light into the painting. It seemed to flow over Mary's hands, bathe her face in the soft glow, and now that she looked carefully, Naomi could see that it was not coming from the lamp she was holding at all but from another source altogether. Catching her breath, she took a step back to get a better view.

"Ferro," she said, "you have caught the angel's ray. It is his light shining on her."

"Well, yes." He put down the jar he was holding. "That's the point, isn't it? That's what the Annunciation is all about."

"I wonder what she felt." Naomi's voice echoed through the church. "I wonder what she thought when that light poured into that dim room and the angel spoke to her. Was she scared, do you think?"

Ferro peered at his artwork. "Well, I should think so. I know I would be scared if that happened to me. I'd sooner believe it was an alien than God's angel, I think. It is rather hard to accept, isn't it? There's an illuminated something standing in your cellar door and it   tells you you're going to have a baby and no, no sex. Ha."

That made her laugh, but her attention was drawn back to the image of Mary. The gentle sweetness of the face touched her unaccountably. "This painting makes me feel so strange. It makes me sad, yet happy. It fills me with a strange yearning and makes me want to spill my heart into her hands."

Out of sheer impulse, Naomi hugged her cousin. "Thank you, Ferro. Thank you for painting this, and thank you for letting me see it."

"Ah, it's nothing." Embarrassed, he patted her shoulder. "This chapel, it is a pilgrimage place. Is that what you call it in English?"

She nodded, and he went on, "Women have always come here to pray to the Virgin. They come to pray for a man, then later, when they are about to get married, they pray for happiness and health." He turned and pointed at the other picture, the one with the Christ Child. "But mostly they come here to ask for babies. They walk up from town and bring flowers, light candles, and pray for children."

The pain hung in her throat like a million unshed tears.

"Does it work?" she asked. "Do they have babies after coming here?"

"That's what they say, yes. I don't know." A small laugh escaped him. "I'm not married. No girl wants to marry me."

Astounded, Naomi looked up at him, but he shrugged. "No woman wants to be second to my art. I've tried it, but it doesn't work. There always comes a point when they demand more attention, more love, and I can't give it. My greatest love, my beloved mistress, will always be painting. My wife would have to learn to take second place." Distracted by Jon coming back, he moved away from her and busied himself with his supplies once more.

"I wish," Naomi said to Jon when he walked up to her, "I wish I could take that painting away with me, the Annunciation one. I wish I could look at it all the time. It's so beautiful it makes me want to cry." Her arms wandered around his waist. "I can feel what she feels, Jon, I can feel the shock, and the revelation and fear, and yes, the joy. He has caught it all, hasn't he?"

Jon laid his chin on the top of her head and contemplated the picture. "Yes, he has. He's a wonderful artist. You should see your portrait. Ferro isn't asking anything for it, says it's our wedding gift; but I'm going to write him one big, fat check."

Naomi didn't reply. There were other ways, she was certain, of thanking Ferro. New York was full of galleries, and no one would send Jon Stone away without at least listening to him. She decided to keep this thought to herself until she had seen the mermaid painting though.

NAOMI DIDN'T WANT to leave. She walked through the house and the park, where she took off her sandals to feel the prickly carpet of pine needles under her soles. Their sharp scent was released with every step she took, and as she moved up the hill and farther into the grove it grew quieter around her, the heat of the day cooling, getting mustier.

When she looked back she could not see the house anymore, or the ocean and the sky. It was just she and the canopy of trees. No birdsong, no cicadas, nothing. Like a tiny melody, a gentle hum, the memory of her coma dreams crept back. She recalled the mossy forest in which she had found herself, and how she had found peace and healing there, and the gentle, calming presence of that other being.

With a sigh, her heart light, Naomi sank down on the ground, her back to one of the huge boles, and breathed in the aroma.

One more day, one last day of reprieve, and then they would have to return, finish the tour, settle in New York and start work on the musical.

Her dream, they were realizing her dream.

She raked her fingers through her locks, felt their ends curls at the back of her neck, then rubbed her hands over her bare knees. They were brown now, after three weeks under the southern sun, with a white ribbon under her rings. Her arms had taken on a golden tan, and they looked less bony, sleeker.

Tentatively, Naomi pulled up her dress and stretched out her legs.

She had gained weight. It wasn't a whole lot, but she did not look as thin as a stick anymore; her shape was coming back.

That morning, standing in front of the bathroom mirror, she had inspected the scar—her zipper, as she called it bitterly—and found that it was indeed fading. The angry red was a pale pink, and it was no more than a fine line. Jon and Kevin had seen to that. They had made sure only the best plastic surgeons touched her, and the care afterward had been ever so thorough. For the first time in six months she could look at her body and not feel disgusted or angry at herself for being disfigured, no longer perfect, not beautiful enough for Jon.

Once, only once, had she taken out the replica of the dress she had worn that night at the Oscars, so lovingly made for her by her designer.

Jon had not been at home; no one had been at home when she had gone upstairs and opened the wardrobe where she kept all her evening gowns, all those lovely clothes Jon had bought for her over time. Her heart had beaten hard when she touched the cream satin, ran her fingers over the dainty embroidery, and recalled how she had stood on that stage, the statuette in her hand, her own Oscar. Jon had laughed at her and pressed her sweaty palm.

Naomi remembered so well how she had felt. The applause had hit her like a wave, and she had soaked it in, ridden that wave, felt the ecstasy of success. For a few seconds, no longer than a heartbeat or two, there had been no doubt, no fear, and she had felt whole.

She had not allowed herself to go any further into that memory. She had held on to the moment of glory and had not followed the path into the darkness and pain that had come right after.

But now, in the warm shade of the pine trees, Naomi carefully opened that door and, for the first time since it had happened, sought out the details of that night, watched it happen, without being inundated in fear and panic.

She remembered being in Jon's arms and kissing him, the Oscar statuette heavy and cool in her hand, and all those people standing around them; and for once she had not cared. Quite clearly she recalled how she had felt walking toward the waiting car, Sal and Sean with her. There had been such lightness, such simple joy in that instant; nothing had really mattered except where they would get a glass of champagne.

And then…Naomi wrapped her arms around her knees and laid her cheek on them.

The taste of blood. That was the worst memory. She had never told anyone, but the sudden taste of blood as it filled her mouth, choking her, spilling over her face, that had been the worst.

THERE WAS MOVEMENT down the hill, and she sighed. He would come after her, always worried, always afraid she had run away again.

"I'm here, Jon," she called, and he came to her.

Naomi looked up at him when he stopped. Jon looked good, rested, tan. His shirt was half open, and he was in Bermudas, barefoot too. He had not shaved, and the black stubble gave him a slightly sinister appearance, which she found very endearing. There was no gray there yet, not one single hair, not in his beard or on his head, and not on his chest either.

"You look nice," she said, "really nice. You look as if your skin would taste of sun."

"Want to try?" He dropped down beside her. "What are you doing here all by yourself? Your cousins are missing you. And, I have to say, I like to see you hang out with them. All of you together, you seem too good to be true. It's like being in a candy store."

She slapped his arm, but it was halfhearted.

"This is a nice place you found here, so quiet." Jon leaned against the tree. "I want to go for a swim. How about you?"

"I was thinking of the shooting."

That made him sit up and look at her, but she smiled and laid her hand on his chest.

"It's okay, Jon. I'm okay. I was thinking of our kiss, and the dress, and how wonderful it felt to be up on that stage and receive the Oscar. You know, with all the horror and pain, it is so easy to push the good part away. But there was a good part to that night, a very good part, and I don't want to forget that."

His skin was warm under her fingers. "I liked receiving that award. I liked it a lot. For a moment I felt important and special, not like myself at all but like somebody who gave something good to the world."

"Which you did, you silly chick. That's what I keep telling you." He wrapped his arms around her. "I keep telling you, over and over again. Come here, kiss me. Now that you mentioned that kiss at the Oscars…"

"Oh Jon, be serious." Gently, she pushed him back. "Just for one more minute? I promise to kiss you then, but let me say this first."

"That better not be an empty promise, my sweet dove. That house is full of girls." But he let her go, settling her on his thighs, and waited for her to speak.

"Do you really think I could write a book, Jon?" Naomi asked.

He dropped his hands from her waist. "Yes, of course I do. Why do you need to ask?"

She pulled up her shoulders. "It takes so much time. And what if it never turns out to be a success, if no one wants to read it? Then how do I justify all the time I spent on it?"

Jon laughed. "You don't. You don't justify anything. You do what you have to do. It's as easy as that, Naomi, and you should know that by now. Can I choose not to write music? Not a chance. Did you put away the lyrics when we were apart? You didn't. Did you ever ask yourself, when you came home from a day at work and you sat down to write another of your forlorn love songs, why you were doing it? Did you step back from yourself and wonder why you kept writing them even though no one got to see them?"

"Well, no…" Her fingers were playing with the buttons of his shirt, opening one after another. "But I didn't write them because I felt compelled to write; I wrote them because I was thinking of you."

"Not so." He caught her hands in his. "Stop that. You're distracting me. You wrote them because you were compelled to put your feelings and thoughts into words. That's a big difference. There are lots of broken hearts out there, but they don't all turn into poets. So the question here is, How can you not, at long last, start the writer's life you were meant to lead all along? Anyway, I thought we were done with this discussion. Why did we go out and buy that computer in Hamburg?"

"Yes. Yes, we are done." She felt stupid, childish, for bringing it up again. "I'll just start and see where it leads me."

"Kiss me," Jon said. "Come on, kiss me."

Surprised, she leaned forward and put her lips to his, but he did not move, did not respond.

She pulled back. "Jon!"

He did not react and just gazed steadily at her. Again she kissed him, but he remained passive and didn't even touch her.

"Jon, damn you! If you want to be kissed, then…then do something!" Naomi took his face between her hands and kissed him, pushing against the barrier of his teeth until his mouth opened. It felt strange, intoxicating, powerful, to be in command for a change when it was always Jon who dictated their lovemaking. She liked it that way, liked to yield to him; but this was heady, wild. Straddling his legs, she opened his shirt and ran her hands down his chest, all the way down to the waistband of his shorts, and tugged.

Jon grasped her wrists. "Right. So you're not afraid to go after what you want at all if you want it badly enough, you little beast. Seducing me here in your uncle's garden!"

"You're impossible." She felt hot, flushed, and quite embarrassed.

"Yeah, impossible. Nice kiss, my sweet dove. I think we should do this more often; I really like being eaten up by you." Tenderly Jon pushed her hair behind her ear. "Go on and write that stupid book already. Stop fretting about it. I promise, it will be okay. You don't have to justify what you do with your time. Not to me, not to anyone." Another thought occurred to him. "Do I justify the hours I spend in the studio, composing? I've never heard you complain about that."

"Oh, but that's different." Naomi's mind was still on the kiss, and where it might have led. "You're successful, famous; you've made your way. You know whatever you put out will be loved by your audience."

"Yes, now, thirty years after I started out. But the point is, Naomi, I did start out. I didn't worry about justification or acceptance. I did what

I had to do. And now it's finally your turn to do what you have to do."

Jon rose and pulled her up with him. "You're on a good path. You give me the lyrics I want, and you wrote the script for the musical. Now it's time for you to do something on your own. Something not connected to me."

"And what if no one wants it? What if I don't find a publisher?"

Jon brushed some pine needles off his legs. "I think, my dear, the danger of that happening is minute."

chapter 28

JON HAD THE pilot fly them into Newark. He grinned at Naomi after the plane had taken off. "You wanted to see New Jersey. Here's your chance."

Leaving Positano had been sad; he was leaving a family he never knew he had. Seeing Naomi's face when she hugged Cesare and Angelica at the airport, he knew she felt the same way. Piece by piece he was picking one brick after another from the wall she had hidden herself behind for so long.

Seeing her now as she peered out of the window at the blue stretch of ocean below, Jon said, "We'll go back soon. We have to. I loved every minute."

She smiled. "And bring Joshua. I could still kick myself for not making him come. He'd have loved it, I'm certain."

Jon was sure it was probably true. Joshua would have loved it, and he would have clamored even louder than Naomi for a Vespa. He could just see his son on one of them, throwing himself down the serpentines.

"We'll bring him next year. I'm thinking we should come back in spring, when it's not quite so hot and we can see the almond trees in bloom. Ferro was raving about that. It's supposed to be very pretty."

Ferro had taken him to his rooms high up under the roof of the palazzo where he kept his paintings and where he had set up his studio.

Among the many canvasses, Jon had found a smaller version of the Annunciation, a perfect copy of the mural. He had asked Ferro to sell it to him. It would be shipped with Naomi's portrait, and he could hardly wait for her reaction, to see the delight on her face.

There hadn't been much time to talk about the house in Brooklyn, and even less to furnish and decorate it. He had to admit that he hadn't cared a lot until now. Buying those paintings had changed his attitude.

"The house."

Naomi stopped tucking the blanket around her legs.

"I'm sure you've planned every room of the Brooklyn house, haven't you?" Jon asked.

"No. Not really. The living room and the bedroom will be finished when we get there, and the kitchen, more or less. Why?"

He had learned, watching her run the hotel in Halmar, not to be surprised at the ease and tempo with which she got these things done.

"Because, little beast, you need a study. You need a place for yourself, to write, to work. Where would you want that to be?"

For the longest time she didn't respond but looked out at the clouds.

"There is one room upstairs, next to the bedroom—" her voice so low that Jon had to lean forward to hear her—"a corner room with a small balcony. It looks out toward lower Manhattan and the Statue of Liberty. I wanted it to be a nursery. But I guess…" She wiped her cheek with the back of her hand. "I guess I might as well turn it into a study."

"A room with a balcony is not a really good choice for a nursery anyway, is it?" He managed to return her gaze steadily enough. "We will have to choose a different room for the nursery."

"Yes." A defeated sigh, nothing more, but the ghost of a smile played at the corners of her mouth. "Yes, you are right. A balcony is not good for a nursery."

She fell silent again.

The flight attendant came to serve drinks, and she asked for bourbon.

NEWARK GREETED THEM with the relentless humidity of an August afternoon.

Naomi stepped out of the plane and stopped in her tracks. She gasped at the hot air; it was as wet as a hot towel right out of the washing machine.

There was no blue in the sky. It shone like a dirty aluminum bowl, the sun hidden in the haze. There was no breeze, no relief. The clothes stuck to her.

Jon gave her a dismal grin. "Newark, baby. It's what you wanted to see."

Naomi stood on the tarmac waiting for Sal to pick them up and tried to take a breath. It felt like inhaling water, pretty foul-tasting water too. The sky, low and gray, hung over the landscape like a dirty dishrag; the tepid breeze touched her face as if the fingers of a middle-aged mermaid were trying to caress her. From the distance, she could hear sirens, police cars howling by on one of the convoluted highways, the echo dropping onto the street.

A black SUV stopped right in front of them. Sal got out. "I wanted," he said, "to get you coffee and doughnuts. Give you a proper New

Jersey welcome, but there was a long line outside Dunkin' Donuts." He picked up their luggage and put it into the trunk.

Without looking in the rearview mirror, he pulled away from the curb and entered a maelstrom of roads, loops upon loops. "I'm taking you," Sal announced cheerfully, "on the Pulaski Skyway so you get a good idea of where you are right away. This is New Jersey, Naomi, and I'm betting you've never seen anything like it."

It was true.

She stared at the scarred, dismal, dingy landscape spreading in every direction: rusty towers and high chimneys; a desolate wasteland of decrepit industrial yards; inlets of water, their limpid, oily waves sucking at dead, marshy earth; and highway bridges in the distance, their iron girders whale skeletons stranded in a world of refuse. Incredibly, there were houses, islands of life, sprinkled around this apocalyptic scene, fingers of suburbia undaunted by the surroundings. She wondered how children grew up there in the midst of this nightmare. Were there parks she couldn't see, some pockets of green, some semblance of gardens, trees, flowers. All she could see from here was gray, brown, black, and dead.

"There," Sal pointed into the distance.

Hovering like a spaceship, the skyline of Manhattan rose above the nightmare of New Jersey.

Naomi gripped the back of Jon's seat, excited, elated, her heart calling out to the glittering towers, certain she was hearing their answering echo, welcoming her back. She could hardly wait for them to dip into the Holland Tunnel and resurface in the city. Her heart was beating fast.

"You and this city," Jon said fondly, "I wonder why you didn't think to come here earlier."

"Me too." She touched his shoulder. "We're getting a box at the Met, aren't we? For the season?"

"Yes, yes." He laughed. "I'll try my best, but it may be hard. No promises, love."

"I know you'll get them to give you one. You have to. Use all your charm and fame and clout and whatever, but I want to go to the Met."

"Oh, that's different," Sal said. "Getting you to the Met now and then is not a problem. Getting you a permanent box will be hard."

"I don't care. I just want to go. And to opening nights, too, so we get to dress up, Jon."

They left the tunnel. Despite the heat Naomi lowered the tinted window and breathed in the humid air, a bright smile on her face. She felt safe, wanted, as if the town had been waiting for her. Even the dingy street vendors and cheap shops on Canal Street seemed to sparkle; and when they stopped at a red light, she smiled so sweetly at a young man hawking fake Gucci purses that he stepped back from the curb in confusion.

"Stop that!" Sal closed the window. "He'll think we're the freaking FBI or something. Or he'll think he can have your credit cards! This is New York, for crying out loud; you can't just smile at people!"

"I can," Naomi replied, "and I will. You just wait and see; no one will harm me."

With a groan, Sal threw her a glare through the rearview mirror. "This is a huge mistake. You in this city, big mistake."

She looked back at the skyline when they crossed the Brooklyn Bridge, at the twin towers of the World Trade Center casting their long shadows over the other buildings in the setting sun.

"I don't think it's a mistake," Naomi whispered. "I think it's just right."

NO ONE WAS waiting for them when they entered their new home. It was dim and cool inside, and smelled a bit of sawdust and paint; but it was clean and neat, and quite empty.

Jon dropped the bag he was carrying on the wooden floor and looked around. He hadn't been here since Christmas, since their first look at the inside, and could hardly remember details. So much had happened since then.

"There was not much time," Naomi said; "I couldn't do a whole lot. We'll have to decide what we want soon or this place won't be habitable."

In the living room there was a couch, a couple of chairs, and a rug, but that was it. The kitchen looked as empty as if it was a store display; there wasn't even a coffeemaker.

"Here." She opened a pocket door and stepped aside to let him see.

The Steinway was brand-new. It stood in front of the bay window; its lacquer shone in the slanting sun beams. There was a desk facing the window with a view of the Promenade and the city, a chair, bookcases, guitar stands, and on top of the grand, a stack of music sheets and his favorite, black pencils. In the bay window, on the broad bench in the niche, lay a load of colorful, soft cushions and a cashmere blanket; a small pile of books rested on a small table, a coffee cup beside them. A lovely blue carpet covered part of the dark hardwood floor.

"A Steinway." Jon realized it sounded stupid, but he couldn't come up with anything else.

"Yes." Naomi was leaning against the wall, her hands behind her back, her feet crossed, just the way she had stood when she had first shown him her apartment in Halmar and given him the time to look around and explore her life. Only this time there was a smile on her face, and the rosy tint of expectation.

"How…" He didn't even know what to ask. Carefully he opened the piano and let his fingers glide over the pristine, smooth keys. "You weren't even gone that long."

"Do you like it?"

"Like it? Are you crazy?" The tone, when he played a chord, was clear and true; it hummed through the space and lingered under the high ceiling like its own memory. "You leave me there in LA, and you don't tell me where you're going or when you'll be back; and then you come here to this empty house, and the first thing you do is buy a freaking Steinway and furnish a studio for me?"

"Well, it was the second thing," she admitted. "The first thing I bought was a bed."

"A bed. You left me in agony, in exile, and you buy a Steinway grand and a bed. Is it big enough for two?"

"It is." A small laugh escaped her. "You are so transparent."

Jon moved through the room, exploring it. He picked up the books to read their titles, touched the mug and noted the dry residue of coffee in it. Half hidden under the blanket, he saw a pink wool sock. "Did you sit here? During your exile, when you were here, did you sit in this window seat all by yourself?"

"I had to watch them paint the ceiling," Naomi replied. "I didn't want them to ruin the stucco."

There were no curtains up yet, and the panes were grimy on the outside. On the patio Jon could see some potted plants, but they were dry, dead; and the small piece of lawn in the backyard needed trimming badly. The brick barbecue was full of leaves from last fall. It would take a lot to make this place shine. "Let me get this straight. These were the most important things to you? The Steinway, and a studio for me?"

"After the bed."

"Yeah, after the bed. There isn't even a coffeemaker, Naomi, and you buy a Steinway?" The stool was just the right height for him; and when he sat down, his hands on the keys, he could see the entire panorama of Manhattan spread out before him: the bridge and its graceful Gothic arches, the river, and the skyline of New York.

She leaned on the piano and looked down at him. Gently she touched his wrist, sighing, smiling. "I can't imagine anything more important, Jon, nothing at all."

"Not even a coffeemaker?"

"Not even a coffeemaker, you silly man."

They walked through the rooms together, hand in hand, exploring every corner of their new home, opening closets and doors and even exploring the musty basement. The house was not as large as the mansion in Malibu, and not as airy, as generous; but it was beautiful in a totally different way with the wooden floors and ornate doorways, the plaster ceilings and the stained glass in the high parlor windows, where Naomi stopped.

"This is where we will put the Christmas tree." She pointed at a space beside the fireplace. "Right there. We need so much for this place, Jon."

"We can go shopping as soon as we're over the jet lag." He put his arm around her waist. "Show me your new bed."

AS A BOY, living with his parents only one block away, Jon had dreamed of owning this house, of using the upstairs room they were entering now as his studio. He had imagined himself stepping out onto the large stone balcony to get a breath of air after working for hours and seeing the city spread out before him. Now, entering behind Naomi, he had to smile at himself. There was no way anyone would have been able to lug a Steinway up the stairs and no way it would have fit through the door. Fondly, he turned the memory of those dreams over and then let go of them.

"It's not much yet," Naomi was saying. "I did all I could, but time was really short, and..." She straightened a fold in the satin quilt on the bed. "And I was in a hurry because I wanted to be back with you. When I left you in LA, when I called you from the airport to tell you where I'd be going, I promised myself not to stay away longer than those three weeks but not to come back sooner either. I wanted it to hurt."

"For God's sake, why?" Sometimes her reasoning was just too much to take.

"Because," she answered softly, "because I wanted the yearning for you to be greater than the pain of the shooting. I wanted to feel the need to fly back into your arms, hear your voice, see your smile. And it worked. That guy on the plane when I flew to London, that reporter, he kept pushing his champagne on me; and all I wanted to do was fall asleep and make the time pass until I could be with you and kiss you. God, I wanted to slap his face."

She walked over to the balcony door. "Here. I want a small couch here, or a settee or something, so I can sit and read or dream and look out at New York. And then, when you're in your studio right below me, I can listen to you play."

He liked the way the bed looked. The sheets were new, cream, fine linen; and there were enough pillows for his taste.

"Your mom was here," Naomi explained. "I asked her to come. I think she also filled the fridge, but we're supposed to go over soon."

Jon knew. He had called Helen while Naomi had been busy breathing in Manhattan from the car. They were expected for dinner, and no excuses. They would walk over; take a stroll through Brooklyn Heights on a summer evening.

Looking out at the dusk, at Manhattan beginning to glitter with the myriad lights in the windows, Naomi beside him, he felt as if he had come a long way to end up where he had started out. Only it didn't feel bad at all. In fact, it felt as perfect as he could imagine.

chapter 29

JOSHUA WASN'T THERE.

"He told me this morning he wasn't coming home for dinner," Helen said, taking a bowl of potato salad out to the table in the backyard. "Said he knew you were coming back but he'd been invited by his other grandparents, and he would see you later."

Naomi, who had been just picked up the plates, set them back down and leaned, her hands on the kitchen counter. She could hear Jon's reply. His voice was quite gravelly, anger swinging in it. "He doesn't think he should be here when his parents get back?"

"Don't blame the messenger, Jon. He called a couple of hours ago. What was I supposed to do?" Helen came back into the kitchen and stopped, seeing Naomi. "Was I supposed to tell him to come home? He's not a kid anymore. He's nearly eighteen, and as headstrong as both of you. He's just returned from LA, where you let him go on his own, his bodyguard in trail. Do you think I'd be able to tell him where to have dinner?"

"But he was with Harry in LA; he wasn't on his own." Naomi sat down at the kitchen table and propped her elbows on it. "Jon didn't let him travel on his own. He went on a private plane, and Harry and Grace picked him up at the airport, and he was staying at their house, well protected."

"You and your private planes, your security men and high fences!" With a huff, Helen pulled open the fridge door and peered inside. "You are so far removed from normalcy, you and Jon, you don't even realize it. You just breeze through life and do as you please. That jaunt to Italy? Maybe you should have come home instead and looked after Joshua yourself."

"But we wanted him to come, and he refused! He said he didn't care for Italy, and he wanted to meet his friends. Are we supposed to trail after him when he goes surfing with Harry's kids? He's nearly grown up!" Helen's words stung badly. "And we don't breeze through life? Jon was working! He did a show nearly every other night in Europe!"

"Yes, yes. I know." Helen dumped a bag of oranges on the table. "I know. And I'm sorry, Naomi. I know your life was anything but a breeze recently. I just feel so bad about this. I know I should have made him come home to greet you. But…" She smelled one of the oranges. "He was hell-bent on meeting his grandfather. Said they had things to do and to talk about. Don't ask me. That boy of yours is just like his father."

Jon, walking in just then, got a dark glance from her.

"He was like that when he was Josh's age. Secretive, determined, obsessive. I never knew what he was up to."

"Well, we do know what Joshua is up to, thanks to Kurt." Jon ignored Helen's words. His phone was in his hand. "Joshua is at your hotel, with your parents, in the dining room; and three waiters are dancing attendance on him. They are spoiling him rotten."

"Which, I can tell you, isn't happening here," Helen threw in tartly. "I make him take out the trash like any other teenager."

"I didn't raise him to be a pop star either."

Both Helen and Jon turned to look at Naomi.

"I didn't raise him to live a jet-set life. Our life in Halmar was pretty small, and very quiet. Until I sent him to boarding school, which I had to do." She pulled down the corners of her mouth, ready to cry. "And that wasn't easy. It wasn't easy at all; but he has all that talent, and I didn't want him to waste it."

"I know, baby, I know." Jon reached out to caress her hair. "I know you always did what was best for Joshua, regardless of your own feelings. Please don't be sad. I'll have a talk with him later."

Just then the bell rang, and Helen went to open the door to Kevin, Jon's brother, and his wife, Sarah.

Naomi rose from her chair with a sigh and rubbed her cheeks. "Get the steaks, Jon," she said. "They'll be hungry."

SHE WAS LISTENING to the conversation with only one ear, her mind on the empty chair where Joshua should have been sitting. Ethan, Kevin's son, wasn't there either. It made Naomi feel old, forlorn, left behind. Listlessly she picked at the steak on her plate; normally her favorite food, but now she couldn't eat it. She watched some moths dance around the candles on the table and breathed in the humid summer air. It had a wet, stuffy smell to it, like an old cellar, hot as a sauna, heavy like clay. It hadn't even cooled off now that it was night.

Jet lag was pulling on her limbs. Not even traveling in a private plane, on their own itinerary, eased the exhaustion of crossing all those time zones.

Jon, beside her, looked tired too. In the murky light she could see fine lines around his mouth, and the skin under his eyes looked gray, smudged.

"So we're throwing this party," Kevin said, "to celebrate our anniversary, and we were wondering if we could make you come? We would like the family there too."

There was a brief pause before Jon replied.

"Sure," he then answered. "Yes, right, darling? Of course we'll be there."

Kevin opened another beer. "I realize it's not something you usually do, Jon. There will be a lot of people you don't know, and you being who you are..." He handed the bottle to Jon, who took it with a nod of thanks. "But after all is said and done you're still my brother, and we want you and your family there. Twenty-five years of marriage is a big deal."

"Yeah, it is." Jon took a sip.

"We considered going on a cruise but then decided to throw a really big party instead," Sarah added. "I wanted that. Everyone goes on a cruise. I want a ball at an elegant hotel."

"Which one did you pick?" Naomi hardly dared to ask, and Sarah replied, "Oh, your parents' place, of course! Actually it was Joshua and Ethan who had the idea, and your father was delighted. And the setting, Naomi, just think! We'll be overlooking the Met!"

"Yes." Sadness as deep as the ocean and as cold as new frost, threatened to overwhelm her.

"I've been meaning to ask this," Kevin went on. "Jon, do you even have any friends outside show biz? Do you meet other people besides the ones you work with?"

"You asked me nearly the same thing last year," Jon replied, his voice quiet and deep. "Funny you should return to this. No, I don't have any friends outside show biz." He stopped and stared out into the darkness of the yard. "Naomi's cousin Ferro and I were talking about this the other day, in his studio. He said his life was gradually getting lonelier. There is the family, some fellow artists, and that's basically it. I know what he means; I know what he's talking about."

"What do you mean?" Sarah watched him curiously, her head tilted and her mouth pursed, making her look even more bird-like than usual.

"Something weird happens when you have success." Pushing away from the table, Jon lit a cigarette. Helen clucked at him, but he ignored it and gave her a guilty smirk in return. "The world shifts. The moment you announce that you've made it, signed your first deal, the world shifts. There is no other way to put it." He got up and began to pace, his head lowered, as if he was trying to gather his thoughts before he could speak. "I've often thought about this. I've tried to write songs about it, but there were never the right words; it always sounded like whining." He took another drag on his cigarette. "Which, well, it is."

"What do you mean, 'the world shifts'? Are you off on one of your songwriter tangents, Jon? You know I never get that stuff." There were some Italian sausages on the grill, and Kevin went to get them. Their aroma reminded Naomi of Positano, of the parties on the terrace and the sweetness of the nights there, compared to the oppressiveness of Brooklyn. She needed, she decided, lots of flowers for the garden of their new house, lots of Mediterranean flowers in terra-cotta pots.

"As long as you're a nobody, struggling, hoping, your old friends will stick to you. But then, once you have some success…I don't know." Impatiently, Jon tossed the cigarette into the ashtray Helen had brought out for him. "It's almost as if your old friends think you don't need or want them anymore once you are a success and get a slice of that fame so many are after. There's all this talk of people leaving everything behind once they get famous and all that; but believe me, it works the other way around too. It's like…" His hands shaped his thoughts in the air. "It's like walking on a path, and when you take that certain turn in the road, some people won't go on with you. And I don't know why. I don't think I've changed that much." He shrugged. "Yeah, I mean, of course I've changed; I'm not a kid anymore, but I'm not a totally different person either." More animated, he sat down again, pierced one of the sausages, and took a bite. "Do you remember Declan from high school? The guy I used to hang out with all the time; the one who would cheer me on like no one else? We would go to the football games, and he'd come downtown whenever I had a gig."

Kevin nodded.

"Well, a couple of months after I signed my first record deal, he told me he didn't want to hang with me anymore because all I did was talk about the studio and the recordings and stuff. He said it in a very friendly and regretful way; but he did say it, and it hurt. I couldn't understand why my breakthrough would change anything. Why being a successful artist would turn me into someone else in my friends' eyes. I don't know. Declan was the worst though. We had been so close, real buddies. We had a great time. And then he dropped me just like that." His hand hovered over the plate with the meat, and he picked out a kebab skewer. "It felt like being punished. It felt like being punished for being successful. And yeah…" The pieces of pork dropped onto his plate when he pushed them off the metal, right into the ketchup. "I've been careful with people outside the biz ever since. I'm not going to waste my time on useless friendships. They don't understand anyway. They don't understand the way we live. They think it's all song and dance and glitzy parties. The work part, the loneliness, the many silent hours spent working on the songs—that they don't see. The drive to be creative, to shape something new—they can't understand that. They only see the stage, the opening nights, the tuxedoes and evening gowns."

Jon stopped talking to pop a tomato into his mouth and wash it down with a good swallow of beer.

"What did Ferro say?" Naomi asked. Everyone was looking at Jon, Helen with a trace of sadness in her face, Kevin in puzzlement, and Sarah with disbelief.

"Ferro?" The bottle empty, Jon placed it on the ground beside his chair. "He said much the same thing. How friendship and love turned into admiration, and admiration into distance. How the expectation that you would move away into stardom made people pull back when you yourself don't mean to distance yourself. And how he stood by and watched in amazement how that happened to him after his first exhibition in Rome. That instead of cementing old friendships, it killed them."

Naomi recalled her own chat with Ferro, when he had told her how hard it was to fit both his art and love into one life, and she lowered her head to gaze at her wedding ring and the diamond Jon had given her that day in London when he had asked her to marry him.

"So yeah, I don't have friends outside the music business." A small, bitter laugh escaped Jon. "Hell, I don't have a lot of friends at all, for that matter. Well, I do, but not buddy friends. Not friends who'd laze on the couch with me on a Saturday afternoon, order in pizza, and watch football."

"Ferro said he had no place for a woman in his life." Naomi's words made him shift so he could see her better.

"No wonder. He hides in that studio under the roof or that church of his all day long." Jon laughed. "I wonder if he can even look at a woman without seeing a potential model in her."

She smiled at him. "You're not like that. You have enough space for a wife."

"Yes." He took her hand in his. "But I don't think I'd be married if it wasn't for you. I don't think I could tolerate anyone else in my life day in day out. I need a woman who would buy a Steinway grand for me before buying a coffeemaker for herself."

"But Jon—" Naomi leaned toward him, ignoring the rest of the family— "you would buy a coffeemaker for me before getting a piano for yourself."

"Yes. Yes. I would. I'd buy you the best espresso machine in the world."

He bent forward to plant his lips lightly on hers until Helen said, "We get it. You may stop, Jon, please. Why don't you go and get us some wine from the fridge instead, please. There's a good boy."

"See?" Jon sighed, rising. "At least here I'm still my old, normal self. Mom always has errands for me to run."

chapter 30

JOSHUA DROPPED BY the next afternoon, just like any high school kid coming home and expecting lunch.

They were sitting in the studio: Naomi in the window seat, laptop on her knees, gazing out at the skyline, lost in thought, and Jon trying the new Steinway, the chords and melodies like the tinkle of rain.

They had spent the entire morning with the interior designer discussing furniture and decorations, carpeting and kitchen appliances. Jon had stood by and listened to Naomi swiftly and easily telling the man what she wanted, and when, and watched with some amusement how he had started to sweat at her demands. She had it all laid out, every detail, the hue of every cushion, the shape of every cup; and she had not forgotten the yard.

"Bougainvillea," she had said. "Jasmine, roses. This garden should be overflowing with flowers and green. I want a gardener, and permanently. Get someone today to clean up the terrace, please. Oh, and send over a bricklayer so we can use the barbecue."

Jon had called his housekeeper in LA and asked her to come over and help them get settled. Amparo would be arriving later in the week and until then they would have to get along by themselves.

He relished the idea. He liked the thought of being alone, of getting to make breakfast for Naomi, cooking her the omelet with mushrooms she liked so much and serving it to her across the counter that separated the kitchen from the dining room while she sat there in her bathrobe and asked for coffee, like he had done earlier today.

Just when he was about to suggest dinner downtown to her, the bell rang.

Surprised, Naomi looked up. "I'll go," she said, but Jon was already up. "No. Stay where you are."

No one could ring their doorbell without being checked by security first, but he still hated the idea of her opening doors to strangers, to danger.

He hadn't seen Joshua in two months, not before Naomi had left LA; and now Jon blinked in surprise.

Facing him was not the slightly straggly, long-haired teenager he had last seen racing along the beach with his friends, surfboard under his arm; this was a young adult in very tidy clothes and with an immaculate haircut.

"What happened to you?" Jon asked. "Are you working on Wall Street now?" He could hardly believe the shirt and trousers, the polished shoes and gold cuff links.

"Seriously, Dad," Joshua replied, and walked past him into the studio, where he gave Naomi's cheek a peck and sat down beside her. "Sorry about last night. I had an important dinner with Grandfather and some friends of his. Ethan was there too."

"Ethan?" Jon felt stupid.

"Yes, Ethan. My cousin." Joshua ran his fingers through his short hair, an echo of his father in the movement. "Grandfather invited us to meet some people, and we really had fun."

"What people?" Naomi closed her laptop.

"Oh, just friends. Some guys from Harvard, a couple of people from Toronto. My uncle Carl was there too. I've been seeing a lot of them recently, and it's really great. We should have gone to Toronto more often, Mom. I wish I knew more of my family there." He grinned at her. "They are quite nice, and I love talking to Grandpa. He is really brilliant, and funny too. And Grandmother loves it here in New York, did you know? She's on a shopping frenzy, took me out to buy new clothes and stuff."

"So I see." Naomi's words dropped into the sudden stillness like icicles.

Joshua threw her a questioning glance but went on. "Okay, so I have something to tell you, and I thought I'd rather do it right away. I'm dropping out of Julliard."

For a moment Jon thought Naomi was going to faint, and he took a step toward her, afraid she would fall off the seat. Her face had turned deathly pale; he could see her struggling for breath and holding on to the windowsill in an attempt to keep her composure.

"What?" Jon asked softly. "What did you say, Joshua?" He sank down on the piano stool.

"I said," Joshua repeated impatiently, "I'm leaving Juilliard. I want to go to Harvard with Ethan. We want to go to business school and then go work with Grandfather in the hotel business." He picked up the briefcase he'd been carrying and put it down on the floor to bring out a stack of documents. "Here's the application stuff. I've been working on this with Grandfather; all I need is for you to sign. I want to start this fall. The Harvard people said I could. I think Grandfather knows them really well; they were quite pleased about the whole thing."

Naomi got up and walked out of the room. Jon could hear her steps on the stairs and the bedroom door shutting, and then he was alone with his son. He folded his hands on his knees, wondering what to say, wondering how to handle this, somewhere deep inside amused by the fact that he had to play father when he hadn't the faintest idea how to do it.

"You are so talented, Joshua," he said carefully, "I'd like you to reconsider before you throw it away. You could become a great composer, a writer of wonderful music. It would be an incredible shame to waste all that."

Joshua sighed. "I'm not throwing anything away, Dad. My talent is my own, and I won't have to turn it in once I walk through the gates of Harvard. But there's more to life than just music." He flicked his wrist at the Steinway. "I know you are nailed to that thing the way Mom is nailed to her desk; you barely even look up from what you're creating. You, both of you, you hardly see anything but your work and each other, and that's okay, because it's nice to watch my parents being so much in love. But I want more. I don't want to be your shadow, and what you expect me to be." His black eyes sparkled. "Hey, did you know I can pick any hotel in the world for an internship? I mean, any of the family hotels? I could travel all over the world!"

To Jon it felt as if little pieces of his heart were breaking off. "You could do that with us, Josh. You could have been in Italy with us the last few weeks, but you opted to return to LA for some surfing with your friends. You could have gone on tour with me, but you decided to stay at school because it was so important to you not to miss a class. And now you want to quit?"

"I'm not quitting." For a moment, for an instant, Joshua looked like a small boy, his lip pushed out obstinately. "I just want to do something else." He jumped up and began to pace the room, his hands pushed into the pockets of the fine trousers. "With Mom, for as long as I can think, it was music, music, music. Every day I had to practice, play the piano, play the guitar, learn theory; and she is one relentless teacher, I can tell you. Kind and nice, but totally relentless. Disappointing her was not an option. With Mom, you really strive to please her or else." His gaze wandered out to the hallway and the stairs. "She is the grand master of friendly oppression."

"She sets high standards," Jon conceded, trying to suppress a grin.

"Dad." Joshua leaned on the lid of the grand in much the same way Naomi used to do. "I really want to do this. It's something that feels like my own choice. Please? What's the harm in going to business school? What's wrong with getting a Harvard degree? I mean, I don't HAVE to work with Grandfather if I decide not to afterward, but why can't I at least try? The music won't go away, and I promise to take a piano with me and keep practicing. But, please? Please, can I do this? Can I go to Harvard with Ethan?"

"Yes." It was as easy as that in the end. There was no reason in the world not to agree. "Give me the papers, Josh. I agree; you should go to Harvard. In fact, I'm rather pleased with your decision. It's a good thing. Yes, you should go. I'm pleased."

"Mom won't be."

Jon took the papers from him. The Harvard logo made him feel proud and, unaccountably, a little sad. "You won't be too far away. We can see you in Boston whenever we feel like it." With a flourish, he put his name on the dotted line. "Boston is pretty. You'll like it there, but Joshua—" he handed the documents over— "Kurt is going with you. You're not going without a guard. Is that clear?"

"Yeah, yeah. I know." Joshua pulled up his shoulders in another imitation of Naomi. "Sometimes it's no fun being your son, I can tell you. I'm never free. I'm always your son, and Mom's. And both are difficult, for different reasons." He reached for the music sheets on top of the Steinway and turned them around so he could look at what Jon had scrawled on them. "You don't really believe in staff lines, do you, Dad? Didn't anyone ever teach you how to write music?"

"Actually, no." Enviously Jon watched how Joshua, with a few deft strokes of the pencil, put order in his wild scribblings. "I didn't have anyone to support whatever talent I had, and no one to push me into practicing as a child. I had to learn everything myself when I was your age, and it was infinitely harder. You see, I never wanted to do anything else, never wanted to be anything but a songwriter. I remember coming home from school, doing my homework and my chores and then settling down to try and write music, practice the guitar; and I hated it when it got too late and I had to stop for the day."

"Use a fifth here." Joshua tapped the paper. "Sounds really mushy otherwise. So, what about Mom? Do I go after her now? I know where that will end. It's either icy silence or she'll yell at me, and I'm not too keen on either one."

This was hard. Jon didn't know what to say. He couldn't even ask Joshua to retreat to his room for a while, because there was no room for him yet.

"When your mother was here, before. Well, when she was here on her own," he said, and Joshua nodded expectantly. "Did you pick a room for yourself? I mean here, in this house? Have you decided where you want your room?"

"Yeah." He waved in the general direction of the stairway. "Way up under the roof. I thought you'd want your studio there; but Mom said she wanted you right here, in the center of the house, where she could always hear you, where you would be close. She even said it with a straight face. So I told her I wanted that space. It's like a loft. Have you seen it?"

"I think it would have been impossible to lug a grand up there. You're welcome to that space." Jon wondered if it would be a good idea to go out for coffee, or maybe even get a coffeemaker right now. He hated not having fresh coffee in the house, and he was sure Naomi hated it even more.

"Well," Joshua interrupted his thoughts, "I'm leaving. I'm meeting Ethan downtown; we're having dinner with the grandparents again if it's okay with you." He looked around at the bare surroundings. "It's not as if there was anything here. There isn't even a microwave. Why are you staying here? Grandfather said he can't understand why you're living in an empty house when there are two hotels owned by the family in town. He thinks you're being utterly ridiculous and blames Mom's stubbornness."

"I think it's rather nice being in my own home, Josh. We really spend enough nights in hotel rooms. It won't be bare much longer. Come back next week, and most of it will be furnished and in working order. Amparo will be here too, so you can be sure there will be proper food." But Jon saw that this did not overly impress his son.

"Yeah, cool," Josh said. "I think Grandfather wanted to drive me and Ethan up to Boston next week. He said something about a condo or something where he wants us to live."

This was too much even for Jon. He had to take a deep, calming breath before he went on. "Okay, listen to me. I don't mind your grandfather encouraging you to go to Harvard, and I really don't mind you going to business school. But honestly, Josh, you're still our son, mine and Naomi's; and if anyone is going to set you up on campus, it will be us, your parents."

Joshua went to get his bag and stuff the signed papers inside. "As if. You never have time for that kind of thing anyway, Father. You are busy doing your own thing. And Mom? My talent was always more important to her than me as a person. She always wanted to see you in me, make me another you, since she couldn't have the original. I've only realized that since you came into our lives, and I'm not holding it against you. It's not your fault. But it's the truth. Being your son was a real pain in the ass for me."

"Are you telling me…" Jon needed a second to sort out his thoughts. "Are you telling me you had a hard childhood? You? When your mother did everything she could to make your talent flourish? And I mean everything, Joshua, including sending you to that school in Switzerland, and letting you go to Oxford while you were still so young? Don't you know what that was like for her? Don't you realize how lonely she was?"

Without looking back, Joshua made his way to the entrance. "I never asked to be sent away to all those schools. And you, by the way…" Doorknob in hand, he paused. "You were quite keen to pack me away to Juilliard so you could have Mom all to yourself. Hey, never mind. I had a great time with Grandma Helen and the family here."

"You know, Joshua, that none of this is true. You know you're twisting the truth. Your mother and I never excluded you, never. You, on the other hand, were always quite willing to go your own way. We never stopped you. I'd have liked to see your reaction if we had made you go to a boring private high school in LA with all the empty-headed showbiz kids instead of being at Juilliard. Five months ago, just after the shooting, I could hardly pry you out of there to come and visit your mother, and now you complain? She asked for you every day; she worried about the impact her injury would have on you, and you complain?" Rather forcefully, Jon slammed the door to keep Joshua from leaving. "Have you ever wondered how it felt to her, letting you go when you were twelve, seeing you go to stay with your grandparents in

Geneva so you could grow into the fine musician you are now and she staying behind alone in that lonely place in Norway?"

"She could have come with me." Joshua raised his chin at Jon. "No one forced her to stay there. Grandfather said it was her own fault if she was lonely and unhappy; she could have had it all: an exciting life, friends, being wherever she wanted, with a private plane to take her all over the place. And she picked the solitude and the cold of Halmar so she could mourn you. That's what Grandfather says. And I think he's right." He turned the doorknob, and Jon stood aside to let him pass. "But I don't mind, Dad. It's okay. Only please, let me go to Boston with my grandfather and Ethan. I really want to."

There was no sound from upstairs.

"You're going to break your mother's heart, Joshua. She will never understand that you want to leave Juilliard; but excluding her even further, going to Harvard with Olaf to get settled, that will break her heart. There's plenty of time for us to go together, and I don't mind one bit if your grandfather comes along. But after all is said and done, we are your parents, and we have the last word. We will decide where you live and with whom."

"Jeez, Dad." Joshua shifted his briefcase from one hand to the other. "You're making such a scene. It's not as if I'm signing up with the marines or anything. I just want to go to freaking Harvard with my cousin, and my grandfather wants to pay. Just chill, will you? And yeah, if you must, come along. If that's what Mom needs to make her happy, sure." He walked away, letting the garden gate shut behind him with a clanging sound.

chapter 31

NAOMI WASN'T, AS he had expected, curled up on the bed hidden away under the covers but busy unpacking their suitcases, stowing his socks in a drawer in neat rows.

Jon stood in the door and watched her for a while, watched how she moved through the room, her body slim and young in the simple rose cotton dress she was wearing, her neck tan from the Italian sun. He loved that color on her. It brought out the ebony of her hair, made her skin glow like a pearl; and for some reason he couldn't figure out, made her look well-groomed, expensive.

"We need a coffeemaker, bad." he said, and sat down on the corner of the bed. "I'm thinking of going out now to buy one. Do you want to come? We could go downtown, have dinner somewhere, and shop for a machine." His gaze wandered out the large windows toward the skyline. Manhattan gleamed in the sunlight, with the towers of the World Trade Center reaching higher than all the others, double fingers pointing into space.

She didn't reply but shook out one of the sweaters he had bought in Hamburg instead, looking at it critically before she folded it again and laid it on a shelf. Jon noted how she had divided up the big walk-in closet. How his things were on one side and hers on the other, sharing the same space and yet neatly divided. There wasn't a lot; most of their belongings were still in LA. He wondered if they would go to the trouble of shipping them here. "Why don't we go out and have dinner somewhere, Naomi?" Dogged, his voice sounded dogged to Jon.

"What did you say to Joshua?" she asked instead without turning to him.

"What did I say to him?" Jon sighed. "I told him it's okay to go to Harvard. Hell, Naomi, what do you expect me to say to him? It's not as if he's running away with the circus or something. I mean, Harvard Business School? Yes, for crying out loud! As least he'll have the ability to control his finances when he comes into his heritage. And you do realize, don't you, that the Carlsson business is coming his way, no matter what you think about it? So yes, I think it's a very good idea for him to want to do that."

She stopped. The silk dress she had worn during the interview with that reporter in London pressed to her chest, Naomi waited for him to go on.

"There is nothing else to say," Jon plodded on. "I signed the papers for him. Joshua is leaving Juilliard and entering Harvard. Your father is paying, and he's buying a condo for him and Ethan. I can't say I'm unhappy. With both your father and me watching them, they'll be safe and comfortable."

Jon could see how her shoulders shook, but still there was no response.

"I know," he said softly, "I know you wanted him to finish his musical education. I know it meant a lot to you, but Naomi...my love. You can't do to Josh what your father did to you. I'm begging you, Naomi. Let him choose his own way. Don't punish him for going a different path than you imagined for him."

Wordlessly, she put the dress on a hanger and put it away.

"I know what's eating you. You think your father is winning. That's what's really eating you. You don't want to give in to him. But Naomi, if your father hadn't been involved, if Josh had come up with the idea all on his own, you wouldn't have had any problems with it; I'm sure of that. This is all about Olaf."

She swiveled around. "Yes. Yes, it is. And you're just not getting it, are you? You're not one whit better than my father, and now you're turning Joshua into another cold, money-obsessed bastard, just like the two of you. Are you really sure, Jon, that you're into the music because of the creativity, or was it the easiest way for you to make a lot of money? I remember you and my father last year, when you were bartering over me as if I was some horse, I don't know, some prized possession neither of you wanted to do without?"

"Good grief, Naomi. He wants to go to Harvard. Joshua wants to go to Harvard, for crying out loud. He has a perspective, a goal, and hell yes. If he wants to enter your family's business, so be it. He'll still be a very fine musician. That talent will never leave him!" He realized, as soon as the words had left his mouth, that he was echoing Joshua's arguments, and it embarrassed him.

She had been holding one of his shirts, and now she threw it at him with all the force she could muster. Jon caught it before it fluttered to the ground at his feet and laid it on the bed beside him. "He should be a shining star, Jon. He should be ruling the musical world, should be dictating his terms to it, just the way you are doing. His melodies should be in every person's head. And you tell me he could just as well run a bloody hotel. I did that, Jon, and for many years. There's nothing, absolutely nothing, creative to running a hotel or a chain of them. Joshua is throwing away a gift."

"Yeah, that's what your father thinks about you too." Jon was so tired. Jet lag was catching up with him, and for a moment he felt as if he was talking about strangers, not about his own son but about someone who didn't concern him, who wasn't his problem at all. He tried to grab that feeling, take a closer look and find out where it came from, when the truth was that nothing in the world mattered more to him than Naomi and Joshua.

"That's what your father thinks. He believes you gave up a brilliant career in the hotel business for my sake, for nothing more than love. Please, Naomi, can we put this behind us? Can you please accept that Josh has a right to make his own decisions? You made yours, remember? And I made mine. We didn't give a damn about our parents' opinions either, and look where we are. Do we have to make this so hard for Josh?"

Her lips were trembling, and in her eyes he could see a world of sadness.

"He planned it so well," Naomi softly said. "He really planned it well. He waited until we were out of the way to come here and ensnare Joshua with his promises. Taking him shopping, wining and dining him. I bet he even stooped low enough to hire a stretch limousine to impress the boys."

Jon tried not to smile. "It's not as if we haven't been in those often enough. Do we go for dinner now, and do we buy a coffeemaker? Please? I think I'll die if I don't get some coffee."

TO PLEASE HER, to show he understood how she felt, Jon asked LaGasse to order a limousine and stay behind herself. They would, he told her, only go to dinner and come right back. No need for guards. LaGasse gave him an icy glance but didn't comment. Jon sighed.

"All right." He said, "You're right. Come along, but…"

"I understand, Sir," she replied, and called for the car.

Jon liked the small, wiry woman with the sharp-angled face and the short, blond hair. She seemed like a knife ready to snap open into a dangerous, glinting blade, a terrier more than willing to bite. He wondered how she and Naomi got along when they went out on their own, if they ever shared meals, or confidences, but he didn't think so. There had been a kind of bond between Naomi and Stewart, the guard who had been killed at the Oscars; but LaGasse, she was different. She was all business, cool distance, constant vigilance. Jon was sure he'd never seen her in anything but the dark suit she always wore, the bulge of her gun in the back.

Naomi came down a few minutes later. She was in a black linen dress, bare feet in high-heeled black sandals, wearing the dark lipstick she had bought in London. Her outfit reminded him briefly of that night in Geneva when they had attended the party at the yacht club, but only briefly, only in the coloring.

In fact, she looked nearly as prim and impassive as she had that very first day when he had found her in Halmar, and it broke his heart. They had come such a long way; they had cleared so many obstacles along the path, and here she gave him the same cool, distanced look. Stillness gathered around her like a cloud. Jon wondered if she had bought the dress for just such an occasion, if she had known deep down in her heart there would be cliffs they would not be able to navigate easily, moments when she would want to hide from him behind the stark facade of a businesswoman.

Naomi walked past him and out the door without a glance, her chin held high, purse tucked under her arm, ignoring him.

"Are you going to play the hating game with me all night long?" Jon asked as the car entered the traffic on the Brooklyn Bridge.

"I don't hate you, Jon." was her reply in much the same tone you might use to tell someone you wanted a divorce, that cool, detached, emotionless. Her hands rested on her lap, neatly folded; her head turned away toward the river passing by under them.

"Yeah, you hate me. Right now, you hate me. I can see it. You'd never wear a dress like that and look away from me like that if you didn't hate me. You hate me for deciding this on my own, for letting you stay upstairs while I talked to Joshua myself. You wanted me to come and get you and let you make a scene, and I didn't and that's why you hate me. You might as well own up to it."

She didn't react.

"So." He wanted to shake her, shake the bitterness out of her, tell LaGasse to turn around and then, back in their bedroom, force her to put on something happier. "Where do you want to go for dinner?"

"You pick." It wasn't as if she sounded angry, upset; Jon was sure he could have lived with that. It was more like she had given up, locked away her hurt deep inside, so deep that she could neither talk about it nor cry. She was like a statue, frozen in her grief.

He was about to suggest the Russian Tea Room, remembering how happy they had been there during their lunch with the theater people last Christmas, when she said, "Let's go to the hotel. It's close to Lincoln Center, and maybe we can pick up a brochure for the season while we are there."

"Oh, so you still want to go to the opera with me."

That made her turn to him. "Yes. Why wouldn't I?"

"Because, dear heart," Jon took her hand. As always when she was upset, it was ice-cold, her fingers as stiff and hard as sticks. "Because you're treating me as if you're thinking of running away again. You look it too, with that severe dress and your chin held at that forbidding angle. You look as if you can't decide if you want to kill me or leave me."

She pulled back from him and picked up her clutch from the seat beside her.

"You really want to go to your parents' place, Naomi? I'm not sure that's a good idea, with the mood you're in right now." His stomach was in knots thinking about a clash between her and Olaf. "It would be a little like gate-crashing, wouldn't it? I mean, Ethan and Josh will be there, and maybe even Carl."

"So now I can't even go and see my son when I want to, Jon? Are you in league with my father in getting him away from me?" Her eyes sparkled with the fury of unshed tears. "I've spent my entire life centered around Joshua and you, I gave up everything, everything, first you, so I could raise Josh in a peaceful place and not in your sex, drugs, and rock' n' roll den, and then I gave up my son so he could grow into the fine musician he is supposed to be; and now you and Olaf turn it against me, use it against me to alienate Joshua. That's what you're doing. You and my father, you are making these decisions, and I'm not having any say. In Hamburg I told you I trust you, but now I'm not so sure." She had to take a couple of deep breaths before she could go on, her voice brittle with sorrow. "I raised Joshua, Jon. Not you. He's only your son because I told him, because I caved and told him my dirty secret. Everything he is, everything he has grown into, none of that is to your credit. The only part you had in Joshua was some heated sex. That's all. He's my son. Not yours."

They had left the bridge a while ago and turned onto Centre. Jon leaned forward, tapped on the pane separating them from the driver. As soon as the car had stopped at the curb, he opened the door and got out. It was hot; the air smelled of dust and fumes.

For a moment he stood, trying to collect himself enough to speak calmly.

"I'm willing to take a lot from you, Naomi. I'm willing to see you run from me over and over again, and wait for you to return. I'll even go after you. But here it ends. I'll not sit here and listen to you telling me that Joshua is not my son and that I have no say in his life. That is more than even I can take."

He slammed the car door and walked away to the next crossing, where he hailed a cab and got into it without looking back even once.

JON REGRETTED HIS actions the moment the taxi had gone two blocks, and he made the driver turn around; but of course the limousine was gone by the time they got to the spot where he had left it. Undecided he stood on the curb, looking up and down the road while the sun slowly wandered toward the west, cursing himself.

She was gone. Again, she was gone, and this time it was entirely his fault.

Jon dug out his cell phone and tried to call her, but as he had expected, she did not pick up.

Rush hour traffic pulsed around him on the sidewalk and the street, and there was no free cab in sight. Slowly walking north, he tried to hail one from time to time, but it was hopeless. He walked west, hoping he'd be luckier once he got to Broadway.

It was a long, lonely walk. No one looked at him; no one noticed the famous man making his way across Manhattan on a summer evening, his hands in his pockets and his head lowered, a cloud on his brow. He walked all the way to Canal and then stood at the street corner, Broadway stretching away along the island and Canal, with its seedy shops, leading into the tunnel, and remembered how only a day earlier Naomi had nearly jumped out of the car, so happy to be back. Her joy in the city had amused him, had made him look fondly at New York and forget its grime and darker side. Her enthusiasm was infectious, like a bright flame, like a flame he needed to give him life, and he missed her already.

His anger washed away. She was right. She was right. She had raised Joshua on her own, in the small, silent world she had created for them in Norway, where time had a different meaning, and love. Just when he finally managed to catch a free cab, Jon admitted to himself that he had no choice.

He had to go after her, find her, make her understand that he would always be on her side, would always stand with her against the world and let no harm come to her again, ever.

Dropping into the back of the cab, he gave the name of the hotel to the driver and told him to hurry.

chapter 32

THE HOTEL ROYAL was situated on a street corner right across from Lincoln Center, with the best possible view of the plaza and the Met.

Jon gazed at the graceful bows of the large windows for a while, recalling their stay last year and how the first small pieces of her wall of secrets had crumbled.

He had walked into love so blindly, let it take him prisoner. He had never cared about her family, where she came from, or even who she was, not for a moment. She had been a mystery, a perfect dream, and that had been enough.

It still was, Jon admitted, entering the lobby of the hotel; he did not care at all about the wealth and the business. He wanted life to be simple: write songs, sing them, love Naomi. That summed it up for him. If he reduced it to bare necessities, that was pretty much it.

"Olaf Carlsson," he said to the girl at the reception, putting his hand down on the counter. "I'm his son-in-law."

She gave him that look he knew only too well. He could see the instant of shock in her young, pretty face, fading into delight and then shyness, before her training won and she turned professional again.

"Right away, sir," she replied, and picked up the phone.

Olaf greeted him at the door to the private penthouse apartment, surprised, delighted, with a bright smile, napkin in hand.

"Jon! We're having dinner. How nice of you to join us; come on in!"

Jon still thought it was suspicous to see him this friendly, and he had to struggle with a response. Before he could say anything, Olaf peered around him and asked, "And where is Naomi? Did she not come with you? Don't tell me she is sitting alone at home, fuming? Jon, going to Harvard is a good choice for Joshua. She should be delighted."

"I thought she was here." The words felt like barbed wire on his tongue. "I thought she'd come here." He did not add that he had expected to find them embroiled in a drama of spectacular dimensions.

"No." Lucia had joined them. "No, Naomi is not here, and she didn't call either. What is going on, Jon?"

"Nothing." His throat was too dry with fear to swallow. "I must have misunderstood her. Thought she said she was coming here."

"Was she coming downtown?" Olaf motioned him to come inside, but Jon did not move. He could hear the voices of the boys from somewhere inside the large condo. The smell of grilled meat and garlic turned his stomach over.

"Yes. No. We were going out for dinner, but..." There was no way he was going to tell Olaf about their fight, about his reaction to her bitter statement. "But our plans changed. We parted, and obviously it wasn't totally clear where we would meet up again."

"So call her," Lucia suggested, "and ask her where she is."

"Yes. Yes. I will do that." The elevator was right behind him and now he took a step back, ready to press the button, but Lucia grabbed his shirt sleeve.

"Jon, stay. You have a funny look on your face. What is going on? I want you to come in and tell me. Come in, have a drink, and tell us why you are here, of all places, looking for Naomi. Has something happened?"

But he shook his head. "No. No, Lucia. Not with Joshua here. I'll call you. I have to find her first. Don't worry. I'll call you." He left before they could go on asking, the confusion and dawning fear on their faces the last thing he saw before the elevator doors hissed closed and he was alone.

Jon was about to ask for a limo at the reception desk when he noticed LaGasse coming toward him, her brow in a frown. "Sir? I can't find Mrs. Stone. She got out of the car and told me to wait for her—she had something to do on her own, and she would be back in a moment—to meet her here in the lobby. But I can't find her. I did exactly as instructed, sir."

"Your orders are to never leave her side." Jon was ready to throttle the thin, pale throat of the bodyguard. "That's your job, isn't it? You are supposed to protect her!"

"That's right, sir, and I do. But when your wife tells me she doesn't want me around for something, then I can't force myself on her. She's not my hostage; I'm her protector." LaGasse faced him squarely, unafraid. "She said she wanted to see her parents and did not need me."

"And now she's gone." He didn't even know where to begin to look. He didn't know what to say to LaGasse or where to turn with his growing fear.

"Sir." She was waiting beside him, as collected as ever. "Sir, if I may make a suggestion."

Jon grunted. The cell phone was in his hand again, and he was pressing the speed dial for Naomi's number.

"Sir," LaGasse said, "the best thing to do is go home and wait. If Mrs. Stone has not returned or contacted you in six hours, it's time to call the police. They won't do anything right now. She might have just gone shopping and lost her cell or something."

He knew.

Abduction scenarios, every aspect of them, every possibility—they had been part of his life for so long now, a constant danger, a daily threat, and one that had only grown with his marriage and Joshua's legal adoption. He and Sal had been over it so often, had carefully discussed the security measures for his new family, had tried to make them safe and happy despite Naomi's desire for freedom. Now, standing with her bodyguard in the lobby of her father's hotel, Jon realized that it was all an illusion. She had slipped away like a wisp of fog, and they had no chance in the world to find her right now.

"Yes." Funny, it was funny how often he kept saying that word today when he hadn't been able to say it to her, to Naomi, knowing so well how hurt she was.

"Yes, you're right. Let's go back." For a second he wondered if he should inform Olaf that Naomi was missing but then decided against it.

London, Hamburg…she did it all the time and then came back with a new lipstick or a different hairstyle, and now that she was in New York perhaps she had just grabbed the chance and gone off on her own to do some sightseeing, some shopping.

Jon held on to that thought as he waited on the steps of the hotel for LaGasse to get the car. She had suggested he go with her to the garage in the basement, but he had refused. He wanted to be here until the last moment, hoping that maybe, just maybe, Naomi would come around the corner, a couple of shopping bags on her arm, and everything would be as before.

HE CALLED SAL, who asked, "What do you mean, she's gone?"

The memory of those words washed down Jon's back like icy slush. Sal had said the same thing to him all those years ago, after Naomi had left him for the first time, and he remembered how he had felt then only too well. In a rush of panic, Jon went to look, but her clothes were there. She had not come back to pack and go for good.

"I'll be right over." Sal's voice sounded raspy. "You know I just arrived today, Jon. We need to get in gear for the tour, and here you are on another drama trip with your wife? What have you done to drive her away this time?"

"Nothing. I've done nothing." Anger replaced the panic. "Get your ass over here, Sal, and quickly."

"Jon." Sal cleared his throat. "I'm still at the airport. I haven't even picked up my luggage yet. I haven't had a decent meal in eight hours, and I'm tired. I'm going to my hotel now, and once I've showered and eaten I'll get back to you. Seriously, Jon. Call the police or something if you think something's wrong. How long has she been gone this time?"

Jon glanced at his watch. "Four hours, and not a word."

There was a pause at the other end of the line. Then Sal said, "All right. I'll be there right away," and hung up.

The bedroom was so quiet. He sat on the edge of the bed where he could see her dresses hanging in the wardrobe, her purses sitting on the shelf beneath them. There was not a whole lot; in fact it was a pitiful collection compared to the LA house. He had loved to go into her dressing room and run his hands over the silk and fine linen of her clothes, breathe in the faint scent of her perfume that seemed to always linger there, touch the jewelry boxes on the table, make sure she had all the luxury and beauty he could provide.

Dusk settled over the city while Jon waited for something to happen, for Naomi to return or for Sal to show up. He was about to call Olaf a couple of times but stopped. Having him around, to hear his accusations and bear his anger was more than he could take right now. He wandered through the house once more, peered into the empty rooms, and listened to the echo of his own breath.

The kitchen was still without a coffeemaker. He had completely forgotten about it, and now he stood staring at the empty counter and wondered if he could risk going out to get a cup and a bagel from the deli down the street, but then decided not to. The fear that she might come home and leave again if she didn't find him here was too great.

Sal arrived some time after nine.

"What did you do, Jon?" He looked around the entry hall. "What have you said or done now? Good grief, I can't take this anymore. Why is it so impossible for the two of you to settle down? What happened? I want to know. If you call me and want me to come here and help you, I have a right to know."

The battery on his phone had run empty. Jon had no idea where the charger was, and that made him smile despite his turmoil. For most of his life, he had done his own packing; but Naomi had taken it out of his hands, saying he was inefficient and sloppy, and using a lot more space than he actually needed. He had loved to give in to her, had loved to sit and watch her handle his belongings. There was hardly anything that had made him feel more married than the small, domestics things they shared, and he wanted that sense of security back at all costs.

"We had a rather bad argument about Joshua and his plans for his future, and we said terrible things to each other. All that could have been remedied, but then..." Jon looked into Sal's face and saw disbelief there. "I walked out on her. I left the car and walked away. It's my fault, Sal. I left her alone, somewhere in the middle on Manhattan." He shrugged. "Well, LaGasse was with her, but I wasn't."

Once the words were spoken, Jon understood he couldn't take them back, nor could he wipe away the trace of disgust on Sal's face.

"You left her," Sal asked softly. "You left Naomi?"

"I was furious, okay?" He wanted coffee so much it was almost a physical pain. "I was so furious it was either walk away or say things I knew I was going to regret forever because she would never forgive me."

"I don't think she'll forgive you for walking away from her either." Sal lit a cigarette, and Jon frowned.

"Outside," he ordered. "She doesn't want smoking in this house."

They stepped out onto the patio where Sal flicked his ashes into the sad ruin of the brick barbecue. "This is all beside the point anyway. You want her back, and she's out there somewhere. So you know what we have to do. We have to call the police. I'll take care of that. And you, Jon—" Sal gave him a sad squint through the blue smoke—"I think you'd better call Olaf. And then put on a bulletproof vest or something, because the old man will have your hide if something happens to her."

IT WAS NEARLY eleven by the time Olaf and Lucia showed up, Joshua in tow. Jon greeted them and tried to offer something to drink before he realized there was nothing in the house. Lucia cast one glance into the fridge, kissed Olaf's cheek, and left again, taking LaGasse and Joshua with her.

Olaf wandered into the studio.

"So what happened? Naomi is an independent soul, Jon; she might just have decided to go to the theater or something. I can't imagine a scenario where she would leave you." He grinned mirthlessly. "She gave up everything for you, everything, including her life. She would never leave you."

Jon closed the door behind him, shutting out Sal. "There is something she would leave me for, and in the blink of an eye, Olaf. She would leave me for Joshua."

Olaf wiped his hand across the gleaming top of the Steinway. "Yes, that. She would probably do that."

"We fought over Joshua today." This, Jon decided, was probably the hardest thing he had ever done. It was much more difficult than going to Geneva on his own to demand Olaf's consent to their marriage, just to make Naomi happy. "And it got really bad. She is very unhappy about Harvard. I signed the papers without talking to her about it. She was very angry about that."

Olaf laughed. "Yes, she would be. It was the right thing to do though. It is a good decision."

"That's not the point."

The towers of the city blinked at him through the darkness; he could hear their hum calling to him, taunting him. Somewhere, somewhere in those canyons, Naomi was wandering around all on her own right now. Jon had the terrible urge to leave the house and the people in it, return to Manhattan, and walk through the streets searching for her. He tried to find the right words, tried to tell Olaf; but looking at the stern, lean face, he stumbled over his own words.

"We took that decision away from her, Olaf. It was hers to make, and we took it away from her. You, by suggesting Harvard to Joshua without consulting her, and me by signing those papers without her consent. She was right. I didn't have the right to do that, and you didn't have the right to talk to Josh without her knowing about it. No wonder she's hurt and angry."

Olaf waved him away. "You don't know that. You don't know what's going on. Maybe she's just shopping and..."—he pointed at the useless cell phone in Jon's hand—"and her battery has run out, just like yours.

You should really get better phones. Those are old and outdated. I'll have some sent over to you tomorrow."

Confused, Jon stared at the thing. He could hardly remember having been in a more surreal situation, ever. Not even when Naomi had been in the hospital, fighting for her life, and he had been alone with her parents at the Malibu house.

"Yes. Thank you," he replied. "I don't think she's just shopping or having a good time. Our parting was too angry for that. And knowing Naomi, I wouldn't be surprised if she's on a plane back to Norway right now. I'm just very worried."

Olaf stared at him. "That's easy to find out, isn't it? Have you called the airports?"

The question was so ridiculous, Jon wanted to laugh. "Not even I would be able to get an answer from them."

"Well." Olaf got out his own phone. "Good thing I have some friends, isn't it?"

chapter 33

SHE HAD NO idea where she was. They'd been driving around for hours once they had left Manhattan through the tunnel, first along the Pulaski Skyway and then toward the shore, where he had taken her to the beach and made her walk through the surf with him. He had even carried her sandals, very gentlemanly and courteous, and offered his hand in support. She hadn' taken it and bent down to pick up a shell instead, pretending to admire it. Parker had smiled and nodded, and commented that this was what he had wanted all along, to spend time with her without all those men who constantly hovered around her.

"Because," he said, "you are way too lovely to waste your time with someone like Jon Stone. He can have any woman in the world, but he shouldn't have you. You are meant to be free."

Naomi did not point out that she wasn't free right now, that he had virtually abducted her and was keeping her away from her husband and home against her will and wouldn't even let her make a phone call. She had tried, but Parker had taken the cell from her, shaking his head. "Don't. Just let it go. I promise, you are perfectly safe with me. Enjoy your new freedom!" He hadn't returned it to her, nor had he given back her sandals but locked them in the car trunk. "Those things," he explained, "looked uncomfortable with their high heels. We'll get you more comfortable ones later."

With a look at her hands he had added, "And those rings. You don't want them anymore. Give them to me." She had hidden her hands behind her back and tried to move away from him, but he had been faster and grabbed her wrist, forcing the wedding band and her diamond ring from her finger to fling them into the sea. Terrified, heartbroken, Naomi had sunk down on the sand and cried.

Parker had comforted her, telling her over and over that they had been her manacles, signs of her captivity, that he would see to it that she would never be a prisoner to anything or anyone at all. It was then that it dawned on her that she was in real danger.

The fast-food place where they had stopped was off the highway, on a small road and surrounded by parking lots. They were mostly empty at this time of night; only the one surrounding the restaurant was busy.

Parker hadn't been too happy about stopping, but she had insisted she needed to use the bathroom, and she was hungry. Pointing at the billboard announcing food at the next exit, Naomi had said, "Go there. You don't want to harm me, do you?" and he shook his head no .

There weren't many people inside but enough to allow her to slip outside without him noticing while he stood in line for her food.

She looked around in the humid darkness, lost and disoriented, barefoot, and totally alone.

Her purse was in the car; he hadn't let her take it, saying she didn't need it in the bathroom and he would get her a burger. He had said it very kindly too, and patted her shoulder. "It's a very nice purse, and you might drop it in that restroom. You don't want it to be ruined, do you?" Obediently, she had shaken her head and let him lead her away.

A car came up slowly and turned into the drive-through lane, a single woman behind the wheel. It stopped at the first window. With a furtive glance to check on Parker, Naomi hurried over to her.

"Help me," she whispered, hunkering down on the side of the vehicle. "Please, help me. I've been kidnapped. He's in there, getting food, and I managed to get away when he let me use the bathroom. Please. Please, help me."

The woman looked at her through dark-rimmed glasses, lips pursed and brows drawn. Then she reached over and opened the door.

"Get in," she said, and stepped on the gas as soon as Naomi had clambered in.

She took the car onto the road and through a number of loops, confusing Naomi even further. Not even in LA were the highways this convoluted.

"You're barefoot," the woman remarked. "Did he take your shoes?"

Naomi wrapped her arms around herself, suddenly cold despite the heat of the night. Her fingers were trembling badly. "He took everything away, everything. My shoes, my cell phone, my purse…" She looked at her hands. "My wedding ring. My engagement ring."

THE STRANGER SAID nothing for a while, just looked ahead into the night. They crossed an overpass and the road turned into the main street of a small town lined with trees and pleasant homes with porches.

"I'm Jane." They took a left turn.

Naomi looked at her. She was a slight woman with short, curly brown hair shot through with gray, somewhere in her late forties or early fifties, her face quite lovely, and very friendly. Her driving was careful, slow, but never uncertain. She glanced at Naomi when she started to cry.

"He threw them away," Naomi sobbed. "He threw my rings away. My diamond…"

"Those can be replaced," Jane replied briskly. "Just be glad you're safe now. We need to call the police. And you have to call your family." She stopped the car outside a white house. "Here we are. Come on, come inside."

They were in a residential area. The house stood on a corner, surrounded by high trees and a clean, neat lawn. It had a small porch, more of a landing outside the door, a few steps leading up to it, also painted white. Naomi, standing on the sidewalk while Jane took her purse from the backseat, was entranced by the blue lights in the posts of the stairway, nearly like small lighthouses, and very pretty. Right now it seemed like the most inviting place she had ever seen.

"Come on in." Jane was waiting for her. "My husband is home, and we have a dog, a rather big and lively dog; but he won't harm you, I promise. He's quite well trained." She paused and added, a little less certain, "I think."

A cozy parlor greeted them, well furnished, tastefully decorated, and with lots of bookcases. They were all glass fronted, which struck Naomi as strange until she saw the dog behind the baby gate, locked in the kitchen. She had no idea what kind of breed he was, but he was large, and he looked like trouble. From the parlor, through the dining room, Naomi could see a TV surrounded by more bookcases, a couch in front of it, and the gray top of a man's head just above the cushions. He was watching baseball.

"HE LOVES BASEBALL." Jane threw a brief glance in his direction. "He won't even notice we're here. Now." She looked critically at Naomi. "Would you like to clean up a bit? You look a little bedraggled. I'll put on some tea and find you something to eat in the meantime. And then you'll have to make those calls."

"Coffee? Could I have coffee?" Naomi felt naked, exposed, in a strange way delivered into strangers' hands, helpless.

"On second thought, maybe you shouldn't be here at all." Jane tapped her fingers on the counter. "Maybe I should take you to the hospital. Were you...did he...your abductor, did he...hurt you?"

It took Naomi a moment to understand what she was talking about. "No." The idea was so terrible, she didn't even want to think about it. "No, I'm not hurt. He never touched me. Well, not in that way. He did take away my rings by force..." Her ring. The diamond Jon had bought for her in London, on the day he had asked her to marry him, on that magical day when she had agreed to be his wife. "I have to call my husband. My father. Oh God, my husband will be beside himself with worry!" She stopped.

For the first time that night Naomi wondered if it was true, if Jon was really worrying about her or if he had stopped caring, stopped loving her the moment he had left her in the limo after those awful things she had said to him. She was so exhausted, so scared and confused, and this thought nearly made her break.

"Yes, please. I'd like to use your phone." Her voice was shaking with this new terror.

Jane nodded. "Come with me. You can use my office. It's a mess, I warn you, but you'll have some privacy there."

The dog waved his tail at her when they walked past the kitchen door to the back of the house, where another door led into the messiest office Naomi had ever seen. There was paper everywhere, piles of books, more piles of paper, and yet more books. In a corner, three cartons stood in a precarious tower, all of them filled with what looked suspiciously like stuffed animals of all kinds. The desk was hidden beneath stacks of more books, more folders; and even the computer was propped on some copies of a dictionary. The wall behind the chair, right next to the window, was covered with notes, postcards, photographs, a Christmas ornament dangling from the curtain rod. It was the most comfortable, friendliest place Naomi had ever seen, and it looked loved.

"Toys?" she asked.

"I juggle a lot of balls." With a shrug, Jane dug out the phone from under a heap of manila envelopes. "Here you go. I didn't even ask; where are you from? How long have you been gone? We should really, really call the police first." She scribbled an address, name, and phone number on a slip of paper. "Here. This is where you are, and that's me.

You'll have to tell them where to find you."

Naomi tried not to sob. "I'm sure my husband will take care of it. He'll...he will take care of everything." It sounded like a mantra, as if by saying it she could make it come true.

"But your abductor is somewhere out there," Jane reasoned gently. "The local authorities should be informed. Really, my dear." She hesitated. "You haven't told me your name."

"I'm Naomi." And that was really all. She had no idea if she was still more than that.

"Right, Naomi. Pleased to meet you. I'll leave you to make your calls and get the coffee going. I'll be in the kitchen, okay? Right down the hall. The bathroom is next door. Join me when you feel you're ready." On the point of leaving, Jane turned back. "Are you hungry? I have some red velvet cake."

Her fingers refused to dial Jon's cell number. For the life of her she couldn't remember it, almost as if her head wouldn't allow her to call him.

Crying, shivering, her hand hovering over the phone, Naomi tried to think of Sal's, or her father's; but her mind was blank.

From one of the boxes a stuffed elephant was looking at her, his trunk raised like a question mark, his eyes big and pondering. For some unknown reason he had pink fur and was wearing a bow with a little bell, like a cat; and he seemed like the most comforting thing Naomi had ever seen. Careful not to disturb anything, she padded over and pulled him out to have a closer look. There was a price tag attached to his little string of a tail, and the badge of a toy shop. All the other animals, she saw, had something similar; but none of them was as cute as the elephant. She pressed him to her face, wondering if he was for sale, if all these things were for sale, and if Jane would sell it to her so she would have something, anything, friendly to hold on to during the night.

Again fear threatened to overwhelm her. Her feet were dirty, she had torn a toenail in her flight across the parking lot of the fast-food place, and there was a cut on her heel where she had stepped on something sharp. The black dress was rumpled, messy from sitting in the wet sand on the beach, stained from the seawater; and she knew her face was smeared with make up and eyeliner from all the crying she had done. She had not taken the time to clean herself up in the public restroom, too intent on getting away.

The elephant clasped to her breast, she made her call.

"Art," she said, her voice wobbly with new tears, "could you please call Jon for me?"

JANE HAD FOUND slippers for her and made a pot of coffee. She placed a huge piece of cake on the table in front of Naomi and sat down across from her, her chin propped on her fists, watching, waiting, ready to listen.

The coffee smelled heavenly. Naomi wrapped her hands around the hot mug and took a sip, breathing in the steam.

"We live in Brooklyn." She picked up the fork and cut off a piece of the red cake. "We just bought a house there. I'm from Toronto. My husband's family lives in Brooklyn; that's why we decided to live there."

"You bought a house in New York?" Jane picked up her own cup.

"Yes, on the Promenade. It's a very beautiful house." The cake was heavenly, and just what she had needed. Naomi let the cream cheese icing melt in her mouth, savoring the sweetness. "I gave it to my husband for our wedding. Last year. Almost exactly a year ago. Well, eleven months. We've been married for eleven months." She was babbling, and she bit her lip to stop herself. The dog had been locked out; he was in the conservatory just off the kitchen, where he had curled up in a dog crate and gone to sleep. His paws twitched from time to time, and he kept making small, funny noises that made Naomi look his way and smile.

"He's chasing squirrels in his sleep," Jane said. "We have so many of them in the yard, little pests. They like to raid my bird feeders."

"I was downtown." Naomi took another bite of the cake, this time a bigger one. It was almost as if the first taste had stirred her hunger. Her stomach was growling furiously. "I was downtown, and I wanted to go to Lincoln Center to check out the price for a box. I wanted to buy a box for the season. And then...I had met him before. He was always very nice; he interviewed me in London, and he was the perfect, charming gentleman. So when we ran into each other in that hotel lobby, I didn't think twice when he asked me to go with him for a drink. It was almost dinnertime anyway, and I really wanted a drink. So I thought it would be better to have one with Parker than go to a bar all by myself, but..." She broke off, realizing that most of what she was saying was totally meaningless to someone else. "That pink elephant."

Jane raised her eyebrows.

"Do you sell those animals? Can I buy the pink elephant?" Naomi asked.

"I sell them, yes. You can buy the elephant, sure." She poured more coffee. "You were lucky. I rarely go to that restaurant at night; but I had a library board meeting, and it ran late. When I got out I wanted a milk shake, so I stopped there. I'm glad I was there to help you. But I really think we should call the police now, Naomi."

"It's being taken care of. I talked to Art, to my husband's manager. Well, one of them. He's in LA, but I'm sure he has called Jon by now, and…" Her voice caught on a sob. "And Jon will take care of it."

Jane nodded. "You know what I think? I think you're in shock. And you need medical attention, my dear. I should really take you to the hospital. Your husband will be able to find you there. Please?"

"No. No." The tears spilled over. "If you're okay with it, I'd really like to stay here. I don't know if I'd feel safe at a hospital. I'll just sit here and not bother you. Someone will be here soon to pick me up. Someone will come."

chapter 34

SHE HAD FALLEN asleep on the couch. A sound woke her, and she looked around disoriented and scared until she saw Jane move across the room to peer through the window.

"Oh my," she commented, "three limos and a row of SUVs? There's a crowd out there for you, dear. I think I'm seeing FBI badges too."

"Is Jon there?" Naomi sat up. "Can you see Jon?"

"Well." Jane opened the door. "There are a lot of men out there, but I don't know which one of them your Jon is. Why in the world wouldn't he be here? He's your husband, isn't he?"

"Yes." Only it didn't feel like that anymore, after he had walked away from her, and without her rings.

"Ah." Smiling, Jane glanced at her. "Yes, I think your Jon is here. At least I see someone I know with that name, and he looks pretty worried. You didn't tell me your Jon was that Jon."

Naomi struggled to free herself from the quilt and rise from the couch. Her legs were shaky, and she had a hard time standing up. Naomi held on to the corner of a cabinet to face Jon when he rushed into the house.

"Are you okay?" He stopped right in front of her, his hands out as if he was ready to catch her. "Are you hurt? Did he hurt you?"

She shook her head, swallowing the tears, mourning that he wasn't taking her into his arms, wasn't touching her.

The others came in; her father, Sal, LaGasse, and a group of men in FBI jackets, hands on the weapons just in case. From the kitchen, Jane's dog howled at the commotion. Jane went to calm him down.

"I'm not hurt." Naomi held up her hand. "But he took my rings, Jon. He threw them into the sea, and we have to go down there and find them, only I don't exactly know where it was, so I'll have to search for them, okay?"

"Yes, yes, don't worry about that now." Carefully, gently, Jon drew her into his arms. "Don't worry about those rings right now."

"Sir." One of the agents touched Jon's shoulder. "We should take your wife to the hospital. She should be checked out for several reasons."

She buried her face in Jon's shirt and closed her eyes. Finally, at last she felt safe again. He was holding her, his fingers stroking her neck; his breath felt warm and familiar on her brow.

"In a minute," he said, and she could feel his voice resonate through his chest, caressing her cheek resting against it. "Give us a moment. Then we'll go to the hospital together. We'll go to Manhattan though, to my brother's hospital, where we can be sure of privacy. And now, if you'll excuse us…"

"Out," Olaf added. "Please, gentlemen. There's nothing to do here anyway."

They wanted to talk to Jane, and she followed them outside to give her report, brief and useless as it was. Naomi could see her pointing, giving directions, running her fingers through the short curls behind her ears from time to time. She was such a small woman, narrow and straight, but she radiated calm strength. "I didn't see him," Naomi could hear her say. "I didn't see anything until Naomi appeared beside my car and asked for help. After that, of course, I didn't bother to look around. We just drove off. She looked distressed and disheveled enough to believe her. No, the place is near here, and yes, it will be open. It's one of those twenty-four-hour places. You can't miss it." One of the men asked something, and she replied, "I really didn't notice any of the cars parked there. I was thinking of what I was going to order; and after Naomi got into my car, all I could think about was getting out of there as fast as I could."

Sal was gazing at her from where he stood in the door, his face old and gray, deep smudges under his eyes, his mouth in a tight line. Naomi could see silvery stubble on his chin and cheeks; and even his usually wild locks seemed subdued, tired.

"I really just want to go home," Naomi said. "Can't we just go home, Jon? I'm so exhausted. Please?"

Jane vanished down the hallway and returned a minute later, a stuffed, pink elephant in her hands. She handed it to Naomi, who took it and pressed it to her body.

"Here." She smiled at Naomi. "I'm giving it to you. Take him."

Naomi let go of Jon for long enough to wipe her face and embrace her. "Thank you for everything. Thank you for the cake; it was delicious."

"Yes," Jon added, "Thank you for helping my wife. I promise, I'll not forget this. Thank you."

"Anyone would have done the same." The blue eyes sparkled at him. "A rather wild night, wasn't it? I'm glad it ended well."

"That piece of paper with your phone number," Naomi said. "Can I have it? Can I call you in a few days and maybe take you to lunch or dinner or something? I'd really like to do that."

Jane pursed her lips. "You can have my phone number, but you don't have to take me out. Really. It's fine." She glanced at Jon. "I'm just glad this is over and you are safe."

"I'll call you." Naomi took her hand and pressed it tightly. "I really want to do this. Thank you."

SHE FELL ASLEEP halfway across Staten Island, nestled into Jon's arms, her head on his shoulder.

He held her close and watched the lights slip by as the limousine sped over the now empty highway.

Olaf, sitting across from Jon, had been gazing at Naomi the entire time, his face inscrutable, his lips set in a stern line.

"She should be in a hospital, Jon," he remarked, speaking in a low voice, trying not to wake her. "They are right; she should be checked."

Jon shook his head. "She doesn't want to. Olaf, she's had enough of hospitals. Let her get some rest. Let her sleep in her own bed tonight, and then if she needs it I'll take her myself tomorrow."

"Insanity. You are as insane as she is. You and my daughter, you were made for each other. Drama, obsession, impulsiveness. There's no talking sense to either of you." Disgusted, Olaf leaned back into the seat.

"Well, thank you, Olaf." Jon grinned mirthlessly. "Thank you for saying that. I really do think we were made for each other, yes."

Sal, in the other corner seat, tapped nervously against the window. "What I'd like to know is how Parker got hold of her. I can't believe she just got into his car. Not even Naomi is that naive."

Jon didn't reply. He'd been asking himself the same thing and then shied away from possible scenarios. The idea of Naomi drugged or forced into a car and abducted, harmed, was more than he could take.

Parker. He hadn't seemed like a threat, a nuisance perhaps, another journalist who wanted a closer look; but nothing more than that. It scared Jon that he had underestimated him, had not looked harder; he had felt spikes of jealousy and possessiveness at the way he had danced around Naomi, but he hadn't felt threatened.

"He didn't seem dangerous." He said it softly, thoughtfully, without looking at Sal.

There was no answer for quite a while, not until they had reached the ramp to the Verazzano Bridge. His eyes closed, Jon listened to the rhythmic thumping of the wheels as they raced over the tar joints in the asphalt. It sounded as if the bridge had a heartbeat, as if it was a big beast that had come to life as their vehicle rode along the ridge of its back.

"It may have been my fault."

Startled, Jon opened his eyes to look at Sal.

"My mistake," Sal repeated. "I should have acted earlier. Only there was nothing tangible, nothing I could grasp..." He shifted uncomfortably. "When I saw you off at the airport in Hamburg, on your way to Italy, he was there. He was on the visitor's platform, taking photographs of the airfield and the hangar where your jet was parked. I didn't think he could see a whole lot, it was too far away, so I just followed him to check-in and watched him leave. And I thought that was that. Seems like I was wrong."

He was so tired. Jon had the feeling that every bone in his body was aching, as if his skin was old leather and his hair had turned gray in a matter of hours. There'd been no rest since they had gotten off the plane.

"It's not your fault, Sal. You can't have every person arrested who trails me. Us. I bet he wasn't the only one lying in wait for us."

"Yeah." Sal glanced at Olaf, who was listening to their conversation.

"You would have to arrest all those fans who hang out in the hotel lobbies, or at the backstage entrances, too." Gently, Jon tried to shift Naomi to make her more comfortable. She muttered and clamped her hand onto his shirt. He looked down at it, at the bare fingers, missing her rings, and covered it with his own. "It's over now. I think Naomi was careless. I don't want to blame her for what happened; I know she was very upset and terribly hurt when we parted. She would never have allowed Parker near her under normal circumstances."

"Why was she so upset?" Sal drew his brows together. "She must have been terribly upset to get into a stranger's car."

"Yes." Jon laid his cheek on her hair. "She was. It doesn't matter, Sal.

It's over. We need a few days of rest and quiet now to get everything sorted out. That's all we need."

"We're here." It sounded like a sigh of relief, coming from Sal; and it almost made Jon smile, because it echoed his own feelings so well.

The house was brightly lit. They could see movement through the curtains, then the door flew open and Lucia came running down the steps, right into Olaf's arms. "Is she okay? Is Naomi okay?"

"She's fine. Just exhausted and pretty grimy." Olaf patted her shoulder. "Don't worry. She'll be her old stubborn self after a good night's sleep. Let's go home, dear. And I think you should maybe bring Joshua. These two have some talking to do when Naomi wakes up."

Joshua, standing at the top of the stairs, his hands pushed into the back pockets of his jeans, watched how Jon lifted Naomi out of the car. "I'm coming," he said. "Let me get my bag."

"You're really leaving?" Jon was sure he had misheard. "You're leaving your mother and me now, after what she's been through? I'm sure she'd like to have you around tomorrow morning."

Naomi opened her eyes. "It's all right. You go, Joshua. And Jon, please set me down. I can walk."

"Yes, I'm leaving. I've had it with the drama." Joshua glared at them. "The more I watch you, the more I think I want to move away, and soon."

He walked away to the waiting car.

Jon set Naomi down. She went into the house and up the stairs without looking back at her father, who was waiting for Jon near the garden gate.

In passing, Joshua brushed his fingers over the back of her hand. "Bye, Mom. I'll be at Grandfather's if you need me. I'm glad you're okay." Joshua hurried into the waiting car before she could reply.

Olaf motioned Jon away from the door, just out of earshot. "We need to find that man," Olaf said quietly. "We can't let him get away with this."

Surprised, Jon gazed at him, waiting for an explanation.

"You're not going to wait for the police to do anything, Jon? Surely you have more clout than that?" Olaf's face was bland, a study in cool aloofness. Without waiting for a reply, he turned and got into the car.

AMONG OTHER THINGS, Lucia had bought them a coffeemaker. A big, silver thing with lots of buttons and a spout for milk. It took up a lot of room on the kitchen counter, but the coffee it produced was excellent. Jon stood and watched it burble and steam while the aroma wafted around him, soothing and fortifying at the same time.

As soon as they had been alone, right after Sal had left, Naomi had gone upstairs, silently, softly, her steps barely audible. The bedroom door fell shut, the sound like a final chord in the drama of the day.

Coffee, he needed coffee, and now. Listening to the hiss of the machine, Jon tried to gather his tired thoughts into coherence. Olaf's words rang in his ears, the mysterious question about his clout, and consequences. He had liked the menace in those words, delivered with a perfectly straight face and without inflection. He liked the suggestion that Parker might get hurt, police or not, that he would see punishment for bringing harm to Naomi. Ice-cold sweat ran down his back, imagining Parker touching her, forcing her rings from her finger, making her cry at their loss.

Jon balled his hands into fists on the counter. He would have another talk with Olaf and find out what he had meant.

With the coffee mugs in hand, he made his way up the stairs, turning off the lights along the way.

The black dress was on the floor, tossed there as if she never wanted to touch it again. Naomi was still in the bath; Jon could hear the water in the shower running. He put the coffee down on the bedside table and went to listen at the door, certain he had heard weeping, he did not go inside but gave her some privacy.

Kicking off his shoes, he stretched out on the bed. His eyes begged to shut instantly, he was that exhausted; but he forced himself to stay awake.

The coffee helped. It was hot and strong, the aroma deep and spicy. Lucia had chosen well; Jon knew he would have to thank her for this.

The bathroom door opened.

Naomi, wrapped in a towel, appeared and stopped when she saw him. "Oh. You're here."

"Yes. I brought you some coffee. Do you want it?" He held out the mug to her. She took it and sat on the edge of the bed, where she waited—her hands wrapped around the coffee mug—for him to speak.

"Feeling better?" Jon knew it was a brainless question, but it was the best he could come up with.

She hadn't looked directly at him since he'd brought her home, hardly spoken to him. It felt as if an abyss of silence had opened between them, and it broke his heart.

"I'm all right, just very tired." Carefully she took a sip of her coffee. "Jane gave me coffee too. I'm afraid I won't be able to sleep. Maybe it would be better if I left you alone and went down to the couch. Then at least you can rest." She got up and wandered over to her dresser; where she dug out a nightgown. On the point of dropping the towel and putting it on, she glanced at him and went back into the bathroom.

Slowly, shyly, she came back, her nightgown on, and stood at the end of the bed.

"I don't know what to say to you," Jon said. "I don't know what to say. We will have to talk about this, about everything that happened today; and I really mean everything. But just for now, Naomi, for this night, can't we just go to sleep as if nothing is wrong? Can't you come into my arms and sleep on my shoulder like always, and can we please pretend everything is all right? And talk tomorrow, when we are rested and calm? Will you please come to me?" He held out his hand to her. She took it.

chapter 35

SHE WAS IN his arms, and that was all that mattered.

Jon had pulled up the quilt some time before dawn, when her limbs had grown cold, and curled around her, his face in her hair, and listened to her breathing. At last he had fallen asleep himself, the comforting warmth of her body close to his, the towers of the city blinking at him through the darkness like sentinels, like giants watching over them..

It was nearly noon when he woke. Naomi was gone, her pillow cold. Frightened, scared that she had, in the light of the new day, decided to leave him after all, Jon jumped from the bed, his heart thumping wildly in his chest. He found a pair of jeans, slipped into them, and hurried downstairs, trying to think where she might have gone, cursing his deep sleep, berating this habit of hers to run away every time something went wrong.

The house smelled of coffee. The familiar, welcome scent drifted toward him through the hall and up the stairs. It was fresh coffee too, the smell hot and heady; and he was sure that the scent of bacon was mixed into it.

Naomi was in the kitchen.

"I made breakfast," she said, wiping her hands on a towel. "I hope it's okay with you. There was a lot of food in the fridge, so I made eggs and bacon." With a shrug she glanced at the frying pan. "They're not as good as your omelette, but I'm sure they are edible. I thought if we can sleep in the same bed we can also eat together."

There was toast and butter, even honey, and it made Jon realize how terribly hungry he was. "Why in the world shouldn't we eat together? We're married, aren't we? We live together; we love each other. Well, I love you. You'll have to tell me you love me at some point today."

Her lips twitched, but she did not reply and instead put a plate down on the table for him, and a stack of bread.

Jon noted how her eyes traveled over his bare chest, and he grinned. "Come here." She was in her bathrobe, her hair still uncombed, and she looked as lovely as she had the first day he had met her.

"No." Naomi folded her hands and stood like a schoolgirl, solemn, a little sad, and very still. "We have to talk first. I want to know if you're only here because of what happened last night or if you have come back to me."

"You silly girl." He nearly choked on the bacon. "I never left you! What makes you think that?"

"But you did leave me! You got out of the car and told me you had enough of me."

"Are you crazy?" Jon lunged for her and caught her sleeve. "Come here. Don't stand there as if you're going to be punished." There wasn't a lot of resistance as he pulled her down on his knees. "I was very hurt, that's true. You, telling me I have no say in Joshua's life, that hurt, Naomi; it really did. I want to be his father; I want to do everything right for him." He hesitated, uncertain if this was the right time, the right moment to talk about this, when they should actually be talking about the abduction and what had happened to her. "Can't you please trust in me? Do you really think my decisions are that bad?"

"No, of course not." With a sigh, she settled against him. "I know you mean well. I was just so terribly hurt when you signed those documents for Harvard without letting me have a say in it. It felt as if…" She hesitated. "It felt as if suddenly everything I had hoped for, everything I worked for, didn't mean anything anymore. As if you and my father had decided that my time with Joshua was over, and it was your turn to take over. I felt pushed aside, and it hurt terribly, when I had never done anything but work toward that music career for him."

"I know." And he did. Jon knew exactly what she meant, and for a moment he felt the hurt himself, shared her grief at seeing Joshua leave Juilliard.

"But the thing is, Jon, and this took me a while to realize." Naomi sat up to look at him. "I don't want to be like my father. I don't want to make Joshua as unhappy as I was because I could never, not once, do anything right or please him. I want to be proud of Joshua for what he achieves, and of the way he finds for himself. I don't want him to be unhappy. Even if it means he's throwing away this great gift of his." Her lips trembled, and she pressed them together to stop it. "Ferro," she said softly, "look at Ferro. He's like me. He doesn't care at all about vineyards or olive presses. All he wants to do is paint. All I wanted to do was love you, and write. Cesare is so proud of him: he eases his path; he thinks it's a great thing to have an artist in the family.

And me? I've always been a great disappointment, the child that went wrong."

"You didn't go wrong. You never went wrong." Jon wrapped his arms around her hip. "You went straight for what you wanted, for me, and I'm very happy you did."

That made her smile sadly and touch his cheek. "Do other parents go through this too, I wonder? Do they make plans and have dreams for their children, and then nothing comes of them?"

"Hell, baby, it's the story of life in this world!" Her question made Jon laugh, even though it was bitter and it hurt somewhere in his chest. "Have you forgotten? My parents threw me out and let me fend for myself when I left college. They were desperately disappointed! Val and Kevin, they were the good children, the children who went the proper way; I was the misfit. The failure." He smiled sadly. "Until I was the big star, of course, and came home in a chauffeur-driven limousine for the first time. Until my mom saw my face on magazine covers and the neighbors asked her for concert tickets. Then, yeah, then I was the good son again, and welcome. Let's not do this to our son, Naomi. I beg you."

"You are right. Let's not do this to Joshua." She thought for a moment. "But it's breaking my heart, Jon. I'm so heartbroken about this, I could cry and cry. Why in the world did I give him up so early if it's all for nothing now? Why did I send him to Oxford? I hardly ever saw my only child, all for the sake of music; and now it's over. And my father wins, at last. I can't believe this is happening. I can't believe I have to give in and let Joshua go, again."

There was nothing he could say to comfort her. Everything was true; she was right about everything she said.

"Yes." The eggs were getting cold, and the bacon. "Let's eat something. I'm sure you haven't had a decent meal since I don't know when; you're as pale as the walls. Here." He rose, planting her on his chair. "Let me see what else Lucia bought yesterday. Isn't that coffeemachine a killer?"

SHE HAD, SHE told him over fried mushrooms, a steak, and eggs on toast that was dripping with butter, gone on to the hotel, ready to storm into her parents' apartment; but then, once inside the lobby, she had changed her mind and decided she wanted a drink.

"I was beside myself, so sad and upset, and I had no idea what to do. I didn't want to call you; I was afraid. I was so afraid you wouldn't pick up, or even worse, pick up and tell me you didn't want to talk to me ever again. I think that would have killed me."

Jon looked at her across the table. "Eat," he ordered gently, and she did.

"I don't know why he was there. But he was. And he was as nice as always, and so surprised to see me."

"Like hell," he muttered, which made her look up with raised eyebrows. "Nothing," Jon said quickly. "Go on. Tell me."

"He said hello and we began to chat and then moved on to the bar and had a drink. I told him I wanted to check out the season prices for the Met, and he offered to come along." She sighed. "It wasn't as if this was in a spooky area or anything; we just had to walk across that open space outside Lincoln Center. We looked around in the Met shop, I asked about the box prices, and then Parker asked me how I liked New York. When I told him how much I loved it, he offered to show me the best view of the city ever, from New Jersey." Embarrassed, Naomi put down her fork. "And I agreed. I couldn't see a reason not to. I know Sal had him checked before you permitted that interview in London, so I never thought I was in danger. It never occurred to me that he might be a stalker. He's a journalist after all, following you around is his job."

It was true; there was no way he could deny it. "So when did you realize this wasn't just a short trip to Jersey City for a view of Manhattan?" His appetite had left him.

"Pretty much right away." Naomi poked at one of the mushrooms. "By then I had decided I needed to talk to you, hear your voice, beg you to take me back, crawl back if I had too."

"Crazy. You know I love you like crazy, Naomi."

"Yes, but…" The fork sank into the mushroom. "But you…I can't even say it. I watched you walk away from me, and I died. Seeing you walk down that sidewalk and get into that cab, Jon, it seemed as if everything ended. Everything."

"You crazy girl," Jon softly said. "How often have you walked out on me, made me bear that; and I do it once and you go to pieces? At least now you know how it feels!"

"It's terrible! It's like seeing your life walk away!" Her fingers shook when she laid down the fork on her plate. "When we were back in the car I got out my phone, and he took it from me. I was so surprised, I didn't even try to fend him off. And he told me…" She had to take a deep breath. "He told me you were my jailer, and he was going to set me free. I had no idea what he was talking about. He locked the car doors and drove off. And then, and then…we just drove around until he took me down to the beach."

Jon noticed how she covered one hand with the other as if to hide the shame of her missing rings.

"I'm wondering, Jon," Naomi said, her voice wavering dangerously, "if we drove down there, if I really searched…"

He laid his hand over hers. "Baby, there's not a hope in the world of finding those rings." A smile tugged at his lips. "Who knows, maybe some day a girl will pick up that diamond and be very happy."

"It's engraved," she replied sullenly. "No one but me has a use for it."

That made him laugh. "Dear heart, I don't think many people would care about a name in a ring. They'd just be happy to find such a lovely treasure. Come on, get dressed. I'll take you down to Tiffany's and buy you a new one. It's only a stone, Naomi."

"It's only a stone." Sadly she echoed his words. "It's only a stone, but it was my stone."

Serious again, Jon asked, "So then what happened? After the beach?"

"Nothing much. He wouldn't give my sandals and my purse back, said I didn't need them anymore, and went on talking about my new freedom and all; and we drove around some more until I told him I was hungry. So he took me to that fast-food place, and I was able to slip away. Thank God for Jane."

"Yes, thank goodness. She is one cool number." And, he thought, he owed her a lot. "So what do you think, do you want to go and shop for a ring?"

Naomi took her time in answering. "Not today." She had another sip of coffee. "Can't we just stay here? At the house, just the two of us, and be lazy? I really need a quiet day. Only a few hours ago I thought my marriage was over. Now I'm back home, with you, and everything seems to be well. I'm tired, Jon. I'm so tired, and for one day I'd really like to lock out the world."

They took a tray upstairs and returned to bed, talking in soft voices, drinking coffee, watching the light change on the towers as the day passed and the sun wandered across the sky. Naomi wanted the window open despite the heat, saying she couldn't understand the American love for shutting themselves in while the weather was nice. She wanted to hear the sounds of the ships, the rumble of traffic from the expressway below the Promenade, the voices of children from the park. Jon's phone rang a couple of times, but he ignored it. She came into his arms when he kissed her, a little hesitant at first, a little abashed even, but he didn't care.

"Let me love you, babe," Jon said. "Everything will be all right," and she softened into his embrace.

IT WAS NEARLY dark again before Naomi remembered. "My purse. I didn't have a lot in it, just my cell phone and a credit card. We need to have it cancelled."

"Yeah, we will. No worries. I'll call Sal." He watched her rise as he picked up the phone. With the sheet wrapped around her body like a robe, she stepped to the window and looked out at the city.

It reminded Jon so much of that first morning in Halmar when she had come down the stairs from the loft that his heart hurt with the love he felt for her.

"I thought I was going to die."

The room was quite still, dark, and very warm.

"When he took my rings away and told me that now I was free, I thought I'd not survive the night. I thought he was going to kill me. And the strangest thing was, when I realized that, I was completely calm. I accepted it as something that had to happen, as the consequence of everything that had come before, as if my time was over. Actually, as if I've been living on borrowed time since the shooting and now it had run out." She turned back to him and sighed. "And then, quite suddenly, I changed my mind. Or rather, I decided I didn't want to die at all. That was when I told him I was hungry and he had to stop for food. And I ran."

The sheet dropped to the floor.

"I didn't want to die, Jon, because I knew I wanted you back. You left me, you left me alone in that car and walked away; and I knew I wouldn't take it. Not this time—I would not give you up without a fight this time. I knew that as long as we lived under the same sun I would love you, and want you. Nothing will ever change that."

He had to take a couple of deep breaths before he could answer.

"You're the one who's always so easy with giving up and running away," Jon said. "It's not me. I'm here all the time; I'm by your side all the time. You are the one who's so easily scared."

"Yes." It was a whisper, nothing more. "Yes, that's true. I'm easily scared. Another thing I have to change."

"You might start right now," Jon suggested. "Come here, come to me. You're standing there just out of reach, wonderfully naked, and I wish you'd come to me." He heard her soft gasp. "Come to me. Let me drive out your last thought of dying. I know I can."

The bed shivered just the tiniest bit when she crept up toward him.

chapter 36

SHE DIDN'T WANT to go out the next day either. It felt good to be alone with Jon, and it reminded her of their time in Halmar, right after he had found her.

"We've been," Naomi said slowly, "always on the move. Ever since we left Halmar to come over for Christmas, we've had so little time to be still, to just sit back and gather ourselves. I need that, Jon. I'm used to it, used to the solitude and the stillness."

He looked at her sitting on the kitchen counter, her feet dangling, a cup of coffee in her hands. They were getting used to their new surroundings. This morning he had gone out early to get fresh croissants and cinnamon rolls. While he was out he'd picked up a newspaper and some milk, chatted with the deli owner who had treated him like a normal, regular customer. Walking back home he had felt good, comfortable, and quite certain they would be able to settle in. As he passed he had waved to his mother, who was washing her windows, and she waved back.

Jon felt at home.

"No reason why we shouldn't stay in," he agreed, "but we need some groceries, and I have to make some phone calls. I'm guessing the police will be in contact too." The last eggs were gently bubbling in the pan, together with the last slices of bacon.

"And we need to talk to Joshua." Her words dropped into the silence.

Jon busied himself with a tomato, cutting it into fine slices and distributing them on the plates.

"We have to decide what to say to him, and what to do," Naomi offered. "I don't want my father to take him to Boston without us. Why is he so angry at me, Jon? I can't figure out why he's so angry at me all of a sudden."

"Maybe he's just tired of this ongoing fight between you and your father." He wiped his hands on a towel.

"I'm not fighting with my father. He's the one who's not happy with me. Have you forgotten, Jon, how you went to Geneva to bring him to Halmar? Don't you remember how mad you were then? Or when I was in the hospital after the shooting! You had him removed and slapped a court order on him!" She slid from the counter when he put the plates on the table and joined him there.

"That was an extreme time," Jon agreed, "and we all reacted in extreme ways. I know he was very worried about you, and furious at me for putting you in danger. I'm surprised he's not blaming me now for your abduction."

"Oh, I don't think he will."

Her appetite delighted him. She had finished off her eggs almost before he picked up his own fork. Amused, Jon watched how she eyed his portion and then pushed it over to her. "Here, have some more. I'm glad to see you eat!"

"I think he'll tell you it was my own fault, for leaving LaGasse behind and getting into Parker's car. And he's right," she said around a mouthful of bacon.

Jon waited for her to go on.

"He's right, because it was incredibly stupid of me." With a shrug, she got up to refill their cups. "It was."

"But you were upset and hurt," he argued. "You know that's the real reason why you got into his car. You had no idea it would end like this."

Coffeepot in hand, she looked at him. "Are you making excuses for me, Jon? Are you trying to be nice and find excuses for my stupidity? Please don't. It's bad enough as it is. And I hope they find the bastard and throw him in jail for the rest of his life."

Jon didn't say that he had a feeling Parker was in for more than just jail. He recalled that cold, bland expression on Olaf's face only too well, and it made him wonder how far his influence really went, if he really had the power to harm someone seriously.

"You know," he said thoughtfully, "I think we should really go to Tiffany's and buy you a new ring. You keep touching that finger as if it's painful. And you're right; it looks very sad without your rings. What do you think? We don't have to go anywhere else, or tell anyone."

IT WAS A beautiful day for late August in New York. A cool breeze had blown away most of the humidity, it wasn't as hot as it had been before, and the sky shone clear, bright blue. It almost looked, Naomi thought as they stood on the doorstep waiting for the car, like early fall, like one of those days when the golden leaves of the trees stood out in such a lovely contrast against the sky. She wondered if they would be able to see the geese pass overhead on their journey south, if geese even traveled over New York or if they avoided the city altogether. This, she was certain, she would miss. Her window had been open through many frosty autumn nights, while she sat wrapped up tightly in her duvet , just so she could hear the call of the birds flying south.

And yet as they drove across the bridge and she could see the glittering water of the East River below, her heart thumped in her chest at the city coming closer. She put Halmar out of her mind and smiled at the towers of Manhattan.

"You're like a child." Jon shook his head at her, but she waved him away and lowered the window.

The entire incident with Parker, even the nightmarish moments in the parking lot and the hours of waiting at Jane's house, left her curiously untouched, as if it had been nothing more than an unfortunate misunderstanding, a strange mishap. She didn't even wonder where he was now or if the police had caught him yet. It seemed as if the whole affair was nothing more than a frame for the one moment that had really hurt, the one instant that stuck in her like a poison dart, seeing Jon turn his back on her.

"You're wearing your wedding ring," she said, touching it with the tip of her finger. "If you buy a new one for me now, it will be as if we're not married to each other at all but just married. It feels very weird. I don't think a wedding ring can be replaced, Jon. This is not really a good idea."

"It's a very good idea, and we're going to do it." Jon took off his own ring and laid it in her palm. "Here. Keep this one safe. We'll just get a new set, and it will be like getting married all over." He caressed her cheek. "And that is a brilliant idea, after this upheaval. This way you'll know I really mean it."

"It's not the same at all." She sighed and closed her hand around the ring. "I know it's only a bit of gold and a stone, but you put that ring on my finger in London, and I promised to marry you that day. Not knowing how it would go, I promised."

"So you did."

They passed the spot where they had parted two days before, and Naomi sat up straight to look; but there was nothing, no sign to mark the drama that had started here.

"You know what I'd really like to do?" she said. "I'd like to go back to

New Jersey and that fast-food place, see where I was in daylight, maybe even go down to the beach and at least go through the motions of looking for my rings and then take a huge bouquet of flowers or something to Jane to thank her. She saved my life."

"You got that right. She saved your life." With a sad smile, Jon drew her into his arms. "I think flowers aren't good enough. After all, we're going to Tiffany's. Let's see if we can't find something better there."

The car stopped right outside the store.

"Now." Jon took her hand in his. "We're going to do this right, Naomi." His chin pointed at Alan and LaGasse, who had left the SUV and were standing beside it, waiting for them.

She didn't respond.

"You know we've been slack; we should always have a guard with us, don't you? We won't have a moment's peace if we go in there at this time of day without protection," he plodded on, his heart slowly sinking. This was not going as he had hoped. Not even two days and again they had reached a spot where they were stalled. "I don't want anything like this to happen again, ever, Naomi. You were incredibly lucky that you got away. Next time it might not go so well."

Naomi blinked at him. "If you would get out, we could go and buy some diamonds. You're holding up traffic."

"Right. Yes." He needed a moment to collect his wits. "Let's go then."

There was nothing left of the exhausted, sad woman he had found at Jane's house. Full of pride, overflowing with admiration, Jon helped her out of the car and watched her gracefully unfold. Her feet were back in elegant sandals, she was wearing the rose dress she had bought in London, and she looked as fresh and clear as a cool spring morning. She had gotten a tan in Italy, but it was more like a dusting of gold than any kind of brown, and it didn't diminish her pale beauty.

They had been noticed. Doors were opening, a senior salesperson welcomed them and led them into a private room where they were offered champagne and coffee while a man in an impeccable black suit listened to Jon's wishes.

"I'm picking your diamond," Jon said to her when they were alone. "It's your engagement ring. You let me pick it last time, and I'm doing it again. And then we'll choose new wedding rings. For both of us. And I want some diamonds for Jane."

"You can't buy her diamonds, Jon." Naomi looked doubtful. "Isn't that too personal?"

"Do I care? How personal can it get? She saved my wife's life. That's as personal as I can imagine." He grinned. "No worries, I won't buy her a ring. But a necklace would be nice. Or better, a bracelet."

With a sigh, she relented and sat back. "All right. But please, can I pick it? I do know her a bit better than you do."

"No."

Again she sighed.

HE WOULDN'T LET her put the wedding ring on. He only let her have the engagement ring when she stretched out her hand.

"Not yet," Jon said, and dropped the little blue box into the bag. "Later. And now we drive out to Jane's, and I'll say thank you again."

His taste, as always, was impeccable; and it made her wonder where he had learned to find exactly the right piece, well-balanced between beautiful and precious. The bracelet he had picked was a narrow gold bangle set with diamonds—simple, sleek, and very elegant—and Naomi liked it a lot.

"You want one." He grinned when she shook her head. "You're hiding your hands behind your back like a schoolgirl stealing chocolate. You want one."

The salesgirl came back to them when he nodded her way.

"Yes, I want one." She could not make herself care. "No, I want two. They are bangles. You're supposed to wear more than one."

Smiling dangerously, Jon put his mouth to her ear. "How about three then? Come on, treat yourself. How many do you want?"

It was like standing at the edge of a cliff; it felt dangerous, heady, exhilarating.

"All right, three." In a show of bravado, she raised her chin at him. "I want three of those bangles. Buy them for me!"

His eyes sparkling, lips pursed in amusement, Jon dug out his wallet again. "All right, Mrs. Stone, three diamond bangles for you it is. And those you may wear right away." He gave his orders to the shopgirl, and she hurried away. "Finally you let me treat you to lovely things without making a fuss. At last, Naomi. What has changed?"

She was shaking, scared of her own daring. "Everything, Jon, everything has changed." There was some champagne left in her glass, and she drank it. "When I woke from my coma after the shooting, I wanted to die. For the longest time I wanted to die. I tried to snap out of it, tried to love my life again, but it didn't work. Somewhere deep down was this blackness, this incredible sadness, like a dark, unfathomable well; and it was calling to me. Even when I came to London, even in Italy, it was still there. It followed me wherever I went, calling."

The champagne bottle stood on the table, and she reached for it, but Jon was faster. For a moment she watched the foam as he poured and then said, "Like my own shadow. It was like a shadow, a deadly sadness. It never let me go, and all the time it just got blacker. I wanted a baby so much; I still do. Don't say it!" She laid her fingertips on his lips when Jon took a breath to reply. "Don't say it; I know what you want to tell me. It may not matter to you, but it does matter to me. A lot. I want this. Wanted this. I wanted to give you this gift, even if only to atone for you missing out on Josh's childhood."

Her hand was a little unstable when she picked up the glass.

"When I was on that beach with Parker, when he took away my rings and my sandals, I realized for the first time that I might not survive that day. And I was terrified. I looked out at the sea and understood that I wasn't ready to die, not ready to let you go, not ready for anything at all but this life with you, and loving you. And that was the moment when I let go of that shadow, when I could finally step out of it like a discarded dress and be myself again. So, yes…everything has changed."

The salesgirl returned, carrying a tray covered in black velvet, five of the bracelets on it, and held it out to Jon. These were the last ones in that size, she said apologetically.

"Give me your hand," Jon said, and when Naomi did, he pushed one of them up on her wrist.

She did not lower her arm, so he put another one on it, and then one more. Naomi gazed at him steadily, and he picked up the last two.

"You glutton. You know wearing five of these is indecent. You'll make other woman jealous." His voice was dark with laughter. "But I love it. I love spoiling you."

The black credit card, the same one she had used in Los Angeles to go shopping with Solveigh, changed hands, and they were alone again.

"I wasn't going to say a baby doesn't matter." Picking up his little shopping bag, Jon rose from the comfortable chair and drained his glass. "Come on, you hussy. Let's go before you want a tiara."

"You weren't?" The gold shone nicely, and the bangles chimed softly when she moved toward the door.

"No, my darling." Courteously, he let her walk ahead. "I was going to say that we aren't working hard enough at it, obviously. I clearly need to take you to bed more often." And laughed when she gaped at him, speechless for once.

chapter 37

IN DAYLIGHT, IN the bright sunshine of an August afternoon, Jane's house was just another small, white house on the corner of two small streets in a residential area of a small town. Across the road, on a school sports field, kids were playing football, watched by some adults sitting on the lawn, picnic baskets between them. The smell of grilled burgers drifted over when they got out of the car.

Jon turned to look when he heard the satisfying sound of a ball being caught after a good pass, the thud of the leather hitting the pocket of the receiver's hands; and he smiled to see the boy doing a little victory dance, holding up the ball, well behind the line.

"Will you look at that." He nearly hummed it, so pleased was he with the view. "What a neat touchdown. Someone should give that kid a contract."

"And here I thought you'd want a daughter if we had another child," Naomi said. "But I believe you need another son, so you can play football with him. I never knew you were such an American dad at heart."

He slung his arm around her shoulder. "Yeah, I am. I think I'm really quite ordinary. But hey, let's not worry about gender, or a baby at all. I'll tell you what. Once we get back from this tour we'll really go to work on this; what do you say?"

"Shut up." Her bangles rang melodiously when she pulled them off and dropped them into her purse.

Jon's eyebrows came up, and she explained. "You're giving Jane one. How would it look if I walked in wearing five?"

They listened to the doorbell, to the echoing bark of a dog, and a female voice calling out to him.

"That dog is really friendly." As if in memory of that night, Naomi touched her wrist, then her finger, and gazed down at the new ring on it. From inside, they could hear footsteps.

Before he could reply, the door opened.

"Oh!" Jane's face was a study in distraction. "What a pleasant surprise! Do come in!" She smiled. "Sorry, I've been so busy lately. Everything's happening at once. Would you like some coffee?"

Before Jon could reply, Naomi nodded. "I'd love some coffee." She followed Jane into the kitchen.

Everything was still there, in the same order it had been when she had sat here; cold, trembling, frightened, and now, during the day, it looked ordinary, pleasant, a normal home for normal people. And yet, and yet, for one night it had been her sanctuary.

"We wanted to thank you," she said. "I wanted to thank you for rescuing me. I owe you my life."

Jane glanced at her from the coffeemaker.

"It's true. You saved my life. I know now, had you not helped me, that I'd probably have been killed. Maybe not that night, but soon." This was more awkward than Naomi had expected. Her hands folded, she stood beside the chair she had sat on two nights ago and stared at a stack of printouts on the table. There were blue markings on them that made absolutely no sense.

"Yes." The machine burbled gently, "I think you were in grave danger." From a cupboard over the sink, Jane brought out mugs but then hesitated. "I should get out proper cups for you."

"No." Naomi took them from her. "These are perfect. We don't want to keep you long either. We really just wanted to say thank you."

"Well, nonsense. I'm happy you're here. I made some madeleines last night; we can have them with the coffee." She brought out a plate with the little, seashell-shaped cakes.

"Proust." It was the first thing that came to Naomi's mind. "Those always make me think of Proust. I love Proust."

The blue eyes regarded her attentively. "Yes, Proust. The madeleines and the childhood memories."

Naomi took one of the madeleines and popped it into her mouth, where it melted in sugary sweetness. "These are wonderful! I haven't had madeleines since I lived with my parents in Geneva."

Jon appeared in the door. "What are you talking about? Is it girl talk? Do I have to stay alone in the living room for much longer?"

JANE REFUSED TO accept the blue box, telling Jon in a surprisingly tart tone that she hadn't helped Naomi to get a reward and that she would do it again at the drop of a hat; and this time her eyes flashed like ice.

"But you could have been hurt." The box balanced on his knee, Jon smiled at her. "You didn't have to get involved, but you put Naomi's safety first. Not everyone would act so selflessly. It might have gone badly for both of you."

With a huff, Jane stretched out her hand. "All right. Since you came all the way to give me that, let's see what's inside." Her lips tightened when she held up the bracelet. "It's lovely, but it's a bit much. Really, I can't accept this"

Jon shook his head. "I don't think so. I think it's not nearly enough. Please accept it. It's only a tiny token of my gratitude."

"Yes, I understand." She held up her wrist with the bangle on it. The diamonds caught the light nicely, throwing their sparkles across the skin of her arm. "Thank you. It's lovely."

"The beach." Naomi's voice sounded distant. "Is it far from here? Parker drove around so much, I lost my bearings completely. I'd really like to go and have a look."

"My dear, there are miles and miles of beach in New Jersey. Where were you?" Jane closed the blue box and tied the white ribbon neatly around it.

"I don't know. There was a red pavilion and a boardwalk. Not many people, for some reason." As if the memory scared her all over again, Naomi gazed toward the kitchen door, toward the place where she had found sanctuary. "I remember the sand was hot to walk on, and the surf was quite high."

"We had a bit of a storm a few days ago." A soft murmur from Jane, accompanied by a thoughtful nod. "Sounds like you were in Bradley Beach. There's a red pavilion there. It's a stretch from here." She glanced at her watch. "It will be getting dark by the time you get there."

Jon laid his hand on Naomi's. "Maybe we'll go another time then. Naomi told me you have a toy store?"

Surprised, Jane glanced at him. "No, no, I don't have a toy store. That's just a small business on the side." She hesitated. "I'm a publisher. I run a publishing house."

With a grin, Jon took another madeleine. "A book publisher?"

"Yes, that kind of publisher." Jane grinned back at him. "I know, we are a rare breed and seldom seen in public. But we do exist."

"What kind of books do you publish, then?" He leaned forward, interested, alert.

From the conservatory, they could hear the snuffling and yawning of a big dog waking from a nap, and Jane got up to check on him. A few happy yelps welcomed her as she slid open the door to the back yard and let him out. Hot air wafted into the house immediately, as if someone had opened a huge washing machine.

"I hate New Jersey." With a sigh, Jane dropped back onto the couch. "I wish I could live somewhere on the beach, where I could spend the day in a hammock, a drink in one hand and a good book in the other. That's my dream. But not yet, I'm afraid. There's still too much to do." To Jon, she added, "All kinds of books. Mostly novels, fiction. Why?"

"Oh, Naomi is a writer," he began, but was interrupted by Naomi, who said, "Jon, that's a gross exaggeration. I haven't even written a book yet. Stop it." For good measure she slapped his wrist, and he laughed.

"All right then. Let's go. I think we've done what we came to do." Rising, he stole another cookie from the plate. "Jane, why don't you come to my concert in New York a couple of months from now? It'll be the last one on this tour, and I have the feeling it may be the last one for a long, long time, if not forever."

"Yes, do," Naomi chimed in. "I'd love that."

"We'll see. I'm not a great lover of the big city." Jane smoothed down the linen pants she was wearing. "Thank you for coming." She thought for a moment, then said to Naomi, "I'll give you my card. Once you've written your book, let me have a look. Perhaps I can help you. Wait here."

A moment later she returned, a business card in her hand. "Here. Give me a call. And about that concert, yes, I think I'd actually like to go."

"Great!" Jon beamed at her. "I'll have the office set it up for you. Don't worry about driving into Manhattan. I'll have them send you a limo. Thanks again, Jane." On an impulse, he drew her into his arms and gave her a tight hug. Laughing, a bit embarrassed, she hugged him back.

THERE WAS THIS special light, this angle of gold and bronze pouring itself over the city at this time of day that made it seem almost alien, something from a painting of another planet, a beautiful, strange metropolis populated with graceful, strange beings.

Again Naomi lowered the window and took a deep breath of the humid, stuffy air.

"Can you hear it, Jon?" she asked. "Can you hear the music of the city? I don't know what it is. It's like a constant hum, as if it's singing. As if it's lying there on its island bed, hands crossed on its belly, eyes half closed; and it's humming an unknown song, content, relaxed, as pleased as a great beast basking in the sun and warmth. It feels alive, and benevolent, as if it wants to embrace every human soul that walks through its canyons, as if it watches out for them."

Jon shook his head at her.

"No, really," Naomi insisted. "Can't you hear it? It's like music."

"Baby, it's crowded, and it stinks of exhaust fumes. Certainly nothing pretty, only boring old Canal, dirty and crowded with peddlers and tourists. I can't even begin to see the beauty you think is there. It's a gritty place, New York is; and trust me, it doesn't embrace its humans." He leaned back into the leather seats, amused by her enthusiasm. "You were never in love with LA like this, and it's a lot friendlier than New York."

"No, you're right. Los Angeles scares me a bit; it's as if it could slip into the ocean at any moment. I think I find the Pacific a bit daunting. It's just so huge, and it leads nowhere."

That made him laugh. "Don't let the Asians hear that. I'm sure they would disagree."

"I can't wait, Jon." Naomi laid her head on his shoulder. "I can't wait until we are settled at the house. It will be so wonderful, you down in the studio, me in my study, working on our projects. We will live a normal life at last."

"Yes." His hand played in her hair. "Yes, we really need a break. We need to find peace and happiness. You're right."

"Let's go to my parents' place," she said, breaking the moment of silence. "Let's go and get this settled. I want to talk to Joshua, and to my father; and I want to know what they are planning."

"Are you sure?" Jon sounded doubtful. "I'm really not ready for another drama. I'd much rather go home. We could have dinner at the Italian place on our street."

"Or we could have dinner at the hotel. It has a rather good restaurant."

"With your parents?" The idea was not really appealing. "Why don't we go home?"

"Oh, okay. Let's go home then." She sighed. "But we have to tackle this, Jon. I want to talk to Joshua. I don't want my father to take him to Boston on his own. I want a say in this."

"And you shall have it, I promise." His grip around her waist tightened. "But let's do that tomorrow, in broad daylight, not tonight. There's still a little matter to discuss between just you and me."

Curious, she sat up.

"Do you want your new wedding ring or not? Did you think I'd just hand it over to you across the breakfast table? Come on, little beast. If you don't have a sense for romance, I do." His dark eyes shone dangerously. "I have something in mind, and it certainly doesn't include your father. It doesn't exactly include a lot of clothes either, but there may be some champagne. And a song whispered in your ear. So, what's it going to be? Your parents or home?"

"Home," she said.

chapter 38

THE CITY SHONE across the water right into their darkened bedroom; the warm night air, smelling of the river and the trees on the Promenade, drifted in through the open window.

Jon had brought a bottle of champagne and two glasses up with them and opened it while Naomi sat on the corner of the bed, watching him. The box with the new rings sat on the bedside table, the bow still around it, and she reached out for it; but Jon shook his head.

"Patience. Wait."

Once the wine had settled he held out his hand to her, and she rose.

Ceremoniously, slowly, he unwrapped the rings and took the smaller one out. For a moment he stood, facing her, collecting himself.

"With this ring I thee wed." The famous voice spoke the eternal words slowly, thoughtfully, well modulated; and it sent a shiver down her bare arms. "You are my music; you are the melody of my life. I need you every day, every moment. Without you, there is silence and sadness. With you, I'm whole."

Just as he had done during their wedding a year ago in the small church in Halmar, Jon took her hand and put the ring on her finger, a small smile on his lips. He kissed her palm before he let go.

That instant came back to her, those minutes when they had stood just like this before the altar, she in her white dress and Jon so beautiful in the cutaway, as elegant as she had ever seen him. She could smell the roses from her wreath and feel the cool Norwegian summer air; it was all there. Deep down inside, in a hidden nook she had almost forgotten about, the memory of delicious happiness unfolded and blossomed into a luxurious, beautiful flower, its perfume nearly overpowering.

Carefully, her fingers unstable, Naomi took the other ring from its white satin bed.

"With this ring I thee wed," she spoke the old formula. "You are my life. Without you, there is nothing. Nothing at all. I promise to love and hold you forever."

There were no bells, no cheering family and friends, and Jon was in jeans; but the feeling was just the same, the wild burst of love, the joy and headiness. Nothing had changed; he was still as entrancing as he had always been.

"I'm allowed to kiss you now. I remember quite clearly there was something about kissing the bride." His arms came around her, drawing her into an embrace. "I recall taking that wreath off your head and opening the sash of your dress. You were quite wild; your hands were all over me. You couldn't wait."

"Yes."

"You made me wait for you. You made me go without you for weeks. You have no idea how that felt." His fingers were tugging at the zipper in the back of her dress. "I could hardly watch you walk by without thinking of holding you in my arms, and you, all soft and yielding, all mine. My only love."

"You, my only love." Her words were like an echo, an afterthought.

"I laid you down on that bed, crushing all the petals on it, and I claimed you, my bride; I made you mine." The dress came off and floated to the floor like a rose cloud. "And that night, at last, I gained what had been missing all my life. That night, when we got married, my life finally was what it was supposed to be. You and me, babe. It comes down to this; it's all about you and me."

"It's about you and me, yes." The new ring glinted in the lights from the Promenade as she began to open the buttons of his shirt and run her fingers over his chest. "You're the most beautiful man I know." It was barely more than a whisper. "How I adore the shape of your mouth, your eyes, even the arch of your brows. You know you can make me wilt with desire with only a glance, by speaking my name, by standing close to me."

"And you." He kissed her, holding her tightly, inhaling her breath, his body pushing against hers, passion rising.

Naomi laid her arms around his neck and surrendered.

JON BROUGHT HER coffee.

He sat on the edge of the bed and held the cup close to her face until she woke, stretching like a cat, and blinked at him, drowsy and tousled.

"Don't get up," he said. "It's still early. The FBI was here."

Leaning against the headboard, Naomi sipped her coffee and listened as he told her about the visit from the FBI.

"I don't know how to tell you." Jon ran his hand over the quilt. "They came to inform us that Parker has been found."

She gazed at him, mug to her lips, waiting. The morning sun was shining on her, highlighting her hair, making her skin glow; and for a moment Jon forgot what he had come to say, the memory of last night flooding his mind.

"Do you feel married to me again?" he asked. "Does it feel real? Did it feel real to you?"

A faint blush crept up her throat. "Yes, pretty real. It always feels real, Jon." She shifted to make more room for him. "Are they gone? The FBI? Or are they waiting downstairs while we talk about last night? That would be embarrassing, I think."

"They're gone." His attention was wavering, seeing the way the sheet was slipping when she moved, exposing more skin. "They left right away; we are all alone again." Hopefully, he tugged at her cover, but she clamped down on it. "What if I came back to bed? What if we just stayed in bed all day?"

"You can hop back into bed," Naomi replied, "but I'm getting out in a moment. I'm starving. I want breakfast, and I'm in a mood for some shopping. It's time we got this house in shape, and I'd like to get some things done before we go on tour again. There isn't a whole lot of time left."

It was true, and he sighed. The desire to go back on the road was minimal.

"So what did they want?" She pushed her foot against his thigh to wake him from his thoughts. "Jon, tell me why they were here!"

"Right." He cleared his throat. "This is a bit difficult. They found him, but they didn't arrest him."

The coffee sloshed dangerously when she sat up. "What? He's still free? They didn't throw him in jail?"

Just like that, the romance of the moment was blown away.

"No, they couldn't." Jon took the cup from her. "He's dead."

Naomi didn't reply but waited, as pale as the sheet now, her hands in a tight knot around her knees.

"They said he had an accident at JFK, where he was trying to get on a plane to London. He didn't even try to hide his trail—bought the ticket with his credit card and all—as if he was totally unaware of what he had done." He took a sip of her coffee. "As if he didn't realize that he committed a major crime by abducting you. He must have been deranged big-time. Crazy, he never seemed that way. Obnoxious, yes. But as batty as a loon? No." His hand cupped her knee and pressed it gently.

"An accident? How can you have a fatal accident at an airport? I'm not getting it, Jon. Was he run over by a plane?"

That made him chuckle. "No, not run over by a plane, even though I must say I like that image. You do have a cruel streak under that gentle and fragile exterior, don't you? No." Serious now, Jon went on. "Apparently, he fell down an escalator. No one knows how it happened. There were other people around, but no one saw it happen. It was just an accident." He didn't say that he thought it was really strange, and actually much too good to be true. Olaf's words and the cold, calculating expression on his face after their drive back from Jane's came to his mind, but he closed that door right away. Not even Olaf, not even Olaf in his anger, Jon was certain, could have somebody killed just like that.

"I'm sorry."

Her soft tone made him look up.

"I'm sorry for him. What a wasted life. What a misguided, wasted life. To this day, Jon, I don't even know if he really wanted me or if I was a means to get to you. It just doesn't make sense."

"Oh." Rising from the bed, Jon patted her knee. "That's totally clear. He wanted you. He wanted you with the same deep desperation that I feel, Naomi. It was quite obvious during that interview in London. He wanted you the way I had you last night. Yeah, babe. That's what he wanted. And he'll never get it, poor asshole."

"Jon!"

He grinned insolently. "What? Can't I call the man who abducted my wife an asshole? Come on and get out of bed if you want to go downtown. It's a beautiful day: not too hot, not too humid. I know because I went out to get you cinnamon rolls."

"I still think it's strange." Naomi began to peel herself out of the bed, but when she saw him watching, his smile turning into an interested, intent gaze, she stopped. "Go away. You're staring. You're making me nervous with your stare."

Jon put his hands on his hips. "I'll stare all I want. You're married to me, and twice. I have a right to every inch of your body."

"And I yours. Watch your mouth, husband mine."

Perched on the edge of the bed, she took a deep breath, the ease of the moment gone. "Jon, I can't wrap my mind around it. He was so nice. Funny too. He made me laugh with his audacity. And now he's dead? Is he dead because of me?"

"No, of course not." The curtain was stuck, and he busied himself with getting the chords untangled, his back to her. "Of course he's not dead because of you. He had an accident. It's weird, that's all. Now what do you want to do today, dear heart? Where do you want to go?"

"Even when we were at the fast-food place, even then, after he had taken my sandals, my phone, everything, he was so courteous, so kind; he never said an unfriendly word. Everything was polite, friendly, delivered in a light voice." She paused. "I think that was the scariest part: the difference between his words and his actions. He would say such nice things, so polite, so gentle, and at the same time rob me of my things, one by one. I didn't want him to take my rings. I struggled. He hurt me."

On the river a barge passed by, a few gulls lazily drifting in its wake. The sky was blue with a few stray clouds in it. The city gleamed in the sunlight. Out on the Promenade, a couple of young women walked, pushing strollers, chatting, laughing. Jon noted these things, saw how the morning unfolded, how everything seemed peaceful and serene while those words rolled in his head, growing, taking on a momentum of their own. She had said it so calmly, as if it didn't matter at all, but those three little words made his stomach roil and his blood churn.

"Well, he's dead now." Surprisingly, his voice sounded calm, even detached. "He'll never hurt you again." Suddenly, quite urgently, he felt a need to see Olaf and look into those icy blue eyes, share the anger and hate with him. It was such a weird, unaccustomed feeling that Jon shook himself.

"I'd like to ask something of you, Jon," Naomi was saying, and he turned his attention to her. She was still sitting in bed, the sheet held up over her breasts, gazing at him.

"Baby, anything you want, you know it. You don't even have to ask." He sat beside her and ran his hand down her bare shoulder, along the length of her arm.

Naomi pursed her lips. "Actually, I don't have to ask you. I can do this on my own. I keep forgetting that I'm as stinking, filthy rich as you are."

"Probably a whole lot richer," Jon mumbled, and gave the sheet a hopeful tug, but she held on.

"I want our friends living close to us. Sean, Art, Russ, Sal. I don't want them spread out all over New York. Don't you think we could do that? I've been thinking about it, and maybe, if we helped them or bought condos somewhere in the vicinity. It would be nice to have them around."

"Yes." He loved the way her shoulder fit into his palm. He could cup it, hold it securely, and it felt a little as if he was enveloping all of her, her essence. "We could offer them that. I have a memory though of Sean saying he wanted to move to New Jersey, quite close to where you…" The name would not pass his lips. It stuck in his chest like a wad of clay: sour, clogging, suffocating.

"Jon." She laid her hand on his chest, on the skin where his shirt was open. "Jon, it's over. We're here. I'm here. Everything is over."

"That's where you're wrong." With a deft flick of his wrist, the sheet came down. "A few things are so totally not over."

AS FAR AS they were concerned, the FBI had told him, the case was closed. They had found his car with her purse and sandals in the trunk, and they would be returned in a couple of days; but there would be no further investigation.

It was over, indeed, like a bad nightmare, as if it had never happened, and only the feel of the new, different ring on his finger reminded Jon of the night he had spent waiting for her in agony, feeling the weight of guilt on his back and Olaf's suspicious stares like needles stuck into his face.

Naomi, when she came down and joined him for breakfast, looked fresh and calm, just like she had looked before the shooting. The blue dress she was wearing gave her skin the pearly luster he so loved seeing on it, and it had an enticing neckline. She was wearing a single strand of pearls with it, and she looked as lovely as a summer day.

"I want to see Joshua today," she announced while she slipped into matching shoes. "I'm still not pleased about the whole thing."

Jon put down his coffee cup. "You said you had forgiven me!"

"You, yes. My father, no. He's done something unforgivable. They came here for just that reason, Jon, to entice Joshua away. I haven't spoken to him about this yet, but it's time."

"He was here all night when you were gone," Jon said. "He was so worried, and so furious. He came out to New Jersey with me and Sal to get you; he wouldn't hear of staying behind, and he pulled some strings to get information from the airports. I don't think the FBI would have been there if was not for him. You know the police don't do anything when an adult goes missing, not for two days or so. I don't know who he called, but it worked."

Naomi shrugged, unimpressed. "Probably his friend the mayor, or his friend the police commissioner, or the attorney general, or even the governor. I have no idea, but you can bet it's one of them. If anyone knows how to pull strings, Jon, it's my father."

"Strange." He put the cup into the sink. "And I always thought it was me who ruled the world. Seems I've found my master."

"Oh, don't put it like that!" She picked up a pink purse from the counter. "I hate that idea! I hate the idea of you admiring my father for his clout when I thought you had way more than he!"

Thoughtfully, Jon gazed at her. "Your father was wondering about my clout too. It's really strange. You and your father, you're the only two people in the world who I've ever heard use that word. It sounds weirdly old-fashioned, like something out of the Roman Empire, and I think it's very scary to measure a man by it."

Naomi shrugged. "I think it's very sexy. And I hate to think of my father like that. I don't mind it in you at all though."

chapter 39

JON COULD HAVE sworn her body temperature went up as they crossed the lobby of the hotel.

He followed behind her, hands sunk in his pockets, amused by the way she carried herself: her shoulders straight and stiff, her chin raised, hands tight around her purse. She kept looking around, taking note of every little thing going on—the flowers on the counter, the uniforms of the doormen and bellboys, the shine of the brass plate around the elevator buttons—and he could have sworn she raised her eyebrows at an empty coffee cup on a table that had not been cleared away instantly.

"You know you scare the living daylights out of these poor people, don't you?" he murmured into her ear when they were in the elevator. "I can see them breaking out in a cold sweat as soon as you walk through the door. I wonder if they do that with Olaf too?"

"I'm sure they don't," Naomi replied with a huff. "And I'm sure he doesn't even bother to check the lobby himself. Want to take a bet that he uses the hotel garage and never goes there? Leaves it all to the manager?"

"Who, dear heart, is paid to do that." He let her step out first. "And maybe your family relies on that."

"Jon." She stopped and turned around. "My hotel in Halmar, the Seaside. There was not a single thing in that house that would have embarrassed me. A guest could have gone anywhere, at any moment, and not found anything to complain about. I was proud to have it that way. Those plates I dropped…"

He raised his hands in defense, laughing at her. "I know, I know. Custom-made in England, and you paid a fortune for them. And you still haven't forgiven me for making you drop them by walking through that door. I've offered to pay for them a million times; stop blaming me already!"

"I have forgiven you." Her lips softened into a smile. "But still. I was trying to make a point, Jon." She waved her hand at her surroundings. "I'm not impressed by this, just the way I wasn't impressed by the Oceano in Positano. Don't get me wrong; they aren't bad places. But they aren't excellent places either. They are not outstanding. If they were mine, they would be outstanding."

Jon nodded, but he didn't reply. Taking her by the shoulders, he gently pushed her forward and knocked on the door of the penthouse apartment.

Lucia opened the door. "You're here; you're here," she said, embracing Naomi and then Jon. "Come in, I'm so happy to see you! Kevin and Olaf are on the patio."

For an instant, before Naomi could answer, Jon felt an echo of her resentment, a stab of anger at Olaf's intrusiveness, at the way he was sneaking his way into his own family and their lives.

Calmly, Naomi answered, "Good. Then we can have this discussion and be done with it," and stalked through the room and out into the sun.

They were sitting at a table set for lunch, Olaf and Kevin, while a cook was grilling steaks for them on a mobile barbecue.

Jon stopped in the doorway.

The roof garden was a lovely place, well kept; set with many terracotta pots, it was a green oasis high above the New York traffic. From where he stood Jon could see the fountain outside the Met, and the graceful arches of the opera house. It was a lovely spot.

"Father," Naomi said, dropping her purse on the table. "You look well."

"As do you, my dear. Have a seat." Olaf pulled out a chair for her, which she ignored.

"You know we have to talk. You know I don't like one bit that you talked Joshua into quitting Juilliard. It was not your decision to make."

With a glance at Jon, Olaf laid his napkin aside and leaned back. "And neither is it yours. It's Joshua's. All I did was show him alternatives, possibilities. No one is forcing him to do anything."

"He's meant to be a musician!" Her voice didn't sound quite as stable as she wanted it. "Joshua has a great talent, and he should be a musician, like his father. You abused Jon's kindness when he retracted that court order by coming here and alienating Joshua from me by putting these ideas of Harvard in his head."

"And you," Olaf replied pleasantly, "should have been the head of the Carlsson business and decided otherwise. So why don't you give your son the same freedom that you claimed for yourself? It's different when your child is concerned, isn't it? It hurts, doesn't it, when they don't go in the direction you wanted for them, don't I know it."

"That is so totally not the point." She balled her fists at her sides. "The point here is that Harvard was NOT Joshua's idea, or his wish; it was yours. You are seducing him into it. I made my own decisions. No one told me to run away with Jon."

"No one would have either." With a sigh, Olaf pushed his chair back and rose. "Naomi, darling. I'm not trying to seduce Joshua away from you. I'm not even saying he shouldn't be a musician like his father. But honestly, I can't see any harm in him going to business school, no matter whether he decides to be a musician or to take over the hotel business. It'll be good for him if he knows what it says in his contracts. I bet Jon here would have liked that knowledge too."

Jon leaned against the doorframe, and grinned. "Oh, I have that knowledge. I didn't go to Harvard, but Columbia doesn't have a half-bad business program."

Distracted, Olaf stared at him. "I never knew you went to college."

"You never asked." Jon sauntered over to the grill. "You never bothered to look beyond the bright lights."

"That's true," Olaf said softly.

There was a very juicy-looking rib eye steak sizzling on the fire, and Jon pointed to it. The cook laid it on his plate, together with mushrooms and onions and a good serving of fried potatoes. A piece of bread in his other hand, Jon sat down at the table, right next to his brother, and began to eat.

"Are you telling me, Naomi, that you think Harvard is a waste of time?" Olaf asked.

She was looking at Jon's food. "Of course it's not a waste of time. It just wasn't your decision to make. You should have talked to me first, before you put that suggestion to Joshua. I'm his mother, after all."

"And Jon is his father." Impatiently, Olaf waved at the cook, who brought over a platter with meat and sausages, grilled tomatoes, more mushrooms, and a bowl of potatoes. "Sit down, Naomi, and eat something. Stop ogling your husband's plate."

"You're..." Her throat was so tight she could hardly speak. "You're treating this as if it doesn't matter, as if I'm making a scene for nothing. You're treating me like an obstinate child. And you're acting as if our wishes in this don't matter at all."

Olaf regarded her thoughtfully before he replied. Then he said, "You know, I actually do think they don't matter at all. Just like mine didn't matter when you made your decisions. It took me a very, very long time to come to terms with that. Indeed, it took me until after the shooting, until Jon threw me out of that hospital and we had to watch from a distance how you made your recovery. Only then, Naomi, only when someone else was keeping me away from you, and not your own stubborn actions, did I realize that you as my daughter meant more to me than the business. I'd gladly have given away everything I owned to see you healthy and happy again."

Lucia came to stand beside him and take his hand, which he pressed.

"Maybe," he went on, "giving Joshua this option, offering him something other than just the music, is my kind of atonement for pushing you all the time, for seeing you as an asset and not as my beloved child."

Naomi took a step back. "I can't take this. I can't take you saying these things. And I don't believe you. You're hatching a new plan to save your precious empire, that's all. You've given up on me, and now you want the boys. You're just skipping a generation."

Olaf threw down the napkin he had been holding. "You know what? Yes. I do hope to pass on what generations of Carlssons built to my grandson, and maybe to my new grandnephew. I'll not lie to you; that's my hope. For the life of me I can't see what's wrong with that. You opted out, fine. Joshua might like owning the Carlsson estate though. He might like being a hotel tycoon. He might enjoy what you resent. And I can't see what it has to do with you. You have everything you ever wanted, Naomi. You have the man you love more than anyone else; you live the life you always wanted to live, married to him; and you make your own choices. Joshua is grown; it's his right to make his own too."

"What it comes down to," Jon said around a mouthful of steak, "is that you should have asked our consent before talking to Joshua about leaving Juilliard and going to Harvard. That's pretty much it, Olaf."

Olaf shot him a brief grin. "I know. It wasn't a planned thing though; it just crept up. And then one thing led to another. We had this dinner party, the one for my birthday. Carl was here, and some friends. A couple of them are pretty important Harvard people, and they took an interest in Josh. That was pretty much how it all started." He shrugged. "Not that I'm unhappy about it. But it wasn't planned."

"And now?" Naomi asked, "is Harvard getting a new library? New labs? A new supercomputer? What did you have to do to make them take both Ethan and Joshua just like that?"

"That's not how it works," Olaf said. Jon choked on his food. "You don't get admitted to Harvard if you're not an outstanding student, no matter how wealthy you are."

"And dogs have wings." Defeated, Naomi sank down in a chair. She took the fork from Jon's hand and pierced one of the mushrooms on his plate with it.

"You could get your own," Lucia remarked. "There's plenty of food." She sat down beside Naomi. "Why don't you join us for lunch. Jon has, as far as I can see."

"The meat is excellent," Jon agreed, "thank you."

Kevin poured wine for him. "I, for one, am very happy about this. This is what Ethan wanted to do all along; and now, with Joshua, it will be even better. For both of them."

Naomi reached for the glass, but Jon took it from her. "If you want some, pour your own. Stop eating my stuff."

She listened to the sounds of the street below: voices, cars, the rumble of buses, a howling siren. The hotel was not very tall by New York standards: only ten floors, low enough to feel a connection to life. This part of the roof was private; it went with the penthouse only the family used, but she knew there was a bigger patio on the other side, one that was open to guests and often used for parties and events.

"The elevator brass plates aren't polished." she said, "And at the hotel in Positano there was stale fruit in the welcome basket. Breakfast was really bad. The bread was downright disgusting."

Jon held out a piece of his bread to her. "Try this; it's a lot better."

She took it and smelled it only to put it down on the table. "I'm wondering, Father, why you never thought of having Cesare deliver the baked goods to the hotel. You know the things they produce at the farms are superior to anything you can buy in Positano. If it was my hotel, I'd change that. I'd buy everything from Cesare."

Olaf smiled but didn't reply. He brought over a glass and poured her some dark red wine and set down a plate for her.

"I'd even arrange tours to the farms for the guests so they could have wine tastings, maybe even let them visit the olive groves and experience a harvest. Something like that. We used to do that kind of thing in Halmar. The midsummer night picnic was one of the favorites, and

New Year's Eve." She held up her plate when Jon offered her meat and potatoes. "That was fun."

"You ran that hotel superbly," Olaf agreed. "You did an excellent job. That's one of the reasons why I kept pushing you into our business. You have an eye for these things, and even though you say you hate it, it's a lie. You did love it. You loved running the Seaside."

Carefully she cut the meat and heaped some fried onions on it. "I didn't love running the Seaside. I loved the quiet and serenity, and the slow, predictable routine. I liked the small, hidden life."

"Yes, but you didn't have to live there. There was no need for that kind of life; you could have had it all." Olaf handed her the salt shaker when she stretched out her hand for it.

"I didn't, Father," she replied softly, not looking at anyone. "I didn't have it all. I had nothing. Without Jon, I had nothing. That's the part you don't understand. That's the part you'll never understand."

"I do understand." Gently, slowly, Olaf reached out to touch her shoulder. "I understand, even though it is hard to grasp how anyone can hold on to feelings for that long."

Before she could respond, before she had even found the breath to respond, Jon said, "It can't be explained. If you lock your heart so tightly around someone that she becomes a part of you, being without her means part of you is missing. It hurts every day. Every heartbeat hurts, every movement, even every thought. You don't want to make plans, go out for dinner, attend a party, anything, because it hurts. All you can do is sit quietly in a corner, develop a slow, quiet routine where every motion is well rehearsed, like a ritual, so you know what will come and you'll not feel the sharp hurt but maybe only a dull pain. You wander through day after day and pray that nothing will happen to upset that small, reduced life you're leading so you'll not be surprised by that knife in your gut." His voice sounded deep and gravelly, and yet there was a sad, melancholy melody in his words. He had put down his fork and leaned back in his chair, his hands folded on his knees; and he was gazing at Naomi, the trace of a smile on his lips. "I moved out of the house where we lived together. The one you saw when you were in LA after the shooting, Olaf. In every room, wherever I went in that house, there was the ghost of Naomi's laughter, the memory of her essence; and I couldn't take it. I found myself turning, thinking I'd heard her speak to me, or grasp for a shadow, imagining I'd seen her. The garden, it was even worse in the garden. I'd walk along the path to the beach, under those high jasmine bushes she never allowed anyone to cut back, and expect her to come toward me, her hands full of seashells and stones she had picked up from the surf— my mermaid, my selkie, and it was an illusion. When Naomi left me that night, my life stopped. And I knew it was my own fault. I had wasted my chance; I had driven her away. And my life stopped. I would have done anything, anything at all, to find her and win her back, every day, all my life. Nothing else mattered."

Silence settled over the table, and even the noise from the street seemed dimmed, as if the traffic had stopped for a moment and the pedestrians on the sidewalk were holding their breath, waiting for a reaction.

With a deep breath Jon took up his knife and fork. "Anyway. We need to plan a trip to Boston. When do you think we should go?"

"Tomorrow, " Olaf said. "Let's go tomorrow. We'll fly. I'll arrange for the jet."

He signaled to the cook, who went inside and brought out a cart with desserts and coffee.

Olaf's eyebrows rose in amusement at Naomi's critical glance. "Naomi, since you seem so unhappy with the hotel in Positano, why don't you take it over? I'll give it to you. To be honest, we hardly stay there anyway. Most of the time we are at Cesare's house, with the family. I'll give it to you, and you can kick out the manager."

She raised her chin at him. "I want this one too. And I want a number of houses in Brooklyn, close to where we are, where our people can live while we work on the musical. I want them close to us."

That made him give her one of his feral grins. "You want this hotel here? As your own? What about your mother and me; are you going to kick us out then? We just moved here!"

"You can stay, of course. But I want it."

"Oh, hang on," Jon said. "You want to own this place? Why in the world?"

Naomi waved at him. "It will still be part of the family estate, Jon, don't be ridiculous. No one's going to tear that apart. And it will all end up with Ethan and Joshua. And whoever has the guts to stand up to them. All right then, Harvard."

Olaf cut a big piece of cheesecake and handed it to her. "Tell me, daughter mine, what's this about houses in Brooklyn?"

Bemused, Jon listened as they launched into a complicated discussion about estate prices, locations, financing, and ownership while he poked at his cherry pie. He felt hungry for a cigarette after the excellent meal; but he couldn't remember if he'd ever seen Olaf smoke, and he had forgotten to bring his own. Kevin had left, saying he had to get back to work and how happy he was at the way things had turned out.

"Can't say I ever wanted Ethan to be a surgeon." had been his parting words. "Even though it's the family tradition. I'm way more pleased with this."

"So," Jon heard Olaf say, "you want it to be part of the Carlsson estate? What would we do with the apartments? Once you move on, what will we do with them? And why can't these people take care of themselves?"

"Because," Naomi replied, laying her hand on Jon's, "they are part of my family. I want them near me," and Olaf nodded.

It still felt surreal. It felt scary and otherworldly, seeing them sit around one table and talk to each other like normal people, pouring coffee for each other, debating the purchase of a Brooklyn Heights building as if they were debating buying a new car for Naomi.

"All right." Olaf picked the phone out of his pocket. "Let me talk to Carl. He's a bit better with that than I am." Once again that shark's grin appeared on his face and made Jon's skin crawl. "I'm only good with money."

"Did you hear," Jon said, "the FBI were at our house today. Seems there won't be a court case. Parker died in a stupid accident at the airport when he tried to leave the country."

"Really." The shark's grin widened.

"Yes, fell down some stairs or an escalator, they said." Jon watched hopefully as a bottle of Scotch was brought in by a waiter and placed at Olaf's elbow, followed by a wooden box and cigar utensils.

"What a pity." Olaf opened the box and gazed down at the cigars. "Would you like one, Jon?"

They were Cuban, the best, and their scent was divine. Jon rolled his between his fingers and listened to the soft, crackling sound of the whole leaves. The brand was the same he had offered Sal and Sean at the Malibu house just before they had left for the Academy Awards, when they had been waiting for Naomi. He remembered how she had come down the stairs, how his heart had nearly stopped at seeing her, thinking for a moment that she was bowing out at the last moment and had not even taken the time to dress before he realized that she was wearing an exquisite, lovely, cream silk dress made to look as if she was wrapped in a bed sheet, as if she had just risen from bed. For an instant Jon thought he could even taste the aged whiskey they had been drinking.

He had been so proud of her, so full of love, and so insanely happy that night, before it all ended in disaster.

"Thank you indeed, Olaf," Jon said, and leaned forward to let him light the cigar.

"Did you have something to do with this, Father? With Parker's death?" Naomi was looking at them, her eyes traveling from one to the other suspiciously, but Olaf gave her a gentle smile.

"Drink your champagne, darling. Do you really think I have enough clout do have someone killed? How silly."

chapter 40

JON WOKE TO what sounded like a door closing.

It was barely light, dawn creeping through the curtains on gray, tired fingers; and once again he was alone, her side of the bed cold and empty.

Panicked, he sat up.

Everything seemed as it was supposed to be, their packed suitcases stood against the wall, her purse on top of them; nothing was missing. And yet, once more, he was alone. His glance fell on the bathroom door, but it stood slightly ajar, and the light wasn't on.

That morning in Malibu came rushing back, the morning a few months ago when she had told him she had to leave, had to find peace, and it could not be with him. Jon recalled only too well how they had stood on the roof terrace of their house while the sun rose over the hills, and how his heart had broken, piece by little piece. For a moment panic took over, the bare-chested, simple fear that she was again gone, again for some reason he could not fathom, gone from his life; and he jumped out of bed, calling her name. There was no answer.

Barefoot, in his pajama pants, Jon wandered down the stairs and into the kitchen. Here too everything was quiet. She had not turned on the coffeemaker, not put bread into the toaster, not taken out a mug. The dishwasher hadn't been unloaded, and the fridge was once again woefully empty. Neither of them was very good at looking after themselves, Jon realized, staring at the single egg left in the carton and the one tired tomato.

Amparo would be arriving later that day, and what a blessing that was. He had not been able to convince her to stay here in New York with them though; she didn't want to leave her family and home in California, but she had offered to send her sister, Lourdes, to run the house for them. Jon could hardly imagine a life without Amparo.

With half his heart beating, the part where hope lived, he walked into the living room, expecting to find Naomi on the couch, asleep again, where she might have come during the night for some reason; but she was not there either.

So much had happened here during the past two weeks.

Furniture, rugs, paintings, and plants had been delivered; and from his perch on the piano stool, well out of her way, Jon had watched Naomi turn the nearly empty house into a home, had watched how she decorated every room, imprinting some of herself into it by her choice of colors, style, the way everything was placed. A couple of times he had trailed after her, entered a space where she had just been, and taken a deep breath, certain he could still feel her there. She had shaken her head at him, saying that she was only making the place livable and that there was nothing special to picking a couch or a piece of fabric, but Jon thought otherwise. For him it was the assurance that she indeed meant to live here with him, share his life, at last unafraid, at last happy to be where she was.

He threw open the double doors to the studio, and to brilliant light. The sun had just risen; it was hovering around the Statue of Liberty like a red balloon, pouring its rays onto the black, gleaming top of the Steinway, but Naomi wasn't there either.

How surprised she had been, Jon recalled, when they had gone to Boston with Olaf and he had shown them the condo he had bought for the boys. It was right on Cambridge Square, an impossibly expensive and wonderful setting, with a view of the campus and right across the street from the Harvard bookstore. Proudly, Olaf had thrown open a door to a salon overlooking a backyard filled with old trees. There was nothing in it but a brand-new grand much like this one. "I never said he should give up the music" had been Olaf's words. "I just want a broader perspective for Josh."

They had walked through the halls of Harvard together, met a few people, signed some more papers; and when Jon had offered a donation, he had received a fine smile and the reply, "But Mr. Carlsson has been very generous. Of course, if you feel you should…"

RETURNING TO THE hallway, Jon called her name.

He listened to his own voice echoing up the stairs and dying somewhere on the third floor, but there was no reply.

Defeated, he wandered back into the kitchen and opened the cupboard to bring out the coffee tin. It was nearly empty too, and he wondered if shopping for groceries would make sense before they left the next morning.

The tour was moving on. Sal had been around a couple of times to keep him informed, to tell him that all containers had safely arrived and that the equipment was in good and operative condition with the exception of two beamers that needed their bulbs replaced. The tour books for the US leg had been delivered, and they were nice, better than the European ones; the office had done a fine job. Ten stops in two months—that wasn't too bad; nothing compared to what he was used to, what he had been doing for many years. This tour was a pleasure trip, planned to entertain Naomi, to give them a good time, nothing more, the cities they would visit those she wanted to see. Over the past few days the others had arrived: the band, Art, and Russ, still without Solveigh, who would stay in Norway until the end of the tour. He had brought a thick stack of photographs and shown them around proudly while telling them every detail about Marisol and what a wonder it was to have a baby. Jon had seen Naomi smile at the pictures, had watched her touch the image of the baby with the tips of her fingers and he had reached out to her, laying his hand on her back.

It had been good to have them all back, find them gathered in this new living room, drinking their wine. The door to the yard had stood open, letting in a fresh, wet breeze after a brief thunderstorm. The terrace looked nothing like it had when they had arrived. Now, there were pots with blooming plants around it and new cedar furniture waiting to be used. Work on the barbecue had begun. Once they got back they'd be able to use it and throw parties for their family and friends.

Jon poured water into the coffeemaker, measuring it carefully so there wouldn't be too much for the pitiful mound of coffee in the filter. He was closing the top of the machine when he heard something, coming from upstairs, from all the way under the roof. Her steps sounded slow and tired, so he returned to the hall.

"I was looking for you," he called.

She was in her nightgown and wool socks, a towel in her hands; and she was deathly pale. "I was upstairs. My stomach was upset. I didn't want to disturb you, Jon, it's so early." Her voice sounded weak and a little rough.

"Are you okay?" Right away, as soon as she spoke, the fear turned into worry. "You look as if you're ready to faint." He laid his arms around her, supporting her. "Do you need a doctor? Do you want me to call Kevin? What's wrong with you, my love?"

Naomi leaned her brow against his chest. "I'm fine, don't worry. Just a migraine or something. I took a hot shower. Now I'm hungry."

Her skin was cold and damp; her hair smelled of shampoo.

"All right." Still doubtful, Jon led her into the kitchen. "Coffee?" He filled a mug and set it down on the table, but she pushed it away.

"I think not. I'm still queasy. Is there any orange juice? And a cookie?"

"A cookie? For breakfast? No eggs, no mushrooms?" He began opening the cupboards looking for cookies, even though he knew for a fact there were none. "You're confusing me. You never want cookies in the morning. You don't even care for the cinnamon rolls as much as I do. I'll have to go out and get some."

"No, stay here." Naomi pulled up her legs and wrapped her arms around them. "If you go I won't be able to look at you, and you're so cute in those pajama bottoms."

"Why in the world did you go and hide in that bathroom on the third floor if you're feeling sick?" There was some strawberry jam, so he buttered a slice of toast and spread some of it on the bread and cut it into squares before putting it down in front of her. "Here, eat something. You look like a ghost."

"Because I was sick, Jon. There are some things even you don't need to witness. And I'm fine now, so stop fussing as if you're my mother, for crying out loud." She poked at the toast with one finger. "I'll be okay in a minute, and then we can get dressed and enjoy our last day in New York for a while. I had the thought about going uptown and buying some clothes. I feel like clothes shopping."

"Hell, you don't look well enough to leave your bed, let alone go shopping!" Critically he watched how she took a tiny bit, as if checking to see if it would stay down. After a minute and another sip of juice, she popped the rest of the piece into her mouth and quite greedily ate the entire slice of bread. "Can I have another one?" she asked, and Jon, sighing, complied.

"When we are uptown," he heard her say while he has watching the toaster, "we could try to get that Met box. I so want to go this season."

"Oh, that."

"You don't want to go."

The disappointment in her voice made him smile. "Yeah, I want to go. I want to go, but I have to tell you; I'm more interested in seeing you in fine evening gowns than in the Met itself. I want to take you out and show you off, little beast. I want all the other men to be jealous of what

I have, of my beautiful wife, the love of my life."

She took the plate from him and balanced it on her knees.

"And the box thing has been solved," Jon went on, retrieving the mug he had poured for her and taking a sip. "We have a box." When she started to respond, he lifted his hand. "It's not totally ours, mind you. Or rather, I didn't buy it. It's your parents'. But they are more than willing to share it with us."

For the longest time Naomi did not respond. Daintily, with two fingers, she picked up one piece of toast after another until the plate was empty.

"It might sound crazy, but deep down I have a feeling that you and my father had something to do with how Parker met his end."

"Hell, babe, no!" He nearly dropped his cup. "Seriously, Naomi, I have no idea why you would think that! I might be famous, and pretty rich, but I wouldn't even know how to go about hiring a killer! I'm a good person. Basically."

"Oh, you are."

It was delightful to watch her unfold, stretch out her legs and stand up, and it reminded him of a flower opening its petals.

"You are a good person, Jon, and a wonderful and loving husband. But I do believe that if you decided to do it, you could very well have somebody killed. And my father? Hell, yes."

Her kiss tasted of strawberries, her lips were sweet and sticky with the jam, and he passed his tongue over them to catch the flavor. She gasped softly, her hands on his bare back when he held her against the counter. "You're really feeling better, aren't you?" Jon said softly. "And how much better are you feeling? Are you well enough to go back to bed?"

"I am." She let go of him. "I am well enough for what you have in mind, but I'm not going back to bed. It's our last day here for a while, and I want to enjoy the city. You can come, or you can lie around in bed alone and dream of me."

"You do this to me all the time," Jon called after her when she walked out into the hall and up the stairs. "You turn me on and then you leave me here to steam. Come back!"

She did not reply.

"I WONDER," NAOMI said when they were on the bridge and she had lowered the window of the limo. "I can't wait to see what it will be like here in the spring. I bet it will be gorgeous. I bet the air will be sweet and balmy, and the sky deep blue."

"Only in your dreams." Her persistence was amusing. "You are such a romantic. I wonder if you really see a different world than the rest of us." That thought made Jon stop and ponder for a while. "Yes," he went on, "I really wonder. I wonder if that thing about different realities isn't really more than just a saying. Maybe you do see things differently. Maybe we do. Maybe that's what separates artists from other people."

"Different realities," she echoed his words. "I don't think it's different realities. I think it's a matter of perception, a matter of love." Pointing at the towers of the World Trade Center, she added, "Beautiful."

"Yes, it is pretty awesome."

The pallor had gone from her face, her cheeks were rosy and her eyes lively, every trace of illness gone.

She wanted, she had told him, a few light things for the tour, clothes that would travel well, and if they were going uptown anyway she planned on dropping in at the Valentino store if he didn't mind.

"Only if you let me pay" had been his reply, and her eyes had sparkled at him.

The memory of their day in London came back to him, that day when he had asked her to marry him and then had taken her to Valentino's store on Sloane Street to heap beautiful things on her.

"You look way better than earlier today. Where do you want to go for lunch?"

"Carnegie's," she replied, and Jon groaned. "I want a pastrami sandwich *this* big, Jon, and an entire jar of pickles. I want a jar of pickles to take home. Or maybe two."

"You are happy." It was more a statement than a question. "You seem as if a huge load has fallen off you. What changed?"

They drove up Madison, past all the fancy stores and the elegant restaurants, up toward Central Park; and again she looked, her head turning from one side to the other like a child's, trying to take in everything at the same time.

"I keep telling you I'm happy, Jon. Not every single minute of every single day, but basically, yes, I'm happy." She smiled at him. "I have what

I've always wanted. I have you. Everything else falls into place."

Jon wished they weren't in a car; he wished they were alone and he could embrace and kiss her, and whisper into her ear how much he loved her.

"I've changed my mind, Jon," Naomi said, "not Carnegie's. Let's go pick up my parents. We can all go out for lunch together…like a family."

The author, Mariam Kobras, with the artist, Eric G. Thompson.

Acknowledgements

MY SPECIAL THANKS TO:

ERIC G. THOMPSON and his wife Hilary, for letting us use his amazing paintings as cover art. I can't imagine my books without them!

MY FAMILY, ESPECIALLY my husband who does the laundry and the dishes and the grocery shopping so I have time to write.

MY BELOVED FRIENDS - Bunny Hipps, Jane Gese, Pea Murrell and Shaleeta Bihari for reading the chapters of *Under The Same Sun* as soon as they were written.

SARAH FULFORD - for the photographs, support, and for being a friend.

FRIENDS AND WRITERS - Johanna Harness of #amwriting, Katie Weiland, Kerry Schafer, Julie Butcher, Zehra Cranmer, Maria Duffy, Jane Travers, Nita Beshear and Rebecca Emin, my Twitter "writing group".

CHRIS DE BURGH, who was the inspiration for this book's title. His song *Same Sun* is one of my all-time favorites!

MY PUBLISHER - MaryChris Bradley, for simply everything.